MXX
AGENT SOLDIER

A Science Fiction Novel By:

DONALD SCHLISING

Tenth Page Books

10 9 8 7 6 5 4

First Edition

All rights reserved.
ISBN: 9780692353776

This book is dedicated with love to my wife Darcy, Mother and Father, sister Toni, and brothers Ryan and Vic. This galaxy, and all others, are brighter because of them.

PROLOGUE

I wiped the spatter of crimson from my face, ignoring the metallic taste of copper pooling inside my mouth. My heart beat so violently inside my chest it outlined my vision in red and pounded an echoing thump inside my skull. I blew out a breath, feeling the pain from my wounds fade under the numbing power of vengeance and the building feeling of pleasure that had eluded me for so many years.

The slaver slumped to his knees, the color in his face draining to match the whites of his widening eyes. As he reached his trembling hands up, his bottom lip quivered, gurgling a froth of red from his mouth, begging for forgiveness, mercy or a quick death. He would receive none of them from me.

His blood coated the edge of my knife, flowing freely down the blade then pattering lightly on the floor; each drop timing the agonizing seconds he had left to live. I held his head in my hand, my fingers locked in his hair like a vice, forcing our eyes to meet. Wheezing a sputtering gasp, his eyelids fluttered and twitched as he peered deep into my soul. Whatever he saw must have scared him more than death.

Fueled by his desire to live, the slaver thrashed at my arm in his final act of defiance. I didn't release him, nor did my eyes move from his. Watching him die, the cold grip of fear clutched my spine. At that moment I'd lost the compassion that made me human, and my body shuddered at the thought.

With his last breath the slaver's body stilled, went limp, then crumpled into a pile at my feet.

The Unified Governments had fashioned a galaxy of wealth and power for the Empire Nations, ignoring the cost of their actions. They created desperation and aggression. They created a galaxy of darkness. They created me, and it's my time now.

"There!" I lanced my finger at the active defense monitor while the piercing shriek of the emergency alarms filled the bridge. Salise reacted to my warning and banked the fighter hard to the left, but it was too late. The forward window flooded with red as three strategically positioned sentry probes targeted our ship with a flurry of precision laser fire, surgically disabling our external thrusters with hundreds of finger-thin beams. The fighter shook against the onslaught, sending my crew of eight, and me, sprawling to the floor. When the rain of laser fire ceased, it left behind the buzz of exposed circuitry and the stench of fused wire and charred flesh.

Angry holes in the ship's hull hissed all around us as deep space greedily sucked the oxygen and cabin pressure from our fighter. Grabbing the scorched bodies of two fallen soldiers, I cursed under my breath then dragged them into the passenger compartment. As I knelt down to check their vitals the crew scrambled around me, sealing off doors and access passages until we were encased in an airtight tube of steel.

Both men were dead; their innards seeped from their bodies through torn layers of burnt leather, cloth, and flesh. We laid their bodies at the back of the room, turning their vacant stares away from us and toward the wall. Salise whispered a few words to honor their passing while my crew bowed their heads in remembrance. I never understood the practice of praying to a god that didn't care. A god that didn't help when it was needed. What good would a few words do for the dead soldiers now?

****

Starlight flickered in and out of view as the haunting stillness of space crept through the port side windows of our drifting ship. Deafening silence consumed us, only interrupted by the crew's labored breathing and an occasional muttered prayer. There was tension in the air and the look of desperation was painted on their faces. Everyone knew we were trapped. Helpless. But no one wanted to say it.

My crew nervously paced the compartment. Salise rubbed her arms and Cooper scrubbed his face for warmth while the cold settled into our ship. A row of emergency lights blinked then failed as the second bank of backup power was consumed. The reassuring drone of the oxygen scrubbers quieted then reactivated when the third and final backup power unit came online. That's when Tank spoke the words that everyone else was thinking.

"Call in the *Beast*, Maxx," he said to me through a cloud of frosted breath.

The *Beast* was my ship, a custom built fortress of fire power, speed, and cargo storage, and was our link to survival. I palmed a communicator in my gloved hand. The decision to contact my ship was not an easy one. I had taken careful steps to conceal our route, yet someone discovered where we were headed - then engineered the perfect trap. The robotic probes were only meant to stop us, not kill us. Why?

Salise placed her hand on my arm and looked up into my eyes. "Please, Maxx, it's our only chance to get out of here alive." Salise was a skilled pilot and had faithfully served under me for five years. Her sunny voice and diminutive frame made her seem childlike, but her cropped, fiery-red hair matched her true, hot-tempered personality. I looked for a hint of that flame, but there was only uncertainty in her eyes.

I shook my head. "Something isn't right," I said, staring out the windows while tapping the com against my chin.

Tank moved to Salise's side and draped his massive arms around her shoulders. Other than rage, it was the first time I'd seen the mountainous warrior show any signs of emotion. "Listen, Maxx," Tank said, his voice even, "there isn't a single damn ship in this system the *Beast* can't handle. Call her in, and get us the hell out of here."

I shook my head. "It's not that easy."

"Damn it!" shouted Travis. "Call in the ship!" The tails of his leather jacket snapped behind his first step as he rushed me from the far side of the room, sliding by Tank and pushing Salise to the floor. His movement was a blur of unnatural speed as he closed the ten-meter gap between us in the blink of an eye. He wrapped his hands around my neck, slammed my back against the hull, and thrust his face within centimeters of mine. His eyes twitched in their darkened sockets and small beads of sweat formed above his brow, freezing as they touched the frigid air.

With a building scowl Tank stepped toward us, but I waved him off with a subtle flick of my hand. "Let go, Travis." I choked out the words as his grip tightened around my neck. "Think about what you're doing."

"Oh, I've thought about it," Travis sputtered as he licked his lips, "and you're going to call your ship! Now!"

I tilted my head to the side and rolled my shoulders in an attempt to loosen his grip. "You better listen very carefully to what I have to say."

His eyes wavered from mine, avoiding direct contact while shifting his gaze between Tank and me.

"As long as I'm breathing I'm still your commander, and you'll follow my orders. Let go, and step away."

"Screw that." Travis' eyes narrowed. "I'm not going to die. Not like this." Releasing his right hand from my neck, Travis reached for the pistol holstered under his left arm.

I caught the top of his hand just as his fingertips brushed the grip of his weapon. I snapped his wrist back against his forearm, immediately draining the strength from his hand. I removed the pistol from his holster, then swept his legs out from under him. Travis screamed as he tumbled to the floor, cradling his arm against his chest while spitting curses. I tore the charge pack free from the pistol and tossed the useless weapon at Travis' feet. Borland and Xavier stood quickly. They had nervous looks in their eyes as if unsure whether they should defend their commander or come to the aid of their fellow solider.

"Stand down!" Cooper shouted as he stepped in front of Borland and Xavier. "Both of you need to take control of Travis before he gets himself killed."

The two soldiers nodded their understanding and snatched the back of Travis' jacket, pulling their friend to the opposite side of the compartment. Borland pinned him against the wall and Xavier whispered something into his ear.

Cooper's arm hung at his side as he rubbed the tips of his fingers together for warmth. His thigh holster's restraining strap dangled loose as the pistol waited to be drawn.

Cooper continued. "Damn it, Travis, you're acting like you're a rookie all over again! You're lucky you're walking away with just a broken wrist. If

I were Maxx, I would have crushed that huge melon on top of your shoulders." Cooper poked his index finger at his temple. Not ready to take his eyes off of Travis, he addressed me while his back was still turned. "It's your call, Boss. What are you going to do?"

I glanced at the communicator now resting in my palm. The ring of lights on the inside of the device was pulsating white, reassuring me the link back to the *Beast* was strong. Though the device was small, the burden it carried made it heavy and cumbersome. My eyes scanned the room only to catch the hopeful looks of my crew waiting for me to press the button and call in our savior. Waiting for me to do what they would've done.

I ran my hand through my hair, paused, then said, "You're all the best at what you do, and that's why you're here. It's the credits that keep you in my employment, and it's your talent that keeps you alive. Many of you have served under me for years, fighting by my side and never questioning my judgment. And because of that, we've never failed. Not once."

"This time it's different, Maxx," Xavier said in a muted tone. "There's only one thing you can do. If you don't make the call to the *Beast*, we all die."

"That's where you're wrong, Xavier. There are always options." I balled my fist and crushed the communicator. The lights on the device faded with an electronic squeal, drowning the room in a deafening silence. The blood ran from their faces, leaving behind pale, sullen looks as their hopes of a rescue were crushed as easily as the com.

"You son of a bitch!" Travis screamed as he fought against the restraints of his two friends. "We're dead! You've killed us all!"

"You knew what you signed up for," I said. I let the remains of the com slip through my fingers to the grated floor, and watched as the pieces scattered and disappeared into the darkness below. "Nothing has changed."

The chaotic, self-serving lifestyle of an agent soldier was defined by risk and reward, taking on contracts no one else would touch. An agent soldier's loyalties lie with their jobs, and those who succeeded understood that crew members were tools used to complete them; no different than the blaster holstered at their side or their battle-torn ship waiting for its cargo hold to be packed with illegal goods. All of your tools were critical components in completing contracts yet dispensable when they'd become a burden or failed to serve their intended purpose. Your only friends were credits, and once you strayed from that philosophy it guaranteed only failure and death. We served together, yet we stood alone.

Cooper lowered his head and mopped his hands across his face. "So what now, Boss?"

"Yeah," Tank said with a hint of growing anger, "what now?"

"Arm yourselves," I said. "They're coming for us."

Four ships of the Unified Governments jumped to our location and rattled our fighter like an ill-fit window struggling against a strong gust of wind. Two clearly marked battle cruisers, a transport vessel, and a command carrier dwarfed our ship, blocking out starlight and enveloping us in darkness. Under the red glow of our fighter's emergency lights, my crew scrambled to draw their weapons and aimed them at phantom attackers.

Tank chuckled while he tugged on his thick goatee. "Well now. The UG sent us a little welcoming committee. Isn't that nice?"

Salise stood at Tank's side almost lost under his towering, muscular frame. Her trembling hands clutched two thin-barreled pistols, their tips scorched black from years of action. "So this is how it ends?"

"If they wanted us dead, we wouldn't be talking right now," I said.

"They wanted you to call in the *Beast*," Cooper said. "They want our cargo."

I nodded. "They were hoping I'd activate the communicator so they could trace the link back to the *Beast*. Once they lost my com's signal they had to move forward with their backup plan."

Xavier tilted his head toward his right shoulder. "Backup plan?"

"Without the communicator they aren't able to call in the *Beast* or trace the link. I forced them to take the next step." My voice was surprisingly calm given the situation. "The UG is coming for us, and they'll want to take us all alive."

"Then cut them a deal!" Travis shouted. "Give them the damn ship!"

A laugh of disbelief crossed my lips. "You don't make *deals* with the UG. They take what they want, when they want. The *Beast* and her cargo are the only things keeping us alive. If I hand them my ship, we're all dead."

As Travis readied his response, the Unified Governments' transport vessel rumbled forward under the power of its blue-flamed thrusters. Built like a steel bullet, the massive ship descended on our location and crashed against our fighter, shearing off a wing and sending everyone sprawling to the floor.

A docking clamp extended from their ship, locked onto our hull and squeezed with all of its hydraulic might. The moaning steel walls of the fighter crinkled under its pressure as easily as someone crumpling a sheet of paper. Like a giant mouth, the docking seal slid down the clamp arm and sucked at the side of our ship. A rush of oxygen surged against our hull as they pressurized the tube.

"Oh God," Salise whispered. "They're boarding us."

The hull groaned as a small spot, no larger than a fist, started to pucker and glow red. Heat built in the room as the steel sagged, liquefied, then dripped like melting wax to the floor. A hole burst through the hull, spitting a waterfall of sparks and metal shards into the air. Two cutting beams inched outwards leaving a trail of molten metal behind them.

I removed my jacket and let it fall to the floor. Reaching behind me, I gripped the handles of the two knives that were secured against my back by a leather cross strap. With a quick twist of my wrists, the blades were freed from their sheaths. The welcoming touch of the balanced steel calmed my mind, reminding me who I was and what I'd become. I was an agent soldier and nothing more.

I pressed the flat of the blades against the inside of my forearms and rested my arms at my sides as I focused on the path of the beams. It would be only minutes before the UG had access to our ship.

"Stand strong," I said, steeling my gaze on our fighter's hull. "Make them regret this moment in their lives." My crew formed a crescent around me, armed with blasters and rifles charged and ready for action.

"I never figured this is how it would end for me," Tank said as he hefted the rifle off of his shoulder and wielded it in his hand as easily as a pistol. "I always thought I'd die in the arms of one of my beautiful women."

Cooper flashed Tank a smile. "Tank, I've seen the women you've been with. Beautiful must be a subjective term for you. Hell, I even thought most of them were men."

Tank grunted his reply.

The cutting beams stopped, leaving behind a glowing arch of red. The section of hull plating teetered, then collapsed into our ship with a thunderous crash. A flood of soldiers burst into our shuttle and rushed toward us as a wave of armored flesh. Their wartime battle armor neutralized laser fire and provided protection in hand-to-hand combat. But the grey mesh suits were bulky and flawed by design. There were too many seams and gaps where the individual pieces met, and my knives found them all. Slashing with precision, soldiers fell around me into bleeding piles of twisted arms and legs. From behind me a torrent of laser fire lit the room in a rainbow of greens, reds, and oranges, but when the energy bolts struck their targets they instantly dissipated with dull hums.

The ineffectiveness of my crew's weapons forced them to engage the UG soldiers in hand-to-hand combat. There were too many. For every felled soldier, two took his place until the passenger compartment of our fighter was engulfed with UG minions. A sea of men washed over my crew, drowning them in soldiers. Even Tank's brutish strength was no match for the small army of men that pinned him to the floor.

I was next. They targeted my arms, grabbing, twisting, and wrenching until my knives were loosened from my grip. My pulse raced as I fought to free myself. I couldn't win. There were too many. They drove me onto the ship's deck, and buried me so deep under a mountain of men that I found it hard to draw a breath.

The screams from my crew rang in my ears, sounds of anger and resistance mixed with cries for mercy. Restraining clamps were attached to my ankles and wrists; chains ran between each to form a rectangle of jingling silver. Crafted in forged titanium, the UG proved they weren't taking any unnecessary risks of an escape.

The UG soldiers jerked me to my feet. I looked around the room at each member of my crew, all restrained and bloodied but still alive - save one. Borland was folded in two. Fragments of his splintered ribs poked through his chest. Soldiers lay next to him, some dead, others wishing they were.

Sprinkled throughout the compartment were dozens of motionless bodies of UG soldiers. They were slowly plucked from the floor and dragged back to their ship. A handful of armed guards were positioned in our fighter, two by the access breach in our hull and a few others scattered around my crew.

A tall, gaunt man strode into our fighter; his body groaned and his joints creaked with each step. He was dressed in newly pressed military blues, decorated with countless metals and ribbons of the UG. He stroked his clean-shaven chin in an inquisitive fashion as his eyes searched the room. His face was creased with a dense web of wrinkles, and his eyes were concealed behind a film of white. The Captain nodded at the UG guards as he directed his focus to me. From the corner of my eye I saw a soldier swing the butt of his rifle, then felt a blaze of pain streak across the backs of my legs as they drove me to my knees. The Captain approached me as two UG guards placed one hand on my each of my shoulders to hold me still.

"So, MXX, how long has it been?" He questioned as he lifted my chin with a long, boney finger. His eyes of white locked with mine.

His words, his look, and the UG symbol on the breast of his uniform brought years of hate and rage to a boil inside me. "Since you murdered everyone in the Lanlin sector?" I replied through gnashed teeth.

"Since you escaped." The Captain tilted his head toward his shoulder. "Ten years? Longer?" My only reply was a burning stare. The Captain paused for a moment then continued. "Where's your ship?"

"Your years of service have taken their toll, Captain. Isn't it obvious you're standing in it?"

He clutched my face in both of his hands and squeezed with anger. He was stronger than I'd expected. Much stronger. "Your warship!" When I didn't answer he moved his face closer to mine and whispered through his yellowed teeth. "You know why I'm here. You're transporting cargo that the Unified Governments are very interested in. Tell me where it is."

I stared into his milky eyes then shook my head.

Using his balled fist he struck me above the brow with a hammering blow, splitting the skin above my eye and releasing a warm stream of blood down the side of my face. "Hell, I suspected as much," the Captain muttered. He tipped his cap forward and wiped sweat from the back of his balding head. "Do you understand the trouble you have caused me? The trouble you have caused so many others?"

"I apologize for your inconvenience," I said.

"Don't mock me." He snorted as he adjusted his cap, leaving it to rest just above his eyebrows. "You may not be sorry now, but you will be." The Captain walked around the room, pausing to inspect each member of my crew. He stopped in front of Salise and smiled as he ran his finger across a gash on her check, smearing blood down to her chin. "We have boarded ship after ship looking for you, packing my carrier's holding cells with dozens of degenerates. The Unified Governments has been searching for you ever since your escape, MXX. Admittedly, you were a tough person to find. That was until we received some recent information."

I bit the inside of my mouth, drawing blood. Even though I already knew someone had sold us out, it didn't make it any easier hearing it from the UG. "Why don't you go talk to your informer and get the rest of the information you're looking for?"

A smirk broke across the Captain's wrinkled face. "I'm confident they have told us everything they know. How about you fill in the gaps for me and I will make this quick for you." His arm made a wide, pointing arc toward each member of my crew. "For all of them."

"You're wasting your breath."

He sighed. "I suppose I am. After all, you have a reputation of being a stubborn bastard." His eyes scanned the room. "Well, if you won't tell me perhaps they will." The Captain motioned to the guards. "Place them in the cells and make sure to leave the big one chained."

"Leave them be," I said. "I'm the only one who can answer your questions."

"Then you'll cooperate?" A raspy laugh rolled over his teeth as his cloudy stare focused in on me. His mouth drew a thin line when I didn't answer. "Take them away." One by one they removed my crew from the fighter. They glanced back at me, their heads hung low and their eyes dimming with the loss of hope. I was left in the shuttle with two guards and the Captain.

"You've caused the Unified Governments a great deal of pain, and now it's my turn to reciprocate," the Captain said as he flashed a smile dripping with malice. "I'm going to make you wish you signaled for your ship. Now everyone on your crew will pay the price for your obstinacy."

I pulled at the restraints, gashing my wrist in an attempt to break free and strangle the smug look off his face.

"Tell me, MXX, have you forgotten what that feels like?" He eyed my restraints.

The guards hoisted me off the floor. "Captain, you have no idea what you've gotten yourself into. Do you?" His eyes narrowed at my question. "I'm not the same man you once knew."

"Nor am I." He shrugged. "Your story is no different than any of the other countless felons I've been commissioned to deal with over the last forty years. The Unified Governments hand me the warrants, and I take care of the rest."

Pushing me into the metal walkway, the soldiers paused when I turned to face the Captain. "The only difference is that you lived to retell those stories, Captain. This one isn't going to end quite as well."

The tapping on the wall reverberated inside my cell, jarring me awake from a deep slumber. *Rap, rap, rap.* The Toad was on his way. I forced myself into a sitting position on my cot, pressing my knees against my chest while struggling to shake off the remaining effects of the drugs still coursing through my veins. The stale taste that hung in my mouth and the ache in my back had me wondering how long I'd been out.

I swung my body to the side of the bed while fighting to free my legs from the twisted sheet. My bare feet were greeted by the sharp protrusions of uneven bolts that lined the floor. The pain in my lower back spread, snaking its way through my spine and settling its grip around the base of my neck and in the tops of my shoulders. Trying to ignore the churning in my stomach, I stood up too quickly; the top of my head reminding me the ceiling was a few centimeters too short, or I was a few centimeters too tall.

Feeling my way through the darkness with my head slumped to one side, I stumbled toward my cell door. I located the seams in the wall and braced my hands against the door in an attempt to stop the room from spinning. It didn't. No matter how hard I pressed my fingers against the steel, the inside of my head swirled like a tornado. My legs weakened underneath me as if they refused to support my weight. I slid down the wall and sat on the unyielding floor. Winding rivers of sweat ran down my neck and back as I leaned my head against the welcoming coolness of the boxed metal cell.

The clatter of a cart's wheels and the tinkling of shifting glass headed toward my door. My cell filled with the familiar stench of Toad, mixed with the odors of his drugs. With the click of a key, and the rusted groan of the sliding access panel, a beam of light shot into my room imploding my pupils into tiny specs and sending me into a new void of blindness.

"Got anything to tell me today, Worm?" Toad's voice croaked under his rolls of sagging flesh. His speech was slow and labored as he gulped down air, attempting to catch his breath.

"You know I have nothing to say," I said. My voice sounded harsh and old.

"That's a pity." His sarcasm oozed into my cell. "You know the deal, Worm. Stick your arm through the slot."

I didn't move at first, fearing I would lose my balance if I forced myself to my knees. Toad waited a moment, ticking the tip of his needle against my cell. "I don't know why we need to go through this every day. Be a good boy. Don't give me any trouble, and I promise to personally see to it that the guards throw you a few scraps of food today."

As he spoke, I ran my hand across my chest and down my sides. My ribs made a bumpy path to my sunken stomach. I didn't know how long I'd been here, maybe ninety days. Possibly longer. My hair had grown out and the stubble once lining my jaw was now a thick beard of considerable length. Consumed by darkness, night and day had blended into long periods of immeasurable silence only briefly interrupted by Toad's feedings.

"I've taken enough of your shit, Toad. Go away before I make you regret your miserable existence."

"All of this time and you still can't come to grips with the fact that you've lost." Toad's voice was thick with agitation, upset with my refusal and because I called him Toad. He didn't like the name I've given him, and the increased strength of my recent injections proved it. "Give me your damn arm, or I'll have the guards pull your fucking body through that hole."

The threat of the guard's punishments didn't worry me. They had beaten me countless times before, and my body had the scars and bruises to prove it. They looked for any reason to storm into my cell, but giving them one only made the beatings more brutal. Some days I welcomed them. They reminded me I was still alive while nothing else around me did. I didn't fear the guards, but that was before I had something to lose. Now I did, and I couldn't continue to press my luck with Toad.

I pushed myself off the floor and onto my knees, then slid my right arm through the slot until my elbow cleared the opening. Peering through the hole I watched Toad waddle to the side of my door. He was only half a meter taller than his cart and wobbled from side to side as he moved, almost as if his excessive mass was losing the battle against gravity. His clothes were stained with food and the poisons that splashed from his jars, his hair was unkempt and his face pockmarked with sores and festering scabs that yawned with infection.

Toad dropped the restraining clamp in place and engaged the locking mechanism by turning a mechanical wheel mounted on the wall outside my cell. The device constricted against my arm, just stopping short of tearing flesh and shattering bone. Flipping a lever, the clamp spun, exposing the black inked MXX letters tattooed on the inside of my forearm. The touch of his plump fingers felt clammy and rough like the skin of a cold-blooded reptile. "Fitting don't you think, Worm?" He snorted as he traced the dull tip of the syringe along the MXX. "Back in captivity where you belong."

A sharp bite stung my forearm and immediately shot a blaze of fire through my arm and up into my shoulders. My fist clenched so tight it felt that I'd broken off each of my fingers at the knuckles. Within seconds my entire right side numbed under a frozen sensation like the prickle of a thousand needles piercing frostbitten skin. The pain crawled its way toward the small of my back and settled its evil at the base of my spine.

"You know what happens when you cage an animal against its will?" I growled through gnashed teeth. Each word I spoke was carried forward by droplets of spittle that sprayed against the cell door.

"Enlighten me, Worm."

"It'll take your beatings and abuse, your torture and punishment, but only because it's biding time. Days, weeks, maybe even months will pass until one day it's ready to fight back."

"Very interesting, yet I still find myself bored." Toad feigned a yawn.

"Eventually it chooses its moment. Fueled by anger and driven by its instinct to survive, it frees itself, killing its obese captor. Standing over him it watches as the last of his life drains from the wretched husk of his body. The last thing his captor sees is a hint of vindication on the animal's face, before everything fades to black."

Toad grunted as he shifted where he stood. "That sounded a bit specific, Worm. Keep those comments coming and I'll put you down sooner than I'd planned." The needle's blunt tip pushed its way through my skin again, burrowing deep into my forearm. "Give me a few more days and you won't be talking so smart any more. These drugs are eating you from the inside out, bit by bit, dissolving brain tissue and muscle mass; slowly they're liquefying your organs until they resemble a glob of thick, black pudding. If you give me the information we're looking for, I can make this all stop for you and your crew."

"And if I don't, the information dies with me," I sputtered in reply, fighting against the pain of the injection.

Toad sighed, either out of frustration or in an attempt to catch his breath. "So be it. The Unified Governments are perfectly content with me melting your brain. If they don't get the information, no one will."

"What you offer me is a mouthful of lies. You'll kill me and my crew the second I tell you what you want to know. Do you think I'm a fool?"

There was no answer.

He didn't need to respond because we both knew the truth. "You'll get nothing from me, or my crew."

Toad peeled his spongy hands from my arm, then loosened the restraining clamp. I pulled my arm back inside my cell and tried to rub away the hurt. Toad tossed the needle into a wooden box at the bottom of the cart, then looked through the access hatch as he spoke. "A few of them spilled some information quite some time ago. Just the sight of my needle had them wetting themselves and crying for their mothers. Unfortunately, they couldn't supply enough details to stop their treatments - or yours. Give most of your crew a few more days and their heads will be no more than bowls full of jelly. It doesn't matter to me who goes first as the outcome will be the same for everyone."

My crew was still alive. It was exactly what I needed to hear. Only I knew the full details of our latest mission and how to locate my ship. I learned long ago you only share information that's necessary for each crew member to complete their job. Lack of trust is a staple in the life of an agent soldier. Plausible deniability was normally a good thing for my crew, but not this time. They were at my mercy, likely praying that I tell Toad everything in hopes of stopping their pain. They needed to remain strong, hold on to the hope that they would be freed. Hope that I would save them.

"Remember, you can make this all stop." Toad choked as he coughed up a ball of phlegm then quickly swallowed.

I wiped away the dots of blood and rubbed the raised bumps where my arm was injected. "You assume I care."

"We'll see," Toad replied. "I injected you with a custom cocktail made specifically for your continued lack of cooperation. If you're not dead in a couple of days, you'll be wishing you were. I was planning on sharing small doses of it with your friends, but today's talk persuaded me to give you every last drop. After all, you know how dangerous those 'caged animals' can be if they aren't properly sedated." The access slot on the door slammed shut and Toad padded his way down the corridor, laughing with each step.

Sliding my hands against the walls, I found the back corner of my cell furthest from the door. An aged metallic odor assaulted my nostrils as my toes slid into a coagulated puddle. The makeshift bandage around my left wrist made a sucking noise as I unwound it, leaking its coppery smell into the air. I bit into my bottom lip as I dug my thumbnail deep into the wound until my arm burned and my fingers grew wet.

A trickle of blood widened into a thin stream, running down my hand and pattering into the growing pool on the floor. The sound made me wonder how much blood I'd lost over the last few days. With little food and water to replenish it, I couldn't play this dangerous game much longer. Twenty seconds of bleeding was all I would allow to clear out as much of the toxin as I could. Any longer and I might die, any less I'd be bleeding myself out for nothing.

When finished, I knotted the cloth around the base of my wound, feeling the warmth of a growing infection. Careful not to touch the walls and leave the stain of my wound behind for Toad or the guards to see, I stumbled through the darkness and crawled back onto the cot. My head was circling faster than before and my body pulsed in agony. Unhappy with the loss of blood, lack of food, and Toad's recent drug feeding, my stomach churned and the inside of my skull pounded. I threw my head over the side of the cot and retched out what little fluid was left in my stomach, then dry heaved for the next few minutes. My body grew colder and my arms and legs twitched against my will.

"Two days," I whispered to myself as I used my shaking hand to wipe my mouth across the soiled sheet. Two more days and I would make them all pay. Toad, the prison guards, and given enough strength, the entire body of the Unified Governments.

Ravaged by poison and beset by fever, the next two days felt like two months in hell. Slipping in and out of a drug induced sleep, my mind raced with dark thoughts and twisted shadows. My nightmares felt real, while reality itself was the nightmare.

Even though sleep numbed the pain, I fought to resist its tempting sanctuary. As it pulled me down into its bottomless void, it felt like I was fighting to crawl my way out of a pit of quicksand. Flooded with mixed visions of peace and torment, I was living in a new world of alternate realities. At one point I was in so deep I felt the boney touch of death and heard the reapers' whispered voices rolling over their pointed teeth. That's when I knew the drugs Toad injected were targeting my brain, determined to induce a slow, paralyzing insanity. I wouldn't let Toad win, and I wouldn't let my crew die.

When I woke, the blackness of my cell greeted me with its unkind embrace. My heart pounded so violently I worried it would loosen my ribs. Gasping for air, I tried to slow my heart and squelch the burning in my lungs while my shaking hands brushed away the layers of dried sweat and blood that caked my skin. My naked body was icy to the touch. Like a sponge it soaked in the frigid air that seeped through the seams of the prison walls. Shivering, I rolled to my stomach and retched.

The room spun as I pushed myself onto my hands and knees. I slipped off the side of the cot and attempted to stand, but my legs were wobbling jelly, giving way and dropping me to the floor. My head bounced off the jagged bolts, sending waves of splintering pain through my skull. For a moment I laid still. I curled myself into a ball and cradled my head in my arms. I was spent and covered in filth. My back ached, my insides were swimming, and every centimeter of my body screamed out from the months of abuse. That's when I started to laugh. If Toad or the reapers wanted to lay their claim to my soul, they needed to try harder.

I bled myself again, but only for ten seconds under a scarily slow trickle. Summoning what strength I had left, I wrapped the sheet around me and staggered across the floor, attempting to sweat the remaining drugs out of my system. The stench of the toxins seeping out of my pores smelled worse than the shit in the corner of the cell. With each step my muscles cramped and tightened like wound steel cables, begging me to stop. But I wouldn't. I didn't.

That's when I was alerted. *Rap, rap, rap.* The Toad was on his way. I used the sheet to wipe the fluids that ebbed from my body and tossed it back on the cot, then placed my hands on the door and worked to steady my shaking legs.

It was exactly what I was hoping for; the familiar rattle of the cart, the clinking of the glass and the odors of Toad and his drugs. A metallic scrape followed by the click of a key and the access door opened. Toad grunted as he bent down with great effort to peer inside. My stomach blocked his view into my cell.

Toad bellowed a flabby chuckle. "I've got to give you credit, Worm. You're a lot stronger than I thought." He groaned as he raised himself off the floor. The clatter of glass echoed as Toad pawed through his vials. "What I fed you days ago would've killed any beast within five systems of here."

"I'm sorry to disappoint you," my voice crackled in reply.

"No worries. I'll get it right this time. That is, unless you've decided to tell me what I want to hear."

I dropped to a knee and thrust my arm through the access slot without offering a reply.

Toad snorted. "No fight left in you, huh? I find that extremely disappointing, though I guess it's time you face the inevitable."

"Do it and get it over with, Toad. I'll welcome the company of the reapers. I'm sick of your drugs, your stink, and the sound of your croaking voice mumbling false promises."

"Y-y-you will not like what I have for y-y-you t-t-today," he stammered in response. The vials clattered as he fumbled to find the right mixture. "Y-y-you won't like it at all."

"You've failed more than once. How can I trust you'll ever get it right?

Maybe that's why you were assigned to work in this lowly UG prison."

Through the narrow access door I could see a nervous tick working the corner of his eye and his lips twitching toward his left ear. He raked his nails across his cheek, catching scabs and drawing fresh blood. When he reached to activate the restraining clamp, I stumbled and fell backward, pulling my arm through the slot and grabbing at its corner for balance. Missing my arm, the device locked around air with an empty thunk.

"Damn you, Worm, push your arm back through and hold it there!" Toad croaked as he reset the clamp.

I pressed my body against the door and slid my arm back through. As Toad released it, I fell backward again, pulling my arm inside the cell. My perspiring hand grasped for the corner of the access slot but slid off the slick metal. My body struck the floor with such force it drove the air from my lungs.

"One more time and I will get the guards!" He sputtered as he worked to reset the clamp. "I swear I will get the guards!"

"Do us both a favor and call the guards, Toad. Maybe they can finish the job you can't." I choked out the words as I struggled to gather my breath. I sat on the floor in front of the access hatch with my legs crossed in front of me. Using my palms, I scrubbed my forehead and eyes, then wiped the sweat from the back of my neck. My stomach churned and I retched.

Toad peered through the slot, his eyes widening as he gazed upon me. His jowls bounced as he talked. "Yes, yes…good. My poisons are still working." His gaze never left me as I fought to keep my balance. "You're an empty shell of who you once were. When they brought you here you were a great agent soldier, now you're just a simple, broken man like the rest of them." He sat on the other side of the door, licking his lips. Staring. Watching.

I struggled to set my feet under me and tried to stand, but the room spun and refused me the balance I needed. "Take your time," Toad said with a relaxed sigh. "I'm in no hurry. Let my drugs punish you for a bit longer while I tell you a story."

Toad pressed his index finger against his double chin as if deep in thought. "When your fighter was captured, we claimed you and five of your crew members. For insurance purposes we removed two of them from the general population. The plan was to hold them until you spilled what you knew, or until you died, whichever came first. The remaining three were killed within hours of your capture."

"You're lying," I said. His words clawed at my insides and I grasped my stomach to stop the sudden burst of pain. "That's not what you told me two days ago."

"Ah, yes. Half-truths used in an effort to play on your sympathies." Toad chuckled at his cleverness. "The military counsel of the Unified Governments authorized the torture of the men and rape of the woman just hours after your capture. Their last moments were extremely painful through the use of medieval, but necessary punishments." Toad narrowed his eyes. "I would be more than happy to give you all of the glorious details if you would like."

"You raped Salise?" My reply sounded more like a growl than words. I could taste the growing rage that formed like bile in the back of my throat. "You watched them torture and kill my crew?"

"Oh, I didn't watch, I participated. The redhead was quite the wild one. It was fun breaking her." A wide smile split his face from ear to ear, breaking scabs and leaking puss. "It only took a few hours to realize your crew knew very little about your mission and nothing about the location of your ship, so they were expendable at the pleasure of others." Toad basked in my burning stare.

He continued. "You need to understand that there's a lot riding on the information that's inside of your head. I thought maybe, just maybe, you had a heart and would cave when you thought I was drugging your crew. I believed compassion would take over, but you proved to be an evil, uncaring bastard. One hundred and seven days of torture and you didn't buckle once."

"You tortured my crew," I mumbled, repeating the words. Forcing myself to accept them. "Open the door Toad and let me show you how evil I can be."

"I can feel the heat of your animosity though the door." Toad mocked me with a fake shudder while rubbing his hands together as if warming himself in front of a fire. "Realize you brought this upon yourself and your crew. Their blood is on your hands, not mine or the Unified Governments." A sharp ache stabbed at my chest and stomach, and I doubled over to the floor.

"Once I'm done with you, your last two men will receive the same treatment as you, one at a time, until we get the information we need or until we bury it with their mutilated corpses."

I rolled to my stomach, then squatted with my arms resting on my knees. I spit the taste from my mouth, crawled my way to the door and slid my arm through the access slot. "Let's get this over with," I said as I struggled to steady my arm.

"Very well," groaned Toad. "It's a shame it has to end this way."

I stumbled twice and my arm swayed outside the slot while I fought to hold it still. Frustration built in Toad's accelerated breathing as he worked the levers of the restraining clamp, attempting unsuccessfully to latch it onto my arm. A third stumble and my arm started to slide back inside the cell when Toad's clammy fingers wrapped around my wrist to brace me. In one hundred and seven days it proved to be his first and final mistake.

Bracing my leg against the wall, I clasped his forearm, twisted my wrist and yanked his arm through the access slot until his shoulder slammed hard against the door. The metal of the tight-fitting slot sheared Toad's arm in an explosion of red mist. The wall and floor were showered in steaming globs of flesh, fat, and muscle.

He cried out as he fought against my grip, but he was no match for me and my one hundred and seven days of building anger. When he realized that he couldn't break away, he started to threaten me with more drugs, beatings from the guards, and other unspeakable tortures and horrible deaths.

"Shhhhh," I whispered. "Let the other prisoners sleep."

"The guards are on their way!" Toad screamed. "They're on their way!" His legs kicked wildly, the soles of his boots squeaking as they were unable to find purchase on the slick stone lining the corridor.

"Let me tell you a little story, Toad."

"You're a dead man!" Toad screamed as he flailed against the cell door. "A fucking dead man! They're on their way! I can hear them now! Let me go and I promise your death will be quick!"

"It's your turn to be a good boy and listen to what I have to say." I pinned his mangled arm against the door inside my cell and held it in place. He would need to chew it off at the shoulder to break free.

"Guards!" Toad shouted. "They see me through the cameras. They'll be here any moment now! You're running out of time!" His voice transitioned from panic to nervous fits of laughter.

"Listen to me, Toad, and listen carefully!" I was trembling. Not from the drugs but from the rush of adrenaline. "I've been watching, listening, and studying your every move since the first day you visited me. I know help isn't coming for you, and you know it too."

Toad stopped screaming and started to grovel like a pleading child through his endless sobs. "Please. Please just let me go…"

"There's no automation in this prison. I can tell your carts are manual because of your physical exertion and labored breathing when you reach my cell. The restraining clamp is activated by levers and dials. The doors to the cells are opened and closed by lock and key. Lighting is sparse. There are no cameras in my cell and the corridors are thick with steel and stone. Shall I go on?"

"But…but…you don't…"

"You're alone tonight and my guess is that no one knows you're here. The cart you're pushing is a second cart, maybe one you hide in your personal chamber and use for these secret visits. I can hear the slight squeak of the lighter wheels and a loose shifting noise as they bounce over the stones. The vials on the cart are lesser in quantity and the thickness of the glass containers cast differing sounds when they clatter together. Maybe these visits are by your own volition, trying to extract information to boost your career, meet a promise, or collect on a reward. The drugs you were instructed to feed me were supposed to kill, but instead you're trying to trick my brain into giving you the information you seek. Shall I go on?"

"No…no, it's not true…"

"When you make your authorized rounds I can hear the scuffing of the guard's boots across the floor and their muffled voices in the distance. You speak differently, more formal, forceful and without sarcasm. The smell you carry during each visit varies, telling me your clothing is different or your visits come after you've eaten. Shall I go on?"

"Please, let me go. Please!"

"I'm assuming that I'm being held in either Paxcel or Hyperion since the UG takes all of their 'special projects' to one of those two prisons. They're the only two in the galaxy where the UG intentionally limits technology. It's the only way they can ensure that no one can hack into their systems and catch them breaking their own laws." Toad was reduced to blubbering whimpers, barely audible under his continuous sobs.

"You've heard enough, Toad. Unlock my cell then hand me the keys."

"No." That word was Toad's final act of defiance. I snapped his arm like a dry twig; bone splintered and burst through his skin. He bellowed a murderous scream while I twisted the shattered appendage in my hands. The grinding and cracking of his humerus echoed off the walls of my cell.

Fumbling through his pockets, he located his keys then unlatched my cell.

I released Toad's arm and opened the door. A rush of air washed over my body while a spray of light took me by surprise, forcing me to shield my eyes. Cowering outside the door, Toad recovered his shattered arm and swaddled it against his chest like a newborn child.

"Get in," I growled. I lifted Toad by the collar of his coat and dragged him inside the cell. The flood of light highlighted a gruesome scene of sickness, blood, and infection on the floor.

"You...you...you were bleeding yourself out to remove the drugs from your system." Toad choked as he stared at the pool of blood. Tears rolled down his cheeks and splashed into the puddle of red and black. "That's why they didn't work..."

"How much were you offered for the information leading to the location of my ship?"

Toad looked up at the ceiling, avoiding my eyes and refusing to speak. His body shook as I continued. "How much?"

"F-f-fifty-thousand credits for the detailed information on the location of your ship and its cargo." Toad replied with a wince.

"And what if I died without supplying the information?"

Shock washed over his trembling body. Toad's eyes drifted from mine as he steeled his gaze on the floor. I kicked his wounded arm, tearing the splintered bone though a new patch of skin. He screamed then begged for mercy.

"Answer my question, Toad."

Toad muttered his response, "P-p-pain, suffering and p-p-paralysis were all acceptable. Y-y-your death wasn't an option."

I stood over Toad. The look in my eyes had him scrambling away from me, his boots pushing and slipping in the pool of dark blood as he backed his way against the cell wall. I gripped his head in my hands and dug my fingers into his skin until his cheeks were mashed together and his lips created a puckered, red 'O.' I looked into his eyes wondering if his gaze was the last thing my crew saw before they died.

"I would've paid you a hundred thousand credits just for releasing me from this cell," I said through gritted teeth. Toad's pupils dilated and his eyelids quivered. "And you would've been alive to spend them." I twisted his head as if it was set on a freely moving swivel. The vertebrae in his neck cracked and popped, his eyes rolled into the back of his head, then his body collapsed to the floor in a pile of lifeless flesh. His death was more merciful than what he deserved.

I recovered his keys and stepped out of the cell. It was time the UG learned what happens when you cage an animal against its will.

The service corridor was narrow but the ceiling was twice the height of an average man, allowing me to stand upright for the first time in over a hundred days. A thin wire stretched between the sconces that lined the stone wall opposite the cells. The hasty tacking of the wire and the unevenness of the fixtures made it appear that the lighting in this area was an afterthought. Though not very bright, it took a long time for my eyes to adjust to my new surroundings.

Before me were six prison cells, each a pocket of steel built into an opening of carved stone. From the outside they appeared identical, equipped with restraining clamps, access slots and key locks. Jagged-cut stone covered the floor and snaked its way along the cells in both directions, disappearing around corners roughly twenty meters from where I stood.

Next to me was Toad's cart, constructed of a lightweight metal with two shelves and four worn rubber wheels. Syringes were tossed haphazardly into a small wooden box on the bottom shelf. Many of the needle shafts were broken and dirtied with crusted blood, and the barrels stained with chemicals and Toad's fingerprints. The top shelf was crammed with twenty-eight glass containers varying from jars to vials to drinking cups to bottles. The rainbow of fluids contained within sloshed and spilled as I pulled the cart near me.

My fingers danced across the tops of the glass as I searched for something that would reverse, or at least slow, the effects of the drugs, but none of the makeshift containers were labeled. My chemistry skills were poor, and to attempt the creation of an antidote based off of color and smell would be dangerous, even fatal.

In frustration I flung the cart onto its side; the containers exploded against the stone under a shower of glass. I raked my fingers across the back of my head as I watched the liquids pool and mix with each other. Their individual vibrant colors morphed into a deadly black stream that found the cracks in the stone and flowed downwards toward the lower cell block. "I need to get a grip," I mumbled, knowing this one stupid act could have alerted the guards.

I wrenched the handle free from the cart, placed it near the hinge and compressed the end by opening and shutting the thick door of my cell. I kept turning and twisting the handle, and opening and closing the door, until I had fashioned a crude point that was strong enough to pierce cloth and skin.

Stepping inside my former cell, I stripped Toad's corpse of his keys, stained coat, surgical scrubs, and military boots. There was room for three more of me inside the coat, pants and shirt, and my toes were slightly curled at the end of his boots, but I wasn't in any position to complain. I stepped out of the cell and closed the door behind me. The satisfying thud reassured me that freedom was within my grasp.

I flipped through Toad's keys until I found one that was imprinted with an 'M' on its base. I tested it on my cell door and the access slot and it opened both with ease. There were forty other keys looped around a tarnished ring of brass, each labeled with numbers corresponding to the markings on the cells. I worked the keys free from the ring and dropped them into the left coat pocket.

I stepped in front of the cell adjacent to mine; the cell of the occupant who warned me of Toad's advancing presence. The hum of a song, barely audible, was coming from inside. Gripping the master key, I unlocked the access slot and slid it open. I was greeted by silence.

"The fat man is dead," I said. A thunderous throb tightened its grasp around my lower back. My heart raced and stomach rolled as I leaned against the cell door.

"By all the commotion I assumed one of the two of you had passed on into the arms of the reapers," a male voice replied, heavy with an outer system's accent. "I just wasn't sure…who."

I glanced down the dimly lit passageway expecting to see a rush of security personnel. I swore I heard something - saw something out of the corner of my eye - but only flickering shadows occupied the otherwise vacant corridor. "He deserved worse than he got."

"It's strange, don't you think?"

"What's that?"

"How one man can determine if another man lives...or dies? That in the end, we are just a fleeting second away from no longer existing." He snapped his fingers.

I exhaled, paused then attempted to rub feeling back into my face. "It's all I've ever known."

"I truly understand," he said. "It's funny how one simple mistake can turn the tide. By all rights he should've won, considering all the toxins and hallucinogens he pumped into your...system." When I didn't reply, he continued. "Don't be shocked at what I know. You'd be amazed at the things I've learned while locked inside these walls of steel."

I dug inside my jacket pocket and retrieved the loose keys. "Your warnings helped, so I'm here to repay your actions with your freedom."

"That's an unexpected act of kindness," he said. "And what about the freedom of the others locked within these...cells?"

"I only pay the debts I owe, nothing more. Their fates are in their own hands, not mine." Grimacing, I knelt on one knee. With a grunt, I tossed the handful of loose keys inside his cell like a scattering of metal rain. "There's your key, along with thirty-nine others. I'll leave the access door open so you can reach your arm through as you try each one. It won't be easy, but if you're careful you'll be able to free yourself."

"With thirty-nine other keys, I could offer freedom to quite a few more prisoners."

"It's your call if you choose to let others out."

"If you don't mind me asking, why won't you open the door for me?"

"There's a reason you're locked behind this door, and I'm not a fool. I'm handing you the key to your freedom as a debt I owe. Nothing more, nothing less."

"Fair enough." His voice carried a matter of fact tone, devoid of emotion. "Let me help you once more - maybe for a future...favor?"

"I never make blind promises."

"Are you in search of your remaining crew? That is, assuming anyone has survived."

"My plans are not your concern."

"Maybe. Maybe not. We'll need more time to determine if that's...true."

He was working me over in hopes that I would let him out of his cell and take him off this planet. As I started to pick myself up from my knee, he called out. "One last thing, Maxx. As I'm sure you already know, the drugs the torturer was injecting you with contained heavy hallucinogens, but what you don't know –"

"How do you know who I am?" I cut him off sharply. When he said my name it hit me like a burst of chilled air, raising gooseflesh on the back of my neck. There was something that felt unnatural about the way it rolled off his tongue.

"Listen to me!" He snapped. His voice carried anger, showing feeling for the first time. "The hallucinogens were laced with small traces of toxins intended to cause a debilitating paralysis. Just like the hallucinogens, they work their way through your bloodstream, but instead of dissolving, they eventually settle and collect at the base of your spine. If you're experiencing lower back pain, the toxins are already destroying your nervous system."

I peered through the access door. A shadowed figure was crouched at the back of the cell, shrouded by the cover of darkness. A single ray of light cast an intruding beam that highlighted his black eyes and light-colored skin. "Who are you, and how do you know me?"

He ignored my question and continued. "If you don't purge the toxins from your system, the torturer will have accomplished at least part of his…commission. If you don't remove them soon, you'll be paralyzed."

I should have been grateful for what he told me, thanked him for the information he provided. But I didn't care about the drugs. Not now anyway. "I asked you a question. How do you know me?"

"That information, my friend, can only be obtained by opening my cell door."

"I don't like playing games."

"Nothing about this is a game, Maxx."

I heaved a sigh as I pushed myself back to my feet, attempting to ignore the stabs of pain shooting through my back. My head spun more violently than before as I attempted to process his warning. Once I regained my balance I crossed to the other side of the passageway and tore the electrical wire free from the wall sconces. The corridor was blanketed in darkness. "Good luck with those keys."

As I walked away I could feel his smile burn into my back.

My eyes thanked me for returning them to the darkness. Although it slowed my progress, I felt more comfortable in its black embrace. It would take some time to get used to the light after spending over a hundred days locked inside a cell.

I crept my way down the corridor, careful not to make any noise that could draw attention. The tight fitting boots were like concrete blocks on my feet, and it took extra concentration not to drag or scrape them across a raised stone. Surprise was my only advantage, and if lost, any hope for an escape would soon follow.

The prison cells were eerily quiet, either empty or converted into tombs for their captives - courtesy of Toad and the UG. There was no yelling or screaming, or beating on cell doors. Not even the faintest shifting of feet or tapping on the steel walls. The stagnant air was dry and gritty and filled my mouth with the rancid taste of death. It felt more like a morgue than a prison.

My progress brought me to a turn in the hall where flickering light cast the shadows of bars and the shifting movement of human shapes on the floor. I stopped to listen, but all I heard was the accelerated pounding of my heart and an echoing thump inside my head. I bit my lip to stifle the pain as I lowered myself flat to the floor and peered around the corner. The passageway made an upward slope that led to a door centered on a wall of bars. Behind the bars stood two guards armed with old-fashioned revolvers, likely loaded with gunpowder propelled rounds. The site of such antiquated weapons intrigued me. *How far had the UG gone to rid this prison of technology?*

One of the two men was a young, athletic-looking rookie possibly serving his first tour of duty with the UG as a prison guard. His eyes were wide and animated, and his chest was puffed with patriotism. The second of the two was older and disheveled; a corner of his shirt was untucked, his boots scuffed and unpolished, and his belt had missed a loop in his unbuttoned pants. His face was tired and uncaring, wearing his years of service like a heavy burden. A veteran assigned the work of a rookie was a clear sign that he had failed as a soldier or was demoted for a breach of conduct.

Suddenly, my lower back tightened into a knot of pain. I pressed my fingers against it as if I could will the poison from my system. If what that prisoner had told me was true, I didn't have much time before paralysis set in. Even if I had only minutes to spare, I couldn't rush into this. I didn't come this far to have six rounds punched through my chest by some snot-nosed rookie or timeworn soldier who had given up on life. *Think, damn it. Think.*

Someone promised Toad a bounty of credits for information leading back to my ship, and I doubted it was the ruling council of the UG. If it was, he'd have no reason to make secretive visits to my cell. He'd done it countless times since I was imprisoned here, and never sounded distracted or worried that he would be caught. Maybe there was another door, a concealed entrance in the prison's halls, or an access hatch in the back of one of the cells that he used.

If there was a door cut into the stone, there was little chance I could locate it under the current shroud of darkness, and opening any of the cells was more risky than charging the gate. There's a reason they transported the most dangerous people in the galaxy to Paxcel and Hyperion. These prisons weren't designed and constructed to hold the common man.

It left me with one final hope. Greed. There were very few people left in this galaxy that couldn't be bought, and none of them worked for the UG. The only question was how much. Maybe Toad was bribing the guards with the promises of his future reward? As the toxins chewed at my spine, I realized I didn't have a choice. I had to try.

I knelt, crossed one leg over the other, then closed my eyes and sucked in a deep breath. The already dim hall grew darker as I shut out the world around me. Bit by bit the pain in my back disappeared, the spinning of my head subsided and my hunger faded. I felt strong and energetic, just like I did the day the UG stormed our fighter.

A decade prior I learned to trick my mind to compartmentalize memories, emotions, and pain, and tuck them away in a part of my brain that was shut off from the rest of my body. It was a useful tool but wasn't without severe risk. There's a reason our brains register pain and emotion, and suppressing its signals can cause adverse, irreversible effects - even death. Compartmentalization acts like a sponge by absorbing select memories, pain, and emotions like water, and holding them at bay until they're willfully squeezed free. The danger comes when there's too much to hold and whatever you repressed frees itself against your will, drowning your brain in a sudden and unsuspected surge.

I only used compartmentalization to store memories when undergoing the most extreme and barbaric interrogations. Even the strongest of men can be broken physically or through chemical means. Never once did I use it to store personal, unwanted memories. That was the coward's way out. Rather I used them as fuel for my hate, for my vengeance against the UG. Memories of my past defined me; they made me who I was. They were memories I would never let go. Never forget.

I broke out of my trance, refreshed and ready. I had to make this work. I had no other choices. No other options. As I stood, I tucked the hastily crafted spike up into my sleeve, holding it securely in my right palm. I drew in a deep breath and turned the corner. I took a few paces up the sloped passageway before both guards drew their guns.

"Don't take another step!" The Vet shouted as he steadied his pistol against the bars.

"Listen to me," I said. My voice didn't waver as I continued forward. The Vet squeezed off a single round that sparked against the far wall, then ricocheted down the corridor. I stopped advancing and continued to play my hunch. "I know what's going on, that you're allowing unauthorized access to the lower level cells."

The Rookie nestled the hammer of his revolver between his thumb and index finger. The cylinder on the pistol spun, and the hammer locked in place with a deadly click. The Vet shot a sideways glance at his partner before his gaze returned to me. As nervous as the Vet appeared, I was more concerned about the unpredictability of an untested youth longing for his first round of combat. The Vet spoke up. "If you take one more step, I'll kill you."

I lifted my left arm and raised my palm. "We can make a deal."

"That's him, Dominic," the Rookie stuttered, wiping tiny bubbles of saliva from his lips. "That's the agent soldier everyone's talking about!"

"Shut up!" The Vet shouted. "Both of you just shut up!"

The Rookie's body was stiff, but his drawn pistol bounced in his hands as he tried to center the gun's sights on my head. His eyes rolled between me, the Vet, and the closed door behind them.

"What did you do to Jark?" The Vet questioned. His voice carried forced un-interest.

"Jark? Ah, Toad...I killed him." The Rookie's cocksure stare melted off his face, and for a moment I was sure he would retch. He removed his left hand from the pistol and covered his mouth.

"You're lyin'!" The Vet's grip tightened around his gun.

"He's dead." I shrugged. "By now his body is colder than the walls of these cells."

"You piece of shit! I'm gonna shoot you in the fuckin' head."

"Think it through," I said, carefully measuring every word that I spoke. I had yet to lower my left palm. "Once you kill me they'll find him dead in my cell with enough evidence to know he was making unscheduled visits. I destroyed his cart, stripped the clothes from his body and scattered his keys." I tugged at the front of Toad's shirt that draped over me like a loose sack. They didn't reply, so I continued. "You can't cover it up. They'll know that you're the two guards that allowed his unauthorized visits - the only guards that were ordered to secure this passageway. Who do you think they'll blame? If you shoot me, you might as well shoot yourselves."

"Dominic, this is all bullshit!" yelled the Rookie. He rocked back and forth and shuffled his feet as he looked for confirmation from his partner. "Right? Both you and Jark said he had authorization."

The Vet fidgeted with his hat and wiped a line of sweat from his brow. He mumbled to the rookie, "Yeah. All of his visits were authorized. This asshole is a liar."

I continued to press the Vet. "Before you pull the trigger, listen to my proposal. Fifty-thousand credits to each of you for letting me pass through that gate. What was Toad offering? The best he was going to get was fifty-thousand credits for breaking me. What was your cut? Ten percent, tops?"

The Rookie squirmed as he digested each of my words. "Don't believe a word he's sayin'," the Vet said as he pointed a gnarled finger in my direction. "We're not fuckin' degenerates like you." The Vet hooked his thumb at the door behind him. "If we let you outta this door, you'll be off this planet doin' the same shit that got you locked up the first time. You expect us to turn our backs on the Unified Governments and what they stand for just because you offer us a handful of credits?"

"That handful of credits is more than you will ever see in your lifetime, and I don't make promises I can't keep." I did my best to keep my emotions in check. The symbols of the UG, emblazoned on their uniforms, were enough to start a roaring fire inside my chest. The UG was nothing more than a contingent of greedy, murdering bastards hiding behind a self-imposed badge of justice.

"Forget it." The Vet shook his head. "Even if you were to pay us off we would be executed by the Unified Governments as traitors for lettin' you leave."

"That's where you're wrong. If you let me pass through that door, I'm killing everyone on the other side." My response didn't calm their nerves. "There'll be no one left to tell the UG what happened. Just open the locked door, name the meeting place of your choice, and give me two days to deliver your credits."

"That ain't gonna happen," said the Vet. The Rookie eagerly nodded at his reply.

"Do you hear stories about every prisoner you lock up behind these walls? Does word of a new inmate spread as quickly as it has about me? You've heard enough about me and about my reputation. You know I have the credits."

They didn't answer, only shared a look between each other before turning their stares back to me. The Vet shook his head from side to side as I continued.

"It's your decision, but know this. It's only a matter of time before my ship, the *Beast*, arrives at this prison. My crew is on their way to free me and what's left of my men. They will kill everyone in this facility regardless if they find us dead or alive. Your only chance of survival is my freedom."

"Then why do you need us to let you out?" The Vet asked with a laugh. "If what you're sayin' is true, why not just sit back and wait?"

"If I become a UG hostage, they won't think twice about killing me if they have to. What I know will lead my crew to unspeakable wealth, and if I share it with the UG, only horrific deaths. Now that they found my location, they won't risk losing me again. I don't wish to wait it out because I prefer to live."

"They have no clue where you are!" the Rookie shouted.

"They don't?" I narrowed my eyes. "It's amazing what implants are available on the black market. Tracking devices are nearly free and easily hidden."

"But…you were scanned for JaCs…," the Rookie whispered.

"Was I? Is that what they told you?" A smile split my face. "I wasn't scanned after they boarded my fighter, or in the transport vessel that brought me here. And this prison isn't equipped with such technology." The Rookie couldn't hold back his sickness any longer and spilled his recent meal on the front of his shirt and down onto the stone around his feet. The Vet had nothing to add, so I continued. "Roll the dice and tell me what you see. Riches and life, or certain death."

The Vet lowered his eyes and spoke down toward the floor. "Go get the Warden. We have an escaped prisoner he needs to deal with."

The Rookie nodded while using his sleeve to wipe the clinging sickness off his lips and chin. It took him a few attempts to work his pistol back into its holster, then turned to leave through the back door.

"Wait," the Vet said, "take this with you." A bullet split the Rookie's forehead as he turned to look back; the report was deafening in the tight space. The flash from the gun's barrel highlighted the chunks of white bone and greyish-red fluid that painted the back wall. The Rookie's body slumped to the floor, twitching and kicking as if he was still trying to leave.

The Vet unlocked the door between us and started toward me; his gun was still readied and pointed at the center of my chest. He took slow steps, keeping his balance while his finger brushed against the trigger.

"Fuck me, I can't believe I'm doin' this," he said as he chewed on his lip. "Fuck me. Fuck me. Fuck me." The Vet shook a finger as he talked. "You will pay up for this. One hundred and twenty thousand credits."

"The deal was fifty," I said.

"I'm taking my fifty and his fifty since he doesn't need it any longer. And for what I just fuckin' did, I'm addin' a little bonus."

"And if I disagree?"

"You'll end up lookin' like my partner."

I glanced at the Rookie. "One hundred and twenty thousand credits then."

"When you get out of here, you'll find me on Torcsa, in the city of Padis. There's a bar in the unpatrolled sector of the city named Neon Tiger. That's where I'll be waitin'." With his empty hand, the vet motioned to the wall of bars behind him. "Walk through that gate, take two rights, and you will find two of your officers under guard. Free your crew, get on your ship, and bring me those credits."

"I propose one last deal," I said. He arched his eyebrow as I continued. "An additional ten thousand credits for the answers to three questions."

He rolled his eyes toward the ceiling as if he was already spending the credits in his mind. "Make them quick."

I rifled off each question as fast as I could ask them. "What prison is this?"

"Paxcel."

"How many UG soldiers are stationed here?"

"About sixty."

"Did you torture my crew?"

"Y...No," he stammered. The burning look in my eyes must have scared him into changing his answer.

I released the spike, letting it drop freely from the inside of my sleeve, and gripped the last of the cold metal as it fell. The Vet squeezed off two rounds, but he was too late. Too slow. The bullets missed my torso as I spun and thrust the rod into his stomach. He grunted as I loosened the pistol from his grip and tossed it aside. I plunged the rod into his stomach again, this time meeting the resistance of his ribs with a sharp snap. A third and final thrust forced the air from his lungs. Blood formed a red line at his lips then spilled from the corners of his mouth.

I kicked his legs out from under him as I grasped his greasy mop of hair. He tried to speak but only red foam bubbled from this mouth. His vacant eyes strayed from mine and fixed on the rod still planted in his gut. A red stain expanded on his shirt and blood ran freely along the metal shaft then puddled on the floor.

I lowered myself and whispered into his ear as I slowly tore hair away from the back of his head. His widening eyes shifted to meet mine. "You slaughtered my crew and raped Salise."

Wheezing like a leaking balloon, the guard mouthed some words but they only sputtered out as gasps and moans. The top of my knee greeted his face with a resounding crunch, dropping the Vet into the puddle of his own fluids and pushing the rod through his back.

I recovered his gun and spun the cylinder open. Two rounds left. I made my way to the Rookie who lay crumpled on the floor, his weapon pinned beneath him. I rolled him to his back and gathered his gun and the keys.

The back gate was unlocked, and opened into a smooth and polished tile hallway. This area must have been reserved for working space, offices, and barracks as the walls were clean, well lit, and lacked the familiar scent of death. At least for now.

When I stepped into the hall, it immediately split into a 'T.' I followed the advice of the Vet and took a right until I came to another split. The passageway was short, ended abruptly, and contained four locked doors. Posted in front of them was a single guard resting his back against the wall only a few paces from where I stood. He lightly tapped a cudgel against one of the locked doors as he stifled a yawn with his free hand.

Wanting to preserve the bullets and avoid the noise, I pocketed both pistols, then removed the coat and laid it on the floor behind me. I leapt around the corner and aimed my first strike at the guard's head. He was quicker and more alert than I had expected. My punch sailed high and struck nothing but air.

He drove his balled fist into my ribs like an angry hammer. A swing of his club caught me under the jaw, wobbling my legs and dropping me to a knee. A second blow struck me on the back of my head and showered my eyes with blinding light.

I recovered, tackled him into the wall, and rocked his back into one of the cell door's hinges. The air emptied from his lungs with a forceful grunt. He reached for my neck but I cleared his hands and thrust my palm up into his face, shattering his nose and sending his head bouncing off the corner of the door. When he stumbled forward, I wrapped his head under my arm and yanked upwards. With a loud snap his neck buckled, and his body went limp then crumpled at my feet.

I tried to massage the pain out of my skull while eyeing the four doors. These weren't standard prison cells. They lacked any type of access slots or visible view of the insides. Three of the doors lined the north wall, one after the other, and were securely bolted behind two horizontal iron latches with manual hand pulls. The fourth door was separated from the others on the south wall and had four vertical and four horizontal steel bars locking it in place.

If any of my crew were locked behind these doors, I had no way to determine who or which rooms they were in. I wasn't going to announce my presence or say their names. I had too many enemies and it was too easy for anyone to acknowledge my call with the hopes of being released. I had to open the doors quickly and be ready to react.

I recovered the guard's baton and stepped in front of the first door.

Palming the latch knobs, I slid them back and opened it. The room was empty but appeared to have been recently used. It contained a bed with crisp white sheets, displaying the indentation of a body that recently slept on top of it. There was a chair near the door and it had facilities with running water.

My movements disturbed whatever was being held captive behind the fourth door, inciting muffled screams and pounding on the cell. I turned to face the noise and watched as the steel bars vibrated each time the door was struck from the inside. Common sense told me to leave this room for last, but I didn't.

I drew in a deep breath and unlocked the eight cross-hatched bars, one at a time. They retracted slowly, groaning as they rubbed steel on steel and sunk back into the walls. The freed door swung open, as if it was spring loaded, and slammed against the outside wall. Standing at the entryway was a mountain of muscle, nearly a half meter taller than me and one and half times my weight. Tattoos of entwined black and red flames were inscribed onto his olive skin, starting at the base of his neck and snaking down his arms and chest. Beads of sweat glistened through the stubble on the top of his shaved head and a thick, twisted mass of ink-black hair cascaded from under his nose and chin. Clothed in the remains of torn pants and a set of broken shackles, his thick corded muscles tensed as the remaining chain links that dangled from each wrist restraint jingled with every forceful breath.

His fists curled and knuckles whitened when he saw me. "It's about time."

Tank stepped out of the cell, careful to duck his head under the low hanging frame of the door. He raised his tree-sized arm, then slapped his paw of a hand on my shoulder, rocking me backwards. "Maxx, I was about ready to give up on you." His voice sounded like a building storm, thunderous and rumbling with anger.

"Tank," I said, "I thought you knew me better than that."

"I suppose I do, Maxx. I suppose I do." Tank's eyes scanned the hall like a hungry predator looking for something to dismember, kill, and eat. Resigned that it was empty, he looked back into his cell and spit in disgust.

There were two doors remaining, both still locked by a set of dual latches. "Who's left?" I asked, tapping one of the closed doors lightly with my knuckle.

"What do you mean?" Tank asked as he squinted against the light and rubbed his eyes.

"I was told that there are only three of us left. Salise was…" I paused mid-sentence. Now was not the time for me to provide too many details until we knew the actual status of the crew. Knowing Tank's feelings for Salise, it would only complicate things.

Tank drew in a deep breath. "Do you know what happened to Salise?" He asked me with hesitation.

"I'm not sure. I've been fed nothing but lies for over a hundred days, so I don't know who's dead and who's alive."

"Then there's only one way to find out." Tank brushed me aside and pealed the iron latches from the wall and door. Bolts popped off the mounting brackets like bullets shot from a gun, and the iron moaned as it was wrenched free. Tank was always inhumanly strong, but his implants

38

morphed him into a dangerous and hard-hearted killer. Living on the edge of sanity, Tank's psyche wobbled between aloofness and brutality. He was the loyal guard dog you wanted at your side, but when his implants flipped the psychotic switch it was best to step aside and let the beast run free.

"Save your anger, Tank," I said as I laid my hand on his shoulder. "We'll have use of it yet." I pulled open the door to find Cooper standing at the entryway, his arms braced against the frame. He yawned as if bored. The hopeful look in Tank's eyes dissolved to disappointment as if he was hoping to see someone else.

Cooper flashed his signature white, toothy smile, which contrasted against his dark skin. His body was riddled with bruises and cuts, and looked as if he hadn't slept in months. He was dressed in threadbare cotton pants and a light shirt, both of which were soiled and torn.

"Well now," Cooper said through a smile. He squinted while rubbing his chin between his index finger and thumb. "Don't the both of you look like shit?"

Cooper was a loyal member of my team and a highly skilled soldier. He'd been working for me since the first day I cut my teeth on this profession, and was the most valuable asset I employed. Captain of my crew, pilot, crafty smuggler, and lethal marksmen, he fit nearly any need our contracts required. Although he's critical to my success, there wasn't a day that passed where I didn't think about punching his teeth through the back of this throat. He's the biggest smartass in the galaxy, and as much as I wanted to crush that trait, his wit was needed to keep the crew's mood light when things got tough. Unfortunately, it's a skill we needed more often than not.

"If you were as quick in battle as your mouth is with words, you may actually be worth something," Tank said. His nose was pinched upward as if he was about to snarl.

"I love you too, Tank," Cooper said as he looked him over. "You may want to take a moment to do a few pushups. Looks like you've gotten a bit scrawny while in captivity." Cooper disregarded Tank's rumbling response. He continued with his smile and slapped me on the arm. "Thanks, Boss, for busting me out. To be honest, I was going to give you just one more day then I figured I would step up and save your ass. I know how good it makes you feel to be the hero, so I wanted to give you first crack."

I ignored him, learning long ago that it was the best thing to do. I never won a battle of words with Cooper. No one did.

"Enough of the little man's talk," Tank said. "Let's get out of here." He rolled the dead guard onto his back and freed his gun from his holster. Rummaging through the guard's uniform, he found a set of keys, a folding knife, and a handful of credits.

"Where the hell are we?" Cooper asked as he scratched the back of his head. "Anyone know?"

"Paxcel," I said.

Cooper's eyes widened. "Wow. Whatever we've done we pissed off the wrong people."

"Fuck 'em all," Tank grunted. "I hope I get a chance to ask them what we did, personally, before we leave." He tossed the gun to Cooper and exchanged the knife with me for the baton. "I don't know about you two, but I don't plan on becoming a corpse at the hands of these UG minions."

I opened the blade on the knife. The greeting of the edged steel was a welcome one. It was utilitarian with a slightly bent blade, yet sturdy and razor sharp. I spun it around my fingers before laying it flat in my palm. "We need to find the docking bay," I said. "The prison area is west and south of here, so my best guess is that the pad is either north or east."

"Where are we headed?" Cooper asked.

"The space station orbiting Kogin."

If it was possible, Tank's eyes looked wilder than before. "Are you fucking crazy, Maxx? That's one of the main substations for the Solonian Empire! No way are we going to Kogin! No way in hell!"

Cooper responded with a series of quick nods. "As much as I hate to admit it, Tank's right, Boss. That's suicide. Hell, that's suicide with a touch of insanity. After failing to meet their contract terms, they'll be looking to tear us apart, piece by piece. We need to head in the opposite direction of the Solonians and lay low for a bit."

"And where should we go?" I asked, shifting my gaze between Cooper and Tank. "Where do you want to hide?" Neither of them replied. "Damn it, think this through. We hold the Solonian Empire's cargo on the *Beast*, the same cargo the UG hunted us down for. We're breaking out of a UG prison! In days we'll have the entire UG and Solonian Empire armies scouring every corner of the galaxy looking for us. The Solonian Empire has a prominent seat on the UG, and a vested interest in their cargo. We have to hope they can pull some strings. It's our only shot of getting out of this mess."

"So your plan is to ask the Solonians for forgiveness?" Tank laughed.

"I'm not planning on saying I'm sorry," I said. "I plan to ask them for credits." The corridor fell silent. Even Cooper didn't have a response. "No one knows where the *Beast* is right now. Not the UG or the Solonians."

"Do you?" Tank asked. "If you do, that's where we should go."

"I don't know where she is, but I know how to find her. I can give the Solonians a guarantee that we still have their cargo and that it will be delivered as promised. We'll just need some of our contract money up front to complete the job."

Tank rubbed the stubble on the top of his head until the skin was irritated and glowing red. "Shit, Maxx, things never get boring with you." Tank closed his eyes and sighed. "If they refuse?"

"I'm hoping their cargo is so valuable that they can't take the risk. There's a reason the UG didn't execute every one of us the moment we were captured. The same reason they've held us for one hundred and seven days. The UG wants whatever's resting inside the *Beast's* cargo hold."

"OK then, let's go for it," Cooper said. "After all, I hear the Solonian prisons are quite nice this time of year."

"Knowing the Solonians, we'll be lucky to see the inside of a prison cell," Tank said. "Whatever. It isn't the first time we've done something crazy."

"What about the others?" Cooper asked.

When my eyes met his, I shook my head, then watched as Cooper's smile melted away. "We don't know for sure, but it doesn't sound good." After a few seconds he bowed his head and traced an outline of a cross on his chest.

"There's one more person that needs to go with us," Cooper said as he raised his head. Before I had a chance to react, he sidestepped me and released the latches on the remaining door. He swung it open and revealed a tall, shapely figure standing at the back of the cell, partially concealed by darkness. "Let's go," Cooper said, motioning to the prisoner.

A dark-skinned female sauntered into the hall, her movement was lithe - almost cat like. Long, tightly-wound braids of sandy-brown hair fell to her shoulders, the ends concealed by dull colored beads that swayed with her hair and rattled against each other as she walked. The shocking beauty of her sharp, statuesque features were surpassed by the large pools of her amber eyes. She had an athletic build with long, sleek legs and well-toned arms. Her body was marred with pale scars and angry red lashes telling their visual tales of a rough life and of recent punishments.

Her inner forearms were burned and scared and she was quick to fold them across her chest the moment I noticed them. What remained of her clothing hung loose from her body, ragged and dirty like the others. Her appearance made we wonder if her treatment was worse than mine.

"This is Terra," Cooper said as he gently placed his hands on her bicep and elbow and escorted her from the cell.

"That's great," Tank said as he rolled his eyes. "It was really nice to meet you, Terra." The sarcasm was thick in his voice. "We don't have time for pets, Cooper." Tank looked over Terra with feigned interest, then spit. "I'll pick up a new, slightly less used companion for you once we reach the Kogin station."

Cooper's eyes narrowed and he ran his tongue across the front of his teeth. "Screw you, Tank!" He shouted as he jabbed a finger in Tank's direction.

I cut in before things had a chance to escalate. "I know where you're going with this, but she isn't coming with us." My stare was directed at Terra as I talked. To my surprise, her face remained unreadable, emotionless. She didn't even blink when I said it.

"You don't understand, Boss. She has to come with us," Cooper pleaded with an unfamiliar seriousness in his voice. "We can't leave her here."

"We owe her nothing," I replied. "And I'm not keen on taking unnecessary risks. We don't know why she's here, or why she's earned those from the UG." I pointed at the cuts and bruises on her body. "You freed her from the cell, which is more than what you should've done."

"Boss, she helped me get through this nightmare," Cooper said. "We'd communicate through the cell walls. Talk when the UG guards rotated their posts. Just knowing that someone else was there gave me a reason to press on. She's the only reason I'm still sane. If –"

"Enough!" I shouted. "There's nothing left to discuss."

Her eyes flickered in the light, changing colors as they shifted in their sockets. Her tongue ran across her lips as if to quench a stifling dryness before she spoke. "You're sick." Terra's voice purred, carrying a soothing and seductive tone. Her accent was thick and it was obvious Common was not her native language. She reached out to touch my arm and I quickly jerked it away from her outstretched fingers. "I can help."

"Forget it," I said, never removing my gaze from hers.

"Damn it, Maxx. If she can help, let her do this."

Terra returned my stare, her eyes scanning mine. Stretching out my arm reminded me of the days I was restrained and forced to take Toad's feedings. My body shuddered in response. The touch of her hand was warm and comforting as her rough fingers and calloused palms brushed across my arm. When she spotted the MXX inked onto my forearm, she retracted as if the letters tried to bite.

"Toxins," she purred. "Yellow skin. Widening pores. Chemical smell." She turned to look at Cooper. "It's poison."

Cooper turned to look at me. "Is that true, Boss? Have you been poisoned?"

"There's something in my system. Some type of neurotoxin that's settling at the base of my spine. I was told I won't have long before paralysis. Maybe a few days."

The braids in Terra's hair clacked together as she shook her head. "Not days. Maybe a day. Likely hours. The pain is great, yes?"

"Nothing I can't deal with."

Tank grumbled, "Let me see if I got this straight. We fight our way to the landing pad and hope to locate a shuttle that's fueled and ready for takeoff. After that we fly into the welcoming arms of the Solonians, search for a medic to remove the shit that's swimming in your bloodstream, then beg for a payout against the job we didn't, and more than likely won't, complete."

I nodded while Tank tugged at the twisted mass of hair that hung from his chin. He smirked then shrugged. "Easy enough. What are we waiting for?"

I grabbed Tank's arm and stopped him before he advanced down the hall. "We're not leaving," I said. "Not yet." Tank and Cooper exchanged glances. "I'm not giving up on our crew until I know they're dead. I won't leave them behind. Not this time."

Tank nodded. "We can start by searching through the cell blocks, but we'll need to be quick. It's only a matter of time –"

"That's not all." I cut Tank off before he could finish. "We have unfinished business we need to deal with. I need to find the location of the UG Captain that stormed our fighter and took us prisoner."

Tank tilted his head and furrowed a brow. "Don't make this personal, Maxx."

"Tank's right," Cooper said. "I'm all in for the search for our crew, but after that we need to get out of here as quickly as we can."

They both knew me well. Conducting business driven by personal feelings was nothing short of a sin to an agent soldier. I'd lost crew members before. More than I cared to admit. Many were slain in battle while others were left behind when I needed to make that call. But what happened to my crew in this prison didn't sit well with me.

"The UG made a choice when they boarded our fighter and took us into custody," I said. "The Captain executed the orders, and now I'm making a decision on how those actions will be repaid."

Tank grunted. "And what purpose would it serve other than painting a bigger target on our backs?"

"Someone sold us out, and he knows who it is."

"I doubt he's here," Tank said, "and if he isn't, how are we going to find him?"

"Maybe there's documentation, travel logs, docking or prison visit records. Maybe there's a soldier who has the information. I don't know, but I'm not leaving until I exhaust every possibility."

"And if you find him?" My quiet stare was answer enough. Tank shook his head as he continued. "You're really going to piss off the UG taking down one of their officers. You know that?"

"Another death warrant on my head makes no difference to me," I said, turning toward Cooper. "Terra is not my problem, and she isn't yours. You need to make a choice right here and right now. Either you secure a shuttle for the three of us, or you find your own way off of this planet with her. What's your decision?"

Cooper exhaled as his eyes found the floor. "You know where my loyalties lie."

"Good. Tank and I will search this facility for our crew and any information leading us to the location of the UG Captain. When we're done, we'll meet you in the docking bay." I recovered Toad's jacket and removed the two pistols and keys from the pockets, then emptied the two bullets from the first gun and dropped them into Cooper's open hand. Turning to Terra, I handed her the second pistol. She looked at the weapon, then back into my eyes as she took it from my hand. "I'm giving you that gun for what you've done for Cooper. Don't make me regret it. If you wait here for a few hours, you'll be safe to make your own escape."

I tossed the jacket to the floor and gripped the knife in the palm of my hand. Thoughts of the UG Captain and my missing crew consumed me as

I stared down the long corridor that would lead us back into the prison. It was time the UG felt my pain, and the pain of my crew. Someone needed to make them pay for their actions, and that person was me.

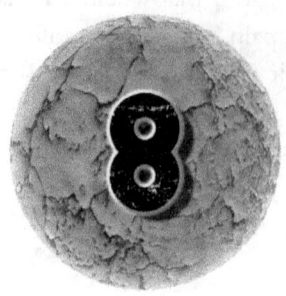

As Tank and I scoured the prison for UG personnel, my hopes of finding our remaining crew diminished with each passing step. I tried to convince myself that Toad was lying about their deaths and that the Vet made a mistake with his response. However, deep inside I knew they were all dead, and that truth burned inside the pit of my stomach like a raging fire. But I ignored that truth, and refused to quit searching until I confirmed it myself.

Outside of the UG, very little was known about Paxcel. Even still, rumors about this prison were widespread, and most appeared to be true. A technology free, maximum-security prison, strategically constructed by the UG to remove all possibilities of outsiders performing remote identification scans, snooping, or hacking of their systems. Only the most treacherous men and women in the galaxy were forced to call this place home, and the UG had every intention of keeping it that way. A rigid set of protocols were in place to ensure that Paxcel was the most secure prison in this sector. It was unfortunate for the UG that greed didn't follow protocols.

Methodically, we moved from room to room, from hall to hall, marking the door of each searched chamber with my knife as we advanced. At first, we discovered very little, and that's what disturbed me the most. Unsecured corridors stretched out before us, leading to offices, briefing rooms, and storage chambers. All of the doors were unlocked and left open. Scattered inside were random supplies, work schedules, paperwork, and tooth-marked pencils. There wasn't one sign of personnel as if the staff had fled the prison.

A yellow beam of light reached into the hall from an open door at the end of the passageway. We entered the chamber and found a desk centered in the middle; a light above dangled by a thin cord and swayed from side to side as if someone had bumped it when sprinting from the room. On top of the desk were pictures, dozens of them fanned out from one end to the other. They were pictures of my crew. Detailed pictures. Pictures of their torture. Pictures they wanted me to see.

Tank backed his way into the corner of the room and slumped against the wall. His eyes were fixed on the desk, his fingers knitted together behind his head. I picked the pictures up, one at a time, and studied them until the images were burned into my brain like a symbol from a scorching iron brand. Buried underneath was handwritten documentation detailing the types of tortures performed, the times they were conducted, the questions that were asked, and my crew's responses. Each document ended with a date and time of their deaths, underlined and circled with emphasis in dark black. Toad told me the truth. They were tortured and killed within hours of our capture.

"This is fucked up, Maxx." Tank rubbed his hands across his face, leaving behind red tracks from the tips of his fingers. "We need to get out. Now."

"The hell we are!" I snapped. The reports shook in my unsteady hand as I read them. "I'm not leaving."

"Why now, Maxx?" Tank arched an eyebrow as he looked up at me. "Why this time?"

"They killed my crew - our soldiers! They tortured them! And for what?" I pounded my fists on the desk then swept the pictures off the edge, spilling them to the floor like a paper waterfall. "They take what they want, impose their will on others as they want!" I shook my head and lowered my voice. "When will it stop, Tank? Who's going to stand up to them?"

"Now is not the time."

"If not now, when? They will hunt us, Tank, until everyone's dead. There's no recourse for their actions."

Tank's eyes drifted to the MXX inked into my arm. "You're too invested in this, Maxx."

"So, we should just forget this happened?" I lanced my finger at the pictures on the floor.

"I didn't say that. But now isn't the time."

I bent down, recovered a picture of Salise and flicked it into Tank's chest. "Do it for Salise. You owe her that."

Tank's lips drew a thin line and his nose crumpled into a scowl. "I only do things for me!" He jerked his thumb at his chest. "Since when do you give a shit about anyone else?" Tank's bottom lip quivered as he drifted into silence. He pretended the death of Salise and the crew didn't bother him, masking his feelings behind a sudden outburst of rage. But I could see his hurt – almost feel it.

"What they did is an attack on me!" I shouted as our heated glances locked. "It's an attack on us! The UG isn't walking away from this. If you don't want to take part, find your way to Cooper and the shuttles and wait for me there."

Tank broke his stare from mine and chuckled under his breath as he tugged on his twisted goatee. He pushed his back away from the wall, stepped next to me and looked down. "Enough talk. Let's kill the fuckers."

I looked up into Tank's eyes. "Anyone in this prison wearing a UG insignia dies before we leave. Anyone who *looks* like they want to wear a UG insignia dies. Understood?"

The knuckles on Tank's hands whitened as he balled them into fists. "Understood."

I took one last look at the pictures, then turned and walked out the door.

The winding passageway led us to a guard; a single soldier manned a gateway that appeared to be the main entrance into the barracks. Behind the soldier were shifting shadows that escaped into the hall through the crack of the slightly open double doors. Muffled voices echoed from the back rooms.

Before I could strike, Tank pushed his way past me and rushed the solider. The UG guard fired an errant round before Tank palmed his head as if it was a small, circular fruit. Tank lifted him from the ground and struck his head against the wall with such sickening force that the guard's skull shattered upon impact and dented the sheets of welded steel. A long streak of red painted the metal as the guard's lifeless body slid to the floor. Tank recovered the gun then cleaned his hands on the front of the guard's shirt. Shadows scattered behind the doorway, and eventually vanished.

"Fuck me," Tank mumbled as he handed me the pistol. "I should've got to him quicker."

I rested my back on the side of the door frame, straddling the guard's body. "We've been locked up for over a hundred days," I said. "We're slow, starving, dehydrated, and our vision is worthless. This isn't going to be easy." I spun open the cylinder of the pistol to count the remaining rounds. "What the hell?" I mumbled. "He had one bullet. Why the hell only one bullet?" I slapped the cylinder back into place and dropped the gun onto the dead soldier's lap.

"Everything about this smells funny," Tank said. "Something's going on."

Tank was right. It was as if the guards and soldiers fled the prison like rats from a sinking boat. Finding a soldier with only a single round in his gun had me wondering if he was really guarding something, or saving the bullet for himself.

We entered the room behind the door and found three men at the back of the barracks, armed with makeshift weapons of pipe and pieces of metal torn free from the frames of their cots. Beds and storage chests were overturned and clothes were dumped onto the floor in a sea of chaos. Tank and I stood in front of the only door, blocking their way out of the room. They were trapped and forced to face us. A rail-thin soldier stood boldly, his arms crossed against his sunken chest. The other two men flanked him on either side.

The Runt called me out. His skin was nearly transparent showing tracks of veins in his boney, rope-like arms. "You're the agent soldiers with all the warrants," he said. "The ones running the illegal cargo."

"Where is everyone?" I growled. The vivid images of my tortured crew played over and over in my mind. I squeezed the grip of the knife so tight that it dug into my palm.

"We're right here, asshole! Don't you worry about the others." The Runt's eyes shifted in their sockets as he talked.

Tank looked at the Runt, then back at me. "Someone cleared out this prison, Maxx."

"You're the ones they left behind," I said as I looked around the room. "The UG left you here to pay for their mistakes." I looked each man directly in his eyes. "I would expect nothing less."

A smile crept across the Runt's face, stretching his pale skin against his high cheekbones and revealing a mouthful of uneven teeth. He exchanged glances with the soldiers on either side of him. "You two take the big one on the left. I'll take the one with the smart mouth."

As Tank stepped forward, I rested my free palm against his chest. "These three are mine."

"I hope you're tougher than your crew." The Runt chuckled. "Those guys were a bunch of pussies."

Tank grunted and took another step, so I moved in front of him. "Their deaths are my responsibility," I said to Tank. "These men are mine."

"Yeah, big dog." The Runt pointed at Tank. "Listen to your master." The two guards next to him joined in, laughing and pointing the ends of their pipes in our direction. "I'll tell you what," the Runt said as he scratched at the patchy hair that lined his chin. "You bring me another one of those hot-tempered women from your ship, and we'll let you two live another few days locked in a cell." The Runt wet his lips with his snake-like tongue. "I can still taste her."

The handle of the knife dug deeper into my skin as my hands clenched into fists. A small cut opened in my palm, dripping blood between my fingers. I tried to bury my anger. I tried to repress my hatred. But I couldn't. My body reacted by instinct. I sprinted toward them. The Runt's jaw dropped while he lost his balance and started to tumble backward. I was there, within a couple meters of sending their black souls to the reapers. That's when it all went to hell.

A fourth UG solider sprang from the cover of an askew cot tipped on its side at the opposite end of the room. From the corner of my eye I caught his sudden movement, and a brief glint of metal followed by an orange flash. I felt two hits. The first was a bullet tearing its way across the top of my shoulder, skimming cloth and flesh. The second was a forearm to my back from Tank, driving me to the floor with the force equal to that of a wrecking ball.

Tank stood over me, his body shielding mine like a towering wall of bronzed muscle. The UG soldier emptied his last five rounds into Tank, a spray of bullets striking his body with muted thumps. Rubbing the stars from my eyes I saw the panicked look on the soldier's face and heard the clack of the hammer dry firing against the empty rounds. Tank took one step forward before his legs buckled and swayed. He crashed to the floor like a broken trunk of a fallen tree.

Tank's fingers scratched at the tiled floor, the tips of his nails broke free as he clawed his way toward the soldiers. He tried to say something, but I couldn't hear him over the screams of celebration. Blood flowed freely from his mouth and nose, leaking onto the floor.

The UG soldiers advanced upon me to finish the job they'd so cleverly started. Their voices burned in my ears and their UG stench churned my stomach. They embodied everything I loathed about the UG. Everything. The next few minutes were lost to a blur of rage. Their screams of joy quickly turned into cries for mercy, leaving me to wonder if my crew's pleas rang similarly in their torturers' ears as they died slow and grueling deaths. Disarming them was easy. Shattering bones and dislocating joints nearly as simple. Their shattered bodies littered the floor around me, curled into balls of blood and pain.

"Please...no more!" The Runt screamed. "I'm sorry. I'm so, so sorry..."

The Runt begged for his life and sputtered apologies for what he did to my crew. He wasn't sorry because of his actions, only sorry because I was here to collect payment for his sins. Sorry because he knew he was going to die.

"Where's the Captain?" I said through gritted teeth.

"What Captain?" The Runt sputtered as he tried to move his legs that were bent at odd angles beneath him. "I don't know..." His voice trailed off into a whimper. He grabbed the frame of a cot near his head and pulled, inching his shattered body away from me.

I stepped on his leg and pinned it between my boot and the polished tile. He howled in pain.

"Who cleared out the prison?" I asked. "Why did everyone leave?"

The Runt's bottom lip trembled as he talked. "I don't know! The orders came from outside of here!"

"Tell me what you do know, and I'll show you the mercy you didn't show my crew."

"Please...I don't know much. They cleared everyone out just hours ago. We were told to stay behind and slow anyone's access to the docking pad. That's all I know!"

"Instead, you hid like cowards and holed up in this room." I looked at Tank's motionless body as I spun the handle of the knife in my hand. Thoughts of my crew and the pictures of their horrible deaths filled my mind once again. "You should've run."

When I was finished, the walls were painted with a brooding red, splashed and sprayed on the tile and steel as streams of crimson trickled down my arms and stung my eyes. My heart raced and thunderous tremors rippled inside my head. I knelt on one knee and braced my hand against the floor. What happened in that room settled inside me like a ball of broken glass that exploded inside my chest. The imagery, the smells and taste in my mouth was death soaked in evil. Yet I felt unsatisfied as if paying with their lives wasn't enough. I started to grow sick.

That's when the inside of my head exploded with the force of a supernova, showering the backs of my eyes with blinding light. Compartmentalizing the ill effects of the torture and drug feedings was too much for me to contain when confronted with overpowering hate. I was able to tuck them away until the bulging walls of the secure container finally burst and spilled its dark contents from my subconscious.

My mind tried to reestablish the misplaced feelings, attempting to work the pieces back into place like a complex jigsaw puzzle it thought was already completed. Leaving no room, it tried to jam in the extra pieces to make it all fit, warping and breaking what was once whole. Synapses fired off in my brain like a raging electrical storm. I placed my hand in front of my eyes and watched as it started to blur and fade. My lungs grew heavy, refusing to draw a breath. The pounding of my heart accelerated and the room started to spin. My last clear memory was a flash of light, and the unwelcome greeting the floor slapped against my face as everything grew dark.

Afterwards, my body took hazy snapshots of the events around me as I slipped in and out of consciousness. I was living in a hallucination. It all felt like a dream in which I had no control, as if I was nothing but a pawn in a nightmare, forced to watch but not allowed to participate with my own free will.

A prickling cold pulsated in the small of my back then crept outwards like an army of a thousand icy spiders, until feeling was lost in my legs and arms. Around me there were explosions, the clanking of boots and loud voices - all muffled as if my head was under water. The look in Tank's eyes was haunting, his body rigidly still and seeping blood from his open wounds. His body was jerked out of my sight. Darkness followed.

I woke to the sound of my boots rubbing across a grated floor. A pair of shuffling legs was on either side of me; my arms, still without feeling, were pulled behind my back. There was a violent roar followed by the stench of something burning. The pungent smell clung to my nostrils and snuck into my watering eyes. Everything around me grew black.

My eyelids flickered open. I was on my stomach, strapped to a cot. There were blinding lights everywhere, above my head, at my sides and directed at my face. I heard the clacking of a cart's wheels, the tinkling of glass, and ringing of metal tools. Off in the distance a blurred figure was flicking the tip of a long needle. My heart raced. We never made it off Paxcel. I was back in the hands of the UG butchers, who were hell bent on finishing the job Toad had started. I willed myself from the cot, but my arms and legs wouldn't respond. I was at their mercy.

As the light faded, I heard a voice as gentle as a warm summer breeze. I couldn't understand the words, but the tone was soft and comforting. Never did I expect to be visited by an angel when standing at the foot of death's door. I always knew there would be countless, darkened souls waiting to greet me, but not an angel. Angels didn't care about people like me. I tried to cry out, to tell her to make her words quick, because when the reapers come for their claim on my soul, no one was safe. Not even an angel. Darkness closed in as her voice warped and dimmed. It was too late for both of us.

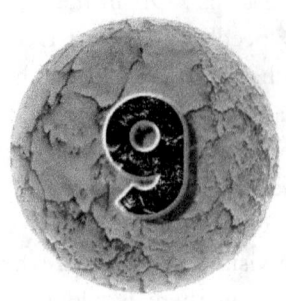

My body vaulted from a deep sleep like a drowning man breaking through the water's surface. I sucked in a panicked breath, attempting to squelch the burning in my lungs. I laid motionless as I concentrated on the whir of vented oxygen that pushed its way through my nose and mouth. My arm felt as if it weighed a hundred kilos as I lifted it from my side and peeled a plastic mask off my face. As I dropped it to the floor it released a relentless, angry hiss. The smell of the air around me was crisp. Fresh.

My eyes were as dry as bone, and when I forced them open, a layer of crust broke free from the corners. I swashed my tongue across my cracked lips, feeling sharp stings with each pass. My joints were stiff and my head felt like a hammer-rung bell, but my thoughts were clear, free of the drugs that had clouded my head for more than a hundred days.

As I sat upright on my cot, a prickling sensation danced around my lower back. My hand found the source - a finger-length incision, stapled and bandaged. Naked with only a thin sheet covering my legs, it was hard not to focus on the punishments I'd taken over the years. My chest and arms looked like a war torn battlefield riddled with pale scars, fresh cuts, and purple-black bruises. Each served as a reminder of how dangerous my profession was, and how every credit I made was earned.

The room gave the appearance of being dipped in white paint. A white sheet, white cot, rounded white walls, and a white marble floor decorated the chamber. Recessed lighting dotted the ceiling, showering the room in a soft, warm glow. A vent on the far wall pumped in oxygen and the smell of antiseptic clean. At the side of my cot was a black coat draped over the back of a white, spindle-backed chair. A black and grey shirt, black pants, socks, and undergarments were neatly folded and resting on the seat.

Underneath the chair was a pair of black military-style combat boots.

The raw aches from too many days of bed rest enveloped me as I stood. I stretched, and my body groaned, popped, and cracked with pleasant agony. My mouth was dry and stale but it was a good taste, a natural taste, assuring me the drugs were purged from my system. I donned the cotton and nylon pants, then the form fitting sleeveless shirt. Both felt durable yet flexible and tailored to fit my frame.

The long flowing coat was crafted out of supple leather and dark as ink, intricately stitched along the edges with a deep blood-red thread. The back was split at the very bottom, into two short tails, and the front was adorned with four silver buckles, three at the breast and one at the mandarin collar. Each buckle cinched the jacket tight around me and tapping the quick release buttons allowed uninhibited movement when needed. Lining the inside of the coat was nylon material, dyed to match the color of the thread, with two pockets and two built-in sheaths for eight-inch knives. Located inside the pockets were two black leather gloves but the sheaths were noticeably empty.

I heard the electronic swoosh of a door opening behind me. "Boss," someone said. It was the familiar sound of Cooper's voice. "I thought you were never going to wake up! That's one hell of a nap you just took."

"What happened to the angel?" I asked, turning to face Cooper. His face was recently battered, sporting a fresh gash on the bridge of his broken nose and an angry bloodshot eye that screamed out in agony. As bad as he must have felt, he hid it well behind his toothy smile. Cooper's head and face were shaved clean and he was wearing a brown, rumpled pilot's jacket, brown combat pants and a black shirt.

"Yeah…an angel. Sure thing, Boss. I think she left to grab us something to drink." He laughed, patted me with mock reconciliation, then took a seat on the chair. "It's safe to assume your pain meds are working."

I shrugged him off. "What about Tank?" The question came out thick as if I already knew the answer.

Cooper placed his arms behind his head and tilted the back of the chair against the wall. His dark skin provided a sharp contrast against the stark white of the room. "To be honest, Boss, it isn't good."

I closed my eyes and pictured the empty look on Tank's face. Running my hands across the stubble on my recently shaven face, I searched for a response. "It's my fault."

"Really?" Cooper asked with an inquisitive tilt of his head. "I didn't know you were the reason he's been whoring his way through this space station."

"Don't mess with me, Cooper." I thrust my foot down on the seat of his chair, slamming the legs on the floor.

Cooper threw up his arms, palms out in front of him as if preparing to stop me from swinging. "You didn't let me finish. It isn't good because the Solonians will be slightly less pleasant to deal with after all the problems he's caused on this station."

"Most days you make me wonder why I keep you around." I attempted to rub the sudden knots of tension out of my neck. "He made it then?"

Cooper nodded. "He's one lucky son of a bitch. Only one of the bullets came close to hitting a vital organ. Hell, he nearly dug those bullets out himself. If his fingers weren't so damn large, and the holes so small, I'm sure he would've tried. I had to use the tip of a screwdriver to dig three of the bullets out, then heated the blade with a torch to cauterize the wounds. Removing the other two was a bigger challenge. They shattered and spread shrapnel across his chest. I had to cut him…a lot, in order to locate all the fragments. He took it in stride and did the best he could, considering I had to do it without any anesthetic. Since then, his healing JaC has done the rest."

I shouldn't have counted Tank out so easily. That bull has survived much worse. "How long have I been out?"

"Four days - give or take a few hours."

"So you played the role of the hero and came back to save us?" I asked. "Were you hoping for a larger than normal cut from our deal with the Solonians?"

Cooper pursed his lips, rolled his eyes up toward the ceiling, then bobbed his head. "Now that you mention it, that does seem fair." Cooper smiled even wider as he stood. "But I can't take all the credit, Boss. It was Terra who saved your asses."

"Terra?"

"Yeah. When she was searching for her way out, she stumbled into the mess you and Tank made. She found the both of you unresponsive on the floor. Eventually she was able to locate the landing pad, and me, and we dragged both of you back to the shuttle - which, let me tell you, was no easy task when Tank weighs more than the shuttle itself."

I lowered my eyes and nodded my thanks. "Where are we?" I asked as I looked around the snowy white room.

"The space station above Kogin. Just like you asked."

"Have you had any discussions with the Solonians?"

The laugh lines around Cooper's eyes grew serious as he closed in and whispered into my ear. "It wasn't easy docking the space station. The Solonians have infested this facility. The guards, business owners, even the damn maintenance personnel are Solonians or on the Solonian payroll. Kogin is no longer just a substation for the Solonian Empire. The only non-Solonian personnel you can be sure of are their slaves."

"Give me the details on how I got here, and keep it short."

"That's where things start to get messed up. When we docked the station, the Solonian royal guard had orders to drag you in front of the Solonian Officials, but the drugs in your body wouldn't pass the quarantine scans. They spent hours debating whether or not to destroy our shuttle and the whole damn launch pad we were connected to."

"But they wanted the *Beast* and their cargo more than they wanted me dead."

"You're right." Cooper tapped the bridge of his nose and winced. "After a *conversation* with Tank and me, they felt confident we didn't know the location of the *Beast* and decided to help."

"So the Solonians purged Toad's drugs out of my system?"

"It wasn't the Solonians. It was Terra. The Solonian Officials weren't keen on parting with one of only four medical personnel staffed on this station. They thought it was too risky sending one of them into a quarantined situation. They sealed off a section of the loading dock, gave us a gurney and medical supplies. She did the rest."

"So my guess is that I'm under guard right now?"

"Once you were in the clear and passed the quarantine scan, they moved you into a secure area of the station." Cooper opened his arms and twisted slightly from side to side. "This lovely, blizzard-colored room. Right now half of their army is standing outside."

I glanced over my shoulder at the door and exhaled. "Why the hell are they letting you and Tank roam free?"

"We'd be fooling ourselves if we didn't think we were under constant surveillance. At this moment I'm sure we're being monitored by Solonian security staff, listening to every word we speak, and watching our every move. They're hoping one of us spills what we know about the ship or that we form a new crew so they can track our route back to the *Beast*."

"Who do I thank for the clothes, and who can help me fill these?" I asked, sticking my fingers into the empty sheaths inside my overcoat.

"We were able to work out a deal with a local tailor on the station, promising him four times his normal fees for the clothes. He took our measurements, asked me some questions and returned a few days later with a new set for each of us. I thought it was best that you look the part of the terrifying, yet respectable, agent soldier for the next time you meet with the Officials." Cooper straightened my jacket, then placed his hands on my face, sniffing as if holding back tears. "You make me so proud."

My tone turned grim. "Where is Terra now? It looks like I owe her more than I would've expected."

Cooper's frown covered his bright, white teeth. "She's gone."

"Gone? What do you mean?"

"Terra was taken as a personal servant slave for one of the Solonian Officials. She was permitted two days of freedom to monitor your health. After that she was escorted directly to them."

My knuckles cracked underneath my gloves as I balled my hands into fists. "I need you to round up Tank."

"Sure, Boss. Then what?"

"We're going to collect our credits and get Terra back."

Within an hour Cooper returned with a stumbling Tank in tow; the stench of alcohol and cheap perfume trailing behind him. Tank's expression contorted into a look of annoyance when he saw me encircled by a contingent of Solonian soldiers.

From the doorstep of my recovery room we were herded like cattle through the space station to the Solonian battle cruiser. The last time I set foot in the Kogin station, it was bustling with activity, rich with life and trade, but this time we were surrounded by an uncomfortable quiet, its occupants subdued by the influx of Solonians. The soldiers, staff, and station residents appeared edgy and avoided direct eye contact as we pressed forward. It didn't help that Tank's drunken stupor had him bumping into the walls and stumbling into the backs of the soldiers. His booming voice belted out slurred, off-tune songs that rang down the halls.

"Holy crap, Tank," Cooper said. "How much did you have to drink? A freighter full of liquor?"

Tank widened his eyes in an exaggerated fashion and brushed his forearm across his face. "I would say...not enough." He shuffled his feet as he took measured steps, swaying from side to side. "Not nearly enough."

"Maybe you should get another healing JaC so you can recoup faster?" Cooper laughed. "Damn man, those must've been some really ugly Solonian woman to have to drink that much."

Cooper's last remark earned him a blistering jolt from the stock of a guard's assault rifle. I turned to catch the soldier's steeled gaze. Their patience was wearing thin, and I knew they'd rather blast us in our backs and leave us for dead than escort us across the full length of the station.

"Control yourselves!" I barked under my breath. Causing ripples now would only amplify our problems later. I grabbed Tank's shoulder and attempted to pull him back toward me. "Tank, I need you to focus." I whispered.

"I promise you, Maxx. I'm focused." Tank snorted and shook his head. "Do you really think the Solonians are just going to hand us a pile of credits and send us on our way with a thank you?"

"I don't know, but we have hundreds of crewmen back on the *Beast* that are counting on us. They need your help." I paused before I continued. "I need your help."

Tank heaved a strong sigh, laced with the smell of alcohol. "It's been a rough few days, Maxx. I thought we lost you." Tank rested his arm across my shoulders as we passed through the shopping district and continued toward the guard station. "It's good to have you back. You know you can count on me."

And with those few words, my team was ready.

Today's meeting with the Solonian Officials was an all or nothing proposition. Four months ago we entered into a contract with them to deliver undisclosed goods to a Solonian contact on Lotress, a planet forty-two jumps away. The route wasn't easy and their generous offer of two hundred thousand credits reflected that. Both parties had agreed there could be some delays in order to ensure a safe delivery of the Solonian cargo. However, they didn't assume "some delays" meant more than ninety days past the negotiated delivery date. Neither did I, and we can thank the UG for that.

The Solonians are one of the seventy-eight Empire Nations which have an equal seat on the coalition of Unified Governments, and like all the other Empire Nations they're as crooked as hell. They hide their corruption well while using the UG when possible to bolster their wealth. They're a heavyweight on the council, quick to judge but not to forgive. Keeping us alive tells me they're concerned about the cargo on my ship, and whatever they contracted with me to move has the keen interest of others, including the UG.

The population of Kogin residents grew noticeably thinner, and the quiet of the space station closed in on us. The muscles of my shoulders and neck knotted when I caught first site of the hatch that blocked access to the battle cruiser's extension bridge. The door leading to the five hundred meter walkway, and ultimately to the Solonian battle cruiser, was sealed tight and locked in place with four cylindrical cross beams of carbon fiber as big around as my thighs.

A guard pushed a pistol into my face and walked us back a few meters while two other soldiers initiated a security confirmation sequence consisting of biometric retinal scans, thermal readings, and DNA samples. When completed, a third soldier traced a pattern onto the lighted panel on the wall. The pressurized seal on the access hatch broke, spewing stale, synthesized oxygen into the corridor, lifting the tails of my jacket under its forceful rush. The all too familiar scent reminded me of business, credits, and a wealth of opportunity. I could only hope that today was no different.

The lead guard bowed at us in a dramatic fashion and raised his hand in front of the open tube to welcome us inside. His polite smile and warm gesture must've been required, because under all the bullshit the twitch at the corner of his eye was clearly telling us to get the hell out of his sight.

The soles of my boots clacked loudly against the walkway when I took my first steps from the station onto the docking bridge. It took a minute before I heard Tank and Cooper approach me from behind. Roughly four meters wide, the base of the bridge was crafted out of reinforced titanium. Attached to the base and looped overhead were titanium rings, spaced apart every twenty meters. Wrapped around the rings was a thin tube of clear cordone plastic; one of the most pliable yet sturdy materials ever manufactured. It allowed an unfettered view of the galaxy around us.

An overwhelming feeling of insignificance showered over me. Burning stars, shimmering planets and long, vibrant stretches of distant galaxies colored the blackness of space, reminding me I was nothing more than a very small and inconsequential part of something so immense. I took a moment to reflect in its humbling beauty, knowing that it was all just an illusion that masked its cancerous insides. A cancer created by the UG.

Years ago the vast openness of space embraced me, granted me freedom and provided me opportunity, and I'm forever grateful for what it offered. While space provided me opportunity, it didn't make me who I was today. My life wasn't about beauty. Far from it. My soul was forged by other people's immorality, greed, and hatred. They created a shuddering darkness that lived deep inside of me. A darkness that would never grow bright. In a universe of visual beauty, I was nothing more than a dark spot of sin.

Tank walked up next to me and brushed his arm against my shoulder as he peered out into space. "Have you ever wondered if you could do more? That maybe you're missing a greater purpose?"

I looked at the letters on my arm and replied by talking down at the walkway. "I haven't taken a single day for granted."

"Understood," Tank said with a quick nod of his head. "But there's always more. We should never be satisfied with what little we have. That's why we're agent soldiers."

"Umm…can we get moving?" Cooper said as he fidgeted with the zipper on his jacket. "This is five hundred meters of death just waiting to happen."

Tank poked the plastic with his finger then smiled. "I'm pretty sure it's safe."

"Seriously, Tank?" Cooper swatted at Tank's hand. "Quit poking the damn tube."

Cooper's concerns were valid. Though rare, tubes have collapsed when ships have prematurely disengaged. Other times parties have made the long walk only to be greeted on the other side by an ambush of enemy fire. But I wasn't worried. The Solonians didn't want us dead. At least not yet.

We reached the access hatch to the Solonian battle cruiser and billowing greenish-brown chemicals poured from two ventilation grids, blending with the oxygen supply and dissipating as quickly as they appeared. The agent was designed to mix with the air supply and cleanse everything contained within the extension bridge, including cargo, weapons, clothing, and the human body - both inside and out. There was no way to avoid it. It penetrated your clothes, seeped into your pores, and was absorbed by your hair.

There were millions of known diseases this agent detected, and far less it cured. If you're infected with a communicable, non-curable disease of any kind, the agent created a chemical imbalance in your brain, shutting it down and causing death within minutes. The last of the agent sputtered from the vents signaling the end of the decontamination process. Now we had to wait it out.

"Looks like you're OK, Maxx," Tank said as he tapped the side of my cheek with his enormous hand. His breath smelled like a stale bottle of grain alcohol. "I wondered what might've happened…happened if Terra hadn't gotten all of that shit out of your system."

"I'm trying not to think about it," I said.

The drone of the ship's electronic message played overhead. *"Decontamination procedure successful. Readings confirm a .00004% chance of inaccurate measurements. Prepare for hatch release."*

"That's funny," Cooper said. "That's the same odds we have of pulling off this new deal."

The port hatch groaned its displeasure when it released the interconnected door modules that blocked our entrance into the Solonian battle cruiser. We were greeted by a red-robed Solonian Ambassador and a smug looking, heavily armed grunt flanking his side. A small army of guards clogged the hall behind them.

"Welcome, gentlemen," the Solonian Ambassador said as he extended his arms out from his sides as if to provide us a remote, but welcoming group hug. The long red sleeves, embroidered with four rings of rich gold thread, draped loosely from his arms and exposed his lean fingers and yellowed fingernails. The word "gentlemen" flowed easily out of his mouth, but the true meaning of it hung heavily in the inflection of his voice.

The Solonians were a predominately human race, extremely tall and wire thin with bubbled facial features as if they wore loose fitting masks of flesh. They draped themselves in long hooded robes, intricately stitched and custom detailed per the owner's choosing, and based on their governmental rank. The higher their political status, the more detailed their robes. Conversely, simplicity in clothing was also used as a tool to signify the unimportance of others. It was the same reason why they held me in a room of white. They wanted to send me a message.

Cursed with underdeveloped immune systems, they took extreme care to wrap their skin in cloth and never touch anything or anyone that hadn't been cleansed. They hired the dregs of the universe to act as their front-line soldiers and security personnel. Mercenaries, bounty hunters, and agent soldiers formed a mixed bag of humanity that they bent to their military will.

"Thank you," I replied.

"Thank you - Ambassador," he snapped back with a frown.

The role of a Solonian Ambassador was a prestigious honor, only a step removed from a seat with the high ranking Solonian Officials. Ambassadors were assigned the duties of trade negotiations, peace settlements, or used to entertain dignitaries and government nationals. He must've drawn the short straw today, sent to greet the unclean savages.

I wasn't in the mood for this game of words, nor did I want to deal with an adult wishing to be treated like a spoiled child. But I had no choice. I had to play along. "My sincere apologies, Ambassador," I said. "By no means did I mean any disrespect. Someone of your esteemed position should be recognized as such." I ended my greeting with a deep, exaggerated bow, which he quickly gobbled up to feed his hungry ego.

"Fantastic!" He cupped his hands in front of his chest. "Fantastic!" His voice was high pitched and pretentious but trailed with a hint of worry. He shifted under his robes, clearly out of his element dealing with "uncivilized folk" such as us. "In order to follow proper protocol, I will need to scan each of you for weaponry and enhancements."

"With great respect, Ambassador, we aren't carrying any armaments," I said. "We were escorted by a contingent of your own men directly to the extension bridge."

"Weapons are easy to pass when traversing through the massive crowds of unclean people on this station." He shivered. "And they're easy to conceal for men of your...stature." He lowered his arms and flicked his wrists toward us. "This is non-negotiable."

The guard to his side stepped forward, his sharply pointed, metal-tipped boots clicked as they touched the titanium walkway. When he moved into the docking bridge I lost sight of the Ambassador, swallowed up behind the guard's hulking frame. He was a man equal in size to Tank, and his face resembled a jigsaw puzzle that had been both burned and stomped in frustration when someone couldn't complete it. The whites of his eyes were overrun with angry tracks of blood vessels that leaked red, and they were fixed on me, sizing me up with rolling glances. The left breast of his tight-fitting military jacket was decorated with a single stripe, indicating he wasn't just a grunt, but a grunt with years of loyal service. Slung over this shoulder was a bulky, military assault rifle, and two T-19 pistols were strapped under each of his arms. Hanging from his belt was a communicator, some buttoned pouches, and a knife. In his right hand he carried a JaC scanner that flashed beams of bright green, recording data as it scanned our bodies.

Jigsaw reviewed the scanner's readings then narrowed his eyes. He grabbed my shoulder and squeezed it like a vice, then spun me into the side of the tube. Tank grasped Jigsaw's forearm and applied his own brand of persuasive pressure.

"Why don't you try to do that to me?" Tank questioned in a suddenly sober fashion.

Tank versus Jigsaw would've been an intriguing fight; both men stood over two meters and carried nearly 150 kilograms of destructive power. Though my credits would be on Tank, you didn't get Jigsaw's boyish good looks without participating in a lot of close combat.

Jigsaw clasped Tank's neck and drew both of them within centimeters of each other. Out of the corner of my eye I saw Cooper creeping toward the two men. I opened my left palm down around my thigh, indicating he needed to stand down.

"Tsk, tsk." A voice squeaked from behind the two behemoths. "Gentlemen, please act as though you have a shred of civility." I could see glimpses of the Ambassador, and the frightful look that made his already white face the color of a fresh snowfall. Both men released each other and took a single step backward. There was a long, uncomfortable pause where everyone just stood quietly and stared.

Never removing his eyes from Tank, Jigsaw took a few steps back and handed the Ambassador the scanner. The Ambassador pulled his sleeve over his hand before he accepted the device. "The big man will stay with my guard," he said as he eyed the readings.

"Ambassador, this is ridiculous," I said. "We're contracted partners of the Solonian Officials. Not pirates. I would expect our treatment to reflect that."

The Ambassador tapped at the screen with his crooked fingernail. "He's a man clearly violating the laws of the Unified Governments. Additionally, four implants prove his mind is unstable at best."

Three years ago the Tise Corporation, the original maker of JaCs, was forced to close under the newly imposed law of the UG, strictly forbidding the production and sale of their implants. Under provision 7.4.1 the UG passed a two-year grace period in which every citizen was instructed to have their implants removed and surrendered. If you're caught with an implant, you're considered to be in violation of UG law, and an enemy of their banner.

When the doors of the Tise Corporation closed, many of their scientists went rogue, designing and selling their JaCs through underground markets. Securing funding from unknown sources, the JaC industry is currently the largest illegal business in the galaxy, and it wouldn't surprise me if the UG had their fingers in that pot.

"You're kidding yourself if you think that isn't packed with implants," I said as I pointed at Jigsaw.

"Questioning the integrity of an employee of the Solonian Empire isn't tolerated. I'll ignore that comment this time, expecting I'll never hear it again." His weepy eyes shot me a glance before returning to the scanner data. "The two implants in your other companion, however illegal, will be deemed acceptable and not a threat." The ambassador tapped the scanner again as his face puckered into a frown. "However, there appears to be a problem with your scan."

"It isn't an error," I replied. "I don't have any JaCs."

The Ambassador reviewed the device once more, then cocked his head to the side. "Besides the fact that you've tested negative for implants, I've never seen this error readout before. Scan him again."

Jigsaw activated the JaC scanner and analyzed me again. The device chirped once and the screen blipped before confirming I was clean. Jigsaw handed the scanner back to the Ambassador. "The error is gone," Jigsaw said. His voice was scratchy, and he winced as he talked. He paused, swallowed a few times, then cleared his throat and continued. "He's clean."

A wry smile crept out from under the Ambassador's hood. "I find it ironic how one of the best agent soldiers in our galaxy doesn't believe in using all the tools at his disposal. How good could you really be?" He tilted his head at me.

"Are we done here?" I asked.

"I suppose so," the Ambassador said, gingerly handing the scanner to Jigsaw, careful not to let it touch the flesh of his hand. He motioned to the army of men behind him and pointed at Tank. "Guards, take him into custody."

Like a grown man lifting a small child, Jigsaw snatched me from the extension bridge with ease, slammed my body against the battle cruiser's hull, and drove the air from my lungs. He forced his muscled forearm under my chin and pushed the back of my head against the ship's hull. The room filled with a loud ringing that matched the one inside my head. Keeping me restrained, he attempted to drive his arm through my neck, cutting off my air supply and beaming a patchy smile while he did it.

Tank and Cooper moved in to help, but were greeted by the business ends of a dozen Solonian rifles. Under gun point they escorted Tank away and left a handful of guards to watch over Cooper and me.

The Ambassador approached, careful to stay out of arm's reach as if one more step would've been uncomfortably close. "You may not be pirates, but your ilk is no better than they are." His voice no longer sounded impish, but relaxed and under control. "You will listen to what I command, or this engagement is over."

A smirk widened across Jigsaw's disfigured face as he increased his efforts to crush my neck.

"Do you understand who's in control?" the Ambassador asked.

Seconds passed and no one moved or said a word. All I could hear was Jigsaw's labored breathing, the gurgle in my throat, and the pounding of my adrenaline-fueled heart. Jigsaw's thoughts grew audible through the reddening scars on his face. Reading them like a detailed map, it was clear he wanted to kill me.

"Need I ask again?" questioned the Ambassador. "Do you understand who's in control?" I hesitated for only a moment longer, then nodded my head the best I could. "Good. Release him."

The look of anger ran from Jigsaw's face, replaced by a glower of disappointment. He paused, then slowly released the arm bar from my throat. I wanted to gulp down gallons of synthesized oxygen but refused to give Jigsaw the satisfaction. Instead, I pulled in short, controlled breaths until my body stabilized and my legs strengthened beneath me.

"Now that we all have a clear understanding, shall we meet with the Officials?" The Ambassador asked as he peered down at us.

Jigsaw pushed me from behind, forcing me down the hall. Cooper stepped next to me, flashing a smile as he watched me slide Jigsaw's knife inside my jacket. "No worries, Ambassador," I whispered under my breath. "I have a very clear understanding of who's in control."

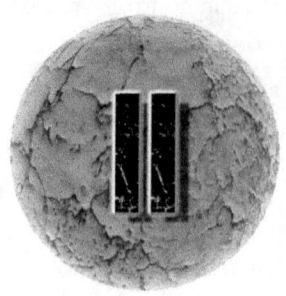

Cooper and I stood at the back of the Solonian council chambers awaiting the entrance of the Solonian Officials. Twinkling starlight dotted the glass ceiling, and an occasional shuttle streaked silently overhead, powered by blue-flamed thrusters. Intricately stitched banners of red and gold hung from the walls, their edges flapped slightly when brushed by the synthesized oxygen circulating through the room. Soft, yellow lights shone brightly on the banners while others placed their warm glow on rare works of art, solid glass tables, crystal drinkware, and hand carved chairs.

The council chambers were refined and civilized; the Solonian Officials were anything but. To the masses they portrayed themselves as kind, gentle, and caring leaders though they were nothing more than corrupt, greed-driven killers clothed in pretty wrappings.

Two decades ago the seventy-eight Empire Nations of the Silor Galaxy united under one ruling party, putting an end to hundreds of years of bloodshed and war. Setting aside their differences, they agreed to form a coalition of governments that would work tirelessly to create a better life for their people. Piece by piece the Unified Governments took the broken fragments of our battle-torn galaxy, shaping, fitting, and melding them together as one.

It took less than two years for the illusion of a new utopian society to rot away, exposing its festering core of greed and corruption. The people of this galaxy were foolish for believing them, but they were blinded by their dreams, their hopes. By the time the signs of treachery became apparent, it was too late. The rulers of the Empire Nations had a plan from the beginning, a plan that plunged our galaxy into a deeper and more sinister darkness than before.

The newly formed Unified Governments created an autocratic galaxy, one that fed its insatiable hunger for wealth and power by granting control to its select leaders while leaving behind only scraps for trillions of others to fight over. Political change ushered in a new order and for many, a new way of life. The universal language was one of influence and credits, and if you had neither, you had no voice.

Countless underground markets sprang to life creating the slave trades, weapons brokers, drug peddlers, counterfeiters, and implant dealers. They needed protection, people to deliver their goods and military services, so opportunities arose for mercenaries, bounty hunters, agent soldiers, pirates, and smugglers.

Even during the bloodiest moments of our galaxy's wars, people fought to preserve their last remaining threads of humanity. But in the new world order, everyone had been reduced to savages who cheated, fought, and killed to survive. The strands of humanity had been broken.

The sole purpose of the Unified Governments was to ensure that each of the seventy-eight Empire Nations received their fair share of the wealth. Every nation had a seat on the Unified Governments, and an equal say when passing laws and governances. The goal was to keep each nation's power in check by measuring and distributing their fair share. While all Empire Nations initially agreed on the terms, many quickly realized their portion of the wealth wasn't large enough, and continued to work their own deals to grow their power and tighten their grips. The Solonians were one of those Empire Nations.

Jigsaw blocked the exit at the back of the room, his arms crossed in front of his chest and his face locked into a permanent sneer. A contingent of well-armed guards lined the halls outside, awaiting Jigsaw's signal to charge into the room and restore order if needed. Standing near the Official's grand entrance doors were two of their royal guard - highly skilled, purebred Solonian marksmen; possibly the most accurate and dangerous gunmen in the universe. Draped in robes of dark blue, the cloth covered every inch of their skin and the hoods devoured their heads, displaying only empty, black shadow. The grayish tips of their readied pistols peeked out from the end of their robes' long arms. Behind the darkness I could feel their watchful stares.

The doors opened and the royal guard escorted three Solonian Officials toward us. They shuffled forward on aged legs, stopping a few meters from where we stood. The identifiable stitching on each of their robes, as well as their awkwardly distinctive gates, made it clear they were the same three I'd originally negotiated with. There were seven seats on the Solonian counsel, seven Officials each ranked by their years of service. In front of us was their top ranking Official, Aphe, and his two lower ranking companions, Modsi and Tocoby.

"Take your seats," Aphe said, lowering himself onto an engraved marble throne with stitched leather cushions. His two companions followed, sitting in chairs similar in look but much shorter and less intricately stitched. The royal guard bowed their heads until all three were seated, then took position on either side of their leaders. Cooper bowed as well, mocking the actions of the guards and taking a nudge from me to finally break his overly enthusiastic greeting. I looked over my shoulder at Jigsaw, then sat on a stone bench opposite the officials. A glass table separated the Solonians from us by more than two meters.

"I appreciate your time and council," I said in the most diplomatic tone I knew.

"As well you should." Aphe sneered from under his hood. "Have you requested my council today to inform us you've successfully completed our contract?"

Aphe took no time to show his arrogance. He knew why we were here and wanted me to grovel before him, speak our story of failure, then beg for our lives. As the highest ranking Solonian Official, he had blessed our docking on the Kogin station and directed the questioning of Cooper and Tank. It was only the start of this mental game by the Solonians - a game I had to win while holding only one chip.

"I haven't completed the contract," I said, my voice steady.

Aphe shook his head in disgust. His hood swooshed from side to side while the other two whispered to each other like nervous school girls. "That's truly, truly disappointing." Aphe's exposed hands clenched into tightly wound fists of pale, wrinkled flesh. "Then I must assume you've come here to beg me for a merciful death for you and your crew."

"I came to this station so we could continue to work together to complete the contract."

Aphe's eyebrow arched at my response. "The terms of the contract were clearly stated; the pickup and delivery of our properties for the price of two hundred thousand credits. We set the details and the timeline, and you were unsuccessful in meeting those terms. I fail to understand what's left to discuss."

"The UG delayed our progress," I said. "Surely this is something you're aware of since you occupy a seat on their council."

Aphe feigned confusion. "I'm a high councilmen, trusted priest, leader, and patriot of our great Solonian Empire. Though it's true the other represented nations of the Unified Governments actively seek my blessed advice, I don't toil in the minor details of their operations."

Cooper leaned over to me and whispered, "At least he's humble."

Aphe continued. "I'm shocked you would think otherwise."

"I've always believed the Solonian Officials had strong ties to the daily operations of the UG. If that is not the case, then you wouldn't know of their tortuous ways, or the fact that they gunned down two of my men with a probe trap then imprisoned and slaughtered my crew while trying to ascertain the location of your cargo?"

"I am appalled and disappointed with your innuendo!" Aphe gasped. "Even the reach of the Solonian Empire only goes so deep. I know nothing of your imprisonment, the death of your crew, or the Unified Governments' involvement other than what I've gathered since your return to the Kogin station." Modsi and Tocoby nodded their agreement.

"It was not an accusation, just a question."

"Tell me, Maxx," Aphe said, stroking his bubbled chin. "Why did you abandon your ship?"

I lowered my arms on the table, slid forward and peered into Aphe's cowl. He sunk back into his throne and clenched the marble armrests as I moved closer to where he sat. "I knew something wasn't right. Someone sold us out." I slid my arms back toward my body and away from Aphe. He acknowledged my retreat by sitting erect and placing the tips of his fingers on the edge of the table. "I took a fighter and moved my ship to an undisclosed location. Our capture by the UG proved that my fears were warranted."

"Interesting. But why not send someone else from your crew as bait for the Unified Governments? Someone beneath you? To me, it appears as though you were fleeing from your responsibilities."

A scowl crept across my face under my narrowing eyes. "I didn't flee, Aphe. I never flee." My anger must have showed because Aphe shifted in his seat as I continued to speak. "Somehow they were able to track me, personally, so I took my best team as a diversion to save the ship and your cargo. What I didn't expect was an engagement with an entire fleet of UG soldiers."

Aphe waved his hand to the side of his face in an attempt to brush off my comments. "I obviously have a vested interest in the safety of my cargo. If I would've known, I would've informed you. It's that simple. The Unified Governments' entanglement would only make things difficult for the Solonian Empire."

He may have stated the truth. Maybe the other ruling nations of the UG wanted the Solonian cargo, and if so, they would've done their best to hide their secretive operation.

"Enough of that," Aphe said. "Your difficulties with the Unified Governments are not my concern." Aphe jabbed his finger onto the table. "Let's discuss the return of my cargo and the termination of our contract."

"I'm not here to cancel our agreement," I said. "I'm here to negotiate new terms."

For a moment I thought Aphe stopped breathing. The exposed areas of his face turned from milky white to a glowing red and his robe stopped moving near his chest. Pounding of his slender fists on the table soon followed. "Preposterous!" Aphe sputtered. "Who do you think you are? I'll have you killed where you sit!"

"You and I know that won't happen. Not as long as I hold your cargo."

"So you've come to my ship brandishing threats at me and the Solonian Empire?"

"I'm not threatening anyone, just here to work out a new agreement we can all be happy with."

"The Solonian Empire doesn't renegotiate contracts!" Aphe pointed a long, crooked finger at my face. His voice rose in anger with each sentence. "You broke the terms! You failed to deliver on your promise! Not us! You will return the properties of the Solonian Empire to our possession and beg for your lives! That is your renegotiation! Those are the terms!"

"Are you done?" I asked, regretting the words almost as quickly as I said them. The grinding of Jigsaw's teeth could be heard echoing through the room and the pistols of the Solonian royal guard were no longer dangling at their sides but pointed at my head. If there was one thing the Solonians demanded, it was respect.

"Keep up the good work, Boss," Cooper leaned into me and whispered. "Things are going well so far."

"You dare talk to me like I'm a slave?" Aphe stammered. "Who are you to speak to the ruling Solonian Official in such as way? You? A lowly agent soldier?" His lackeys shook their heads in agreement.

"Relax," I said as I exchanged glances with Jigsaw and the royal guards. "This is business, and business only. It isn't meant to be personal."

Aphe burst into a deep, throaty laugh. A surprising sound generated from such a tall and lanky frame. "Ahh…business. You wish to conduct business? Then let's be direct. Tell me, Maxx, what do you propose we do about our failed contract?" Folding his hands, he laid them on the table and leaned forward as if eager to hear what I had to say. His anger appeared to wash away any fear of drawing too close to someone who they considered to be "unclean."

"I will complete our contract within thirty additional days."

Heavy breathing fluttered Aphe's cowl as he talked. "So you propose the contract terms remain intact, and as promised, with a gracious time extension?"

"Here it comes," Cooper mumbled under his breath.

"And, I need half of the payment up front," I said.

Aphe paused, then laughed. Modsi and Tocoby followed his lead. "That's ridiculous. Utter foolishness. You wish for me to pay you up front for an uncompleted contract?"

"You didn't let me finish." The room grew silent as I continued. "I need one hundred thousand credits up front and require Terra to be returned to me."

Modsi and Tocoby laughed as I finished my sentence but Aphe waved them off into silence, his lips curled back exposing his gnashed teeth. "I do not appreciate your humor, agent soldier."

"It wasn't meant to be funny. The UG delayed our contract, destroyed my fighter, and disarmed and killed my crew. I need the credits for purchases so I can return to my ship and complete our contract."

"And why do you require the services of a worthless whore of a slave girl?"

My fists tightened as I watched those words slip off his moist, wormy lips. "She's part of my crew, and has medical knowledge that's critical to our success."

Aphe shrugged. "Why is all of this the problem of the Solonian Empire? I grow tired of your mumblings."

I could feel the edged steel of Jigsaw's knife resting against my chest, begging to be lodged in the middle of Aphe's bubbled head. "It's your problem because I have your cargo. And until I return to my ship, that cargo will remain hidden. And, if I don't return to my ship within another sixty days, it will be dumped."

"Forget about the cargo." Aphe waved his hand to show its unimportance. "It isn't worth it."

"I'm not stupid, so you can quit talking to me like I'm one of your underlings." And with my last statement, the gloves were finally off. This somewhat peaceful negotiation took a nasty turn. "Nobody contracts to pay two hundred thousand credits to move worthless goods. Nobody."

Aphe licked his lips as I continued. "The UG believed the cargo I was hauling was important enough to send a war-sized squad to hunt down my fighter, imprison and slaughter my crew, and torture me for more than one hundred days. No more games Aphe. You won't find your cargo without me. There's no doubt in my mind you've searched for my ship, and if you've found it, we wouldn't be having this conversation right now. Pay me what's needed for me to join my ship, and in return I will safely deliver your cargo."

Aphe eased against the back of his chair, his cowl consuming what was previously visible of his ghostly face. He held his hands out in front of his chest, his fingers created a steeple while he tapped his index fingers together.

"So, you come into my ship not to ask, but to dictate new terms of a previously agreed upon contract. An agreement we trusted you to complete." Aphe's voice was short and deliberate. "Now you sit before me with a new list of demands, not negotiations."

"You've seen to it that I've little choice."

Aphe leaned forward. "You will receive fifty-thousand credits up front, half of what you are requesting, as well as your precious slave whore. And in return, I expect you will deliver my properties to our previously agreed upon destination within thirty days." I nodded my response as he continued. "But I have a few terms of my own."

"Fair enough."

"Once delivered, you will not receive the additional one hundred and fifty-thousand credits. For those credits I will broker a trade, offering each member of your remaining crew a full pardon from the Solonian Empire for their failure to deliver on our original contract."

"I accept –"

"Do not interrupt me until I am finished speaking!" Aphe hissed. "You will not be included in that pardon. Within two days of the completion of our contract, there will be a warrant placed upon your head for the same one hundred and fifty-thousand credits I won't be paying you. That bounty will be paid upon the delivery of your body to the Solonian Empire - dead, not alive."

"Agreed."

"Maxx, wait!" Cooper shouted as he stood. "We won't agree to these terms!"

"Who is this who speaks to me?" Aphe questioned. "Is he your master, your leader?"

I looked at Cooper. "He's just a crewmate who needs an occasional reminder he isn't in charge." Cooper readied his protest but stopped when he saw the seriousness in my eyes. "He has no authority to engage or dictate terms of the contract."

"Learn to control your subordinates," Aphe said. "The fifty-thousand credits will be delivered to you in tangible rather than electronic form so they can be spent without complication. I don't want the transaction to transpire on my ship, so I'll have someone deliver them to you in a bar called the Starlight Room back on the Kogin station."

"We will make our way there and await our contact," I said.

"I will not authorize the purchase of any weapons while on board our battle cruiser or on Kogin. Once you depart you are left to your own devices to acquire such goods. Additionally, I will not allow the use of the Unified Governments' vessel you illegally acquired during your escape from Paxcel. You will need to purchase another ship. When you're ready, we will provide provisions and medical supplies for your journey and will load them onto your new vessel once it's acquired. I will have the slave girl you speak of delivered to you at that time."

"I'll notify you when we have our new ship."

"Maxx, there will be no further negotiations. No other terms. Thirty days is all you have to complete this contract. After that, all terms of the agreement are voided, and every member of your crew becomes a listed enemy of the Solonian Empire. I will unleash every asset we own to hunt you down and recover my cargo, even at the expense of revealing our secret to the Unified Governments. Do you understand?"

"I do," I said as I stood. Cooper followed my lead as I nodded at Aphe then turned to the exit. As we reached the door by Jigsaw, Aphe called out to us. I turned to catch his fiery stare blazing from under his hood.

"One last detail you should be aware of. My trust in you and your team was thin from the very start of this deal, so I engaged in an insurance policy by hiring someone to track you and your ships movements. That second contract I executed on behalf of the Solonian Empire will remain in place until my properties safely reach their destination." Aphe stood, lowering his gaze on me. "However, as of today their contract now authorizes them to engage and recover our properties by any means necessary. The first of you to deliver the cargo to Lotress will receive credit for completing the contract. At which time I consider the terms of the other contract immediately terminated."

I nodded. "We'll arrive with your cargo on Lotress in less than thirty days."

"Not if Tompkins has his say in it." Aphe's parting words sent a rolling chill down my spine.

Cooper, Tank, and I located a secluded table at the back of the dimly lit Starlight Room. From this position we could see only a small section of the tavern and its patrons, but were well protected by placing our backs against a walled corner.

The establishment was larger than I had expected, filled with a mix of Solonian soldiers, lower ranking officers, and local residents. Most of the station's natives appeared despondent; their faces were as weary as their tired frames, hunched over quickly emptying glasses. The seating areas were filled with white tables and chairs, marred and scratched from frequent use. Walls of dirty white surrounded us, stained with dried sickness and hastily-scrubbed brown patches that I could only assume were blood. The Starlight Room was constructed in the shape of a cross with four individual rectangle rooms and a rounded bar and serving area located in the center. Three tenders worked feverishly inside the service area, passing drinks to customers seated at the bar and to the tavern's servants to deliver to their assigned tables.

Once we were seated, a young servant girl took notice and limped her way over to us. Her top lip was split in two places and her right eye socket carried a purpling bruise. Concealed behind her dark eyes was a deep sadness. Even still she forced a smile. She couldn't have been much older than fifteen years, but the harsh toll that slavery had taken made her appear twice that age.

I informed her that we were instructed by the Officials to meet a Solonian contact at this establishment to conduct unspecified business, and that we didn't need anything except a place to sit and wait. She retreated back to the service area and talked to a portly man filling pitchers and mugs with liquid courage. After a few moments she returned with a round of drinks and a note that she set on the table and gingerly slid toward me. Her hand trembled as it drew near mine. She pulled her arm back quickly and grasped the serving tray. I smiled at her and retrieved the note. It read: *Your contact will be here within an hour. While you wait, enjoy your bottomless drinks. On the house.* The server placed the drinks on the table, paused for a moment, then left.

Since we had an hour to wait, I decided to take the time to inform Tank about what he'd missed during our meeting with the Solonian Officials.

"Really fucking dumb, Maxx," Tank said. "Lately, it feels as though I'm constantly reminding you that you're an agent soldier and need to look out for yourself. Why were you so quick to throw your life away? Just fucking dumb."

Cooper nodded and added, "I told him the same damn thing."

I ran my hands through my hair and sighed. "Neither of you get it," I said. "Do you really think they were going to let me walk away from this? I was already a marked man. I didn't give them anything more than what they were already planning on taking."

"We could've worked something out, Boss," Cooper said. "There has to be another way."

"You don't *work* anything out with the Solonians," I said. "There's a reason they were paying two hundred thousand credits for this mission. I failed. It's as simple as that. We've got thirty days to complete the contract to get everyone their promised pardons. Once that's done, I'll figure things out."

"*We* failed, Maxx," Tank said. "Not just you." He took a long drink from his mug then wiped the bubbling froth from his goatee. He motioned to our servant to fill his half-empty glass. "You could've dropped the credits. Credits always do the talking."

When he took another drink I saw a dotted field of purple and black bruises on his knuckles. "What the hell happened to your hand?" With Tank's healing JaC, those types of injuries heal fast, so whatever he recently punched is either dented, dead, or both.

Tank continued his long draw until there were only patchy streaks of foam settling at the bottom of the mug. "You mean this?" he said, flexing his hand with a grimace. "Let's just say that when they hauled me away, I got a little angry." He looked at me as I narrowed my eyes. "Yeah, yeah. It's all good."

Tank's outbursts had become more frequent and intense since his most recent JaCing; one of the many byproducts of unnaturally tinkering with the human body. He had four enhancements including a pain suppression modification, healing module, and two strength boosters - hence the nickname Tank. Able to dish out an abundant amount of pain to our enemies, while not being able to feel it, makes him an invaluable asset. The man is a mountain of rage, and he pushed the limits on modifications making him unpredictable, and at times, a liability. I put him on notice that a fifth JaC gets him booted from the team. No questions and no discussion. He didn't take it well, and I didn't expect him to.

Cooper's look shifted between Tank and me. He knew both of us too well, and cut in on the conversation before it escalated. "So what do you make of the Tompkins' contract?"

The muscles in my neck knotted when Cooper said Tompkins' name. "It's nothing more than a small inconvenience," I said. It was a weak attempt to convince myself it was true.

"I don't know, Maxx," Tank said. "He's caused us more trouble than anyone else - ever. He could really fuck this up."

"If we get this contract completed as quickly as I expect, we should be able to avoid him altogether," I said. "He's a non-issue."

Cooper tilted his head back and took a drink from his mug, suddenly spitting the alcohol back into the glass. "It appears that it's not our lucky day." Cooper pointed at a table across the bar.

Standing no more than fifteen meters away was Tompkins, owner of the Off World Mining Expedition (OWME) and lapdog to many of the UG's Empire Nations. His company consisted of a fleet of mining vessels and resource extractors that jumped from one nutrient rich planet to the next, stripping them of all their natural resources and leaving behind only a crusted orb of infertile soil. It's not surprising that his license to operate was sanctioned by the UG, and the planets he decimated were worlds that openly resisted their rule. When he wasn't raping worlds of their resources, he played the role of bounty hunter and soldier for hire.

Tompkins and I had a storied history of bad blood between us, and this wasn't going to make our relationship any healthier.

A few years ago Tompkins bid against me on a contract for the Thoddis Empire, and lost. I was hired to rescue one of their governors who was captured and held captive by a group of anti-government rebels. Our mission was simple. Locate the governor, extract him from the situation, and deliver him safely back into the hands of the Thoddis Empire.

All went well until Tompkins interfered. My tactical team had located the governor, neutralized the threat, and was ready to transport him off the planet. That's when we were engaged by Tompkins' team. He killed a dozen of my men with the sole purpose of preventing my mission's success. He wasn't hired by anyone, or paid for the attack. He wanted me to fail, and ultimately become a listed enemy of the Thoddis Empire.

He's on a short list of people I've vowed to personally send back to their maker. No matter the payback, it won't be enough to rectify what he's done. If there wasn't so much at stake, I'd put him down here and now.

My hatred radiated, and drew the attention of Cooper. He reached over and grabbed my bicep as if to reel me back in.

Tompkins was alone, likely relishing in the fact that he had the protection of the Solonian Officials. I doubted I was the only person in the galaxy who wanted Tompkins dead, so he's smart enough to take necessary precautions to keep himself on this side of the dirt - breathing, scamming, and murdering.

I emptied my drink, ready to find a table with a better view, when Tompkins looked my way. Our eyes locked and both of us refused to break the contest of wills. He knew I wanted him dead, so I'm sure it made his contract with the Solonians that much sweeter. My short timeline didn't leave any room for error and instead of me hunting him, he'd become the rabid dog nipping at my heels.

Cooper spoke between swallows. "We can't leave, Boss, until our contact arrives. Don't let him mess with you."

I ran my tongue across the front of my teeth. Cooper was right, and for the first time showed that he was the sensible one in the group. I couldn't let uncontrolled hatred complicate what was left of this contract. There was too much riding on the successful completion of this deal. Too many lives. I couldn't fail again.

I put up with Tompkins' mocking stare until our contact arrived at our table. He was human, dressed in worn miner's clothes with long pants that were frayed and dusty near his feet. I assumed his look was intentional to deter any suspicions of the Solonians striking a deal with an agent soldier.

He carried two tattered cases, one tucked under his arm and the other in his hand. He dropped both on the table, looked over his shoulder, then cracked open the first. Digging out an electronic device and a mound of papers, he tossed them onto the table and delivered the details of our new agreement through muted whispers, rushing through a series of statements that could either be construed as terms or threats, depending on my mood.

I noticed Tompkins watching our activity from a distance. When we locked eyes again, his smirk grew to a face-splitting smile. I did nothing in return, keeping my gaze fixed on him until I was forced to break our ocular combat for a series of DNA signatures. When I looked back up, Tompkins had left the bar.

The newly agreed upon deal for fifty-thousand credits was granted and passed to me across the table in a slim, electronically sealed case. Our Solonian contact stood up, collected his documents and electronic scanner, then handed me a paper-thin microchip with the necessary credentials needed to gain access to the credits. As I slid the chip into one of my inside jacket pockets, he gave us all a polite bow then shuffled out of the bar. Tank reached over, scooped up the case and nestled it between his chest and the table.

I eased back in my chair, rubbed my temples and sighed. As hellish as the last three months had been, things would only get worse from here.

Now that we had the credits, our biggest need was a ship. Something in the fighter class would be ideal - fast with formidable firepower, and designed with seating for a minimum of six passengers and light cargo. For the next hour we ironed out the details over a few drinks and the first solid meal I'd eaten in months. In the end we agreed that Cooper and Tank would do the work necessary to acquire the ship, so I could deal with other pending issues.

"Don't spend any more than thirty thousand," I said. "We'll need a good chunk of the credits for weapons."

"Twenty-thousand credits will buy a small army's worth of weapons," Tank said.

"Yeah, and I expect we'll need them."

"Thirty-thousand will get us a nice ship," Cooper said. "But why do we need something so large? Wouldn't it make sense to get something small and quick?"

"There are a couple of people we need to pick up along the way," I said. "Let's leave it at that."

Banter continued between the three of us as we drank heavily. Much more than we should have. There was a calming feeling between us, a sense of ease that had settled in. We had escaped one of the harshest prisons in the galaxy and struck a new agreement with the Solonians. The most dangerous part of our mission was still ahead, but it felt good to be in control of our own destinies once again.

The feeling of contentment was short lived. While Tank boasted of his recent heroic actions, I spotted Tompkins returning to the bar.

Cooper followed the look in my eyes and found Tompkins approaching us. "Here's the deal, Boss. Any violence, illegal, or offensive actions on this station gets us jailed then shot. Or shot, then jailed. Neither of which is ideal."

"I understand," I muttered while taking another drink.

"Good. Those rules also apply to Tompkins. Please remember that."

"Of course they do."

He ignored my response and continued. "I can't let you do anything stupid, Boss. You've risked too much already with this contract, and you can't throw it all away over some senseless vendetta."

"Senseless vendetta?" I slammed my mug onto the table then turned to face Cooper. "The Thoddis Empire rescue mission is only a very small taste of our past. If I told you everything, you wouldn't sit there and lecture me."

Cooper mopped the beads of sweat that dotted the top of his head. "Fine! But there will be another place and another time."

"Will there be? Can you give me a guarantee?"

"I'm with Maxx," Tank added with a growl. "We take him down now."

"Why don't you drink a little more, Tank?" Cooper said. "What stake do you have in all of this?"

"No stake at all. I work for Maxx. He wants it done, so we do it."

"He wants it done, so we do it?" Cooper fumbled for words. "That's nonsense, and you're both crazy." His pointed finger shifted between us as he continued to sputter. "We're in the middle of a space station infested with Solonians, and you want to break their laws because you're either pissed off or drunk. One swing and most of these people in the bar will be using us for target practice."

"And?" Tank said.

"And? So you want to kill one of the Solonian's guests, in one of their stations, with no chance for escape?"

"We'll do it…discretely," Tank said, wobbling slightly in his chair.

"Sounds like a great plan," mocked Cooper as he stood. "Do both of you need a history lesson on the Solonian Empire? You know they have ties to everything and everyone; all of the governments, politicians, businesses, shipping docks, criminals, and even the goddamn elderly hobbling down these halls. They have eyes and ears everywhere just waiting for us to slip up. Right now they own us and we need to see this deal through."

Tank chuckled. Reaching up, he placed his hand on Cooper's shoulder and shoved him down onto his chair. "It's true I'm not the smartest one sitting at this table, but maybe we should finish this discussion a little later." Tank cut off the conversation before our approaching guest heard what we were discussing.

"Maxx!" Tompkins said with an overabundance of happiness. He pulled a chair up to our table and sat next to me. "It's great to see you, my friend. It's been awhile, hasn't it?"

Tompkins leaned back and stretched his arms over his head. His chair groaned its displeasure while the stitching of his clothing screamed from the strain. He was dressed in black cotton pants and a tan shirt crafted out of fine silk. The armpits of his shirt were sopping wet, tracing a stained trail to the logo of the OWME (a mining vessel circled in a single red stripe) on his left breast. An occasional cough rippled his cheeks and forced him to use his sausage-like fingers to slick back his greased, shoulder length hair as it fell loosely in front of his face. His appearance, arrogance, and ego all painted a clear picture of the life this man lived. A privileged life he didn't earn, but had taken off the backs of others.

"For health reasons I would suggest you find yourself another table," I said.

Tompkins struggled to turn his torso in the chair, taking a great amount of effort to look over at the bar. "Well, I would be happy to do so but it looks like most of them are filled up."

"There are plenty of single seats available. That's if you can find one that will support your weight."

"Petty, Maxx. Very petty." Tompkins slowly shook his head from shoulder to shoulder. "I see you continue to carry such pent up hostility. I'm sure there are open chairs available for the taking, but I have a few others joining us." His face cracked a wicked smile. "People I would so dearly like you to meet."

"What a strange coincidence," I said. "There are at least a dozen of my dead crew members I would like you to meet as well, and I'm looking to arrange that. Soon." Cooper shifted in his chair while Tank flexed his fingers, balling them into fists then slowly releasing them.

"I'll give you credit for one thing, Maxx. You aren't the typical agent soldier, at least the kind that would be successful anyway. The way you carry the burden of your emotions is phenomenally intriguing. I'd be lying if I told you it isn't fun watching them gnaw at your insides. You need to learn how to relax, my boy, and let those feelings go. This is all just business."

"I'm not your boy," I snarled. He chuckled, clearly attempting to provoke me into doing something stupid. Tompkins carried on as if he wasn't afraid of me snapping, but the twitching at the corners of his eyes told me otherwise.

"I know what you're wondering, but may be too afraid to ask," Tompkins said. "You're wondering how I'm going to locate your crappy little ship and collect the Solonian cargo to complete my deal."

When I didn't respond, he continued. "Let me be honest - I can do that with a good friend, can't I?" Tompkins squinted and smiled. "I've been looking for you and your ship for quite some time now and haven't had any luck. When I heard you were on this station I figured this was my chance to make good on my Solonian contract."

Tompkins leaned on the table. The mixed smell of his sweat and cologne assaulted my nostrils. "When I first engaged with the Solonians, I knew my old crew wouldn't cut it. Most of them have grown complacent and sloppy from all of our successes. So, I decided to recruit some new blood. Some of the very best assassins this galaxy has to offer. You thought I was good before –"

"I never thought that," I said, cutting him off.

"Ha!" Tompkins snorted.

"I couldn't care less who you've hired, Tompkins. It makes no difference to me. Once the three of us leave this station, you'll never find my ship or the Solonian cargo."

Tompkins arched an eyebrow. "Oh you will care! Trust me when I say you shouldn't be so dismissive."

I had to separate myself from this discussion before my fist emerged from the other side of his skull. As I stood, he placed his hand on my arm. I reacted, bending his fingers back toward the top of his wrist, fighting the urge to tear them off.

Tompkins gasped as I held my grip. His face turned serious and the words flew rapidly over his fat lips. "Maxx, you truly don't understand the danger you and your crew are in. I know how to find your ship. I'm putting all of the pieces together. And once I do, I will storm the *Beast* and kill every last fucking one of your crew."

"I'd wipe my ass with your best-of-the-best team," Tank said.

"That's big talk," Tompkins continued with a grimace, "but it's only talk." Tompkins attempted to wriggle free of my grasp, so I wrenched his fingers back slightly more. The tendons tightened and the bones creaked under my grip. "I have something powerful backing my contract. Inside information, and the benefits of JaCing."

Tank laughed and took a long draw from his recently filled mug. "Maxx, are we done listening to this idiot?"

I released Tompkins' fingers then watched him cradle them with his other hand. "That's your secret?" I asked. "The entire galaxy is JaCing, Tompkins."

"True," he replied as he did his best to pretend he didn't feel any discomfort in his swelling fingers, "but to what extent? Most people have two, three, maybe five tops before the JaCs start to cook their brains. What if I told you two of my lead assassins have six, and my number one killer has ten?"

"Impossible. Even if they weren't transformed into drooling piles of human flesh, there would be no way that you could control them. No way."

"Is it impossible?" He smiled. "Unfortunately for you, it's true. Their speed, strength, endurance, and pain thresholds are off the charts; especially that of my number one. They're special, and not even you could stand toe-to-toe with any one of the three."

I've always been able to read a liar's facial expressions and unconscious tells. Nervous ticks, dilated pupils, scratching, shifting eyes, involuntary sweating - all kinds of maps that lead to their inner truth. Tompkins displayed none of these.

In my lifetime, I'd seen only one individual fitted with six implants, and it took less than two days to erase any trace of his humanity. He lost the ability to think rationally, to reason. Consumed by a foul, animal instinct, he slaughtered seventeen men, women, and children with the spade of a shovel and three meters of rope. It was a gruesome event and an eye opener for the UG and the big businesses that supported the sale and implanting of JaCs.

"Tompkins, I don't scare easily," I said. "You can recruit an army of these JaCed soldiers and they still won't be able to protect you from me."

"Who says I need anyone's help? Even I have a few of those implants," Tompkins said.

"You know that you aren't supposed to eat them?" Cooper said, breaking his forcefully restrained silence.

"If you're all lucky, you'll get one more day to live!" Tompkins pushed himself away from the table and shot up in anger. He tossed his chair to the floor then stormed away.

"Job well done, Cooper!" Tank said with a laugh. "Well done!"

As Tank and Cooper conversed, I couldn't help but mull over what Tompkins just said. Most of my crew had at least one JaC and some, such as Tank, had as many as four. The implants range from simple to dangerous; some boosting the pleasure center while others mask pain as severe as the loss of a limb. They enhanced your strengths, but in the process magnify your weaknesses. In Tank, anger, rage, and hostility are all amplified and mostly unwanted byproducts of electronic chips telling his brain and nervous system how to act. In most scenarios, a single JaC would introduce only slight personality quirks. However, there are times when I'd banished members of my team who couldn't handle their side effects.

The causal user has them attached at the back of their neck just above their shoulder blades. They are easy to identify as a flat, black strip with intertwined patterns of gold circuitry, roughly three centimeters long and a centimeter wide. This location is normally reserved for junkies, with limited funds, seeking a quick boost of pleasure. The process is simple and inexpensive, but the total number of implants is limited to one.

Most hardcore users have them surgically implanted at the base of their spines directly above their buttocks. Depending on the person's body type and size, they're able to implant up to four JaCs, which are then tied into the central nervous system through a complex melding process. This location provides the benefit of concealment and improved effectiveness because of the direct attachment.

The last option is to have JaCs fused directly to your spine. This process is still considered experimental due to the danger and complexity of the procedure. For the users who are able to live through the process, it becomes the perfect location because it doesn't restrict the total number of implants while providing a direct path to the nervous system and neural circuits. The measured performance of JaCs implanted at the spine is more than double.

I rubbed my right forearm as I recalled my unpleasant history with JaCing. It was a past I didn't wish to revisit. I made a promise long ago that a JaC would never be allowed to pollute my body ever again, and I'd kept that promise. My crew knew it, and the circles I traveled in knew it as well. It could have been a detriment, but I choose to rely on my own natural speed and instincts, not trusting that a JaC wouldn't deaden my senses or cloud my thoughts. There were many people that were stronger than me, but very few were faster - at least on the draw of a blaster or when wielding a knife, and I'd proved that time and time again.

"Heads up," Tank said, breaking me away from my thoughts. "They're here."

Three figures entered at the front of the bar, clad in flowing black overcoats hanging low enough to brush across the tops of their boots. A moving wall of patrons made it difficult to get clear views of any of the three. Tompkins scurried up to them like a neglected pet excited to see its owners. The way he groveled in their presence had me wondering who was really running the operation. The commotion and buzz that filled the room only moments before suddenly deadened as floating whispers drifted amongst the masses.

The man in the front appeared to be the leader of the three. He dealt with Tompkins directly, nodding as they talked. The other two were standing behind him, shrouded in the bar's shadows. The group's leader was of average size and build, with a spaded goatee jutting from his chin. His shortly cropped, jet-black hair matched the color of his jacket and soulless eyes. Tompkins pointed at our table, and the man tipped his head toward my direction.

After a few minutes of conversation, they headed toward our table. His two companions broke from behind to flank him on either side while Tompkins led the parade. The first was short, slightly taller than a meter and half, with a slender build and brown, shoulder-length hair. His face brandished the tracks of three reddened scars that ran from one ear to the other, as if some creature clawed an angry path across the middle of his face. The end of his nose was torn away and the lid under his right eye sagged in the direction of the scar.

The second of the two was a shocking beauty with long legs and an athletically fit build. She approached slowly with her head down, staring at her feet as she walked. Her long, raven-colored hair fell in front of her face and drifted lightly from side to side. As she drew closer, she raised her head and brushed her hair to the side with slender, gloved fingers. My breath caught in my throat. Liriana.

I flinched when I saw her. It was slight, but still an obvious tell of my feelings. Tank caught it, and so did Tompkins who was pleased to see my reaction and acknowledged it with a half-smile.

Liriana locked her deep-brown eyes to mine then quickly looked away; another signal that Tompkins was quick to notice. It had been years since...since we last worked together. I thought I would never see her again, and now that I had, to find her working for Tompkins made it only that much worse.

"Please, find a seat!" Tompkins said to his crew as the people in this section of the bar abandoned their chairs and scampered toward the exit. "I believe it's time we all got acquainted with one another." Tompkins nodded at the scar-faced assassin, who bowed in response then disappeared into the mass of people.

"Now my friends," Tompkins said, "where were we?"

I refused to answer Tompkins' question, or even acknowledge that he was speaking to me. It didn't seem to bother him as he sat across the table working the broken end of a toothpick through the gaps of his uneven teeth. Cooper couldn't take his eyes off of Liriana, and if I was alone with her it wouldn't have been any different for me. Tank sat erect in his chair, stroking his goatee as he looked around the table. I noticed a hint of fear in Tank's eyes, and that sent a creeping shiver up my spine. Tank wasn't afraid of anything.

Tompkins drew in a deep breath then sighed. "Well, there's no need to be rude. These, my friends, are our prey - Maxx, Cooper, and Tank." He pointed at each of us with a stubby finger as he said our names. With a sudden jolt of excitement, he clasped the shoulder of the male sitting to his right. "By formal introduction this is Rothet, a highly skilled and accomplished tactician, recently hired by the Off World Mining Expedition."

With groaning effort, Tompkins turned to his left and continued with his introductions. He opened his palm and swept it in front of Liriana. "And this fine lady to my left is Liriana, also a new hire for my corporation." Tompkins' face split into an evil grin when he looked at me. "Maybe you're familiar with Liriana, Maxx?"

"Cut the bullshit, Tompkins." I said.

I needed a little more time to gather my thoughts, but Rothet wouldn't give it to me. He splayed his elbows and forearms on the table, and leaned next to me. Cooper started to rise up from this seat, but stopped short of standing.

"Let's not make a...scene," Rothet said. "We're all friends here."

My eyes met his. "I think it's best you remove your arms from my table."

Rothet smirked then forcefully exhaled. "For everyone's benefit, I've talked Tompkins into working out a deal that won't lead to...bloodshed. Your bloodshed. I recommend you listen to what he has to say."

Rothet's face looked youthful, lacking any scars and the unavoidable weathering an assassin receives from years of training and combat. If he was an assassin, and half as good as Tompkins boasted, he should have obvious blemishes marking his experience. His speech was an off-world dialect, and the patterns were unique but familiar. Very familiar. He talked in loud whispers, emphasizing key words while taking long pauses to finish many of his sentences – which created a sense of unease.

"I'm not in the mood to make a deal."

"Don't be stupid, Maxx!" Tompkins blurted out. "You can't beat what you're up against. Take us to your ship, hand over the Solonian cargo, and we'll let you and your crew go free. It's that easy."

"And if I don't?"

"Then you just signed a death warrant for everyone on your ship."

"So that's your threat, Tompkins?" I stared him down. "You aren't getting my cargo, so why don't you try and settle one of those warrants right now?"

My response turned Rothet's joyful grin to a look of irritation. "Tompkins doesn't have to deal with the minutia, Maxx. That's my job, and your death would come...by my hands. All Tompkins needs to do is utter the words."

I smiled at Rothet, my eyes locking with his. I didn't remove my stare as I talked. "Tompkins, pull your puppet's strings. I'll be happy to kill him in front of you."

Tompkins sat motionless as if contemplating my request and the consequences of performing such an act on the Solonian space station.

"This is idiotic," Liriana said. Her words cut through the tension. The sound of her voice hit me like a sharp uppercut to the chin. "This isn't the time or the place."

"Maybe, maybe not," Rothet said. He shifted his look to Tompkins as he drummed the tips of his fingers on the table.

For a brief moment Liriana and I exchanged glances. Her brown eyes poured out all of the hatred she felt toward me. She had a right to harbor those feelings. I'd earned them, with interest.

"Listen, fucker," Tank said as he grabbed Rothet's wrist. Rothet's forearm was devoured in his monstrous hand. "One more word out of you and I'll break you in two!"

Rothet smirked at Tank, then used his free hand to slowly peel Tank's fingers away from his wrist. "I'd welcome that challenge, sir," Rothet said. A moment of shock consumed me. I've never witnessed someone that matched Tank's strength, let alone surpass it.

"That's enough for now," Tompkins interjected, taking rushed glances at the people in the bar. "We've already drawn enough attention to ourselves, and to continue to do so would only complicate matters." He stood and motioned Rothet and Liriana to follow. "We'll see you soon enough, Maxx. Keep that cargo warm for us." Tompkins spit near my feet and slicked his hair back against his head. He gave me a slight nod, then the three made their way to a table on the other side of the room.

"Boss, that was some messed up shit," Cooper said, taking a dramatic pause. "I don't think I've been that quiet for years."

"I'm sorry to have put you in that position," I replied.

Cooper rubbed his hands around his chest. "Feels like I'm burning up inside. All of the pent up comments are slowly eating at me, clawing their way out."

"Can't you ever be serious?" Tank shouted. He slammed his fists on the table, which bounced his mug off the side, sending it crashing to the floor.

"Both of you need to focus," I said. "Right now I need you to work on acquiring a ship. Tompkins has made things more urgent."

"Ah, who cares anyway?" Cooper shrugged. "Once we leave, there isn't any way he can track us."

"Yes there is," Tank said with a growl. "He has Liriana."

"So what?" Cooper said. "She hasn't worked with us in years."

"It doesn't matter though does it, Maxx?" Tank questioned as his muscles tensed.

"She knows everything," I said, my voice low.

Cooper's smile quickly faded. "How?" He asked. "I don't even know where the *Beast* is."

"She doesn't know where it is," I said, "but she'll know how to find it."

"Bedroom secrets." Tank spoke behind narrowed eyes.

"It's best both of you leave," I said. My leather gloves creaked under the strain as I clenched my fists. "Right now."

"Hmmph." Tank grunted and leaned into my face. "I'd fight for you until my last dying breath. You know that. But this one mistake could cost us everything."

"I don't need to apologize for my past."

"Whatever," Tank said as he leaned back in his chair. "She's dying anyway. Hopefully sooner, rather than later."

"Huh?" Cooper said.

"She's dying from the JaCs. You can see it."

Cooper looked over at me, then back at Tank. "What do you mean?"

"When you JaC, your body is forced to answer the call for whatever the JaCs demand. Eventually you'll reach a point where there are too many calls on your system, and they'll drain you dry."

"And how can you tell?" I asked. "How can you tell that she's dying?"

"You can see it in her eyes. How she carries herself. Her body is too small and too weak for the implants she has. She's always had the unique ability to control her JaCs' side effects, but doesn't have the capability to slow the drain on her system. They're eating her up."

I didn't know what to say. I shouldn't have cared, but I did.

Tank continued. "Maybe there's a way out of this. For all of us."

"How?" Cooper asked.

Tank turned and looked at me. "The compensation JaC, Maxx. Give it to her if she promises to leave Tompkins."

I looked at my right forearm that rested on my lap. "I can't, Tank."

"You have to."

"Wait a minute!" Cooper said. "You still have that JaC?" I nodded my head as Cooper continued. "But, you were going to destroy it. You said you destroyed it."

"It doesn't matter," I said, shaking my head. "I can't give it to her." I paused for a few moments to think it through. If what Tank said was true, I could save Liriana, remove her from Tompkins' employment and complete the Solonian contract. On the surface it all made sense, but it was too dangerous. Too risky. I couldn't give the JaC to anyone. Not even it if meant saving Liriana's life. "I won't do it."

Tank sighed. "Whatever. If we wait it out long enough, we won't have to worry about it. She won't last much longer."

Cooper tapped Tank on the arm as he stood. "We'll take care of the ship, Boss. Give us a few hours to work out a deal and contact the Solonians for the delivery of Terra and the supplies. I'm also going to settle up with the tailor. When you're ready, we'll meet you at the docking bay." I located the chip that contained the case's security credentials, pulled if from my pocket, and placed it in Cooper's extended palm.

Tank started to speak, but this time it was Cooper who restrained him from talking. Cooper nudged him forward and away from where I sat. Tank grumbled as he stood, then tucked the case under his arm.

As Tank left he cleared a path through the bar directly at Liriana, Rothet, and Tompkins. When he reached their table, Tank lowered his shoulder into Rothet, who only glowered back while straightening his jacket, allowing the mountainous man to pass without retaliation. Tank walked out the door of the bar and disappeared from sight.

"Boss," Cooper said, "I know what you're thinking right now. Just remember when you reopen a closed door, you may not like what you find behind it." He rapped his knuckles on the table then turned and walked away.

The drunken rumble of the crowd continued around me as I sat at the table in stunned silence, unwinding the jumbled mess of new thoughts tangled inside my head.

I was pissed off, consumed by my emotions and left with a mind that felt as thick as mud. I tipped the mug back to take another draw, only to find it empty. I tossed it to the side letting it wobble across the table then tumble to the floor. I took a deep breath and raked my fingers through my hair. Whatever choices I made in the next couple of hours would shape our mission's success or failure, and right now everything pointed to failure.

The same young servant girl approached me and placed three vessels of brightly-colored, alcoholic liquids on the table.

"Those aren't mine," I said, muffled and uncaring. "Please go away."

The lights from the bar danced between each of the decanters, casting vibrant colors on the scratched white tabletop. A slender, crystalline glass, intricately etched with Solonian symbols, was placed in front of me as the servant brushed her hands by the decanters. The dark letters inked into her inner forearm changed colors when her arm passed by each of the available choices. She waited quietly for me to choose the one I wanted.

"I said, those aren't mine," I repeated a little more gruffly. I settled my chin into my chest, closed my eyes, and rubbed my temples.

She tapped me lightly on the arm to draw my attention then pointed her finger at the bartender. He nodded and mouthed, "On the house."

She turned back to me, once again running her hand across the fronts of the three decanters. I wasn't accustomed to fancy drinks, so I shrugged my response. "How the hell does he stay in business giving all of his drinks away? Maybe I should just stay here for the next thirty days and drink myself into oblivion."

She acknowledged me with a restrained grin that she was quick to hide, then placed her hand next to the tall blue vial. I nodded; she smiled and poured it into my glass stopping just short of the rim.

"Thank you," I said. She bowed, waited a moment for a command, then turned and walked away. I drew back a deep swallow of the beverage and placed my right leg against Tank's chair, tipping my back against the wall. The drink had a strong, fruity flavor, and enough of an alcoholic punch that it sent a warning with each sip.

I found myself stealing glances at Liriana. Tank's words about her impending death stuck inside my mind, and I couldn't shake those thoughts free. I could tell she sensed my looks, but chose not to acknowledge them. I really didn't care to hide it anymore. My lack of concern was fueled by how much I had to drink and a building 'I don't give a shit' attitude. It didn't take me long to find the bottom of the crystal glass and less time for the servant to refill it.

Halfway through my second glass, I watched Tompkins pat Rothet on his back and eventually wobble out of the bar. Rothet leaned into Liriana and spoke into her ear. She appeared to be comfortable and calm, occasionally nodding her understanding or acceptance of what he was saying.

Rothet finished speaking and ran his hand down her arm as he backed away. He placed two fingers on his forehead and sent a salute in my direction before vanishing into the crowd. Liriana was alone, her back turned to me. The lights in the room embraced her shapely figure clothed in layers of black cloth, tight fitting leather, and light armor plating. Her dark hair rested on her shoulders and spilled down to the middle of her back, curling slightly at the ends. She was as beautiful as I had remembered, maybe even more so. I had to remind myself that her beauty was only surpassed by how dangerous she was - a trained and deadly killer, amped with more JaCs than anyone else I knew.

She turned to look at me over her shoulder, briefly losing me in the deep pools of her shocking brown eyes. Her features, distinct look, and the way she carried herself separated her from any other woman in the galaxy. Finding beautiful women was easy. They're on every planet, every ship, and around every corner. But Liriana was different. She wasn't just beautiful; she was striking, intelligent, and confident. She embodied perfection. Liriana was a woman that all other women wanted to be - until she started to JaC.

An innocent smile crept across Liriana's face as she walked toward me. I had a tough time pretending I wasn't interested.

"May I have a seat?" she asked.

"Please," I said, pointing to the chair on the opposite side of the table.

She arched an eyebrow and sat down. "Are you afraid of me sitting any closer?"

"I have rules about getting too cozy with someone who's trying to kill me."

The servant girl rushed to Liriana's side and motioned at the vessels.

"I'll take what he has," she said.

The servant handed Liriana a crystal glass identical to mine, filled it with the light blue liquid, bowed then stepped away.

We sat in uncomfortable silence while our gazes shifted between our alcohol and each other's eyes. I could tell she wanted to say something and was fighting to hold it back.

"Nice bar," I said, finally breaking the silence.

Liriana snorted out a laugh and shook her head. "That's a really great attempt at small talk, Maxx. After three years that's all you've got?"

"Maybe." I took another drink.

"Maxx, what happened between us is unforgivable, but it doesn't mean we can't be civil to each other."

"Civil?" I sighed and shook my head, then rested the front legs of my chair back on the floor. "Civil, as in let's settle the score by hunting me down, stealing my cargo, and killing me and my crew?" Her eyes shifted, moving away from mine before finally settling her gaze on the table. "I'm not sure how to be civil when talking to my potential killer."

Liriana's head snapped up and her eyes engaged mine as she reached across the table and lanced her index finger into my chest. "You made your own damn bed, Maxx. Now you get to lie in it!"

"Liriana, there isn't a day that goes by that I don't second guess my decision."

"Really? Is that supposed to make me feel better?" she replied with a thin, mocking smile. "If you were to do it all over again, would you still abandon me? Would you still toss me aside like trash?"

I'd run this scenario through my head countless times, and each time I came back with the same answer. "Yes, I would."

Slowly shaking her head, she let out a sigh followed by a muted chuckle.

"You were a risk to everyone on my crew, our missions, and my ship. You gave me no choice."

"I was a risk to *you*. Only you, and that's all you cared about. I know it, and your crew knows it."

"How many times did we talk about your JaCing? How many times did I tell you when you push the limits of the JaCs you became more of a liability than an asset? Damn it Liriana, we had that discussion a hundred times yet you still disobeyed my orders and went forward with yet another JaC. You forced my decision."

"Your orders?" She replied, moving her hair away from her eyes as she tilted her head to the side. "So you were my commander when you gave me those orders?"

"Our involvement with each other was a mistake." Those words stung the moment I said them. "I was your commander, and you worked for me."

"I see..." Liriana smirked.

"No one can handle six JaCs, Liriana. No one."

She eased back in her chair and finished her drink, then motioned for a refill. Liriana leaned forward as the servant poured the blue liquid into her glass. Her hair fell to the sides of her face and rested on top of the table. The stark contrast of the two was like a raven soaring across a field of newly fallen snow.

"I told you I could handle them, and you didn't listen." She took another draw from her glass. "And now, I have ten."

My mind raced and a lump rose in my throat. The thought of a single individual with ten JaCs was above my, or anyone else's, comprehension. It couldn't be possible. The effects of JaCing isn't a simple one to one ratio you compound with each new JaC added. No one had passed the mark of six and lived. How the hell could she possibly have ten?

"You heard me," Liriana said, once again easing back in her chair. "Ten," she whispered, holding up her fingers. "Ten, Maxx, and you worried about my sixth. You took away my friends, my family, and my life. You left me. Just like that." Liriana snapped her fingers.

"How are ten JaCs possible? I don't believe it, Liriana."

"Believe what you want. After all, you always have." She took the last swallow from her glass then cast it aside. When our servant approached, Liriana snatched the decanter out of her hands and motioned her away. Liriana tipped it back and took a long drink before she rested it on the table. I was only halfway through my second glass, and was already woozy from its effects. My vision started to betray me, casting doubles of nearly everything I saw.

"So, you're Tompkins' number one assassin?" I said in an attempt to change the subject.

"Does it really matter? We make a pretty damn good team. He sees the value in my JaCs. The value in me."

I tried to ignore her last biting comment. "Why, Liriana? Why would you go to work for Tompkins?"

"Why do you care? You dropped me from the team and from your life. You cast me out on my own. What was I to do?" Liriana rested her elbows on the table then placed her chin on her closed fists. "Tell me, Maxx, what was I to do?"

"You don't need him."

She took another mouthful of the blue liquid then slammed the towering pitcher on the table, spitting droplets of light blue alcohol into the air. "You don't get it do you?"

"Liriana, you're only a pawn being used by someone who's pure evil. You're better than that."

"And your heart isn't black? You, the man who kills in the name of credits? Who are you to judge me or Tompkins for that matter?"

"There are difficult decisions we all need to make in our lives. Get out now. Choose a new path. This is your time."

"Do you really believe that? When you cast me aside I accepted my new path. Thank you for helping me discover my real self. I couldn't have done it without you." Liriana pointed at herself. "Take a look. Do you like what you see?"

She wasn't evil, and she shouldn't be working for Tompkins. She was playing a distinct role in a madman's wicked plan. In the end, she would be a liability. One he would need to address. When he was done with her, he would just cast here aside, or kill her. I paused for a moment as that last thought ran though my head. *Were Tompkins and I really that much different?* I winced as I considered it.

Liriana continued. "I know how to find the *Beast*, Maxx. I know the protocols you follow to hide your ship when things go bad. You don't know where the ship is, but you do know the location of the two crew members who have the information that will lead you back to her."

"I'm not sure I know what you're talking about."

Liriana laughed. "Each soldier carries partial coordinates of the undisclosed location of the *Beast*, and they'll be positioned somewhere within a few jumps of your ship."

She was right. Liriana knew my strategies well, and there wasn't any reason to continue to deny it. "Even if you're right, how do you propose finding them? It could take you decades to hunt them down. It's an impossible task."

"Maybe. Unless I know the location of one of the two already."

I felt the blood drain from my face. "It won't do Tompkins any good if you can't find the second."

"It won't do you any good if we kill the first. Without both crew members' coordinates, you'll never be able to locate your ship."

The alcohol was much more potent than I had originally expected. My heart started to race and the room swirled around me. I reached out and grabbed the edge of the table before I lost balance and fell off the chair. I tried to disguise it, but knew I was failing.

"How are you doing, Maxx?" She asked with a slight tilt of her head. "I don't feel a thing."

"Me either," I said. I swiped my hand across my face and continued. "You're here to try to cut a deal. So what do you and Tompkins want?"

"Just what he asked you for before. The Solonian cargo. That's it. You lead us to the cargo, you keep your ship, and you and your crew go free."

"If I don't?"

"We find your contact and search for the second. If we find both we'll take your ship by force. If we can't locate the second, the first will die along with your hopes of finding the *Beast* and completing your contract with the Solonians."

"Liriana, if I don't deliver on the Solonian contract my entire crew dies. The same people you fought side by side with. Members of your team."

"My old team, Maxx, not my new one," she replied softly. "You get to keep the *Beast* and have the opportunity to get as far away as you can."

"So you propose that we all go into seclusion and hide from the Solonian Empire and the UG?"

"Do you think the Solonians will let you and your crew live, even if you complete the contract?"

"I just negotiated a new deal with the Solonians. Everyone receives a pardon when we complete the contract."

"I'm surprised," she said, arching an eyebrow. "Maybe Tompkins underestimated you. That's some serious negotiations to pull your ass out of the fire after the catastrophic failure of your first contract."

"Everyone receives a pardon but me."

There was a look of shock on Liriana's face as she stumbled to find the right words. "Why would you do that?"

I ignored her question. "Tell Tompkins that there's no chance of cutting a deal. I'm done talking."

Her look changed to one of sympathy and concern. What I couldn't tell was if it was genuine. "You can't be serious, Maxx? This is the best deal you'll get. Either way you're a marked man. If you make this deal, you buy yourself some time to run."

"Liriana, I can't trust you and I'm surely not going to trust Tompkins." I forced myself to stand, using the edge of the table to support most of my weight. "It's a race then. The first to recover my two contacts wins."

"That's insanity. Let me talk to Tompkins. Maybe we can work something out with the Solonians? Let me help."

"Tompkins won't help me, and the Solonians won't change my deal. The only way my crew lives is by completing this contract."

"You're foolish and just throwing your life away."

"That isn't the first time I've heard that." I brushed my jacket sleeve across my face in an attempt to scrape away the haze. I looked down at Liriana and set my hand on the table near hers. "Are you dying?"

She looked vulnerable for the first time today. She replied softly. "Don't –"

"The JaCs? Are they killing you?"

She steeled her gaze on her hands, which were folded together and resting on the table. She attempted to say something a few times, lips parting then quickly closing.

I placed my hand on her shoulder. "Remove the JaCs. Get them out of your system before it's too late."

Liriana jerked away from me as if my touch burned her skin. "It's too late. They're part of me...they are me. You can't fix the past by just cutting it out and tossing it away."

I steadied my feet and closed my jacket. I reached out to her one more time, to provide whatever comfort I could, but stopped short of touching her. I placed my hands at my sides and walked away.

She called out to me as I left. "No matter what you think, Maxx, and no matter what happens, always remember you gave up on me."

As I exited the bar, I felt that I left part of me at the table. I still felt the guilt for what I did, for driving her to Tompkins, for not helping her when she needed me the most. But I'm an agent soldier. Life goes on.

I stumbled out of the Starlight Room and down the space station's passageways using the welds on the walls as my guide. The look on Liriana's face, when I asked her about her impending death, was burned into the backs of my eyes. The alcohol surged through my system, pumped through my veins by my pounding heart. My depleted blood supply made drinking dangerous, and it was all that I could do to keep myself upright. I used both of my hands to brace myself, sliding them against the cold steel as I edged my way forward. The taste in my mouth, the spinning of my head, and the cold metal walls reminded me of the one hundred and seven days of Toad's hell. Just the thought of Paxcel made my hands shake.

Stupid, Maxx. Stupid. This was exactly what Tompkins wanted. What he counted on. He knew he could play on my emotions simply by making an appearance and by introducing Liriana. I shouldn't have drunk so much after the recent fight for my life. I shouldn't have sent Cooper and Tank away to locate a new ship. Getting messed up drunk is one thing. Getting drunk and leaving the protection of the bar, while hunted by three assassins, is another. I just dug a two-meter hole for myself and placed one foot over the edge.

Staggering forward, I caught the blur of people passing me in the hall, careful to lower their voices as I came near. Two people spoke, but I only saw a fuzzy mass of color streak past. The sounds in the hall echoed inside my head as if I was locked in a steel-lined room with hundreds of people shouting in unison.

I stopped, steadied my breathing and focused on compartmentalizing the alcohol's effects. Slowly, my vision cleared and my feet stabilized for a few seconds before the spinning and blurriness returned with a vengeance.

My stomach roiled and I stumbled, thumping by shoulder hard against the corridor wall. My thoughts were too muddied and slow, and no matter how hard I attempted to focus, I couldn't suppress the alcohol's effects. I couldn't ignore the thoughts of Liriana. Things had never been the same for the crew since I forced her off the team. Things had never been the same for me.

I needed to get my bearings, figure out where I was and how to get to the dock. Closing my eyes I visualized my path from the Starlight Room, through the maze of hallways, and back to the docking bay. It was a straightforward progression, a fairly direct path that was easy to reverse, but the visions in my mind twisted and ran together like a young child's finger painting project. *You can do this, Maxx. Focus.*

I created a small tunnel of clarity amidst the frenzied chaos in my mind. That tunnel helped map the route from the bar to where Cooper and Tank would be waiting. I moved as quickly as I could through the halls. The people I passed slimmed in number with each turn in the passageway.

Each corridor grew darker and quieter until all I heard was my breath and the clank of my boots against the station's deck. I was nearly there. The ends of my fingers started to prickle and the building warmth in my chest grew outwards, sending its burn into my arms and legs. When I stopped to work feeling back into my hands, I heard the muffled breathing of another person.

"How are you feeling, buddy?" echoed a voice from behind.

I turned to locate the source of the voice, but the darkness didn't let me see more than a couple meters from where I stood. I squinted as he continued to talk.

"You don't look so good." It was Tompkins. The smell of his cologne filled my nostrils and his voice was all too familiar even under the puffing of his labored breathing. But it wasn't just him. There was someone else as well, standing close, silent and unmoving except for the soft sound of cloth sliding over leather. Tompkins stepped near me. Only a meter from where I stood, his figure was nothing more than a rounded shadow. "It's over, Maxx. I've won."

I gnashed my teeth. "Enough!" My punch was wild, but my fist found his soft cheek, splitting skin and breaking teeth. It sent him flailing against the wall then bounced him to the floor with a booming thud. There were scuffling sounds as he scurried away on all fours, fleeing back into the darkness to where his silent partner stood.

"Alright!" He screamed. His speech was distorted and he talked with a lisp through his split lips and broken teeth. "You took your one shot!"

"You like to talk, fat man, but that's all you're good for." I rested my shoulder against the wall, keeping my body stable and providing security on my left side.

"Why don't you chew on this, Maxx?" He spit something wet onto the floor. It splashed as it hit and clattered with something that sounded like splinters of bone. "You're all by your fucking self, in an area that doesn't have any guards, cameras, or body scanners."

"That's all the better for me," I shot back, "though not such good news for you."

Tompkins slowed his speech and carefully spoke each word. "The Solonians are going to scream in horror when they find what's left of your body."

"Just more talk."

"It's time we said our goodbyes." He spit again. The sound was followed by a dull groan. "Before I go, I want to leave you with one agonizing memory, as short as it will be. When you dumped Liriana, you broke her mentally, worse than when you first discovered her years before. She was a wreck, seething with betrayal."

I exhaled sharply and narrowed my eyes as he continued. "When I found her, she was at the worst possible point – both mentally and physically. When you gave up on her, she found a friend in me. I helped her recover, and supported her desire to continue to JaC. I became her friend. Her only friend. I was everything you promised to be, but weren't. Soon, Maxx, your crew on the *Beast* will regret the day you dropped her from your team."

His words tore through me like point-blank blaster fire. The leather gloves tightened around my hands as I balled them into fists.

Tompkins continued. "The biggest payoff I've ever earned was seeing the look on your face when you found out she was working for me. That fuck up of yours has to be a tough pill to swallow." He spit again. "The second biggest payoff will be your death. And that's coming very soon."

"I'll make you this one promise, Tompkins," I said. "I promise to deliver you to the reapers myself. No matter what you offer me, no matter how much you beg for mercy, I will kill you."

"Goodbye, Maxx," Tompkins said. "This is the end for you and only the start of the terror your crew will experience." His voice trailed off as he plodded down the hall.

Before I could act, I heard the wisp of a wire cutting the air behind me. I slid my left arm next to the side of my face before a garrote was cinched around my throat. The wire dug into my forearm just a few inches below the wrist.

A sharp lash whipped across the backs of my legs, driving my knees to the floor and slamming my torso and face against the corridor wall. The attacker pushed their leg into the small of my back, keeping my chest pinned so I couldn't move.

Whoever it was they were incredibly strong, and I knew right away I would be no match for their strength. But I was lucky. The garrote caught underneath my jacket's collar, and my forearm gave me enough slack to continue to breathe and avoid decapitation. I was quick enough to turn my forearm sideways to protect the veins in my wrist and the soft flesh in my arm. It all happened so fast that I should've been dead.

The leather of my jacket helped as padding, but my sleeve slowly relented to the saw-like motions each time they moved and twisted the garrote. The wire sliced its way through the leather and bit into my arm, cutting skin then muscle. I felt a sharp burn then the flow of warm, wet liquid.

My arm throbbed as my heart pumped streams of blood on my face and on to the wall, spilling the sickly smell of copper into the air. The wire grew tighter and tighter, then suddenly stopped. That's when I felt a stinging punch to the side of my ribs, accompanied by the sound of punctured leather and torn cloth. I screamed out, but the garrote silenced me.

The attacker must've slipped the garrote into one hand, and was using their other to knife my side. They struck again. I clawed behind me with my right hand, only finding air. Searing pain erupted from my side as they slowly twisted the blade. There was a new darkness closing in on me. A darkness that carried the whispered voices of the reapers.

I gasped for air as my side grew numb. My heart pounded, surging adrenaline through my veins. I pushed against the wall with my right arm creating some space, then forced my way back to my feet. The noose of the garrote didn't loosen, and the legs of my attacker soon wrapped around my midsection. His blade rattled against the deck, then I felt an increased tug on my arm and my collar giving way as they pulled tight with both arms. My neck was basted in the hotness of their breath as they pulled me in closer. Wrenching. Tightening.

Reaching into my jacket, my hand fumbled through the inside pockets until I located the knife I lifted from Jigsaw earlier today. I pulled it free and grasped it in my palm. My first blow was under the attacker's right kneecap, splitting bone and slicing ligaments. The second plunged deep into the top of their thigh, and the third severed the hamstring. Their leg dropped limply at my side. Not even the slightest whimper was heard and the garrote didn't loosen from my neck. The assassin had to be JaCed - inhuman strength, blazing speed, and an insane tolerance for pain.

I stabbed and swiped at their hands but they shifted them away too quickly. Reaching across my body, I dismantled their other leg much like the first, removing any leverage the attacker had. I lifted them off the ground, spun around and crushed them against the wall, driving their back against the steel with a resounding thud. One of their hands must have slipped as the garrote loosened enough to allow me to free my left arm. In a single motion I flipped them over the top of my head, and slammed their back onto the floor. They released an explosion of exhaling air as their appendages splayed outward.

I moved to hammer their chest with my clenched fist. They blocked my attack with both arms but left their right side exposed. *Sloppy.* I buried the knife deep into the soft tissue of their neck, twisted clockwise then counter clockwise. My attacker's response was nothing more than a wet gurgle that seeped through the cloth mask that covered their face. I balled my fist and struck the hilt of the knife like a hammer, driving the blade through their neck, stopping at the pommel. Their arms wilted and head rolled to the side.

I scrambled to my feet. My body was running on a surge of adrenaline that was sure to fade. I didn't know how badly I was hurt, and needed to take advantage of my newfound strength while I could. I left the body and the blade behind and worked my way down the hall, attempting to stem the flow of blood from my forearm.

As I limped my way through the maze of passageways, one hollow thought lingered in my mind. *Did I just kill Liriana?*

"What the hell?" Tank's voice boomed as I approached hunched over and clutching my leaking side. Everything was still a blur and shrouded in shadow. Two people stood from their seated position on what appeared to be a stack of banded crates.

"We need to go," I sputtered. "Now."

"Over here, Boss." Cooper's voice fought against the noise of the robotic maintenance crews moving supplies and making repairs. "This way." He opened the access hatch to the fighter and helped someone inside.

Tank rushed over and wrapped his arm around my shoulders to keep me from falling. My body wanted to quit, but I wouldn't let it. I fought to move forward, dragging my feet and occasionally slipping in a puddle of red that splattered at my feet.

Stepping into our new ship, I worked to remove my jacket and shirt against the protest of my shredded arm and punctured torso. The blood soaked cloth of my shirt tugged at sections of torn flesh, sending ripples of agony through my body. Someone hurried to my side as I lowered myself to the floor. I tried to flush away the blurriness by opening and closing my eyes, but couldn't regain focus.

"It's me," Terra said softly. She pressed her hands against my ribcage to help slow the bleeding. Blood flowed between her fingers like water leaking through a sieve. Cooper ran over to us carrying a large bag that swung wildly at his side.

The high pitched whine of the ship's engines pierced my ears until the whooshing burst of the ignited thrusters drowned it out. Our fighter lifted from the platform, then turned awkwardly. Each unexpected jolt of the ship sent my head spinning and my sides throbbing. Digital clearance codes pumped through the overhead communicator as our takeoff from the Kogin station was granted.

"Cooper, I don't need you hanging over me like you're my mother," I snapped. "Get your ass into that cockpit before Tank puts this ship into one of the docking bay walls."

"Are you sure you don't need my help, Boss?" Cooper knelt next to me and placed his hand on my shoulder. "I should've stayed with you at the bar."

I forced a laugh then winced. "Most of these wounds are surface scratches. The blood just makes it look bad." Cooper remained still. "If you don't get to the damn cockpit everyone on this ship is going to look worse than me."

"Yeah, Boss. OK."

"Tesid," I said. "Take us to Tesid." Cooper paused for a moment, then stood and raced to join Tank.

"He's a friend," Terra said calmly. "He cares."

"We're not friends." I grimaced as Terra applied a medicinal agent to my wounds that fizzed and bubbled as it made contact with my skin. The holes in my side cauterized and sealed almost immediately. "I don't have any friends."

"Your bond with him is strong. Friend is just a word you choose not to use. Pick your own word, but the meaning will be the same."

The pool of blood underneath me filled the air with a sickly, metallic smell. Terra tied a rubber tunicate around my forearm to stop the bleeding and examined the wounds near my rib cage.

"The agent sealed the wounds," she said, gently tracing her fingers along my side. "They aren't deep, so they will heal quickly. You're lucky there wasn't any damage to your ribs or internal organs." She reached over and took my left arm into her hands. "This one though, is not so good." Terra picked at the shredded flesh below my wrist then turned it from side to side to inspect what she was about to work with.

"Can you fix it?" I asked.

"Fix?" She asked with a tilt of her head. "I can stop the bleeding. Patch the muscle. Stitch the wound. Your arm will be weak and it will hurt for a long time."

"Do your best," I muttered. "I have a feeling I'm going to need it soon enough."

Terra sprayed something on the gash then doused it in an orange liquid. My arm felt as though she was applying it with a blowtorch.

Cooper stepped back into the compartment as I spit curses into the air. "We've plotted our route to Tesid," Cooper said. "It should take about three days of travel."

"Hmmph," I grumbled back, not able to speak while my arm burned with fury.

"What happened to you, Boss?"

"Are you sure you aren't burning my arm off?" I yelled at Terra through gritted teeth.

"I told you it would hurt," she said.

"Yeah...hurt," I mumbled. I checked my arm to see if it was still there, afraid it had been burned to cinders. I took a deep breath and exhaled. "I had a little run in with Tompkins on my way to the docking bay. He had someone with him."

"Who?" Cooper asked.

"I'm not sure. The only thing I know is that they're no longer on Tompkins' payroll." My mind shifted to thoughts of Liriana, wondering if it was her that I fought in the corridor. I didn't want to believe that she would try to assassinate me. I didn't want to believe that I killed her. Suddenly the hurt in my arm moved and settled inside my chest.

I stared at the fighter's deck for a few moments as I tried to compose myself. Dwelling on the past wouldn't serve any purpose, so I tried to clear Liriana out of my mind. "I have two crew members waiting for us, each at different locations carrying partial coordinates for the whereabouts of the *Beast*. Jackson is on Tesid."

"So we're in the clear then," Cooper said.

"Maybe. Maybe not. Liriana claims that Tompkins knows the location of one of the two crew members."

"So Tompkins knows where Jackson is?"

"I don't know for sure. All I know is that Jackson is closest, so we're going to him first. After that, we'll worry about what's next."

"I'll let Tank know." Cooper turned to Terra. "Take good care of him. He gets a little grumpy when he's in pain."

Terra smiled and motioned Cooper to her. She whispered something and planted a soft kiss on his cheek. He nodded and exited the room.

"Drink this," Terra said as she placed a vial in my hand.

I swirled the liquid inside and crinkled my nose at the smell when I sniffed the top of the bottle. "What the hell is it?"

"It will cleanse the alcohol from your blood."

I drank it, burped half of it back into my mouth and swallowed again. I kept my eyes closed tightly, willing the liquid to stay down. "First you try to burn my arm off, now you try to poison me."

"You need blood."

"Is there something wrong with mine?"

"Nothing is wrong, but you've lost too much."

She was right. My blood supply was dangerously low from the intentional bleedings on Paxcel. That, compounded with the loss from these recent wounds, and I was running on empty. Bodies have a way of alerting you of danger and mine was screaming for help by growing cold and numb; my hands shook and the room spun around me.

"When we land on Tesid I'll find someone to perform a transfusion," I said, balling my fist against the fire still blazing through my arm. Terra trimmed the ragged flesh then worked a needle and thread through my wound.

Terra gently touched the side of my face as she spoke. "You will fight when we land, will you not?"

I shrugged. "I'm not sure, but it's likely. Things never go as easy as I hope."

"Then you need blood now, you need the time to heal. I'll give you mine." I chewed on the inside of my cheek, not knowing how to respond. She laughed at me and said, "I sent Cooper to bring the medical supplies we need."

"Why?" I asked. "Why are you doing this?"

Terra tilted her head at me, her braids clattered as they fell to the sides of her face. "I don't know why you would ask. It's what friends do."

The planet of Tesid was the familiar, desolate wasteland I'd visited a few years ago. Crusted with ice and snow, its frigid temperatures blanketed the surface under a frozen cover, slowing civilization to a crawl. Located in the northern hemisphere was the only populated city on the entire planet; a city no one cared to name.

After years of careful study, the UG determined there was nothing of value on the planet of Tesid and declared it independent of the UG nations. Their declaration opened the floodgates to the criminal world, allowing it to grow unchecked and unmolested. It was now the most popular destination for the galaxy's outcasts.

"I planted Jackson here in hopes of avoiding any UG entanglements," I said. I felt the frigid bite of cold that seeped through the hull of the ship as I leaned against the access hatch. "That decision may pay off considering the mess we're in now."

"We need weapons and coms," Tank said. "And it wouldn't hurt to equip this fighter with some firepower as well." Tank banged his fist against the hull. "The Solonians stripped off the cannons as soon as we made the purchase."

"Tank, you know what we need. Take care of us and the ship." He gave me a reassuring nod. "Cooper, I need you to locate six coms. They all need to be programmed and encrypted for the same secure channel."

Cooper arched his eyebrow. "An encrypted channel? Should I contact the UG to see if they're OK with us breaking their laws?"

Ignoring Cooper, I continued. "While you guys track down the gear, I'll locate Jackson."

"What if Tompkins and his team are already here?" Cooper stroked his chin. "You can't go out looking for Jackson on your own. Wait until we get back and we'll go with you."

"If Tompkins is here, we'll have to deal with him. We need to get to Jackson before Tompkins does."

"Then let's look for him first, and get the gear later."

"The weapons and coms are just as critical. The UG is combing each planet across the galaxy looking for us and the Solonian cargo. If they show up, they'll lock this city down tight, and if they do that, we're screwed. Use the underground tunnels. Any skin exposed to these harsh winds for more than a couple of minutes will frostbite and die."

Tank nodded. "Watch your step down there. The tunnels are filled with beggars and criminals waiting to score quick credits."

"Everyone needs to be back on the ship in six hours," I said. "Not a second later." My look shifted between Cooper and Tank. "Everything is riding on this. You understand that, don't you?" They slowly nodded their responses. "This is the start of the most dangerous mission we've ever attempted. Treat it as such."

Tank clapped his hand against the hull in acceptance.

"Take care of yourself, girl," Cooper said to Terra. He wrapped his arms around her in a quick embrace. "I'll be back soon."

I punched the code into the panel and released the access hatch. A spray of white, carried in by sub-zero temperatures, sprinkled the floor of the hatch near our feet. "Take this," I replied. I pressed a microchip into Cooper's open palm. "There are some other things I'll need you to take care of besides the coms."

"Got it." Cooper smiled and dropped the chip into a front breast pocket of his jacket. "Before I go, let me thank you for this rare opportunity to spend six hours in the anus of the galaxy." Terra laughed, then covered her lips with her fingers as if attempting to hold it in. Tank sighed, then shook his head and followed Cooper out the door.

I turned to Terra. "Keep the hatch locked and don't open it unless you can clearly identify one of us on the monitors," I said. "Do you understand?"

"Yes," she said. "Thank you."

"For what?"

"For everything you've done for me."

"Terra, you have a distorted sense of who owes who." I clasped the buckles on my jacket and cinched it closed, sending a burning wave across my ribs. I slid on my gloves and flexed my left hand, feeling the pull of the stitches accompanied by a sharp sting each time I moved it. "Plus, you shouldn't be thanking me. There's a good chance we're all going to die." I stepped out of the access hatch and sealed the door behind me.

The hangar doors were open, allowing Tesid's elements to extend their cruel reach into the cavernous building. The bitter arctic air nipped at my exposed flesh, while the tails of my jacket danced in the swirling winds. The cold intruded through the knife holes in my coat, blowing against my wounds and sending a numbing sensation across my side. My cheeks reddened and became prickly to the touch.

Outside, the locals shambled from building to building bundled in bulky layers of black and brown furs, giving the appearance of beasts roaming freely among civilization. The lights of the city flickered and danced behind the drifting snow, providing their welcoming promises of shelter and warmth. The city was built in a circle with a web of interconnecting underground tunnels used to transport goods and provide shelter from the harsh conditions. Most of the city was buried deep under the planet's frozen crust and only a few outdoor entrances were cleared for the people brave enough to face the weather – or too afraid to traverse the tunnels.

There were three distinct districts in this city, separated by their form of criminality: drugs and prostitution, electronics and hacking, weapons and JaCs. If you had the credits, you could purchase nearly any illicit good you desired. That was if someone didn't kill you and steal your credits first.

A single flickering light marked the entrance into the tunnels, buzzing its warning as I walked underneath it. Even in the harsh cold, the air reeked of urine, vomit, and human filth. Mixed together they gave the truest sense of what this place had become. The floor was littered with junkies huddled around makeshift fires. A few reached out, clawing at my jacket with their soiled hands and dirt-packed fingernails. I brushed them away with a kick of my boot.

The sea of wasted human flesh eventually thinned and parted, opening into the deepest part of the tunnels. Like the spokes on a wheel, each passageway carved a dirty path to a large center expanse which became another city in itself. Made up of hundreds of misfits cast out from the general population, it was a dirty version of what awaited me above. Most of the wares they peddled were stolen or counterfeit, merchandise too risky to purchase unless you were desperate or poor.

"Hey buddy! Wait up!" Someone shouted from behind. I turned and watched a man limp his way toward me on a stiff right leg he was unable to bend at the knee. His combed-over hair sailed erect as he hurried to my side. "You need to see my selection of JaCs," he said between labored breaths. His reflection shown in a polished brass box he clutched tightly against his heaving chest.

"I don't have the time," I said, then continued down the passage.

"You can't afford not to make the time, sir." He scurried behind me, moving his precious box to one arm. He dug through his pockets, eventually emerging with a worn implant reader. Thumbing the device controls, he activated it and scanned my body. He took one look at the reader's display and frowned. "Error," he mumbled. "What the hell?" He snorted, struck the reader against his thigh then rapped a finger against the display monitor twice. Reactivating the device, he initiated another scan and smiled at the results. "You definitely need what I'm selling!"

"I doubt that." I stopped to gather my bearings and find the most direct route into the city. The eastern spokes led to the districts that would offer shelters such as brothels, safe houses, and drug dens; the most likely spots where Jackson would hole up and wait.

The man hobbled in front of me and flashed a greasy smile as his eyes examined me from head to toe. "A fit man like you needs speed, perhaps endurance or strength." He rubbed his pointed chin as if in deep thought. "I can help you with all of those."

"Get out of my way." I headed toward the eastern spokes and the man stepped in my path again.

"I assure you that the quality of my implants are far superior to anything you'll find in the city above us." He nervously licked his lips and gave me a reassuring nod. "Your body is an open canvas, ripe for two or three."

I snatched his shirt into my hand, popping off buttons and tearing away a small section of cloth. "I don't have time for this!"

Masked by the commotion around me, someone stepped from behind, wrapped their arms around my neck and constricted like a hungry snake until they forced the air from my throat. "You make the time," he grunted. His breath smelled like rotten eggs and alcohol. "Buy somethin' from Jake. Buyin' is good."

The dealer squealed. "Yes! This is my lucky day! You will buy something from me! And of course, the prices of my JaCs just went up!" He placed his closely guarded box on the floor and released the two latches that secured its cover. His trembling fingers raised the expanding shelves until three trays of JaCs were revealed. Each of the implants were individually sealed in solid glass cubes and clearly labeled with their unique function. "Which three would you like?"

"I'm going to offer you a deal," I choked out, "but only once." The merchant's stooge tightened his grip around my neck. "Give me that implant scanner, and I'll let both of you walk away from this. Speak to me once more and the deal is off."

The merchant dangled the implant reader in front of me. The stooge laughed at the 'error – null' statement flashing in green across the display.

The merchant smiled and said, "As –"

The excitement in the merchant's face drained when I shattered the leg of his stooge with the heel of my boot. Under a swift crack, the bone snapped and sent him to the floor howling. He clutched at the center of his awkwardly bent shin; the broken bone was splintered backward as if he had a second knee on this right leg. My fist found his face, busting his already misshapen nose under a spray of red. I continued to hit him until the screaming stopped.

Stunned, the merchant turned to run. I grabbed the back of his grubby collar and jerked him to the floor. The contents of his box spilled, sprinkling the JaCs to the ground like glittering cubes of ice. Kicking them with my boot, they scattered into the open area around us to be crushed under people's feet as they passed.

I recovered the implant reader, turned it off, and dropped it into my pocket. "Do you have a problem with me taking the reader?" I asked.

He answered with a quiver of his lip as he shook his head from shoulder to shoulder.

"Good." I patted his face. "Then you're right. This is your lucky day."

When I cleared the tunnel and stepped into the city, it was as if I had entered another world. The voluminous passageway opened into a splash of bright lights, bustling life, and the smell of credits. People moved past me with purpose, knowing what they were looking for and how they were going to get it. Voices, heavy boots on metal, and the swoosh of opening and closing doors blended together and filled the area with a dizzying buzz.

What services and products the shops offered were kept discrete, yet identifiable if you were familiar with the black markets. Universally known symbols were etched on the walls near the store doors, partially covered under graffiti and years of dirt and grime. It was a way for the merchants to advertise what they sold, while supplying some plausible deniability if confronted by the UG. It provided a small level of comfort for the merchants, but that was about it. The UG knew the symbols, and they were the only ruling judge, jury, and executioner in the galaxy, and playing ignorance would buy you nothing. The UG didn't rule here, but it didn't mean that the residents were immune from their tyrannical grasp.

Just like the merchants, Jackson would've disguised his own symbol by combining it with others in a confusing mess of shapes and colors. And that's what I was looking for; a single symbol directing me to where I wanted to go. It wouldn't be obvious, so I had to work my way down the hall, slowly, carefully, and examine every marking I could find.

The section of merchant shops, that greeted me upon my entrance to the city, transitioned into the housing district as I headed southwest. It was as if someone drew a line in the corridor to separate one section from the other. When I stepped over that line, the noisy buzz of bustling life was drowned out by the darkness of another world. A world of flesh for

117

credits.

Women lined the halls like cheap decorations, arching their backs and rubbing their thighs, barely hiding their skin under a few strips of narrow cloth. Many were young and beautiful. Others displayed the severe tolls their bodies took by dealing in the flesh trade. They worked hard to sell whatever they had to offer. A tender brush of a man's shoulder with their long, brightly colored fingernails was the bait; naked skin and painted smiles were the hooks.

While I searched for the markings, I spotted a man pinning one of the prostitutes against a wall, eagerly striping what little clothes she had from her body. His pants hung loose past his knees, and his belt buckle jingled as he moved in closer. The prostitute's body trembled at his touch. She turned away from his aggressive hands and impatient lips as he forced himself onto her. Her sad, wet eyes locked with mine as I stepped toward them. She slowly shook her head at me. This was her life. What she needed to do to survive. The look in her eyes screamed out with years of regret. They told her sorry tale without uttering a single word. We've all been there. This was the galaxy we lived in. I bowed my head and turned away.

Three doors down the hall was the entrance to a brothel, lit by the waning red of two sconces that cast their welcoming light on a circle with a cross in the center that was scratched into the wall. Unlike the others it didn't show spots of aged rust. The symbol was no larger than my fist and placed amongst the others as a random act of graffiti. I rapped my knuckles against it. He was here.

I pushed open the only entrance into the brothel and was greeted by the rolling smell of sweat, alcohol, and cheap sex. The grand hall was enormous, adorned in plush carpets and vivid tapestries, all muted under the dim lighting. A bar occupied the far end of the room. On either side were staircases that spiraled their way upwards to a second level balcony of rooms. A dirty heaven for the customers.

Two dozen couches were scattered throughout the chamber, filled with patrons hollering like little boys who got their first look at a naked woman.

A finger leisurely ran along the stubble of my cheek. "And how may I be of assistance?" A calming, sensual voice said from behind. Her hands started to rub my shoulders, kneading the tension from by body.

I turned to greet her. She was tall and curvy, with bright yellow hair that spilled onto her breasts and spread curls across her chest. Her lips were pouty and red, and her eyes as green as emeralds. She smelled like flowers on a summer day and her smile filled me with uncomfortable warmth.

"I'm looking for someone," I said softly, almost lost in her beauty.

"Looking for someone or for *something?*" she asked. She slid her hands down my shoulders to my biceps, rubbing as they descended. Her tight fitting, scarlet dress hugged her curves and revealed just enough skin to make you wonder what was underneath.

I looked her over one more time. "I'm looking for someone...someone else." The lack of lighting created a horrible mix of shadows and flickering images. All I could identify were blobs of moving darkness and blurred shapes in the corners of the grand hall. Finding Jackson, while standing here, would be impossible.

"I'm intrigued." She smiled as her hands worked down my arms until they rested in my palms. I flinched as she grazed my left wrist. "Maybe we can have a drink and talk about this person? Who is she?"

"It's a he."

Her eyes widened. "I see. Well, we do provide services for all of your wants and needs at my establishment."

"Your establishment?" I arched my eyebrow. "It's a nice place you have here. I like the way you decorated it with all the naked women."

She closed her eyes and fluttered her long, black lashes as a smile spread across her full lips. "Thank you. It's the best of its kind on Tesid."

"I'm sure it is." I was running out of time and I needed to speed this conversation along. "I'm not here to look for the services of a man, nor am I looking to bed one of your employees. I'm here to recover one of my crew."

"Oh." She removed her hands and crossed her arms in front of her chest. "You work for the Unified Governments? I don't need any more trouble."

"You just ruined our moment." I squinted against the darkness, turning the dark shapes around me into large, darker blobs. "I don't work for the UG. I run my own business."

Relief washed the concern from her face and returned a look of natural beauty. "You're familiar." She rested her chin on the heal of her palm and drummed her fingers against her cheek. "I've seen you before..."

"I'm sure you've seen a lot of people, but trust me when I say you don't know me."

"Maybe," she said, running the point of her tongue across her top lip while studying me with her welcoming eyes. "What's your name?"

"Names only complicate things, and mine is guaranteed to cause you trouble."

A smirk crossed her lips as she tilted her head at me in acceptance. "Who is this crewman you're looking for? Maybe I can help."

"Slightly shorter than me, black hair –"

She sighed and pressed her index finger on my lips. "You're about to waste our time by giving me a description of everyone who visits this place. Tell me something unique."

"His face is heavily scarred, torn and patched back together by someone who couldn't mend a hole in a shirt. His tongue and lips were carelessly reattached, making it hard from him to speak, causing him to occasionally drool and mumble when he talks too fast. He carries a cloth with him, subconsciously dabbing at the corners of his mouth." Her eyes shifted, scanning the parlor as I continued. "He has a kind and forgiving heart. One that sets him apart from anyone else in this godforsaken galaxy."

Her painted fingernails snatched the leather around my elbow and tugged me forward, escorting me through the brothel with haste. She flipped up a small section of the bar and led me to a door. Punching a code into a lit panel on the wall, the door slid open and she motioned me inside. She whispered something to two of the women tending the bar then shut and locked the door behind us.

"How did you know to come here?" She asked. The pace of her speech quickened, tripping over her words as she talked.

"The symbol outside your brothel door," I said. "The cross set in a circle."

"And what does it mean?" She turned away and rushed over to a cabinet at the back of the room.

"My contact has a strong faith, both in the humanity of people and in his god."

"Tell me more about him," she said as she dug through a drawer. "What's his name? I need to know more..."

I didn't like where this was going. "It's best that you don't know any more. I've already told you enough."

Her hair whipped in defiance as she spun her head toward me. Her lips were tightly pursed. "If you want my help, you'll answer my questions!"

She clearly knew who Jackson was and where he was hiding, so I indulged her. "His name is Carter Jackson, a crew member of mine for nearly four years. During one of my contracts I stumbled across his captors and freed him and a dozen other slaves. He vowed to fight by my side from that day forward."

"His name is unique...old fashioned."

"When you're born and raised as a slave, you're never given a birth name. So I gave him Carter Jackson; the first names of two of the greatest men I've ever known."

Her uneasy stare never left me, so I continued. "He's served many roles on my ship over the years. Spiritual leader, cook, and medic. About anything he can do to help."

"So you're Maxx," she said with a twinge of anger. Before I could respond she pointed a blaster in my direction, the barrel staring at my face like an ugly black eye. In her other hand she clutched a small metal box no larger than a bar of soap. The box was streaked with patches of red.

"It doesn't matter who I am."

She bit into her bottom lip, not releasing it as she talked. "Show me your arm."

"My arm?" I ran my tongue across the back of my teeth.

"I want to see your markings." She shifted her stance as her finger massaged the trigger. "I want to know if I'm about to kill the greatest agent soldier that has ever lived."

I looked down at my arm then shook my head. "No."

The pistol hummed as she flipped the booster switch on the charge pack. "I'll ask you one last time. Show me your arm."

"It's obvious that Tompkins or the UG has beaten me here." I stepped forward and reached out my hand. "Hand me the blaster, or shoot me and collect the reward. I don't have time to talk."

The gun trembled in her hand as if it suddenly weighed ten kilos. Contemplating her options, she raked her nails across the back of her neck. She let out a sigh and tossed the blaster and box at my feet. I knelt down, picked up the pistol and turned it on its side. It was Jackson's. I turned off the booster switch and watched the green digits grow from seventeen to forty-three. I released the buckles on my jacket and placed the gun inside one of the pockets.

I recovered the box from the floor and pried open the lid. Inside was a crusted cloth that cracked and shed flakes of brownish red as I unfolded it. Encased within the cloth was a single JaC, still adhered to a sliver of bone and a patch of torn skin. I lifted it to the light, then closed my eyes and bowed my head. "What happened?" I asked.

"Months ago he came to me seeking refuge in one of our rooms." Her eyes never left the floor as she talked. "Every day he sat in the far corner of the grand hall, waiting to meet someone - waiting to meet you. He paid me in full for room and board while passing on our services. Day after day he sat at the same table from early morning to late evening."

I stood up and walked over to her, lifting her chin with my finger and looking into her eyes. Deep inside her there was a sense of caring and passion I'd believed no longer existed in this galaxy. Our eyes locked as she continued. "I was intrigued by him, by his dedication and his kindness. I got to know him well, and he became a friend. We shared a bond I've never felt with anyone else."

She pushed herself away from me, paused for a moment then turned back. Her voice transitioned from sadness to anger. "Recently, the Unified Governments came sniffing around here looking for your ship. People heard us talking and it wasn't long before he was ratted out as one of your crew."

"He should've known better," I said.

"He opened himself up because he trusted me! It's my fault he's dead." She narrowed her eyes and pointed a finger at me. "It's *your* fault he's dead!"

I pulled in a deep, settling breath. "So the UG killed him." I wrapped the JaC in the cloth, placed it inside the box, and dropped it into my jacket pocket.

"He knew he wasn't going to get away, and still refused to sell you out. Carter begged me to cut that JaC out of him before they killed or took him into custody. He said it contained information you needed, and no matter what happened I had to deliver that JaC to you and only you." Her purposeful stare became vacant. "It all happened so quick. They stormed into my brothel and cornered him in the grand hall. Eight or nine of them. When they tried to take him away there was a fight for a soldier's gun. He took down two of the soldiers before they shot and killed him."

"What's your name?" I asked as I retrieved the pistol.

She hesitated, then said, "Elizabeth."

"Elizabeth, when did this happen?"

"Only a day and a half ago."

"Who's leading this squadron of UG soldiers?"

"I...I don't know his name. An older man, tall and thin with eyes of white."

"What did they tell you do to?"

"The man leading them, the older man, told me I had two choices. Either I persuade you to tell me the location of your ship, or I lure you into my office and lock you inside so they can arrange for your capture themselves. If I was successful, they promised me three hundred thousand credits and to move my business to an off-world location protected and sanctioned by the Unified Governments."

"And if you failed?"

"I was told that failure was an option I wouldn't enjoy."

"These men. Are they still here?"

Her body shuddered at the question. She crossed her arms over her chest as if to provide her some comfort. "A handful of them remain behind."

"How many?"

"Only five. They're sitting in the grand hall as we speak. I don't doubt that they called more soldiers the moment you stepped through my office door."

"It seems as though the second choice was an easy one. Why didn't you just play along longer to keep me occupied?"

Elizabeth bit her bottom lip. "Because of Carter. He told me that he owed everything to you, and had no way to pay you back for what you did for him. This is his payment, Maxx. You're even."

I walked over to Elizabeth. "Thank you for what you did, but there isn't any way out of this for you. You understand that? There isn't anything I can do to help. The UG will be back here with more ships and more men." She nodded her response.

I turned away and walked to the door, pausing before I opened it. "You need to leave. You need to gather your girls and get off of Tesid. Once this is all done, I'll find you and pay you back for your part in this."

"I only want one thing," she said with a growing darkness in her voice. "I want those Unified Governments soldiers to feel like I do right now."

"You don't have to worry about that, Elizabeth," I said as I tightened my grip on the pistol. "They're going to feel worse. Much worse."

I activated the panel on the wall that opened the door of Elizabeth's office. The shaded darkness of the bar, and the sounds of lust greeted me the instant the door slid into the wall. Streaks of laser fire lit up the room, shattering bottles, torching wood, and scorching the walls. The UG was anxious to claim their prize and fired on me too early. Their eagerness to put me in the ground would be their undoing.

I charged forward and leapt over the bar, tucking myself into a ball then rolling onto the floor. My left wrist buckled when I pushed myself back onto my feet, and my side burned each time I moved. I traced the paths of their blaster fire - two soldiers to my right, one near the exit door at the far end of the room, and one only ten meters to my left.

My first shot from Carter's pistol found the crown of the head of the UG solider near the exit door. The orange bolt of laser fire burst his skull like a ripe melon and sprayed its contents on the wall.

Patrons screamed, shouted, and stumbled over one another as they scrambled for the exit. Their arms flailed with terror, creating moving barriers that blocked my view of the remaining UG soldiers. I tucked my head and sprinted toward the exit. Laser fire exploded around me and splintered the wooden planks near my feet. I dove to the floor and rolled onto my back, allowing momentum to carry me forward. I aimed and squeezed off a second shot. It found the center of a UG soldier's chest with a lighted thump. His torso imploded, dropping what pieces remained onto the floor in smoldering clumps. He looked like a candle dripping wax until his body collapsed on top of his sizzling jacket; the trails of wispy electronic smoke fighting to escape.

I scrambled to locate cover and dove behind a couch to shield myself from the remaining two soldiers. Laser fire punched holes through the fabric above me. The red material burst into flames, billowing smoke into the air. I crouched down and dragged myself on my elbows across the room and behind another row of velvet couches.

The legs on the couches were high, allowing a clear view of the scurrying feet around me. The blazing fires brightened the dim room and highlighted a pair of standard issue UG boots creeping toward my position. I squeezed off two shots. The first separated the soldier's foot at his ankle. His shin crashed onto the floor with a bone-shattering snap. He fell, curled into a ball and clutched his bleeding leg. My second shot ended his murderous screams.

Green lasers blistered their way through the backs of the couches, missing my head by only centimeters. The heat of the blasts singed my hair and burned the skin on my face. I flipped the booster switch on the pistol's charge pack and waited while the violent hum of the weapon peaked. I wrapped both my hands around the pistol's grip, blew out a breath, and sprung from the back of the couch and fired three times. The pistol bucked in my hands with each pull of the trigger, sending shockwaves through my left wrist and arm. Orange light washed over my body as the blaster found its mark. The first two shots melted wood and metal, and the last found the final UG soldier who had sought cover behind the bar. It showered the back of the room in red.

Most of the brothel had cleared. All that was left behind were a handful of shaken service girls and a few drunks who didn't trust their wobbly legs to get them through the exit. Across the room, seated in a corner, was a lone man, still and quiet; his face illuminated by the single click of an electric lighter. He took a draw on a cigarette then blew the smoke into the air. The tip of the cigarette burst to life with each puff, then slowly the ash burned free, fell to the table, and faded his face back into the darkness.

"You need to give me one minute to speak before you do something rash." His voice crackled with age.

I raised the pistol and thumbed the booster switch. "Captain, you have five seconds before I pull the trigger. Three of which I just used."

"You need me, MXX." The white eyes of the Captain stood out from the cloud of grey smoke, until the ash fell from the cigarette and he vanished back into the darkness. "I'm here to make a deal."

I walked toward the Captain, the pistol site focused on the center of his skull. When I reached the table I grabbed the edge, turned it over, and sent it crashing to the floor. He didn't flinch, only took another pull from his cigarette and blew the smoke from the side of his mouth. I picked him up by his decorated military collar and slammed his back into the wall. He grunted, but never moved his eyes from mine.

I spit the building anger from my mouth. "You authorized the murder of four members of my crew. You imprisoned and tortured me. There will be no deal. Only answers." I thrust the pistol into his chest and brushed my finger across the trigger.

"Then no one wins," he said. "Pull that trigger and we all lose. Me. You. Your remaining crew."

My vision clouded in red just before I slammed my head into his. A long gash opened above his brow and his legs wobbled. I didn't say another word, just watched the gash spill red down his face.

The Captain cleared his throat and regained his footing. "Clearly, you don't understand." The blood from above his brow streamed into the corner of his mouth. He corralled it with his tongue and spit to his side. "I'm the only reason you're still alive. The Unified Governments is here in full force. More than a hundred soldiers, and I'm the reason that there were only four in this brothel."

I slammed his body against the wall again, fighting the urge to break him in two. He coughed, wiped the stream of blood from his eye and continued. "Kill me if you wish, but you won't make it out of here alive. I'm the only one that can keep the soldiers at bay while you make your escape."

"Why should I believe one word that comes out of your mouth?" I asked through gritted teeth.

"Do you think I would make my way to this worthless planet with four soldiers? Is that how you think the Unified Governments operates? You're just lucky there are only a hundred of us." He paused as his white eyes burrowed their way into my soul. "They want what you have in your cargo hold, MXX, and they want it badly."

"And you wish to broker a deal with a hundred men at your disposal?"

"The Unified Governments has their wants, and I have mine. I want to see you go free."

"Why?"

"Knowing why isn't part of this deal." The Captain licked at the free flowing stream of blood and spit again. "Where were all the guards when you made your escape from Paxcel? Who would clear out most of the personnel manning one of the Unified Governments' most secure prisons?" The Captain lifted his arm and looked at the communicator wrapped around his wrist. "You should know that you don't have much time left."

"Before?"

The Captain rolled his eyes toward the ceiling as if he were in deep thought or searching for the right words. "Before this entire city is burned to the ground. Before everyone who lives here dies. Before you're killed, or captured and confined back in a cell." I didn't know how to respond. His eyes and his face were honest. They were going to murder everyone in this city. A thin smile cracked his wrinkled face as he continued. "And it starts just outside of this brothel door."

I looked over my shoulder at the entrance to see the fire that blazed from the outside and snaked its way inward; orange and red tongues licked at the curtains and couches near the door. Embers blew into the room then danced around us, driven upwards by the waves of heat and vented oxygen.

Elizabeth emerged from her office. She stopped and grasped at the edge of the doorframe for balance; her right hand covered her mouth. All she could do was look on in horror.

"Elizabeth!" I shouted. Stuck in a stunned trance, she didn't respond. "Elizabeth!" Her head snapped in my direction. "You need to get out of here! Get off of this planet now!" She took one last look at the room around her as if saying her goodbyes to a dear friend, then nodded at me in understanding. She shouted some instructions to the girls that remained in the brothel, circling her arm to motion them to her. One by one they disappeared through the door of her office.

Elizabeth was the last to leave. She stood motionless under the frame of the office door, shock rendering her helpless. Her fingers wove through her long hair as she brushed it away from her face, revealing tears welling up in her eyes and streaking down her cheeks. She eventually broke from her trance, then stepped into her office and closed the door.

"Interesting...," mumbled the Captain. "An agent soldier taking precious time to save the innocents." My head found his again, opening another gash near the first. The Captain's legs buckled, but I didn't let him go. I kept him pinned to the wall as he shook the fog from his head. He looked up at me and whispered, "You need to take advantage of my kindness, before it's too late."

I pushed the pistol into the center of his chest and took a long, deep breath.

The Captain raised his arm to my meet my eyes, and turned his wrist to show me his com. "I can route the soldiers away from here, buy you enough time to get back to your ship and get your men off of this planet. But each second you waste is one less you'll have for your escape. I can only do so much."

I played with the booster switch, toggling it on and off. I took another breath, released my grip on the Captain, and placed the gun inside my jacket. "There will be another time, Captain. There will be payback for what you've done."

The Captain straightened his jacket and wiped his sleeve across his bloodied brow. "I'm counting on that moment, MXX, when you attempt to deliver on your threats. And don't worry. You'll have the opportunity soon enough."

Flames twisted their way out the doors and windows of the merchant shops. The halls were full of people, pushing and shoving their way to safety. The already darkened corridor grew black from the rolling smoke that blew through the city's ventilation system. I paused to rub the stinging from my eyes and to gain my bearings. I reached inside of my jacket, fumbled through my pockets, and located the hard outline of the metal box. The touch of it reassured me. We were halfway there - halfway to finding the *Beast*. I attempted to cough the smoke from my lungs and spit the burning taste from my mouth. I choked and gagged as I pushed my way through the masses and back to the ship.

This city was a powder keg of crazed people just waiting to explode. I couldn't be concerned about the UG soldiers that may have been only paces behind me, or whether Tompkins' goons were waiting around the next bend of the tunnel. I just needed to get back to the ship. Even so I couldn't shake the thoughts that beat inside my head like a drum. How the hell did the UG figure out where Jackson was, and how did they know we were headed here to pick him up? Hell, they arrived a day and a half before we landed on Tesid. If Tompkins knew the location of one of our contacts, I could understand stumbling into them here, but not the UG.

What worried me most was the fact that the UG had upped the ante. They had no qualms about venturing into non-federated space to search for me and my crew. And their insane bounty of three hundred thousand credits told me they were pulling out all the stops to acquire the Solonian's cargo. Whatever their motivation, the size of the bounty reeked of desperation. None of it added up, and the only answer was lying in the cargo bay of the *Beast*. Whatever I was hauling had to be worth a fortune.

As for the UG Captain, what role he played in all of this was still an unknown. Why he aided our escape from Paxcel, and why he would help me get back to my ship now didn't make any sense. He captured me, then helped me escape - twice. He had his own motives, which added yet another layer of danger to completing this contract.

My body trailed with the stench of smoke and death, but that smell was lost in the stink of the underworld. As I continued my path back to the ship, hundreds of people were running frantically, creating moving walls that concealed me from the UG soldiers. Walls that would soon be trampled by an army of UG minions.

The smell of crisp air and the grasp of the bitter cold assaulted me as I emerged from the tunnels and sprinted toward the ship. The open hangar door had a dusting of salt and pepper colored snow, filled with dark, blowing embers still reddened as they fluttered then settled on the concrete pad. Outside the city was engulfed in flame, spread by Tesid's unrelenting winds. There was no way to contain the fires, and it was only a matter of time before Tesid's residents would be driven from their home. They would be desperate to find a ship to take them off the planet. So desperate, they would easily kill and take what they wanted by force. Anyone left behind would be reduced to ash or frozen and consumed by Tesid's harsh elements.

The skin on my face grew numb and my joints stiffened. It didn't take long for my sprint to the ship to turn into an old man's hobble. Open crates were strewn outside our fighter. Frosted metal frames and the wired circuitry of armaments peeked out from the boxes. As I approached someone spotted me from inside the ship and activated the hatch, which responded with a hydraulic groan. Limping inside, I found Tank standing near the door. Schematic prints littered the floor around his feet.

"We have to go," I blurted out with a gasp. The frigid temperatures stole my breath as my lungs contracted and fought against it. "Now!" I continued my path past Tank and stepped onto the bridge. I had to stop for a few seconds just to rub the feeling back into my legs before I continued to limp forward.

Tank followed in haste. He screamed something at me from behind that I failed to recognize. His thunderous footsteps raced to catch up as he continued to talk. "We can't leave for a few more hours. It's going to take at least that long to attach the weapons to the ship."

The bridge was empty. "The city is burning, Tank, and the rats will be fleeing the sinking ship." I pointed out the bridge windows then headed back to the passenger compartment.

"Huh?" It was all Tank could muster in response. He froze in place as he looked out the windows.

I found Terra sitting in one of the flight chairs in the passenger compartment, her long legs propped up on the seat next to her. She rolled a small electronic device between her hands, occasionally stopping to pluck a wire from the circuit board. Her brow was arched and the tip of her tongue poked from her lips.

"Where's Cooper?" I asked.

She continued working on the device, turning it in her hands while carefully inspecting the circuit board. She shrugged without looking up. "He's not back yet."

"Holy shit, Maxx!" Tank yelled from the bridge. "What the fuck happened?"

I left Terra to join him. "Do you have our personal weapons on board?" When he didn't reply, I yelled out. "Damn it, Tank! Focus! Do you have our personal weapons on board?"

His head snapped back to look at me. "Yeah, they're in the storage area. Only the ship's weapons are outside."

"Arm yourself. Quickly!"

Tank's eyes moved away from me and back to the bridge window. "We need to get the hell out of here."

"Not without Cooper. Get us some blasters and meet me by the access hatch."

I curled around the door frame and hobbled back to the passenger compartment where Terra's focus remained on the electronics in her hands. "Terra, I need you on the bridge." She raised her head to look at me. When she saw my face, she knew not to ask any questions. She tossed the device on the chair next to her and followed me to the bridge.

"Do you know how to pilot a ship?" I asked out of desperation, realizing it was a stupid question the moment it left my lips.

"Yes," she replied with a reluctant whisper. My eyebrows creased. I watched her for a moment. Her eyes widened as she soaked in the visual horror of the burning city. Nearly the entire town had been set ablaze. Orange dots streaked through the roads as people streamed into the outdoors, engulfed in glowing suits of flame. They ran in panic, driven by an instinct to survive yet with no plan for what to do next. Each dot spiraled out of control until it finally fell, quiet and black, into the blowing snow.

"You can pilot this fighter?" I asked.

She nodded at me. "I think so. Yes. I've flown before. Not this model, but ships similar to it." She examined the panels in front of her.

"The ship needs adequate time to warm the engines and charge the thrusters. In this extreme cold it doesn't have enough power to ignite both thrusters at the same time so they must be activated in sequence." I pointed to the two separate banks on the control panel. "In two minutes I need you to start with the left panel. Flip these two switches, wait five minutes then press this button. Once the thruster ignites, start the same process with the one on the right."

Terra watched silently as my fingers moved between the panels, her eyes shifting back and forth.

I gripped her shoulders and shook her lightly. "Are you able to help?" I asked.

"Yes."

"Good. No matter what you hear and no matter what you see, do not leave this bridge. We need to have both thrusters activated before we can take off." She nodded then took a seat in the pilot's chair.

"Go," she said to me. "Get Cooper."

Tank was waiting for me near the access hatch. Leaning against his body was a large UG auto-repeating cannon, a gun normally mounted on a military ATV. Its outer casing was dented and scratched and there were numerous spots of patchy rust etched into its grayish frame. Dangling in his hand was a gun belt that holstered two TW-34 blasters - my weapon of choice.

I snatched the holster from Tank's hands and secured it to my waist and thighs. I removed both blasters and turned them on their sides for a quick inspection. Both guns were heavily used, scratched with a buildup of grime in the creases, but everything appeared solid and in working order. A quick review of the ammunition counters confirmed I had slightly less than a maximum charge and only twenty rounds. The TW-34 blasters were unique weapons, offering a dual barreled combination of laser fire and old school uranium bullets, propelled by gun powder and activated by a firing pin. One flick of the toggle switch, resting directly above my thumb, provided instant access to either ammunition.

"We need to find Cooper and get the hell out of here," I said.

"You can't go back out there," Tank said. He placed his hand on my chest and shoved me back as he opened the access hatch of the ship. He raised his hand and pointed his finger at the chaos outside. The entrance to the tunnels looked like the end of a well-lit cigar, burning red and spewing smoke. Hundreds if not thousands of crazed people were filling the hanger, creating an unthinking mob that trampled everything in its path.

The rumble of an ignited thruster rocked the ship under us. "I can't leave Cooper here. Give me five minutes to find him."

Tank grabbed my arm as I started to exit the ship. "The cold will kill you," Tank said as he hoisted the cannon off the floor. "My healing JaC can handle five minutes of this fucking cold. I'll find him."

I shook my head. "This isn't your responsibility, Tank. Secure the ship and I'll be back soon."

Tank didn't let go of my arm. "Fuck that. You're no good to anyone dead. If I don't make it back, you need to get off this planet and complete the mission. You're the only one that can. The crew on the *Beast* dies without you."

I nodded. I didn't want to send Tank out into that mess, but he was right. "Only five minutes," I replied. "It's all the time we have."

"I'll find the little prick." Tank smiled. He clapped me on the shoulder then followed the barrel of the gun out the access hatch.

I left the hatch open knowing that Tank and Cooper would need quick access to the ship. With both blasters resting comfortably in my hands, I stood at the side of the entryway to shield myself from the blowing winds. Every thirty seconds I stepped in front of the hatch to look for Tank and Cooper. The biting winds attacked my face and the blowing snow and ash pelted my body.

A growing black cloud of rolling smoke filled the hanger outside, consuming the masses fleeing the city. The state of panic escalated as quickly as the desperation. A man with a wild-eyed look stopped at the base of our fighter's platform, and motioned to two of his friends. My gloves creaked as I gripped my pistols. I stared down all three of the men then shook my head slowly from side to side. They considered it, then decided to move on.

The rumble of a second thruster shook the ship. Time was up. I holstered one of my pistols and inched my way down the ramp, holding onto the iced hydraulic extensions for balance. The cold gnawed its way through my glove, and my hand burned with a dull, numbing throb. The suffocating smoke that filled the hangar crept inside the ship, watering my eyes and forcing me to squint against its oppressive wave. The streaming mob continued to break through the wall of smoke only becoming visible once they were within a few meters of where I stood.

We needed to leave Tesid, but I couldn't. Not yet. I edged my way down the ramp trying to catch sight of Tank or Cooper. Halfway down my foot slipped on the buildup of ice and snow, melted by the fires and re-frozen by the harsh winds. My back slammed against the slick steel and jarred the pistol from my grasp. I caught the edge of the ramp and stopped myself from sliding down into the hangar. I reached across my body to draw my second pistol, but it was too late. Angry hands pulled me from the ship and dragged me out. Six men stood over me, transformed into frigid pillars of black soot. The whites of their murderous eyes were the only thing visible against the curtain of billowing black.

A volley of fire cut a swath through the angry mob. Each pulsating shot split the smoke, determined to find its target. The air filled with the stench of burned flesh and heated blood. A tree-trunk sized arm reached out to me, plucked me from the floor of the hangar and tossed me inside the ship. The air was forced from my lungs as I landed on my back and slid to a crashing stop against the hull. Tank backed his way up the ramp, never releasing the trigger of his cannon. Cooper was slung over his left shoulder, his body motionless and covered in soot. Tank continued to launch a volley of bolts into the smoke as I scrambled to my feet and activated the close sequence on the access panel. The spray from his auto cannon ceased as the door sealed shut.

"You found him." I gasped in attempt to catch my breath. "You found Cooper."

Tank threw the cannon aside, showering the room with sparks as it slid across the grated deck. He wiped the soot from his face, revealing splotchy patches of pink and black skin. His hands shook as he laid Cooper at his feet.

"He's dead," Tank rumbled as he slammed his fist against the hull. "He's fucking dead."

The drone of the thrusters was the only noise heard in the bridge. None of us spoke a word. Tank's mood was dark, matching the black soot and ash that streaked his skin and covered his clothes. Other than a single swipe across his face to clear his vision, he left the dirtied remains of Tesid on his body. It was a visual reminder of our failure to save Cooper.

Orange flame leapt from Tesid, lashing in anger at the snow-filled sky as if claiming thousands of lives wasn't enough. Fighting against gravity, the ship climbed through Tesid's atmosphere and shrunk the fires from view.

I programmed the ship's autopilot for a direct path to the *Valkyrie*. Needing to clear my head I left the bridge, walking past two empty seats that would never be used. The two reserved for Cooper and Jackson.

I braced my arms on the door frame of the passenger compartment and stared through the darkness of the room. Cooper's lifeless body lay on the floor, covered by a thin sheet. I willed the sheet to move, waited for Cooper to take a breath, but he didn't.

Cooper knew what he signed up for. He knew that one day he would die on a mission. I'd lost countless crew members and this wasn't any different. I was an agent soldier, and I shouldn't have cared. I promised myself I would keep repeating those words until I finally believed them.

I rubbed the back of my neck then bent down next to Cooper's body. I pulled the sheet back to take one last look. Cooper's head was mangled, his body badly burned. His skin had turned multiple colors and was sloughing from the bone, an effect of the harsh Tesid weather. I opened his jacket and patches of his skin peeled free from his chest as the material crumbled and broke free in my hands. I slid my index finger into the inside of his jacket's breast pocket. The microchip was gone. No metal, plastic, or ash, just an empty pocket. I pulled the sheet back over Cooper's head and rested my palm on his shoulder. It had been years since I felt such pain; the true pain of loss. Terra was right, he was my friend.

A soft glow pulsed from the storage compartment down the hall. My boots scraped the floor as I moved toward the light. The room housed a pair of footlockers and a few canvas bags that contained our weapons cache. Tank was sitting on the opposite side of the room, his knees bent and pushed up against his chest. He scrubbed his face with his hands, smearing the black soot.

I dug through the bags, located a maintenance kit, and pulled the remaining TW-34 from my holster. I sat on one of the footlockers and disassembled the pistol, breaking it down into its individual components, cleaning the parts and repairing the damage. Weapons were simple. They were things I could fix.

"I got these for you," Tank said in a muted tone, his arm outstretched in front of him holding something wrapped in a soiled cloth. "You'll find them familiar." I stood, took the item, and sat back down and placed it on my lap. "So you weren't able to locate Jackson?" Tank asked.

"He's dead. Killed by the UG." The words burned in my mouth as I spoke.

"Fuck me. We're screwed then?"

I ignored Tank's question. "What happened to Cooper?"

"I saw him making his way back through the tunnels. I couldn't tell if he was being chased or if the mob just got to him. Before I could clear the area they took him down. Someone rocked the back of his head with a club." Tank covered his face and talked through his fingers as he continued. "It was gruesome. They bashed his skull in, took what he was carrying, and trampled across his body like it was a muddy field."

I continued to assemble my pistol. "You saw it then?" My voice was dry, the words catching at the back of my throat.

Tank looked at me, his face curled into a frown. "I tried, Maxx. I did everything I could." Tank threw his hands into the air and placed them behind his bowed head. His elbows touched the tops of his bent knees. "There were dozens of them. I mowed them down, one after another, but I was too late. I failed."

"You did what you could, Tank. This loss..." I didn't continue.

Tank pushed his way to his feet and stood over me. "Look, this loss is just as hard on me as it is you. But it's one loss. We have to move on.

Don't get soft on me now. The crew on the *Beast* is counting on us. They're counting on you."

Tank took a step backwards when my eyes met his. "Don't doubt me. Never doubt me." I stood, keeping my eyes steeled on his. "We'll get this done."

Tank's fists tightened and his veins expanded like twisted vines around his biceps and forearms. He set his massive hands on my shoulders, his fingers grasped my shoulder blades near my neck. "We'll get even with the UG," he said through a scowl. "We'll make them pay for what they did. I don't care what it takes, they'll pay." I nodded. He clapped my shoulder then left the room.

I looked down at the rag that I was clutching in my hands. A section of the cloth was open, revealing a glimmer of silver. Unwrapping the cloth I removed two knives, rotated and stacked on top of each other from blade to hilt. They didn't show the wear our other weapons did. Everything about them was perfect - the weight, balance, and length of the blades. Each knife had a dual, razor-sharp edge and were forged in one piece but split in the middle where the fuller would be located. It created two separate blades on each knife with two cross-sections of metal connecting each of the blades near the center. I slid them into my jacket, listening to the satisfying sound of metal rubbing against cloth.

I rummaged through the bags and found some spare charge packs for my TW-34 and a handful of uranium rounds. I tossed Jackson's pistol in the bag and removed one of the holsters from my thigh. I cinched my jacket tight, feeling the welcoming cold of the blades against the sides of my chest. This was what I knew. This was who I was.

I found Terra and Tank whispering to each other as I entered the bridge. When they saw me they stopped talking and eased back in their chairs.

"We're headed to the *Valkyrie*," I said. "The last of our two contacts is there."

"We don't have Jackson, so we're screwed anyway," Tank said. "We should be discussing other options to locate the *Beast*."

"Jackson took steps to make sure I received the coordinates," I said. My hand involuntarily moved to the inside of my jacket until I located the metal box. "Now we need to recover Ava."

"So once we locate Ava, we can find the *Beast*?" Tank arched an eyebrow and smiled. "The *Valkyrie* is a large space station. It will take some time to track her down."

"Liriana told me that Tompkins knew the location of one of the two crew members I sent out with the *Beast's* coordinates. If that's true, there's a chance they already have her."

"Maybe they knew about Jackson and were heading to Tesid. Maybe we got there before they did."

I rolled my neck on my shoulders. "Maybe. But Tompkins has some of the fastest ships I've seen, and plenty of manpower to spare. I can't see how they wouldn't have made a break for Jackson before we did."

"So, what's our plan?"

"The *Valkyrie* is a two story space station leaving a single floor for each of us to cover. We dock the station and split the two levels between us."

"What about me?" Terra asked. Her face reddened, and her eyes were squinted as she talked. "I will not sit back and wait again!"

"I can't take responsibility for you Terra. You'll slow us down."

"Don't underestimate me," she said. "I can fight!"

"You want to help?" She nodded quickly at my question. "Then learn the ship. Learn everything about it. There's a chance one of us, or neither of us, will make it back."

"But –"

I cut her off before she could continue. "Prepare what medical supplies are left in case one of us needs medical attention. In case Ava needs it. That's how you can help."

"But, I want...revenge." Terra's jaw was clenched. "For Cooper."

I sat next to her in one of the open chairs. "Once you start down that path, there's no turning back. You'll become everything you despise, everything you hate. You'll become one of us."

We were nearing the fourth full day of our journey to the *Valkyrie* and hadn't encountered trouble of any kind. Our ship's systems were functioning properly, the engines were responsive, and hourly health checks resulted in above average results. There hadn't been any signs of the UG, Tompkins, or a tail from the Solonian Empire, only the darkness of space dotted by flickering pin points of blue and white starlight. When things go this well, I grow uneasy and wonder what we've missed.

Even though I no longer talked about it, the thoughts of Cooper weighed heavily on my mind. For a brief moment I considered compartmentalizing any emotions related to him, but keeping them fresh in my consciousness forced me to accept responsibility for his death. When I refused to talk about Cooper, Terra eventually stopped talking about him too. She just sat quietly in the pilot's chair, studying the ship's controls and diagnostic readouts. More than once I noticed the reflection of her wet eyes in the forward facing monitors.

It took me awhile to come to grips with the internal conflict I was dealing with. Losing a member of my crew resulted in either my casual acceptance, or drove me to seek revenge. There was no in between. When I sought revenge in the past, it wasn't because I cared about the crew members that lost their lives. It was because an enemy bested me, and I needed to make them pay for their victory. But Cooper's death was different. I shouldn't have cared that he died. I shouldn't have dwelled on the loss. But I did, and it haunted me.

****

We were five minutes from the *Valkyrie*. As with planets, space stations were aligned with neutral factions or placed under UG rule. The *Valkyrie* was a neutral faction space station populated with civilians that hadn't yet been forced to align with the UG. The declaration of a neutral faction was different than being declared an independent. In the UG's eyes, neutrality was officially permitted as long as the local populace remained democratic in nature, and obeyed the laws set forth by the UG. They received no benefits from UG, such as protective services or military aid, but were still required to follow all of the laws and governances they imposed. Neutral faction sites were one step away from being devoured into the collective whole of the UG. It's just that the UG hadn't found a lucrative enough reason to do so.

Neutral faction planets and space stations were located on the fringes of the populated galaxy, in locations that proved too costly for the UG to travel to and maintain. Most civilians had the intentions of operating respectable businesses in these democratic locations, though much like the independent sites their neutral alignment acted as a magnet for the undesirable, drawing in anyone running or trying to hide from the UG. As the UG slowly consumed the neutral faction planets and stations, many of their populace who once called them home migrated deeper into space to avoid their rule. The worst of them moved into the Dark Quarter.

The *Valkyrie* is the last active station orbiting the barren, water-covered planet of Disic. Disic's seas once concealed thousands of rich veins of titanium ore that prompted a flood of miners and prospectors to this desolate section of the galaxy. Mining coalitions banded together to construct three space stations, each with the capacity to house ten thousand people. For decades this area bustled with commerce and attracted travelers from every sector of the galaxy with the promise of wealth. Once Disic was stripped of its most precious resource, most people moved on, and two of the three stations were abandoned.

A small group persevered, and worked hard to maintain the last of the three stations. They discovered a sustainable niche and turned the *Valkyrie* into a hospitality location for space travelers as a source of fuel, repairs, supplies, rest, and some basic forms of entertainment. Although the mining operations have dried up, it's still home to a number of permanent and traveling prospectors hoping to discover a rich deposit of titanium that may have been missed.

I stood on the bridge of our fighter with Tank and Terra. The two abandoned space stations surfed the solar winds like weather-beaten flotsam drifting across a calm sea. Their dull metal shells refused to reflect starlight, and their lightless windows looked like eyes, watching as we intruded into their space. As we approached, the *Valkyrie* hinted at signs of life through speckling beams of light that twinkled from the occupied compartments. The station had two levels, each the shape of an independent circular tube. Elevator shafts and spiraling walkways connected the two levels through dozens of vertical spindles.

A tinny, pre-recorded message played across our ship's communicator as we neared the docking bay. Its voice scratched with static as it spoke. *"Identify your order of business."*

"We have trade to conduct over the next two days," I said. "I also need to refuel my ship."

After a pause, the recording continued. *"Upload ship data using secure channel X1.7B."* Tank entered the channel identification and submitted the requested information to the *Valkyrie's* docking system. As we waited for its response, I noticed Terra watching our every move with keen interest. Though her head rested idly in her open palms, her eyes fluttered between our movements and the ship's controls.

The automated docking system took a few minutes to process our information, then fed us the details. *"Fuel level currently at thirty-one percent for fighter model ND1. Three passengers for two night's stay. One hundred and forty-two credits. Do you authorize this transaction?"*

"Yes."

"Incomplete information," the system chirped. *"Please standby."*

The scratchy sounds of the automated docking system were drowned out by a sharp, electronic squeal as a human took control of the communicator. "There's an error with your uploaded data. I have ship particulars and clearance information but it doesn't contain your crew's IDs."

"There's no requirement to supply identification when visiting an independent station," I said, confused as to why they were asking for our IDs. I intentionally picked the *Valkyrie* as Ava's location to avoid such complications.

"We're no longer classified as an independent. Our station was recently annexed to the Unified Governments' mining operations division. New law requires IDs for anyone docking this station."

My mind swam in circles. There was no way that a station in desolate space could afford to turn away our business. I had to try and press him. "I have no interest in docking to a UG military complex," I shot back. "I will take my business and credits elsewhere."

"Wait one moment, sir," the docking attendant said. "Please understand that we're not a Unified Governments occupied station at this time, and aren't staffed with any military personnel currently. We're still operating as a civilian run, free-trade station."

"I'll double your asking price."

He cut me off before I could continue. "Before you go any further, I won't...I can't accept your offer. I can't let you dock or refuel without the proper identification."

"Great," Tank mumbled. "This docking attendant is the only clean person in the entire galaxy, and he holds our boarding pass to this station."

"How far out do you think the UG is?" I whispered to Tank.

"Hard to say," he said, stroking the mass of hair under his chin. "They could be a jump away, or days away. Who knows?"

"As big as the UG is, they can't visit every station and every planet. They don't have enough soldiers or ships. We need Ava. We've got to take the risk."

Tank sighed. "Then we have to move fast. Once they ID us, the UG will know we're here."

I nodded. "Please stand by for our biometric identifications," I said to the *Valkyrie* docking attendant. "This changes our business plans. I need immediate refueling and our stay will be less than one day."

We each pressed our hands onto our ship's scanner. With a flash of green light the scanner captured our DNA so it could be searched against UG databanks for a match. My heart rocketed against my chest as our connection with the *Valkyrie* went silent. Ten seconds. Thirty seconds. A minute of silence. If the attendant had UG personnel watching over his shoulder, our ship would be docked and stormed with brute force or immediately destroyed. I sat in the pilot's chair with my hand hovering over the thruster controls, ready to engage at the first sign of danger.

The com barked with a belch of static. "Thank you. Please move your fighter to port F5 and wait for further instructions." You could almost hear the ship sigh in relief as I guided it to the fueling dock.

Within minutes the refueling process was in full swing. I powered down the ship as two restraining clamps engaged and locked it securely in place. Two of the *Valkyrie's* crew floated toward us, attached to long tentacles of undulating conduit and safety cables. After initial inspections the technicians were forced to remove the ice-covered fuel port with chisels and space-ready torches.

"This setback could add hours to our stay," Tank said, staring out the bridge window.

"We don't have a choice. Locating Ava won't do us any good if we don't have a fueled ship to make it back to the *Beast*."

Tank grumbled as he cracked his knuckles. "Let's get moving, shall we?"

I buckled my jacket and turned to Terra. "I need you to prepare the ship for a quick exit."

Terra chewed on her bottom lip. "A quick exit isn't possible. The restraining clamps are locked to the hull of our ship. Their power dampeners will keep the engines dead until they're done. It will take more than an hour to initiate and complete the disengage sequence."

I headed toward the bridge door, ignoring her comments. "Monitor the local com traffic for any signs of the UG. Once we're in the station, we'll acquire coms for Tank and me and link them back to the ship. If we run into trouble, I may need you to work with the docking attendant to end the refueling process early."

"Do you know what would happen if we attempted to leave before they disengaged? There's a chance we would lose our fuel tank. Destroy the fuel port seal. What's the sense of it?"

I stopped at the door and rested my hand on the access panel. I spoke with my back facing Terra. "Everything is riding on us finding Ava and getting back to the *Beast*. If one of the three of us messes up, we all may die. Us, and the crew back on the *Beast*. Your role in this is no less important than Tank's or mine."

"I don't agree with your plan. I don't like being excluded." Muted words, in what I assumed was her native tongue, followed before I heard the faintest of sighs. "I'll do it."

"Thank you, " I said as I left the bridge, wondering if Terra was fully engaged. Wondering if she could be counted on. Wondering if this is where it all falls apart.

The staff on the space station was welcoming and helpful, a clear sign that the UG integration was only in its infancy. I purchased two coms and programed them for secure communication with each other, and back to our ship, using a private channel. I kept one and gave the other to Tank. We made our initial entries into the space station before I tested the coms.

"Tank and Terra. Can you hear me?" I said through the com.

"I'm on the top level now, Maxx," Tank said. "Let the fun begin."

"Both coming through," Terra said.

"Good. If either of us locate Ava, or if we run into any trouble, make sure to notify the group right away. Otherwise, keep the traffic on the coms light." I slipped the com into my pocket as I entered the service elevator and selected the bottom level.

The top level of the *Valkyrie* contained modest rooms, dining facilities, and gambling halls for any visitor that had expendable credits. The lower level was designed for mining recovery operations when Disic was still actively mined for ore. Half of the lower level was equipped with mineral extractors to remove recently mined ore from transport vessels, freighters, and mining haulers, to be placed into temporary storage. The other half was converted into offices and inexpensive, long-stay rooms for visiting prospectors.

Stepping out of the elevator, my feet stirred dry clouds of filth that billowed upwards creating a thick, orange haze. Banks of lights lined the floor and walls, and strained to illuminate the room through the clutter of debris and grainy powder. I covered my eyes and forced back a cough as I opened the door into a service passageway.

The well-travelled corridor was empty. The carpet was worn in the center and small bits of ore gathered at the base of the walls. Eventually the path led me to a closed door that screamed for lubrication when I opened it. On the other side was a long hallway, noticeably clean by sight and smell. As I stepped into the corridor it transitioned from worn carpet, chipped paint, and warped floors to painted walls and plush carpets. Purposely positioned spotlights were recessed into the ceiling above, showering anyone traversing this passage in their bright light.

The doors of the first two rooms I passed were open. They were offices, clearly marked on the outside with the employee's name, title, and a room number. Both were empty. I didn't give it a second thought until I passed the first visitor room, which was also open. The door's secure access panel in the hallway had small bends around the outside of its frame, as if it was pried from the wall then set back into place.

I stepped into the room as quiet as possible. The entryway opened into a dining room where shards of broken glass and droplets of blood sprinkled the floor. The blood created a dotted trail that I followed down a hall and into a study. Inside I found a woman bound to a chair. A torn cloth was shoved in her mouth and tied around the back of her head. Her neck was slit from one ear to the other creating an ugly red smile under her chin. Her wound was still leaking fresh blood. The fingers on her hands were gnarled and broken, and her palms were marked with deep gashes. Purple and black blotches surrounded her eyes and dotted her cheeks. Someone had questions, and didn't like the answers.

I continued down the hallway and found a young man prone on the bedroom floor, his face buried in the carpet. One of the walls was streaked with red; his fingers had scraped bloody tracks as he fell. The back of his shirt was riddled with a dozen holes, burned from a spray of laser fire. I rolled the man over. Crushed underneath him was a child. His tiny head was marked with the sole of someone's boot. They were casualties of being in the wrong place at the wrong time.

On their bed I noticed a small tented notecard resting on the pressed sheets. It read: *Thank you for five years of unparalleled service, and congratulations on your first anniversary! Please accept this room, and your stay aboard the Valkyrie, as a small token of our appreciation.* I tossed the card to the floor and knelt next to the baby. I removed my gloves and brushed his impish face with my calloused finger. He was cold; a defenseless child who never had a chance to create his own mark on this sickening galaxy. His mouth gaped open like a small red 'O,' and his glazed eyes stared blankly at the ceiling.

I gently turned over his right forearm. It was bare. Untouched. Unmarked. This child would've had a chance at becoming someone important. Maybe he would've done something to help others. Enabled change. But that opportunity was taken from him.

I laid the child on the bed and made my way back to the infant's mother. I cut her free from her chair and carried her into the bedroom. Placing the father next to her, I rested the child in their arms and covered them with the comforter from the bed.

Everything about this was the signature brutality of Tompkins and his goons. I've seen this before. Countless times. No matter the mission, everyone was expendable and no one was innocent. I drew the TW-34 pistol from its holster and checked the ammunition counters. Thrusting the gun back into place, I opened my jacket and released my knives from the custom made sheaths. Gently resting the flat of the blades against the insides of my forearms, their flash of steel crested from the base of the hilts and stopped just short of my elbows. I mouthed a promise to myself that the bite of these blades would even the score.

Back in the corridor, I located an emergency panel mounted on the wall. Similar bends and small scratches marked its cover where someone had pried it free. I loosened it with my knife and found all the wires cut from the touchscreen. I pressed the panel back into place and continued forward.

I rounded the first bend in the passageway and stopped. My heart pounded against my chest as I looked on. People's lifeless bodies stretched out from their rooms and spilled into the hall, lying motionless in expanding puddles of dark red. Tufts of wet, matted hair displayed evidence of vicious blunt force strikes to their heads. The men were brutally beaten or gunned down, and the women showed the clear markings of torture. Some of the rooms were entered covertly, hacked into through the security panels, while others were pried open with force. I didn't find one person alive, just a trail of winding death that snaked down the hall.

I grabbed my com. "Terra. Have you heard any com traffic from the staff of the *Valkyrie* about a security breech?"

An electronically scratchy voice responded. "Negative."

"Tompkins' men are here, Tank," I said as I stepped into the next room. "They're killing everyone onboard, and by the look of it, their patience is wearing thin. They're disposing of the men quickly and the women are beaten and tortured. They're looking for Ava."

There was a long static-filled pause until Tank finally spoke. "There's nothing unusual happening up here, Maxx. I've passed a few security personnel and there's no urgency in their appearance. I have to assume that they're not aware of what's going on in the lower levels."

"Keep looking, and let me know if you find her," I said, then slid the com into my pocket.

I pressed forward until I heard muffled voices from around the corner of the hall. I kept the flat of the blades pinned against the leather sleeves of my jacket. I inched my way toward the voices. As I neared the ninety-degree bend, I could hear the brushing of feet across the carpet, and an unintelligible discussion between two men masked by heavy accents of an unfamiliar dialect.

There was a scream for mercy, then the roar of a blaster exploded in my ears as its sudden flash lit up the bend in the corridor. Silence. I stepped around the corner and stood within a few meters of the two men. One of them clutched a blaster in his hand, standing over a pair of motionless legs that jutted out of the room and into the hall. The second stood near the first, his back facing me and his arms dangling at his sides. His hand rested less than a finger length away from the pistol holstered on his hip.

I unleashed my knives and rotated them in my hands. Their silver blades bent the reflecting glare of the hall's spotlights at their will. The actions of both blades were simultaneous, artfully dancing together as they sliced the air. The goon closest to me drew his blaster and turned to fire. With an overhead swing I severed his hand at the wrist. His pistol dropped harmlessly to the carpet, followed by a stream of blood that sprayed from the stump. Using the same blade, I speared the head of the second goon, and pinned him against the hallway wall with a weighty thunk. Only the handle and half buried hilt were exposed from his ruptured temple. I returned to attack the first goon, spinning in place and burying my knife into his sternum, punching a hole through his chest and snapping bone. A sharp twist pushed a wheeze of air from his lungs before he dropped to the floor.

I pressed my forearm against the soft neck of the goon I stuck to the wall, and worked my knife back and forth from his skull until I freed it from the bone. His body thumped to the floor in a twisted pile of arms and legs.

I gathered their blasters, disabled the charge packs, and tossed them aside. I dragged both of them into the room and shut the door behind me.

I cleaned my blades across the OWME logos then spat.

I searched their bodies and found a handful of credits, a communicator, and a holo-device. When activated, the holo-device projected detailed information about Ava and a hazy picture that was likely lifted from security camera footage from years back. I slid the communicator into one of my jacket pockets and tossed the holo-device across the room.

This wasn't the work of only a couple of Tompkins' goons. The station would be full of them, and I only hoped I wasn't too late.

I stepped out of the room and back into the passageway to be confronted by the sights and smells of callous death. I bowed my head, and focused on one of the dead bodies on the floor as I retrieved the goon's communicator from my pocket. We would be lucky if Ava was still free and alive, and if she was, I didn't have the luxury of time to track her down when the station was crawling with OWME goons. I pressed the distress key on the goon's com, waited a moment then released it. A garbled response soon followed, illuminating the lights on the device. When I didn't respond, the same message was repeated again.

I activated the distress button one more time, brushed it back and forth against the folds of my jacket, then released it. The com lit green - they had locked on to my location and were tracking my coordinates. Another jumbled response blurted through the communicator, though this time it was accompanied by the background noise of troop movement. They were coming.

Not knowing which direction they were coming from, I settled for a position in the center of the hall, activated their com, then dropped it at my feet. As I closed my eyes, visions raced through my mind. First it was Cooper, Liriana, Jackson, and my tortured crew, then the UG, Tompkins, Toad, and the Captain. They all slowly faded behind the recent images of these sadistic murders, and the tormented looks on these innocent people's faces. My veins surged with adrenaline, pumping a sustained rush of hate. I gathered my composure, drew in a deep breath and exhaled all of my cluttered thoughts. My mind was enveloped in darkness. I drew my pistol and flipped the toggle switch from the clean killing force of the lasers to the flesh-ripping explosives of the uranium bullets. Then I waited.

An array of noises filled the hall; rushed footsteps and the clatter of armaments, flapping straps, and clacking metal buckles worked their way toward my position. I kept my eyes shut and focused on their labored breathing - the sound of building nerves from at least a half dozen men. The darkness was comforting to me. It was my second home away from the *Beast*. As they drew near, the smell of evil preceded them, greeting my nostrils as if it was their battle standard. Only seconds away from rounding the corner of the passageway, their pace continued to quicken, their aggressiveness leading them to a fitting end.

I raised the pistol; my outstretched arm held the sure weight and deadly balance of the weapon, and delivered a dose of justice into the unsuspecting goons. The bullets split the air, tore through metal, leather and cloth, biting and shredding flesh and bone. The pistol pumped out bullets and silenced the goon's pleas for help, drowning their cries in the explosions of gunpowder and the detonation of uranium. The darkness held me in the tightness of its grasp, only briefly welcoming the flashes of light that burst from the barrel. I didn't let go of the trigger until all of the rounds were spent.

The confrontation ended as quickly as it had started. I raised the pistol near the front of my face and opened my eyes. The air in front of me was warped from the heat that radiated from the glowing, reddish-tinged lower barrel. Wisps of smoke snaked their way out of the pistol, making their escape from deep within. The room grew silent, save for the moans of the mortally wounded as they drifted into the arms of the reapers.

Reaching down, I recovered the active com which had broadcasted the demise of Tompkins' goons. "Tompkins, why don't we end this today?" I said, squeezing the com with such force it started to emit an electronic squeal. "I'm coming for you."

The answer was immediate, but it wasn't Tompkins. It was the thick, off-world accent of Rothet. "So, you're finally here, Maxx," he said. "I would've expected you to be a little more...discrete."

"I'm not hiding from you, Rothet. Bring what's left of your goons and come and get me. I snapped the com into two pieces and watched the lights dim as its electronic life trickled out in a rain of sparks.

I walked over to the first group of wounded goons, the empty shells from my pistol clinking against each other and crunching beneath the soles of my boots. The ones that were still alive tried to escape. They scratched the carpet beneath their bloodied fingers as they attempted to pull themselves free from the tangled pile of bloodied meat. Broken limbs, severed appendages, and shattered torsos pinned the living under their dead weight, suffocating their movement.

I watched the soldiers reel in agony and flounder in their fear. They deserved so much worse, and I desperately wanted to give it to them. Unfortunately, I didn't have the time to deliver proper compensation. I flipped the toggle switch on the pistol and with a few squeezes of the trigger the blaster fire finished off the rest of the men under the scorch of heat and the smell of burned flesh. Seven of Tompkins men were laid to rest, with many more to go.

Tank's voice crackled inside my jacket. "What the hell is going on down there, Maxx?"

I dug the com out of my pocket. "I'm waiting for the second OWME welcoming party."

"We need to find Ava, quick, and get the hell out of here!" Tank's voice was rushed and carried an unfamiliar sense of urgency. "It's getting crazy up here! Security personnel are attempting to secure the station by locking everything down. Whatever the hell Tompkins started is spilling onto this floor."

"Do whatever's necessary to find her, Tank. I'll join you on the top level soon." I ended my transmission with Tank and attempted to raise Terra. The com stayed silent.

I turned it off just as the bend in the hall grew dark with advancing shadows. Four of Tompkins' goons appeared, empty handed, and wearing a look of concern on their faces. They stopped when they turned the corner and noticed that my pistol was zeroed in on their skulls. I drew one of my knives and pressed it tightly against my forearm then positioned my left side near the hallway wall.

I watched the goons form a living shield in front of their leader. "I see that you place an extreme amount of value on your troops, Rothet," I said.

"They know their roles," Rothet said, "and are paid well."

I detected the faintest noise from behind me, stealthy and deadly quiet, but just enough to know that I had an unannounced visitor within only a meter of where I stood. I didn't react. Turning my back on Rothet would have been a bigger mistake. If the person behind me wanted me dead, they would have killed me already.

"Why don't you tell your friend behind me to leave so we can settle this between the two of us?" I asked. The cold touch of a barrel parted the hair at the base of my skull, brushing against my skin just enough to let me know it was there.

Rothet laughed as he stepped through the wall of goons. "That's not going to happen. It's clear you hold the advantage." Rothet's gloved hands hung loosely unencumbered at his sides; his flowing and unbuttoned coat revealed the occasional glimpse of dark metal holstered at his waist. When he shifted his head, I noticed the handles of two weapons reaching over his back.

"Interesting how you consider my position an advantage when your goon is standing behind me ready to splatter my head all over the this hall."

"You intrigue me with each passing moment. Your ability to anticipate your enemy's every move is rather extraordinary, though your tactics are a bit...chaotic. Do you think I can't see the blade in your left hand?" I narrowed my eyes as he continued. "The one ready to carve a hole in the chest of the assassin behind you?"

If Rothet was honest, and it was an assassin, there was very little chance I would be able to take both of them out.

"Leave," Rothet said as he folded his arms behind his back. His goons acknowledged his command and disappeared down the hall. "So, let me ask you a question, Maxx," Rothet said as he advanced toward me, slowly pacing the hall from side to side. "Where is...Ava?"

"Ava?" I tilted my head in response.

Rothet smirked. "I think we both know why we're here. Can we at least agree upon that?"

"If I knew where she was, I wouldn't be standing here exchanging pleasantries with you."

Rothet arched an eyebrow and nodded his head. "Fair enough. We'll continue to search for her and force her out of hiding." He brought his arms out from around his back and folded them across his chest. He raised his right arm, then rested it on his left and tapped his chin. "Maybe you could answer one last question for me then?"

"You're wondering how I'm going to kill Tompkins?'

Rothet sighed. "Well, that would mean that you killed me first. So, no, that's not my question." He continued his pacing. "Tell me, where's your second...crewmate? The one with the other half of the coordinates to your ship? You've gotten here late, so I'm assuming you went to recover them first? Maybe they're here with you? I would desperately like to meet them."

"Since we're spending time getting cozy with each other, why don't you answer something for me first? You've been here for days and haven't recovered Ava. How come?"

"Simple. We can't find her. We started by bribing the locals for information and conducting our own covert searches as to not scare her into hiding. But as you can see, we didn't have any...luck."

"So you decided to slaughter everyone instead?"

"You act like this is something foreign to you. What you see here is nothing different than what you would've done if the roles were reversed."

"That's not true."

"*Hmm*," Rothet replied, stroking his chin and shaking his head. "I think you know better. Anyway, Ava seems to be fiercely loyal to you and your cause, even to the detriment of everyone on this station. So we have no choice but to question then torture and kill everyone on this station until we find her." Rothet stopped and cocked his head to the side. "It would be a shame for all of us if we...accidentally killed her along the way."

"I don't think that matters much anymore, Rothet. My other contact is dead, and I don't plan on being killed, so where does that leave us?"

"You're lying." Rothet frowned. "If what you say is true, why would you come here?"

"I won't abandon my crew. I came for Ava."

Rothet sighed and shook his head. "Now I know you're lying. What about Liriana? You abandoned her, did you...not?"

My heart stopped when I heard her name. "I've had enough of this, Rothet." My hand tightened around the grip of the pistol. "What now?"

"Touchy subject?" Rothet smiled. "I am a man of honor. Toss your weapons to the floor, and I promise you a fair fight - just you and me."

"A man of honor? That's an interesting assessment you have of yourself. The dead in these halls say otherwise."

"This was a necessary...evil. Business." Rothet opened his arms to me. "You understand that all too well, Maxx. You killed one from my team back on the Kogin station. You left him to bleed out on the white floors of the Solonian Empire."

Him. It wasn't Liriana I killed. My shoulders suddenly felt lighter. "My only regret is that Tompkins didn't send you."

A voice echoed from the assassin, leaving no doubt that it was Liriana behind me. "Tompkins sent Sterger to kill Maxx?"

There was a chill in Rothet's voice. "I didn't know of the attack until after it…happened. It was Tompkins' decision to take Sterger with him. Not mine." Rothet paced the hall, his anger building with each step. He stopped, then continued to speak through a sneer. "Maxx, if it would've been me in that hall, we wouldn't be having this conversation now. You're a pitiful man, slow, and weak, relying on your aged, un-JaCed body. You're an amateur, at best!"

"Rothet!" Liriana shouted. "What the hell happened back on Kogin?" The barrel of her pistol pulled away from my head, but still brushed against my hair. Rothet didn't answer. His soulless eyes were focused on mine, and his once calm exterior was shed away like the skin of a snake. "Answer me, Rothet!"

"I don't owe you any explanation, Liriana!" Rothet growled. "You work for me and Tompkins, and we'll share information with you as it's needed!"

"I was recruited as part of the lead team and was told that no decisions were to be made without my input."

Rothet brushed off her statement with a wave of his hand. "You know your place, Liriana! You'll listen to me! Subdue him now!"

The barrel of the pistol returned, pressing so hard against the back of my head that it broke skin. I could feel Liriana's elevated breathing on my neck as she moved closer to me.

We all remained still as if waiting for the endgame to unfold. The points of my blade rested just below Liriana's chest, the tips set on her ribcage, tearing at the fabric of her shirt and occasionally catching her skin as her breathing stirred her chest. My pistol was aimed just below Rothet's neck, the biggest area on what I expected would be a blazing-fast target. My finger was begging to pull the trigger and end his miserable existence.

I knew what I needed to do, but couldn't act on it. Liriana was distracted, and an easy kill with a simple thrust and twist of my knife, and a follow up shot from my TW-34. Rothet's hands were empty, and any action initiated by me would force him to make a split-second decision of his own. He would either reach for the weapons underneath his coat, or dive for the cover of the corner of the hall. My instinct told me that he would play it safe.

Years of combat screamed at me to act before I was dead, but for the first time in my life I ignored the call to action and tossed both of my weapons to the floor. A smile crested Rothet's face as he made his way toward me.

"Stop," Liriana said. She removed the pistol from the back of my head and repositioned it alongside my right cheek. The black barrel reached over my shoulder and stretched past my nose.

"What?" Rothet questioned. That single word erased the confidence from his face.

"I believe you heard me." Liriana's breathing settled and the blaster held as steady as her voice. "We had a deal, Rothet."

"Deals are, can be, a little...subjective."

"Then it's time to make a new one."

Rothet's response was filled with rage. "You were broken! A pawn of your addictions! You owe us girl, and you better not forget that. Maxx discarded you without any regard, and you're going to defend him now? You're going to come to his...aid?"

"Rothet, I won't forget what you and Tompkins did *for* me, or what Maxx did *to* me. All of those memories will remain until I draw my last breath. But we had a deal." Liriana's voice remained calm. "Maybe my best option is to dust both of you right here and now, then negotiate a new deal with Tompkins on my own?" She paused for a moment as if considering her recent words. "But I have a better idea. Toss me your guns, Rothet."

Rothet's cocksure smile returned, spreading across his slender face from ear to ear. "So this is it? You and I both know, Liriana, that if I draw now, both of you are dead before you can even blink."

"Give it a try Rothet," Liriana taunted, "please."

The growing din of battle spilled from the upper level, echoing through the air ducts and in the stairwell behind us. Things on the station were getting ugly all around the *Valkyrie*. Rothet wasn't ready to relent, and Liriana wasn't about to back down. Conveniently, both appeared to have forgotten about me; the wild card in this standoff. I didn't know who was the fastest on the draw, or the most accurate, but the way things were disintegrating, we may find out soon enough.

"OK, girl, take my blasters," Rothet said.

"Slow, with one finger only," Liriana said. "And I warn you, Rothet. If you move in any way that makes me think you're going to draw on me, I'm pulling this trigger."

Rothet worked his jacket over his shoulders and dumped it on the floor, revealing two snub-nosed blasters holstered on either side of his hips. The blackened blades of two swords peeked from behind his ribcage, fastened to his back by a leather cross strap that stretched across his chest. Using his ring fingers, he released the security straps that held his pistols then slowly removed the weapons until they cleared their holsters. He let them drop at his feet.

"Kick them over to me," Liriana said.

Following orders, he kicked the pistols next to Liriana's feet.

"Happy?" Rothet smirked.

"Quite," Liriana said. "Maxx, take a step toward Rothet."

As I moved forward, she gathered up the three blasters on the floor and tossed them into a satchel, keeping her pistol vigilant and focused on Rothet. After she slung the pack over her left shoulder, she retrieved my knife and slid behind me

Liriana reached her gloved hand around my waist and ran her fingers up my side and across my chest. Her familiar touch was welcome, but brutally painful as she raked my wounds while quickly examining each with the tips of her fingers. She released the second knife from the sheath and pulled it out of my jacket.

"Take off your jacket and put your palms out in front of you," Liriana said. "Slowly."

My injuries lit on fire as I worked the jacket off my frame, forcing an uncontrolled wince as I removed the coat and tossed it to the other side of the hall.

"Looks, and sounds like Sterger did a number on you," Rothet said. Though most of my injuries were covered, my forearms and wrist were exposed and revealed the recently patched gashes.

I glanced down at my arms then back to Rothet. "And look what it got him."

"That's a very nice accessory inked into your right forearm, Maxx. I never knew your...history."

"Enough!" Liriana shouted. She reached out and placed both knives into my open palm then backed away. "It's time you boys settle this on your own. Rothet, if you win, I'll see you back on our ship to discuss the new terms of our deal. Maxx, if you survive, I'll deal with you later."

"I'm right behind you, girl," Rothet said, blowing Liriana a kiss.

I shifted my eyes only enough to watch Liriana leave through my periphery, keeping my main focus on Rothet. She backed her way down the hall, pistol still readied and her satchel in tow. She eventually faded into the shadows of the long corridor, consumed by the darkness.

Rothet reached behind him and wrapped his hands around the handles of the swords strapped to his back. "Now my good friend, where were we?"

Rothet released the two short swords from the scabbards strapped to his back. His weapons were modified katana, space-black from hilt to tip, straight bladed, double edged, and slightly longer than a meter. They looked cold and unrelenting, refusing to reflect the light cast from the fixtures in the hall.

"Maxx, my friend, this will prove to be the worst day of your miserable life," Rothet said, twirling the blades around the outside of his arms. He paced from wall to wall in the pathway, occasionally taking a step closer to me. "After I'm done, I will have you kissing my boots, and begging for mercy. Mercy that will never...come."

The once bright blades of my knives still flashed their occasional brilliance between the patches of dried blood that coated the edges. I reversed them in each hand and pinned the flat of the blades against my forearms. I didn't know what Rothet was JaCed with, but from what little I'd seen and heard, speed and strength boosts were a given.

"She doesn't know it, but Liriana did me a favor my...friend," he said. "If she took you down, I wouldn't have had the pleasure of doing it myself." The slightest of grins split his face. "I've been thinking about this since our meeting on Kogin."

"This all ends here, Rothet," I said. He laughed. I didn't.

He set the blade of one of his swords on his shoulder and pointed at my arm with the other. "Take a good look at those marks on your forearm, Maxx. If those letters don't remind you of your inglorious past, of your pathetically dismal existence, my blades will. You're property of the Unified Governments. Nothing but a worthless slave." Rothet's face pinched into a snarl. "And after I'm done with you, I'll take care of Liriana and our little…disagreement."

His words burned inside me, dulling the pain of my wounds and drowning out the noise around me. My vision tunneled on him and him alone. I wasn't sure what triggered the smoldering rage - the mention of my past, his comments about Liriana, or that he actually believed he could best me in battle. I had enough of the delays. Enough of his words. Enough of the needless death I'd caused. It all needed to end, and I was the person to end it.

Rothet met me in the center of the hall; his swords slashed with shocking speed and force. The dark blades moved so quickly it was as if someone drew solid black arcs in the air behind the path of each of his swings. A rain of sparks followed each of my blocks as the metal of our weapons relented under the pressure of impact.

The tips of his katana tore at the cloth of my shirt and pants, and the razor sharp blades caught me twice - once on my right thigh and once on my left lateral muscle. I disengaged, wiped the sweat from my face, and steadied my breathing. So far I was nothing more than a practice dummy to his superior offense.

He advanced, creating a moving wall of blades that carved the air and spit tiny fragments of metal when his swords nicked the walls. I dodged a dual scissors swing at my head then rolled back across the carpet, creating four meters of distance between us. I stayed down on one knee, my head up and my palms and knives resting on the floor. I could feel the friction heat on my blades working its way up to the hilts and into my hands.

"You disappoint me," Rothet said. "From what I've heard about you, I would've expected…more. There's no mystery as to why people JaC." He smiled and advanced on my position. "Too bad it's a lesson you'll learn much too late."

Cockiness appeared to take control of Rothet. He took a swift, but careless lunge with both of his swords. I rolled again, but this time toward him. I caught his right shin with both of my knives, the blades sliced into his leg, cutting a single buckle and strips of leather strapping free from his boot; the edges of my blades tasted his blood for the first time.

He didn't cry out or even wince from the blow, rather he just moved his injured leg behind the other. Either he tried to hide the damage that my crippling blow caused, or he had a JaC that nullified the pain. Regardless, him placing his power leg behind the other was an obvious sign of the structural damage I'd caused.

Rothet came after me again, his blades as swift as before but his blows not nearly as powerful, as he attempted to generate force from his non-dominant leg. I blocked his advances while watching his wounded shin regress from a deliberate shuffle, to a stutter, and eventually a painful drag as it painted a dark red trail on the carpet beneath him.

Even with the wound, he didn't tire. He didn't slow. His attacks were driven by a boost of adrenaline, pumped through his system by JaCs. I was breaking down, slowing, and exhausting the last of my energy. He backed me down the hall as I concentrated on parrying his swings.

Suddenly, a blast rocked the *Valkyrie* and knocked both of us to the floor under its violent concussion. Emergency strobes lit the halls with blinding flashes of white, accompanied by hazard sirens and mechanical warnings of danger. *"Hull breach. First floor life support bays one and two. Emergency containment measures in progress."*

Both of us worked our way back to our feet and readied ourselves for continued battle. The entire station could have been imploding but I refused to run. Rothet was thinking the same thing. I could see it in his face

The strobes continued to flash as the sirens blared overhead. *"Oxygen levels at eighty-eight percent. Evacuate level one. Emergency containment measures in progress."* The angry groans of bending steel surrounded us, and the station started to shudder under our feet.

Two of the *Valkyrie's* security staff burst through an access door behind Rothet. "You need to clear out of here!" one of them yelled, his voice muted by the sounds of the explosions, twisting metal, and mechanized warnings. They both froze. In their haste they didn't notice the halls lined with death - until now. Their eyes moved to us and our weapons. Rothet broke free of our engagement and turned to face the two guards. He dispatched both under a swirl of black and an arch of red. The men didn't even have time to scream.

"Danger! Oxygen levels at sixty-eighty percent. Evacuate level one. Emergency containment measures in progress."

It took less than a couple of minutes for this floor to lose thirty-two percent of its oxygen. There must have been a crater sized hole in the hull to drain oxygen supplies so quickly. Space was sucking the life out of the station.

Rothet lunged toward me. I crossed my knives like an 'X' and caught his blades on the downswing. He swiped the swords out from his body, freeing his blades from my block then returning with relentless fury. Red and white sparks danced under the strobe lights as I blocked blow after unrelenting blow. His last attack came in quick, and dislodged the knife from my left hand. Two swings followed. He slashed across my chest, tearing cloth and slicing flesh.

"Danger! Oxygen levels at forty-five percent. Evacuate level one. Emergency containment measures now active. Door seals commence in two minutes."

Rothet backed me into the corner in the hall. I blocked his swings and dodged his blows, but took a flurry of cuts on my arms and upper body. I rolled away from the slashes and thrusts.

He swung high and missed. I lowered my shoulder and tackled him into the wall and down to the floor. His blades spun free from his hands. I drove my knife toward his head, but he caught my hands and stopped them. Forcing my arms down was like trying to push my way through a wall of stone. He tossed me aside like I was a child. My back collided with the floor and drove the air from my lungs; my blade skittered down the hall and out of reach.

"Danger! Oxygen levels at twenty-nine percent. Evacuate level one. Emergency containment measures now active. Door seals commence in one minute."

I vaulted to my feet then caught an advancing Rothet with a side kick to his solar plexus. Air leaked out of him through a forced wheeze as he dropped to one knee. He knelt, staring me down with eyes of fire. I pressed my shoulder against the wall and gulped down the heavy, oxygen-depleted air.

"There will be another time," Rothet said. He stood, placing all of his weight on his good leg. "Consider yourself...lucky. He recovered his swords from the floor then limped down the hall away from where I stood. The strobe's flashes highlighted his sleek frame for nearly ten paces down the pathway, until he opened a door and disappeared from view.

"Critical Warning. Oxygen levels at eleven percent. All personnel must evacuate the first level."

Rothet was right. It was my lucky day. However, if I didn't make my way to the second level, that luck would end pretty damn quick. I scooped up my jacket and knives and ran to the nearest exit. Only seconds after I cleared the opening, an emergency door closed behind me, stopping short of sealing.

"Critical Warning. First floor sealed due to breach in life support bays one and two. Station pressurization normalizing. Please report to emergency check points."

A rush of oxygen pushed past me and out the opening in the jammed door. They must have opened the bottom level of the *Valkyrie* to the darkness of space. Doing so would stabilize the station, but would pull all the oxygen out of the lower level, and more importantly, from this stairwell. I slid on the jacket, sheathed the knives, and sprinted up the stairs as my fingers searched my body for major wounds. The cuts on my chest, legs, and arms were wet and throbbing, but none of the gashes were life threatening.

I searched through the pockets of my jacket but was unable to locate my communicator. It must have fallen out, or was taken by Liriana. The lights in the stairwell dimmed. The only illumination was the occasional flashes from the emergency strobes that bathed me in white then cast me back into darkness.

As I worked my way up the stairs I could smell the drifting stench of charred flesh that was carried on sheets of blackened air. The walls of the tight passage were marked with burns from heavy blaster fire and sprays of red. Further up the stairwell, near the exit door, I found a dozen bodies torched beyond recognition. The walls and stairs were scorched black. Whatever weapon was used in this hall, it was meant to incinerate everything.

When I reached the top of the stairwell, I was greeted by a brightly stenciled '2G' painted on a closed door. The access pad dangled loosely from the wall, attached by only a few wires. The door panels were closed, but off the tracks, dislodged from the sliding mechanism that drew them into the walls.

I pushed my fingers between the door panels. Leather burned away from my gloves and my skin sizzled as soon as my fingers touched the metal. I jerked the gloves off and tossed them down the stairs, then clenched my hands and placed them against my chest as I doubled over. Shaking off the pain, I pulled one of my knives from its sheath, slid it through the door opening, and tried to pry the panels open. They didn't move. The door was stuck tight.

I trudged back down the stairs as I flexed the pain from my fingers. I stopped at each body and searched for anything useful. Most were burned so badly that whatever they had with them was fused to their skin or clothes, melted or damaged beyond use. Their bodies were still hot to the touch, their flesh slipping from the bone.

My lungs grew tight and each breath came in thick and heavy. I was running out of oxygen. I was running out of time. Tearing through the bodies I cast aside anything that came loose in my hands - patches of cloth, warped weapons, flesh, and pieces of metal. Nothing of use. My vision blurred, and my head pounded with each beat of my thumping heart. Adrenaline surged through my body like liquid fire, igniting my insides.

I crouched and rested my arms across my thighs. Panic wouldn't help. I had to clear my mind. I closed my eyes, took a calming breath, and slowed my heart. There had to be something here that could help.

I broke from my trance and continued to dig through the remains. Something caught the corner of my eye, concealed by what appeared to be a piece of charred leather from a boot or jacket. I brushed the material aside and recovered the device. It was a com. I scraped the bits of black from its screen and activated it. Only two of the twelve lights lit. It was a weak signal, but it worked.

"Can anyone hear me?" I said into the com. The device remained silent and dark.

I pressed the button again. "I'm trapped in the stairwell leading to the upper level. It's marked '2G' and I need assistance opening the door. There's a breach in this passageway and there's not much oxygen left." The lights dimmed when I released the com, briefly lit for a second then grew dark. I pressed the com one more time, but the lights remained off. The other end was no longer receiving the signal. I kept activating the com. No luck. I dropped it into my pocket and continued to search through the bodies.

There was nothing useful left in the charred remains. I ran back up the stairs, consciously shortening my breath. I had to pry the door open myself. It was my last and only hope.

I drew both knives from my jacket and jammed them between the door panels. Bracing my back against the extended frame of the door, and placing my foot against the other side, I pulled with everything I had left in me. The right door panel groaned in resistance. I sucked in what little oxygen remained and tried again. The door shifted with a grinding thump, rocked forward then realigned on its track. The mechanism in the wall squealed and engaged, then closed the door on my blades. The door was set to lock, not to open. I lowered my head and gnashed my teeth.

I left the blades in the door and wiped the sweat from my face. If the door was set to lock, I wasn't sure even Tank would have the strength to open it. And the way the access panel was destroyed, I doubted anyone would be able to operate a working set of controls from the other side.

I wrapped my hands around the hilts of my blades, and using the last of the strength granted to me by free flowing adrenaline, I pulled. A small gap separated between the two panels as the muscles in my legs and arms felt as if they would tear free from the bone. A sliver of light crept into the stairwell. I didn't relent. I kept pulling. Sweat ran down my forehead and pooled in my burning eyes. My arms and legs started to shake as the door slowly closed. My head spun and vision blurred. The gap was growing dark, the light pinched off from the closing panels.

Suddenly, gloved fingers slid through the opening, sizzling upon contact with the metal. My strength-sapped arms cried for me to stop as I kept pulling at the doors. The panels groaned and the mechanism inside the wall squealed and popped. A burst of oxygen spilled into the stairwell as the door opened.

I crawled through the opening and collapsed on the other side. I gulped down oxygen, hacked and spit, then sucked in some more air. I scrambled to my knees and wiped the sweat from my blurry eyes. As I blinked my vision back into place I noticed a gloved hand extended in front of my face.

"Thanks," I said. I reached up and placed my hand in theirs, and they helped me up off of the deck. "I owe you one."

"You owe me more than that," Liriana said.

I stood silent as my mind raced to find the right words. My body grew rigid and my arms dangled stiffly at my sides. Her welcoming eyes provided a fleeting moment of sanctuary, filling me with a flood of memories and generating emotions I didn't know I was capable of feeling.

"Why?" I asked.

She removed the burned gloves from her hands and tossed them aside as she spoke. "Why, what?" She asked. "Why did I come?"

"Yeah."

She frowned at my question. "Someone used one of our communicators and called for help. What did you expect me to do? Ignore a call for help from someone on my team?"

I brushed the ashen flakes of the dead goons' skin off of my jacket while keeping both knives firmly griped in the palms of my hands. "So, you didn't know it was me?"

"The transmission was too weak. I had no idea who it was. I tried responding, but your com's signal wasn't strong enough to accept the transmission."

I started to respond. There were a million things I wanted to say, but decided against it. I looked down at my forearm as I spoke. "I can save you." When she didn't speak I continued. "I still have the compensation JaC in my possession, Liriana. I can stop your JaCs from killing you."

Her eyes briefly found the tops of her boots. "Carter's little invention, huh?" she asked. "You told us years ago that you destroyed it. We all thought it was gone."

I shook my head. "I wanted to destroy it. I should have. I've come close so many times, but I haven't."

"I never understood why you wanted to destroy it. Think of what you could do with that one single JaC. The credits you could make if you sold it to one of the Empire Nations to reverse engineer the technology."

"Never," I said. "That JaC will never fall into the hands of the UG or any of the Empire Nations." I looked into Liriana's eyes. "But I will give it to you, Liriana. It will create a stable balance between all of your JaCs' transmissions and your body's responses. I know that it works. It will save you."

"So, what's the catch?"

"Come back with me to the *Beast*. We complete the Solonian mission then we find someone to implant the JaC."

"That's it?"

"That's it. After the JaC is implanted, you're free to go wherever you like."

"Wherever I like…as long as it isn't with you?"

I paused before I spoke. My mouth and tongue were suddenly thick. "The Solonians and the UG will be hunting me, Liriana, and they won't stop until I'm dead. The farther you get away from me, the safer you will be."

She smiled and brushed the hair away from her face. "So you swoop in like the hero, save the damsel in distress, then send me on my way to live happily ever after?" Liriana shook her head. "Not a chance."

"But –"

Liriana cut me off. "No buts, Maxx. I'm finishing this mission."

"You'll die without it."

She narrowed her eyes. "I have no reason to trust you."

I exhaled and tightened the grip on my knives. "So what now?"

"I don't think we have a choice, do we?"

"There are always choices," I replied grimly. "Though it's not always easy to know what the right one is."

Liriana snorted a sigh, shook her head, and clenched her hands into fists. "Did you kill Rothet?"

"Unfortunately, no."

Her eyes scanned me from head to toe as if searching my body for wounds. "Have you found Ava yet?"

I shook my head and spat ash from my mouth. "You know her well enough, Liriana. She's too good at what she does to be found so easily. Tompkins made a big mistake busting in here and trying to force her out of hiding. She knows we're here, and she'll find us soon enough."

Liriana nodded. "I tried to tell him, but he didn't listen until it was too late. Until too many lives were lost." She started to circle me as she continued. "That's why we're forced to move forward with our backup plan."

"You need to kill me."

"I need to take you back to Tompkins' ship, Maxx. I'm forced to finish what Rothet started."

Liriana's fist was an arching blur of black leather. I turned away from the punch just in time to avoid a fractured skull, but her knuckles still grazed my jaw and bottom lip. A streak of pain blazed across the side of my head and dotted stars in the back of my eyes. A second blow caught me in my stomach, doubled me over and drove the air from my lungs. Her knee caught my forehead and launched me backwards; I slid across the deck for a few meters before I finally came to rest. Upon impact, one of my two knives was jerked free from my hand and spun out of my reach.

She came at me quickly. The heel of her boot connected with the floor, just centimeters from my eye. Ramming my forearm against the side of her calf, her knee buckled under her and she tumbled to the deck. I scrambled back to my feet to find Liriana already recovered and ready for round two.

I spit a stream of blood and wiped the sticky red ropes from my mouth, stopping to touch my lip where it was split. "You know I don't want to do this," I said, securing my grip on the remaining knife.

"What's that?" Liriana asked with a smirk. "Suffer?"

"We can both walk away from this, Liriana."

"No, we can't."

"I can save you. Just let me help."

"I don't need your help, Maxx," she said as her voice trailed off to a whisper. "I don't want your help."

"I'll kill you if I have to. You know that."

Her eyes turned cold as if my words drained the life from them. "You killed me years ago."

Her leg sprung at me like a bullet shot from a pistol. I ducked, avoiding her kick, but before I could step back, she spun and thrust her boot into my chest and forced the air out of my lungs with a loud grunt. I dropped to one knee. The flat of her fist struck the back of my head and drove me down to my hands and knees with so much force I felt like a nail being pounded by a sledge hammer.

I heard a creaking swoosh of leather then a wave of fire blazed across my back. My legs and arms couldn't stop my body from bouncing off the deck. Rolling to my back, I grabbed her ankle, twisted, and dropped her next to me. Her elbow caught the center of my chest before she rolled away. She shot back to her feet while I recovered to one knee, gasping and spitting blood.

The vision in my left eye was blurred and fuzzy as if someone had placed a piece of clouded plastic over top of it. I closed my eyelid in an attempt to regain my balance and depth perception.

"Are you ready to give up?" I asked. She didn't find my question amusing.

She watched as I struggled to my feet. "You know I would've never given up on you, Maxx."

"I know," I said spitting another stream of blood, "but you left me no choice."

"There are always choices," she replied. "Though it's not always easy to know what the right one is." She paused for a moment letting my own words sink in. "I loved you, Maxx."

She was too quick and too strong for me to beat her in hand-to-hand combat. Because she needed to take me alive, I was able to buy some time, and catch a few of her body's tells. A twitch in her eye before she punched - a slight shift in her shoulders to balance her body for her kicks. I held still, waiting for a sign. Her eye twitched, and I was ready.

Her attack came at me, quick and powerful. I slid to the side, avoiding her swing and allowing her punishing fist to sail by my head. Sliding my arm around hers, I spun around to her back, wrapped my other arm around her neck and pressed the blade against her face.

With a sharp pop I kicked her in the back of the knee. Liriana fell; my arms and weight of my body pinned her to the floor. My blade grazed her cheek and turned its edge bright red.

"I'm sorry," I said as I tightened my grip around her neck, cutting off her oxygen. My blade was pressed against her temple. "I'm sorry...," I whispered.

Her fingers wrapped around my forearm as she tightened her grip like a powerful vice.

"Don't make me do this." I pricked her temple with the tips of my blade, cutting her skin and pattering blood on the floor. "Your death can be clean."

MXX: Agent Soldier

There was a moment of hesitation, my arm still locked in her grasp, before her grip released. Tears streamed down Liriana's face and over the fresh cut on her cheek, eventually pooling on the arm of my jacket. Accepting her fate, she removed her hands from my arm and placed them on the deck in front of her. Her fingers scratched at the steel as I tightened my hold around her neck. I could feel one last gasp for air and heard a gurgle snake through her throat before she grew limp in my arms.

"Tompkins told me you were a monster," Rothet's familiar voice shouted from behind me, "but I didn't believe the stories to be true. You will answer for what you have...done."

Vivid memories of Liriana flashed across the backs of my eyes, playing in fast forward like videos across a monitor. Memories I tried to forget. Emotions I never knew I could feel. I didn't look up at Rothet as I laid Liriana's body on the floor. I watched as her long black hair spilled to the sides of her head. Her eyes were closed, her face calm and peaceful. Grasping my knife I scraped it across the grated metal deck, creating a trail of sparks as I stood.

"You think I'm a monster, Rothet?" I replied with darkness in my voice. "You have no idea."

I turned to face him. Rothet's head tilted to one side and his nose pinched as he looked at Liriana's body. His right palm covered his mouth as he raked his fingers across his cheek. He sighed, then drew a pistol from its holster.

"Tell me." His soulless eyes rose to meet mine. "How does it feel to have the blood of someone you loved on your hands?"

My hand was wound so tight around the hilt of my knife that my palm started to ache and my knuckles throbbed. I didn't speak; my stare told him everything he wanted to know.

"Ahh...quite painful then." He pursed his lips. He took one step in my direction then stopped. He pulled in a deep breath, pointed the pistol at my head, squinted, and then lowered the gun to his side. "Liriana was faster than anyone I've known. Stronger than your brutish sidekick, Tank. Yet you were able to take her...down. Kill her. How?"

I looked at her face, motionless and quiet. "It's time to finish this, Rothet."

Rothet raised his pistol at me, brushed his finger across the trigger, then lowered it again. "I will finish it, my friend." Rothet paced around Liriana's body. Through the cuts in his boot I saw the metal staples and glossy refection of the glue that bound his wounds. He had only a slight hitch in his gate. I've never seen someone heal so fast. Never. "You made her pay the ultimate price in the name of your survival. You traded one life for yours. That's something any agent soldier would've done. Maybe I've underestimated you."

My chest heaved as I sucked in angry breaths. "You brought her into this. You and Tompkins."

"There's no reason to lie, Maxx. She played an extremely important part in our mission." Rothet stroked his bearded chin, closed his eyes for a moment, then opened them to gaze upon Liriana's body. "A mission that was quite dead until you helped us."

I stood silent, staring at Rothet as he continued. "You haven't pieced it together yet, have you?" The pistol shook in his hand as he talked. "The Unified Governments caught us trailing you and intercepted our ship before we had a chance to make our...move." Rothet released a sword from the scabbard on his back and swung it down in front of him. "You released me from my cell on Paxcel, and gave me all the keys to free my men. And it was you that cut a swath of carnage through the prison letting us walk out...unfettered." Rothet shook his head. "You took pity on me because I notified you when the torturer was on his way. You freed me, and along the way broke the only code an agent solider lives by." Rothet placed the tip of his sword on the floor, leaned on the pommel and whispered. "Trust no one."

With those three words, Rothet flooded my mind with memories of my past. Flashes of when the black letters were inked into my forearm. My escape. The purchase of the *Beast* and how I formed my crew. The promises I made to trust no one but myself. How it all changed with Liriana's tender touch, her love, and her caring.

I laughed. It wasn't a laugh of humor, rather one that vaults you awake from a nightmare. "You have two choices," I said. "You either attempt to kill me, or you run." Rothet's eyes widened as I continued. "If you run, you'll need to find a place to hide. Somewhere obscure in this galaxy, because I will hunt you down and kill you in the most horrible way I can imagine."

Rothet peeled back the corner of his jacket and holstered his pistol. He lifted his sword off the floor and rested the flat of the blade against his shoulder. "You're no good to me dead," Rothet said as he ran his tongue across the front of his teeth. "And I won't run..."

We lunged for each other in unison, our blades slashing streaks in the air and locking at the hilts. I grabbed the corner of his jacket and tossed him to the floor, away from Liriana's body.

Rothet rolled to his feet wearing a look or surprise. "Impressive. But adrenaline will only carry you so...far."

He came at me again, sword tip aimed at my chest. I parried the attack to my side. Rothet spun his blade and slashed at the backs of my legs. I flipped backwards to avoid the sword and caught his chest with the edge of my knife. When he followed with another slash, I rolled away from his strike, stood, and braced the knife against my forearm.

Rothet used both hands and swung his blade at my torso. I stepped into the attack and let the handle of his sword strike against my side with a dull thump, then I pinned his hands under my left arm and slammed my forehead against the bridge of his nose. The cartilage shattered and sprayed a mist of red. I struck his wrists with my hand, snapped them to the side and forced the blade from his grip.

I reached down for his sword just as someone shouted my name. I turned to see Tank standing over Liriana with Ava half hidden under his mountainous shadow. Rothet took advantage of my mistake, and swept my legs out from under me. As he reached for his pistol, red bolts of energy blasted the floor around us, splattering small molten shards of metal against our clothes. All I heard was an incessant buzz in my ears and the hiss of melting steel.

"I wouldn't do that," Tank said, his laser cannon pointed at Rothet. The tip of the barrel was a glowing cherry-red, slowly darkening with each passing second. His finger brushed against the trigger, waiting for Rothet's next move.

Rothet lowered his arms to his sides and backed away from me. His steps were slow and measured, as if his body was wound tight and ready to pounce on his prey like a wild beast.

"Is this how you fight, Maxx?" Rothet smirked. "With the aid of your friends?"

I pushed myself off the floor and wiped the sweat from my eyes. "No,"

I said. I turned to address Tank. "Let me finish this."

"We don't have time," Tank said. "This was all part of their plan. Tompkins and his goons are on their way."

I spat on the floor. "Then get ready to greet them." I looked down the passageway and watched as the station personnel scurried in and out of the halls, then shifted my gaze to Liriana's motionless body. "It all ends here, Rothet. For you and Tompkins."

Rothet smiled. "The only people you'll end up killing is that pathetic...girl." He pointed at Liriana. "And your crew."

A slim beam of yellow sliced the air and struck Rothet in his chest, crumpling him onto his knees with a loud gasp.

Ava's face was stoic, her pistol raised in Rothet's direction. A small wisp of smoke snaked from the barrel. "That's for Liriana."

As Rothet fell to the floor, a silver gleam off a small circular device caught my eye. It rolled free from his left hand then wobbled to the side of his knee. The round object, about half the size of a fist, pulsated green then magnetized to the station's deck. The lights in the hall flickered then went dark, along with the bright green charge counter on Tank's laser cannon. "A power dampener," I mumbled under my breath. "Go!"

The sound of leather on steel, the rattle of weapons, and the rushed grunts of men echoed behind us. Within moments a group of Tompkins' goons flooded the halls, spilling from the interconnected passageways and pushing their way through a panicked crowd of the station's residents.

"Go!" I shouted. The three of us ran toward the docking bay. Tank held the communicator in front of him until the lights activated, indicating we cleared the power dampener's radius. He raised Terra on his com and instructed her to ready the ship for immediate take off. The armored goons continued their pursuit, but were unable to close the gap between us. We twisted and turned through the halls as blaster fire lit the air.

We boarded the fighter just as Terra engaged the thrusters. The ship screamed, and steel groaned, as it fought to tear itself free of the docking clamps. The fighter lurched underneath our feet as we rushed to the bridge.

"Ava, take over the ship," I said. "Terra, back her up." Terra moved over to the co-pilot's seat as Ava slid into the pilot's chair.

"I got this," Ava said. She routed all the fighter's power to the starboard thrusters. The ship turned to the left, wrenching the docking clamp free from our port. Ava deadened the power, then engaged the portside thrusters. The fighter pushed hard to the right, breaking free from the remaining clamp and spinning our ship away from the space station. Sheets of metal tore free from our fighter as Ava righted our ship through a series of corrective thruster bursts. Once she stabilized our trajectory, Ava engaged full power. Within moments the station was lost from our view.

"What the hell happened back there, Maxx?" Tank gasped to catch his breath.

I leaned my head into my open palms and covered my face. "You found Ava," I mumbled through my fingers. "Thank you."

"I can't believe..." Tank stammered. "I can't believe you killed her." Tank looked away from me, his face was red and his teeth clenched. He opened his mouth to speak, stopped, then slammed his fist into the hull. "I said some things back on Kogin. Things I didn't mean. I didn't want her to die, Maxx! I didn't want that!"

"None of us did, Tank," I said, "and that's why she's still alive."

"What did you say?" The words spilled from Tank's mouth.

"She isn't dead," I said.

Tank grabbed me by the shoulders. "How do you know?"

"I never planned on killing her." Tank stepped away from me and rested his back against the hull. He held his breath as I continued. "I restricted her breathing just long enough to render her unconscious. Why all of the concern for Liriana now?"

Tank's eyes grew wide as he blew out a breath of air. "Why the hell would you say something like that?" Tank's face turned red and his muscles knotted in his arms. He stepped forward, grabbed my shoulders again and tightened his grip. "Don't forget that I fought by her side for years, Maxx, just like you!"

"Just days ago you were happy that she was dying from her JaCs. Hell, you would've put her down in the Starlight Room had you been given the chance."

"Those were different circumstances, Maxx. Tompkins pushed us to the edge, and it was an easy decision if I needed to choose between her or our mission."

I ran my hands across my face. "I understand."

Tank exchanged a glance with Ava then turned back to me. "What happened?"

I shrugged. "She threw the fight. She had me, but she let me win. Then she trusted me enough not to kill her. Why?"

Tank arched an eyebrow at my response. "Hell, I don't know. Maybe all those JaCs are messing with her head."

"Maybe," I stammered as I tried to patch together the recent events. So much of it was lost in a fog, scrambled together with memories of Liriana's and my past. "I offered her the JaC, Tank. The compensation JaC, and she wouldn't take it."

Tank narrowed his eyes. "You have it with you?"

"I asked her to come back to the *Beast* with us. Told her we could get it implanted after we finished our mission. But she refused, then threw the fight." I scrubbed my face with the rough palms of my hands. "None of this makes sense."

A smile broke through the twisted mass of hair on Tank's face. "Now ain't the time to worry about it, Maxx. We have Ava, the coordinates from Jackson, and we'll be back on the *Beast* soon. We've done it!"

I nodded my response. Tank clasped my forearm and clapped me on the back. "Ava, how do things look?" I asked.

"Commander," she said from the pilot's chair. Her eyes were fixed on the forward display monitors. "I'm fairly certain we aren't being followed."

"Good," I said. "Keep it that way. What's the damage to the ship?"

"Minimal," Terra replied. "We lost some hull plating to the docking clamps, but the refueling process was complete. She'll be fine." Terra rubbed her hand in a circular motion over the bank of controls in front of her as if to reassure the ship.

"Where's the *Beast*, Maxx?" Tank asked.

"That doesn't matter right now," I said. "Ava, your job is to make sure that we stay off of Tompkins' and the UG's radar."

"Aye, aye, Commander," Ava said with a wink.

"Maxx, how can I help?" Terra spun in her chair so she could meet my gaze. She looked childlike, curled up with her knees pressed against her chest.

"Terra, you can help Tank reroute the ship's power from its shields into its thrusters. It'll take two people to decode and reroute the sequences on the ship's database."

"Can't wait to get back home to the *Beast*!" Tank clapped his hands and rubbed his palms together. "Come on, Terra, let's lower you into the belly of this ship! Being large has a lot of benefits, but fitting into small spaces isn't one of them."

Terra uncoiled her long legs and stood. The beads in her hair clacked against each other as she walked up to me. She looked at my wounds, then at my face. Her amber eyes locked with mine, shifting as if she was studying my feelings and reading my thoughts. She placed her hand on my shoulder then walked past me and out the bridge door.

I sat in the chair Terra had vacated, placed my elbows on my knees and cupped my head in my hands.

"You've had better days I would guess?" Ava snorted.

"Actually, this was better than most," I said as I eased back into the chair. I pushed my palms against my forehead and kept my eyes closed tight as if my thoughts would leak into the bridge if I opened them. "You did well, Ava."

"How so?"

"For staying hidden for over a hundred days. For not abandoning your mission. For staying alive when Tompkins' crew came looking for you."

I opened my eyes to find her smiling at me. Her natural eye on the left side of her face was a muddy brown and her artificial eye was a flickering silver. Her auburn hair twirled in spiraling curls in front of her slender face, covering parts of a long scar that started as the top of her forehead, traversed down the front of her face and across her right eye, down the side of her cheek and finally stopping at the base of her neck. At the top of her head a small patch of white hair surrounded the base of the scar. Even after all of these years the injury remained pink and appeared tender. Ava's facial features were slight and sharp with high cheek bones. Her nose was a small bump on her face and her chin ended in a point. Her ears were lost under the mass of dangling curls.

"It's no big deal," Ava said. "Sitting on that station was like a vacation. Better than serving back on the *Beast* without you there running things." She was using her smile to hide something. Pain? Uncertainty?

"What happened back on the station?"

Ava bit her bottom lip. "Tompkins crew was going to do whatever it took to find me." She drew in a deep breath then continued. "They were questioning every woman they found on the station. When they denied that they were me, or couldn't tell them where I was hiding, they tortured them just to make sure. And if they had a spouse, or children, they killed them. They killed them for fun."

"You did what you had to do."

"I know, but it doesn't make it any easier to live with."

"It's the situation we're in now. Tompkins, the UG, those are things we can't control. We'll get through this." I placed my hand on her arm.

She nodded as if trying to accept that everything was OK. "They were closing in on me, Maxx. There were so many of them and I was running out of places to hide. That's when someone detonated the oxygen scrubbers on the lower level. Without the distraction, I don't think I would've made it."

"How do you know someone intentionally destroyed them?"

"If there was one spot on the *Valkyrie* that was closely monitored, it was the life support bays. There were so many sensors, backup systems, contingency plans, and precautionary measures taken that if even the slightest issue was detected it would have been addressed. A catastrophic malfunction was highly unlikely if not impossible. The detonation was so large that it blew out a section of the hull. No accidental explosion would cause that much damage."

My eyes searched the bridge as if to find the hidden answer to this question. "You're probably right."

"If it wasn't for that, they would've –"

"It doesn't do you any good to think about what could've happened. You did your job as you were asked, and you made it back safely. That's all you should think about."

Ava swallowed hard. "I just wish there was more I could've done for those people."

"Once this mission is complete, there will be retribution. That much I promise."

"Good," she whispered.

I patted her on the shoulder then retrieved the box with Jackson's implant along with the implant scanner. Removing the lid, I produced the JaC that was sitting inside, still wrapped in the blood-encrusted cloth.

"What's that?" Ava asked.

"What's left of Jackson," I said, adjusting the settings on the implant scanner.

"Looks like my assignment went a little better." Ava choked out a heavy sigh.

"Yeah." I nodded, drawing a frustrated chuckle from Ava. "Jackson was a good man. He served us well."

I scanned the JaC and downloaded the contents into the scanner's memory unit. Other than the necessary coding of the JaC, there was a sizable amount of encrypted data stored on the tiny chip. I located the *Beast's* coordinates and punched them into the navigation system. The rest of the data would require systems I had on the *Beast* to break the encryption.

"Do you need me to scan a JaC?" I asked Ava.

She snorted at me. "You know me better than that. It's all right here." She tapped at her temple with an index finger.

"So, you continue to hold out? We may be the only two people in the entire Galaxy that don't have one."

She winked. "That's why I got this." Her finger traced the scar from her forehead to her neck. "Too slow."

Ava reached forward and entered her coordinates into the navigation unit. The data needed for the location of the *Beast* was complete.

I removed the memory component from the base of the JaC scanner and tossed the unit to the floor. I placed Jackson's JaC back in the small metallic box and slid it in my pocket.

"If I give it hell, we have less than four days of travel," Ava said. "I wouldn't have guessed you would have left her so close."

"I didn't choose the location. It's a random algorithm generated by a program that Roger created. It's the only way to ensure that even I don't know the exact location of my ship."

"What would've happened if you couldn't have located us?"

"Roger would've dumped the cargo, disbanded the crew, and sold the *Beast*."

Ava's eyes opened wide. "You would lose everything."

"It was too risky for me to know the *Beast*'s location. Everyone can be broken."

"Even you?"

"Even me."

"You did it to protect the crew," she whispered.

I stood from the chair shaking my head. "Don't kid yourself, Ava. I did it to protect my interests." I saw a smile spread across Ava's face as I walked out of the bridge.

I'd spent the last three days isolated in a back room of the ship, walled off from the others. The darkness and solitude offered me an unexpected sense of peace and a chance to rein in my emotions. With great effort I fought to come to grips with what happened over the last hundred days.

I ran my hand over the inked MXX letters on my forearm and stopped on the first 'X.' My fingers pushed against the outline of the letter as I thought of Liriana. The loss of Cooper. The death of Jackson. The murder of my crew. The senseless slaughter of hundreds of innocents. The toll this mission was taking on everyone. We were only hours away from docking with the *Beast*, and eventually completing the Solonian contract. It would all come to an end soon.

My insides boiled with the thoughts of Tompkins, Rothet, the Captain, and the UG. At that moment I was reminded of what my former partner, Drauq, told me years ago. "We all have a heart," he said. "Everyone cares about someone, or something in their lives. Even the shadow of one's own evil can't choke out the light of their good. It's there. You just need to find it."

I was young, and considered it to be credible advice offered by a fulltime smuggler and self-proclaimed philosopher. Drauq thought the Silor Galaxy was only as dark as you made it. Only as dark as your mind and heart. I believed him, and his lifetime of experience. I was a fool.

Drauq died collecting on a contract. I found his body a day later; his head was separated from his shoulders by the same man who had hired him. That's when I knew Drauq was wrong. This galaxy was nothing but evil, filled with darkness, greed, and corruption. He was a good man, and that's why he's dead. His trust in the inherent good of people cost him everything. It was a mistake I promised myself I would never make. In the end, I would only trust one person - me.

After his death, the loss of Drauq haunted me. I couldn't eat or sleep. Every time I closed my eyes I saw his cold, dead eyes staring back at me as if they were trying to speak. I knew what I needed to do. I had to make things right.

I gave up everything, and spent all of my credits just to track down his killer. It took me months to find him, and when I did I made him pay his debt in full. Even though it didn't bring Drauq back to life, I found that his killer's agonizing death filled an empty void inside of me. At that moment my transformation was complete; an internal metamorphosis from what I had believed to be true into the reality of what the galaxy really was. The darkness embraced me.

I shook the thoughts of Drauq from my mind as I stood at my cabin door and stared at the control module set into the wall. I was always able to drown my feelings inside of a well of hate and anger. Brush away my emotions with purposeful revenge. But the death of Cooper and my feelings for Liriana wouldn't leave me. This time it was different.

Relief and a sense of familiarity washed over me the moment I stepped on the dock of the *Beast*. It felt good to be home.

"Commander," one of the dock attendants said with a smile as he extended his hand. I shook it as he continued. "It's good to have you back."

A few deckhands gathered around our fighter and took notice of the missing members of our crew. The collective look on their faces said it all. Eight were lost from our team; leaders and soldiers that couldn't be replaced. Their losses would be felt across the ship.

Tank shouted, "Get back at it everyone! We don't have time to feel sorry for ourselves. The fun part of this mission has yet to begin." A rolling murmur worked its way through the workers as they stepped away.

"Tank," I said. He tugged at the twisted mass of hair that hung from his chin as he turned to face me. "Take Ava and introduce her to our tactical point team. She's taking over for Cooper."

Tank chuckled, glanced at Ava then back at me. His mouth drew a thin line when I didn't relent. "Seriously?"

"Do you have any other suggestions?"

"Hell, I'll take both squads. Anything is better than turning the tactical team over to her."

Ava stepped up to Tank, the top of her head barely reaching his chest. Her eyes flashed a blur of brown and silver as she read his face.

"I can do it, Tank, and better than you," she said. Her hands were firmly planted on her hips.

"She's more than capable." I nodded at Tank. "Make it happen."

"Listen, Maxx, this is a mistake," Tank grumbled. "She doesn't have any experience running point. Hell, she's a co-pilot, not a leader of men. She doesn't have the training. We would all be better served with Ava back in her position on the bridge."

I pointed at Terra. "We have a new co-pilot." Terra's eyes grew large and her mouth opened as if she wanted to speak but didn't know what to say. She exchanged looks with Tank as I continued. "You can't handle two teams. I need your team ready the moment we touch down on Lotress."

"Ready for what?" Tank said. "We don't even know what the hell we are running into, if anything."

"Exactly," I said. "That's why we can't put anything to chance. Your team is the only squad we have left intact, and I intend to keep it that way."

"It's a tough time to introduce so many unknowns. A really bad, fucking time, Maxx." Tank spit. "I don't know that the men will follow her lead."

"Ava will make it happen." She crossed her arms in front of her chest and nodded. "She'll do just fine."

"It's on your head," Tank said with a sigh, then spun away from me as if he needed to remove himself from our conversation. After a few steps he paused, scrubbed the stubble on top of his head then turned back. "Where are you headed?"

"To the bridge to talk to Roger and set our course for the delivery of the Solonian cargo. I have to confirm our current coordinates, but I'm estimating we have a week to a week and a half before we reach our destination. Take Terra to the officer's quarters, get her a room and have someone sit down with her to review the layout of the ship." I turned to face Terra. "Are you up for this?"

"Why are you doing this?" She asked with a tilt of her head. "I'm no one. You don't even know me. Why the trust?"

I looked down at her scarred forearms then back at her eyes. "You saved my life. Twice. I know you well enough to see that you cared for Cooper, and that you've done everything you could to help us every step of the way." She crossed her arms across her chest and bowed her head. "We...I need your help."

Terra nodded and chewed on her bottom lip. "Thank you."

"Go," I said to Tank. "Every minute we waste is another minute Tompkins and the UG have to track us down."

Tank, Terra, and Ava headed toward the elevator shaft that would lower them into the bottom levels of the *Beast*. Tank led the charge followed by the two women. His eyes were focused on the floor as he flexed his hands open and closed at his sides.

I shared some of those doubts with Tank, but what choice did I have? There were more competent people on our ship to fill those positions, but I'd been away for so long that I didn't know who I could trust, or who would sell me out. Maybe assigning Ava and Terra to those roles would prove to be a fatal mistake. But I had a gut feeling it was the right thing to do, and that feeling was worth the risk.

I made my way through the tube-like tunnels to the command deck. Crew members rushed past me, forcing me to turn sideways to allow them to pass. These tight fitting, dimly lit corridors served multiple purposes. Most importantly they created a confusing passageway for any unwelcome visitors boarding our ship. There was no logical path from any main section of the ship to another, and the winding, single-file lanes prevented an organized, military raid by an enemy.

It would take some time for Terra to learn how to navigate through the *Beast*, but it was critical that she learned quickly. The bridge was the command center, but in-depth knowledge of the ship's inner workings was a must for any pilot.

When I reached the bridge, I went through a battery of security scans: DNA, retina, and facial structure analysis, then entered my eleven digit code on the sensor screen. A high pitched squeal rang from a speaker overhead followed by the ship's distorted, electronic greeting. *"Welcome, Commander."*

"Roger," I said as I entered the bridge.

"Commander," Roger said. He spun in his seat and arched his eyebrows with an upward tilt of his head. "Good to have you back." Roger's focus shifted back to the control panels spread out in a semi-circle in front of him. His fingers worked over the ship's controls with a blur of button presses and screen taps, perfectly choreographing the *Beast's* thruster adjustments.

I'd owned the *Beast* for seven years, yet manning this vessel was still foreign to me. I used to ask Roger questions, a lot of questions, on how to operate this ship. I figured that someday I would have to pilot this monster to save our asses. But Roger's brain worked faster than his hands and worse yet, his mouth couldn't keep up. He's brilliant, but when it comes to piloting the *Beast* he's extremely quirky and struggled to relay his knowledge in common terms. That would pose a challenge for Terra to learn, and I needed Roger's most focused effort to make the training a success.

A warship of this size took two skilled pilots to maneuver, however we haven't had that luxury for over half a year. Ava had been filling in when needed, but never participating during the critical stages of any of our missions. When we lost our co-pilot, Roger's trust in anyone else's ability to pilot the *Beast* went with her. It was a personal issue with Roger, not based on the professional skills of potential replacements. Roger not only lost his co-pilot, but also his wife, and he took her death hard. He asked for the opportunity, and I gave him the chance to prove himself as the sole pilot. Things were fine for a short while before Roger's metal stability and physical health deteriorated. When he stopped eating his body reacted by consuming his muscle mass, leaving him with a pale and emaciated frame resembling one of the ship's thin support beams.

He grew increasingly distant and bitter then started to fail some of his assignments. At first he underestimated travel times by only a few minutes, but then those windows of time started to grow. Our clientele are particular about scheduled meetings, and tend to get nervous when you don't show up on time and as promised. Then he started to guide us into unfamiliar territories while missing his navigation points. My plan was to remove him from his post during this Solonian mission, but that's when everything went to hell.

I eased myself back into the command chair as I watched the vastness of space through the forward window. I spun my chair to get my first good look at Roger. His face was sunken, his eyes surrounded by dark circles.

"When's the last time you slept?" I asked.

"Don't know," he muttered in reply. "How about you?"

I took in a deep breath. "I didn't stop up here to talk about me."

"Yeah, I figured."

I stood and made my way for the co-pilot's chair next to Roger. "You know why I'm here."

"I suppose that I do." His voice was as heavy as the bags under his eyes.

"I have a recruit. Someone I need you to train as your co-pilot."

"Ava and Tucker have served well enough when I need a break." Roger sniffed, then rubbed his sleeve across his nose. "There is no need to complicate things any more than we have to."

"And you still haven't accepted either as your co-pilot. You're killing yourself, Roger. Do you think she would want that?"

Roger looked at me. Red tracks marking jagged patterns on the whites of his eyes made them look like worn maps. "Please don't tell me what she would want."

"I'm not going to tell you how to battle your personal demons. You need to do that on your own. However, I am going to tell you how to do your job and you'll accept that."

Roger replied with a hesitant nod as his eyes returned to the controls. "What's their name?"

"Terra," I replied as I stood.

"Someone new to our crew…" Roger slowly shook his head from side to side. "What's so special about her?"

"She has experience piloting fighters. She's smart and picks up on things quickly. She'll prove to be an asset."

Roger snorted out a *hmphh* then scratched at his sideburns. "How can you be certain?"

"Honest, I can't," I said as I made my way back to the command chair. "She's been with us since our escape from Paxcel. She has saved my life twice. I've seen her piloting skills and her willingness to help and learn. It's a feeling Roger, that's it." I eased back into the chair and continued. "She needs full access to everything, a thorough review of the ship's controls, mapping, and emergency systems."

"What about Ava or Tucker?"

"I need Ava to cover for Cooper, and I want to keep Tucker's focus on the *Beast's* engines. I know this is going to be difficult Roger, but I have faith you can pull it off."

"Of course." Roger slouched back in his chair, bowed his head and nestled his pointed chin against his chest. His eyes drooped closed. "So they imprisoned you in Paxcel? We're in deep then, aren't we, Maxx?"

"We are."

"You left here with eight of our crew and sent two others out with the coordinates of the *Beast.* You've returned after a hundred and twenty-three days and seven hours with three - two from our crew and this new girl, Terra. Mix in the complications with the UG and things look really grim."

"And that's just the start. I had to negotiate a new deal with the Solonians. A deal that we need to complete to make sure that everyone receives a full pardon from their empire."

Roger opened his eyes and rested his head on the back of the chair. "You renegotiated with the Solonian Empire? I highly doubt that the new terms didn't come without a steep price."

"It's one that we can afford," I said. "They gave us another thirty days to deliver their cargo, and we've already eaten into that time locating Ava and Jackson."

Roger sighed and thoughtfully licked his lips. "How much time do we have left?

"Less than twenty days."

"Is the drop point still on Lotress?"

"It is." I leaned forward, resting my elbows on my knees and clasping my hands together in front of me. "You've had a long time to analyze the best routes to Lotress. What's your flight plan?"

Roger punched instructions into the ship's control panels and displayed his research on the forward monitor. "I gave consideration to time and distance, refueling options, and safe locations for the necessary downtime needed for the hyperdrives, then coupled that with trips through the Dark Quarter, and avoiding sectors that contain the most hostile Empire Nations and high traffic areas for the UG. With all of that, I've come up with two potential routes. This first is a more direct path, eliminating our need to refuel by greatly reducing the distance we need to travel. That would ease the strain on the *Beast's* engines and hyperdrives, but would require twenty jumps through the Dark Quarter."

"And the other option?"

"The second option is a longer route, bypassing as many of the hostile areas as possible and eliminating travel through the Dark Quarter entirely. The downside is that we would be pushing our new timeline very tight. One incorrect jump, or any system failures, and we may not make our destination on time."

I lowered my head and massaged my temples as I considered the two options. The *Beast* can run without fuel as long as the engines stay functioning and engaged. The eight engines emit renewable electrical discharges that are harvested, processed, and reapplied as fuel. In the event that our engines go dormant, we have to rely on two battery towers to jolt them back to life. It's a one-shot deal requiring enough charge to drain both towers on a single attempt while injecting a reserved mixture of highly combustible fuel.

In order to vault great distances in short periods of time, we need to activate the ship's hyperdrives. The hyperdrives are powered by liquid fuel only, and each jump takes an enormous amount of fuel to complete. After each jump the hyperdrives must be disengaged, and allowed to rest for a minimum of twelve hours. They are never activated before the rest period is complete. Ever. If you do, your best scenario is covering a portion of the jump distance and fusing the circuitry and mechanical components of the hyperdrives into a solid mass of worthless scrap. If you aren't lucky, your drives could rupture, spraying the fuel into the ship and setting off a wave of rolling fire and flame that will puddle steel in seconds.

The *Beast* is a warrior in the truest sense of the word. She has taken a beating unlike any other ship I've seen and has dealt out even worse. But even she has her limits, and expecting her to handle rippling solar winds, engine strain, and an onslaught of potential laser fire without a tick of downtime, was simply unrealistic.

I wasn't thrilled about traversing the Dark Quarter. The twelve hours between each jump would leave us drifting in the most dangerous sectors in our galaxy. What roamed free in the Dark Quarter made the UG and Tompkins look like a schoolyard of playful children.

Rubbing the back of my neck, I widened my eyes and sighed. "There's really only one choice."

Roger nodded. "Unless you're willing to take the risk of another failed timeline, I believe traversing through the Dark Quarter is our only viable option."

"The Dark Quarter it is," I said as I drew in a deep breath, stood, then headed toward the bridge door. "Terra will be joining you soon. I'm dumping a lot on your shoulders, Roger. Make it happen."

"I can handle it as long as she can." Roger's focus went from me back to the control panels. "Let's just hope the *Beast* has it in her."

The moment I stepped into my personal cabin, I noticed that it had been searched. It was executed by a professional, discretely and thoroughly. I nearly missed detecting the slightest shift of my personal effects, and the small indents in my clothes that had been picked off shelves and set back in place. What I saw didn't surprise me. We were sold out to the UG, and whoever searched my cabin was still on the *Beast*. What I didn't know was what they were looking for.

As big of a threat as this person could be, I couldn't share my suspicions with the crew. Not yet. I couldn't have them second guessing each other, questioning if the man next to him had their back. The open knowledge of a potential traitor on our ship would destroy what little morale was left. It was too dangerous.

****

So far our voyage had been quiet and uneventful. It gave me much needed time to reunite with the crew and set them at ease about our recent losses. The medics had tended to my wounds by sewing up the holes in my body like a mom caring for a child's abused stuffed animal. I had some quiet moments to spend by myself to think over how this mission was going to play itself out. I even found time to get a few hours of rest.

I made my way down through the winding tunnels toward the cargo bay. My breathing and clanking steps on the deck were the only noises in the otherwise vacant passages. The banks of lights that lined the halls flickered on and off, casting my shadow on the floor then erasing it with every other step. It seemed like an eternity since my head was clear and free like these passageways, instead of muddled with burdens and regret.

When I entered the cargo hold, towers of Solonian crates greeted me. They filled the hold from end to end and were stacked over twenty meters high. Each crate was secured with extreme care, banded with straps and chained to the hull. The lids were secured with tamper triggers installed by the Solonians. If any of the seals were broken, it would activate the sensor and alert our contact on Lotress, once they were delivered, that the contents were compromised.

"What's in them?" a voice said to me from behind. I turned to face Terra standing only a few meters away. An innocent smile crept across her face. "Sorry. I didn't mean to startle you."

"No worries," I said. I'd been too lost in my thoughts to notice that she had stepped into the room. The *Beast* had made me more comfortable than I should've been. I turned back to the crates and rubbed my chin between my fingers. "I have no idea what's in them."

Terra stepped to my side. "Have you ever wanted to open any of the cargo you transport?" Her amber eyes widened as she scanned the towers of crates.

"It's bad for business." I laughed. "And normally bad for your health. My customers don't take too kindly to us tampering with their cargo."

Terra nodded her understanding. "Whatever we're carrying, it appears that it's all very similar." Terra pointed to the crates spread around the room. "They are all the same size."

She was right. They were roughly two meters in length, a meter tall and a meter wide, and based on the scales, weighing between a hundred and a hundred and fifty kilos each.

"How has your training progressed?" I asked. "And your familiarity with the ship and its crew?"

"Very well, I think. Most people have been helpful. Roger has been...understanding."

"I've put him in a very difficult situation. I hope you understand that."

"I do."

I turned to face Terra. "I'm trusting you. Everything I've learned throughout my life has told me not to. But I am. You need to succeed at whatever I throw at you. There isn't any option for failure. No room for mistakes."

She touched my arm, her hands warm and gentle. "Your trust is well placed. I will make good on it. I promise you."

"Cooper thought the world of you. He trusted you when I didn't." Terra remained quiet after I mentioned Cooper. Her eyes moved from side to side, unwilling to meet mine. "I've seen your arms. I know about your past. You continue to try and cover the pain, but you can't hide it. This opportunity for a new life is because of him."

Terra crossed her arms below her chest and buried the scars against her shirt. "I've come to grips with my past. What's done is done."

I shook my head. "I'm not sure you're ready to embrace it. I can see it in your eyes, and in your actions. Just like you, I live with it every day of my life. When we're at our lowest point, what emerges is who we really are - a warrior or a coward, a survivor or a victim. You can follow your heart to your own destiny or let your past control and manipulate you. Who are you, Terra?"

Her amber eyes flickered with a hint of darkness. "I've always been a survivor. I make my own decisions, choose who I am, and what I want." She unfolded her arms and stretched them out for me to see. Jagged scars were cut across the dark, soft flesh of her forearms. "I've made my own path and buried my demons. No one will speak for me again. Ever!"

The pain, the hurt, was just below the surface and my words had scratched them free. It wasn't my intention to release such feelings, but it had to be said – even by someone that was more broken than her.

As she spun, the beads in her hair clacked in unison, echoing her anger. She started to walk away then turned back to face me. "Never underestimate what I'm capable of." Terra stormed off through one of the side tunnels and vanished from sight.

They say time heals all wounds, which are nothing more than flowery words people use to make you stop feeling sorry for yourself. I knew personally that Terra would carry the ache of her psychological scars for eternity. Many of those scars had never healed for me, and many others were slowly splitting and leaking bile. It wouldn't be any different for Terra.

I made one last round in the cargo hold reviewing the digital manifest and checking the security of the crates. Only a handful of days in the Dark Quarter and this mission would be complete. Only then would I be forced to make decisions about my new life and leaving my crew. Shrugging off those thoughts, I made my way toward the exit from the cargo hold. The same passageway Terra just used.

A familiar, high-pitched whine filled my ears after I took a few steps into the tunnel. The sound of an active detonator. I turned and ran back into the cargo bay. My heart pounded as I fumbled with the door access panel trying to punch in the code to seal the door. I was too late. A flash of light and a thunderous wave of fire launched me across the room. My back slammed against the hull, blistering my spine with pain as I tumbled to the deck. The room warped and swirled as my vision tunneled on the white and red flames that lashed out from the passageway. The stench of burned electronics were carried into the room on rolling clouds of black smoke.

I fumbled though my jacket, searching for my communicator under the darkness of the caustic smoke. The com felt clumsy in my numbing hands as I slid my thumb over its surface. Jagged shards of metal snagged my skin as the device crumbled in my hand, destroyed from the impact with the wall and floor.

Another explosion rocked the *Beast*. The deck rippled and shuddered as sheets of steel folded like paper. The ship's hull groaned its displeasure, followed by the hissing rush of oxygen that seeped out of popped rivets and torn welds. I felt the push of air from behind as the ship's emergency detection systems attempted to compensate for the loss of oxygen by doubling the output of the oxygen scrubbers. It fueled the fires and created a bright tunnel of flame that raged into the cargo hold.

I had to secure the cargo. Pushing myself to my feet, I removed my jacket and held it out in front of me as a shield of leather. The flames crept around the door frame in all directions like hot fingers clawing their way inside.

Drawing in a smoke-filled breath, I pushed my way toward the door's access panel. My lungs burned and the surge of smoke forced my eyes closed. I groped the wall for the panel, touching it for only a fraction of a second then removing my hand before it burned my fingertips. My fingers caught its edge, and I traced over the screen and fumbled to enter the lock code. My jacket relented to the extreme heat and ignited into a shield of white hot flame.

Just as I confirmed the code I heard another squeal, a high-pitched whine barely audible above the roaring din of the blaze. That's when everything went black.

Every sound was muffled as if I was submerged under water. I was surrounded by garbled screams; the undeniable sounds of suffering. The lids of my eyes fluttered open like wounded butterflies, breaking a crusted seal and allowing a stream of blinding light to lance its way into the back of my skull. The muffled voices grew louder, but were just as unintelligible as before. The piercing light was replaced by a contorted shape floating above me as it moved close to my head then backed away.

I worked the feeling back into my hands and fingers by flexing them into fists, then releasing. They felt like stones, heavy and stiff, the tight skin tugging and cracking at my knuckles with each flex. Feeling was returning to my lower extremities. The biting numbness started at my toes and inched its way up my legs to my waist like a creeping blanket of prickling electricity.

The blur in front of me started to take form, and the words it spoke were less muffled but echoed in my head like the heavy hiss of static. "Maxx..." The snapping of fingers and light slaps against my cheeks increased with intensity.

My eyes were fully open now, but everything around me was unfolding like a slow motion dream. The room was towering in size; so tall I wasn't able to focus on the ceiling. To my left was an empty cot with a blood-soaked sheet, pulled back from the mattress and spilling onto the floor.

On my right were rows of wounded men, my crew, stretched out as far as my eyes could focus. Many bared bloodied stumps of severed appendages, gruesome and gaping wounds - the types of injuries that made you wish you were dead. There were stacks of men, piled on top of one another like cordwood. Their empty eyes staring back at me. When my hearing returned to normal, the sounds of the wounded made me wish it hadn't.

Sliding my hand off of my chest, I found a cylindrical bar at my side. I wrapped my numb fingers around the metal and gingerly pulled myself up into a sitting position. Almost immediately a hand pushed hard against my chest and forced me back down.

"Rest for now," the voice said.

"Where am I?" The words came out thick.

"In the corner of the cargo hold," the female voice answered.

I rubbed my face, feeling the unshaven stubble against my palms and the calloused skin of my hands. My heartbeat quickened from a sluggish pound, to a steadying beat as my breathing leveled. When feeling returned, it came with rolling waves of pain that rippled through my core.

Scores of injured soldiers littered the cargo hold, some lying on blankets or piles of bundled clothing while others were forced to make do on the unyielding steel. Ava stood over me, carefully looking into my eyes for signs of a head injury.

"Enough," I said as I pushed her hands away.

"You're in rough shape, Maxx," Ava said. "I'm not a doctor but you're suffering from a concussion, obvious burns and –"

I cut her off by extending my open hand in front of her. "Help me up."

"You need to rest."

"I need to command my ship. Help me up, and that isn't a request."

Ava was apprehensive at first, scanning the room as if trying to locate someone to hold me down, or at least convince me to stay on the cot. After a few seconds she released a sigh, extended her arm, then struggled to pull me up. She was strong for her size, but much smaller than me, giving up a good forty kilos. My legs wobbled and I used the bar on the cot to hold me upright.

"How many?" I asked. I used my forearm to wipe the soot from my face.

"Most of them, Maxx."

The pain that flowed through my body had found its way into my head. A deep, throbbing, weighty pain. "Give my cot to a soldier who needs it." I took a few steps; my feet clunked like bricks of lead, jarring my legs and knees and sending shockwaves up my spine.

Looking around the room, I paused, sucked in a deep breath then closed my eyes. For every twenty injured, there was one man or woman tending to their needs. "Where's the medical staff?"

"Dead," Ava said. "They're all dead."

"What sections of the ship were targeted?"

Ava shook her head. "I'm not exactly certain. The engine rooms, medical bay, and munitions storage for sure. Maybe this cargo hold." Ava pointed at the scorched tunnel and the remains of the door, now just a crumpled sheet of smoldering steel. "They didn't set detonators in here, but if you hadn't closed that door in time, there was a chance we would've lost the cargo as well."

"Where's Tank?"

Ava summoned a soldier to her side to assist her, then the two of them placed one of the wounded men on the cot. "On the bridge with Roger. I'm assuming he's assessing the damage and reviewing our progress to the drop point."

I turned to face the solider helping Ava. His right cheek was swollen and bright purple, and a few of his teeth were missing. "Soldier, you're now in command of this medical operation. Take as many of the healthy men as you need to help the wounded. Understood?"

He nodded his response.

"Where the hell are you going?" Ava asked with a furrowed brow.

"Where are *we* going?" I responded. "We're headed to the bridge to regroup." I pointed to the soldier I just talked to. "Help him round up some able-bodied crew members. Brief him on where you left off and meet me there."

Ava nodded then turned away before I had a chance to finish. She wasn't about to let any more of these men and women die.

I'm still not sure how I made my way to the bridge. There were periods of my trek that I couldn't recall. Passageways I wandered off in. Blackouts. One of the few things I remembered were some of my crew squeezing past me in the tunnels with carts of supplies and packs in tow. I stopped a few times to purge my already empty stomach, and to use the wall as a brace until the spinning in my head subsided.

When I finally made it to the bridge, I punched in the secure access code - three times, and was finally permitted entry. Tank, Roger, and Ava stood in a circle whispering to each other. The looks on their faces made my head feel worse than it already did. Tucker was off to the side of the bridge running status reports where Terra should've been. She was noticeably absent.

"Maxx, I was worried," Ava said. "I didn't see you in the tunnels."

"I'm fine," I replied. Seeing Ava here made me realize that I lost a large chunk of time while trying to find my way to the bridge. Minutes, maybe hours. "Tucker, please leave for a moment."

"Yes, sir." He gathered an electronic report reader from the console and brushed by me on his way out of the bridge. The door sealed shut behind him.

"Give me a status report," I said.

Roger spoke through his hand that covered his mouth. "How are you doing, Commander?"

I waved him off. "We don't have time for that now. Status."

Roger sat quietly as he slid his hand under his chin. He tapped his boney finger against his lips, occasionally stopping as if he was going to say something but needed more time to contemplate how it would best be delivered. Tank tugged at the mass of hair that fell from his face, and Ava avoided looking me in the eyes.

"How many men did we lose?" I asked.

Tank gripped his goatee and spoke. "If we count the dead, incapacitated, and gravely wounded, we are down to roughly thirty percent of our crew."

My legs buckled. "How?"

"Explosives rigged throughout the *Beast*. Engine bays, barracks, med station, and heavily traveled passageways. Some of the detonations were stronger than others. The only areas that remain completely untouched are the cargo bay, bridge, and officer living quarters."

"Why wouldn't they target those areas?"

"We were just talking about that, Maxx. The best we can figure is that the bridge was left alone because Roger more or less lives here. It would've been nearly impossible for someone to get access without him knowing about it. And the officer living quarters? Hell if I know."

I made my way to one of the bridge seats, eased back into the chair and cupped my face in my hands. Less than a hundred and fifty men left? So many killed...so many good soldiers and crewmen.

"Do we have enough coverage to man the critical areas of the ship?" I asked.

"Yes," Ava said, "but it will be tough." Her eyes rolled upward while she mumbled some numbers. "We'll need to repurpose the entire cargo bay crew for general maintenance and repair duties. We'll shuffle some people to address system repairs. Everyone else will need to tend to the wounded. It's a skeleton crew, but we'll make it."

"I'm sure those charges weren't set just to kill our men," I said. "So tell me what they damaged."

Roger spun in his chair. "We were partially lucky, if I can use that word. The ship diagnostic scans revealed that we lost one of our two hyperdrives, substantial fuel stores, both battery towers and five of the eight engines. The explosions collapsed the passageways to the lower decks. There's so much structural torment in that area that I believe we won't have a choice but to seal those levels off. Our docking clamps and platform landing gear took severe damage; to what extent I can't say. As bad as all of that sounds, we're still stable and able to continue our path to Lotress. We can continue to make our jumps assuming that the last remaining hyperdrive holds up."

"And if the remaining engines stall or fail, we are nothing more than a hunk of floating steel."

"Might as well hang an "open for business" sign outside the ship for all the pirates to see," Tank grumbled.

"How much fuel do we have for the remaining functioning hyperdrive?" I asked.

"Not a lot, and it will be close based on the number of jumps we have left," Roger said. "We were able to stop the loss by rerouting the fuel from the damaged hyperdrive to the functioning unit."

"Are we still on schedule to reach Lotress in time to complete the contract?"

"Yes, assuming we don't encounter any additional setbacks. I would recommend one refueling stop to be safe. If we can refuel, and we don't experience any further system failures, we will arrive with time to spare."

"That's a really big *if*, Maxx." Tank said. "We can still bail on this contract. Take what days we have left and use them to run. It isn't too late."

"Abandoning the Solonian contract isn't an option. That just signs the death warrants for the crew that's still alive. We didn't come this far, and lose so many to quit now." I worked my neck around my shoulders. "Where's Terra?"

My answer came back as empty stares and silence. I looked at the three, shrugged my shoulders, then opened the palms of my hands. "Anyone?"

"We think she's responsible," Tank said, his voice just louder than a whisper.

"Why?"

"She's gone."

"How do you know she wasn't killed in one of the explosions?"

Ava sighed. "There was a single shuttle that ejected just after the explosions took place. Most of our security recordings were destroyed in the blast but we've pieced together sufficient data that shows her direct path to the docking bay. It was her clearance access code that was used to open all the doors and to launch the shuttle."

"That's all you've got?" I asked. "Even if she was the person manning the shuttle that doesn't mean she set the explosives. It wouldn't be the first time someone evacuated the ship when things started to go to hell."

"Commander, I shared a lot of information with Terra," Roger said. "Gave her access to data that very few of us know. The areas that were targeted were very specific. The explosives were strategically set to target primary wire clusters and critical electronics." Roger handed me a data pad. I scrolled through the reports as he continued. "There was a well thought out plan behind all of this. Everything leads back to Terra."

The ship's logs recorded all of Terra's authorized access over the last few days. She spent much of her time roaming through the ship, and she had visited every area that was targeted in the explosions more than once.

How did I not see this coming? I was reminded about what Rothet said, that he and his team were captured with us and imprisoned on Paxcel. Terra must have been one of his. She worked me over and worked me good.

I tossed the data pad onto the chair next to me. "Even if we agree that Terra did this," I said, "there's still something we're missing."

"What's that?" Tank grunted.

"She wasn't the only one. Someone sold us out to the UG before we encountered her, and someone had to give her access to those explosives. She didn't bring them with her."

"Maybe they left with her in the shuttle," Ava said, "or were killed in the explosions."

"Or maybe they're still onboard," Tank said. "Trusting an outsider, Maxx. You really fucked this one up."

"What good is pointing fingers going to do?" Roger cut in. "I don't know about the rest of you but I would like to live through this." Roger spun his chair to face the ship's controls. "Can we continue discussing a plan that leads to the successful completion of this mission?"

Tank's words stung, but he was right. Ill placed trust had cost us dearly.

"Where the hell are we currently?" I asked Roger.

"We're about seventy-two hours away from our destination, but I'm flying the *Beast* at about half speed," Roger said. "I'm not certain that the remaining three engines can handle the stress."

"Maintain our current speed for now," I said, "until we've had a chance to analyze the damage and patch our hull." I continued to rub sensation back into my head, cheeks, and neck. My nausea persisted, but was fading and leaving me with an uncomfortable stomach and a knot of pain in my head.

"You're fucking crazy," Tank said. "A fleet of UG ships and Tompkins' destroyer will be faster and better armed. We'll never outrun them."

Roger knitted his brows together. "If that's true, we're in serious trouble in our current state. Though there's Tank's pending assumption that they know where we are, and how to find us." Roger twisted in his chair to face Tank. "How can you be certain?"

"I'm not," Tank said, "but the way things have gone, I'd expect to see them jump to our position any second now."

"We should be concerned," I said. "If by chance Terra or someone else is working for either Tompkins or the UG, you can bet they hid transmitters."

"Let me gather a few people and conduct a sweep of the ship," Ava said as she walked to the bridge door.

"Wait a minute…," Tank yelled out to Ava as she left the bridge. "She's back on the ship for a few days and you would think she's running things."

"Tank, I need you to assess the extent of the damage to the *Beast* and its crew," I said. "I don't want estimates or rounded figures. I need an exact count. I need to know what weapons on the *Beast* are still functional and what's available for manpower."

"Got it covered," Tank said.

"Roger, you and I have our work cut out for us," I said. "The lives of everyone on this ship are riding on your ability to get the *Beast* to Lotress on time."

Roger looked up at me though his weary eyes. "I would expect nothing less."

The *Beast* limped onward, propelled by her remaining engines that spit clouds of smoke into space. In her current condition we couldn't rely on her brute force or speed to save us. Our mission's success rested solely on the shoulders of my skilled crew.

My main concerns revolved around the stability of our remaining engines, our last functioning hyperdrive, and the integrity of our hull. Once we determined that the *Beast* was space worthy, we swung our attention to the crew. How they would hold up through the completion of this contract was something I couldn't predict.

There was no doubt that the explosives targeted key areas that would disable and slow our ship, but the main target was personnel. The wounded littered the floors in the lower levels of the *Beast*. We had three distinct levels of devastation - dead, dying, and may die soon. We didn't have a medical facility or medical supplies, and the constant groaning from the *Beast*'s hull didn't ease the minds of anyone onboard.

Roger and I agreed that one refueling stop would give us enough fuel to make our destination on Lotress as well as a few additional jumps to get us away from the planet. Out of necessity, I contacted Terrell, a former shipmate of mine who left my employment to start contracting his own services as an agent soldier. He was known to traverse the outer reaches of the Dark Quarter, and was an obvious choice from a shallow pool of options. He agreed to refuel the *Beast* and take on the burden of the dead and dying on my ship. In turn I would pay him a ransom in credits and owe him one favor to be redeemed in the future. Terrell knew I had no room to negotiate, so I accepted the terms.

We were too deep into the Dark Quarter to add new crew members.

Terrell offered to sell me some of his men, but now was not the time to take on the additional risk of untrustworthy soldiers. So we were left with no other choice than to work with the crew we had through the completion of the Solonian contract.

Anyone who was able to work had been assigned to eighteen hour shifts. Even then it wasn't enough. The three functioning engines required constant attention and maintenance. We salvaged as much as we could from the damaged engines and created a cache of spare parts. What we couldn't scavenge we cannibalized from less critical areas of the ship. Morale was brittle, crumbling and falling away like rust from aged iron. I only hoped it would hold out long enough to complete this mission.

I instructed Tank to lead a handful of the crew and patch any gaping holes in our hull, and close off sectors of the ship where the breaches were too large to repair. Reports showed that the lowest two levels sustained the most damage and needed to be permanently sealed before the *Beast's* life support systems were unable to compensate for the loss of pressurization and oxygen. The *Beast* constantly moaned as we drifted across space, leaving me to wonder if she would eventually give up on us.

I tried to piece together what happened, and who was to blame for the sabotage of the ship. If it was Terra, she received help. It was too big of an undertaking for one person to accomplish in such a short period of time. Especially for someone new to the layout of the *Beast*.

Since they didn't directly target the cargo bay, I had to believe they wanted to save the Solonian's goods. If Tompkins were to kill us and deliver the cargo himself, he would win a lifetime of debt and gratitude from the Solonians. The bridge was possibly left untouched in the hope that he could still transport the cargo using the *Beast*; probably the same reason the life support systems were left intact.

I decided that the bridge would become my new home. The first day of our trip, after the explosions, proved uneventful. The eerie quiet added to the stress. We encountered a handful of ships, pirates, and scavenger class vessels. There were a few tense moments during our encounters, but in the end they chose to avoid us. Our massive size was intimidating, and even in her battered state the *Beast* could still tear smaller ships apart with little effort.

Our refueling stop with Terrell was tricky, but successful. Before we departed we were able to procure medical supplies, some scrap steel and titanium, and basic welding torches and cutters. As agreed, he took a few hundred corpses for incineration and seventy-three of the wounded. Another dozen men left under their own volition, believing their chances of making it in the Dark Quarter with Terrell were better than staying on the *Beast*.

It took less than two full days before my officers became a bit edgy as we waited for the hammer to drop down around our already bruised and battered heads. Tank had been unruly at best. Ava was quiet and reserved. She picked up more than her share of the load and was doing her best to fill the role of a leader; the role that Cooper once held. Roger became matter of fact and focused, but at times distant.

My head swam with the thoughts of everything that had happened in such a short period of time. I stared at the letters on my arm. They were there to remind me of who I was, what I had become, and how I got there. What Tompkins and the UG didn't realize was that their tactics wouldn't break me - it fueled me. And soon, my pain would become theirs.

Two jumps remained. It was just a little more than twenty-four hours before we reached our destination on Lotress, and the crew started to eye our success. Three days of uneventful space travel returned the lost feeling of comfort and the swagger we all used to have. Everyone continued to work, passing on sleep and burning off the last of their nervous energy. I was satisfied that things had gone so well, but tempered my feelings. Deep inside it didn't feel right, and I refused to acknowledge a win until the cargo was off my ship and in our contact's hands.

I decided to wait out the rest of our trip in the cargo hold. After a few days on the bridge with Roger, I felt as though I had worn out my welcome. I paced around the towers of crates until Ava approached me from across the room. Her face was a welcome sight.

"Maxx, don't you want to open just one of these?" Ava said as she slid her hand across the smooth wood of one of the crates. "Just to know what's inside that's causing us so much trouble."

"More than you know," I said. She stood at the center of the cargo bay floor where a dozen individual crates rested. Crew members were weaving between them, slowly moving the crates to the other side of the bay and away from the damaged hull. I walked over to her, brushing my fingertips across the lids.

"Tompkins must really want the favor of the Solonians."

"We still don't know that it was Tompkins."

Curled locks spilled in front of Ava's face as she cocked her head at me. "Who else would it be?"

I shrugged my shoulders. "We've been traveling for three days untouched. You weren't able to find any tracking devices. Who knows?

Tompkins isn't the only one that wants me dead. Maybe someone tried to take us out and didn't get the job done. Either way, I'm betting they're still on the ship."

"What would make you think that?" Ava's head was still tilted at the floor, but her eyes scanned the towers of crates as if she expected to see someone jump out from behind them. "You're not sold on the fact that it was Terra?"

"I don't know. There was something about Terra. It just doesn't seem to fit. You wouldn't cause all of this damage and then just run. There has to be more to it that we're just not seeing."

"I think your bond with Terra was based off of your friendship with Cooper and her slave past. If you don't mind me saying so, I don't think your head is clear. Everything that happened on the *Beast* since we've been back leads to her."

"I do mind," I said.

Ava didn't back down. She stepped up to me, her sharp chin jutted out and her finger pointed at my chest. "You claim you don't care, pushing your "me first" attitude on all of us. Maybe it fools them, but I can see through it, Maxx. You've changed. I see the compassion and pain. The hurt you feel because of the loss of Cooper and Liriana. It's your past that drives —"

"If there's going to be a fight, I want in," Tank shouted from across the cargo bay, his hands cupped around his mouth. He entered through the access hatch across the room, avoiding the buckled passageway where the explosives were detonated. He rolled his head around on his shoulders as he approached.

"Looks like things are heating up over here," Tank said as he rubbed his hands together. Ava flashed him a sideways glance and walked away.

"Looks like you saved me, Tank," I said as I watched Ava leave the cargo bay. "How did everything go?"

"Lower three levels are welded shut and air tight."

"Three? I thought that we determined that we only needed to close off the bottom two?"

"Yeah." Tank nodded his head. "That was the original plan, but the damage was worse than we thought, and I needed one more level to contain the breach."

"That seals off the officer sleeping quarters and weapons storage."

"Yup, pretty much." Tank yawned. "It's not like anyone has any time to sleep anyway. I removed as many of the weapons as I could before we sealed it off." Tank stretched and his glassy eyes watered at the corners. "Anyway, I didn't come down here to talk about my welding skills. Roger said he needs you on the bridge."

"For what?"

"Not sure. He seemed a little panicked. Even more than usual. He said he's been paging you for a couple hours." Tank looked around the cargo bay. "Coms must be out down here."

I closed my eyes and shook my head. "Thanks," I said. "Things sound like they're looking up." My sarcastic tone wasn't wasted on Tank. He smirked then slapped me on the shoulder.

"I had a few men organize what's left of our weapons," Tank said. "I'm headed over to get a final count now." Tank's voice was swallowed up by the cavernous cargo bay as I headed toward the tunnel to the bridge. "Looks like some of the repairs on the *Beast's* gun turrets were successful. We have four usable laser cannons…" I gave him a thumbs-up as I walked away.

When I reached the bridge, Tucker was pacing outside the door like a child just banished from the grown-up's room.

"What's going on?" I asked.

"Don't know," Tucker said as he bit off the tips of his fingernails then spit them onto the deck. "We received a broadcast message then Roger kicked me out."

"Take some time to get something to eat, and get some rest. You've done a great job filling in, Tucker."

Tucker nodded, but it was obvious he didn't want to leave. "Raise me on the coms when you need me back up here. I don't feel comfortable leaving my post." He crossed his arms in front of his chest and nervously rubbed his shoulders, then headed down the passageway.

I watched Tucker disappear around the bend in the hall, then I processed the ID scans and entered the bridge. The lights on the consoles and panels were dimmed to a faint glow. The forward monitor was turned on, flooding the room with flickering, blue static. I stood next to Roger, but he didn't acknowledge me. His face was solemn, his gaze fixed on the screen.

He spoke the moment I sat down on the commander's chair. "We received a message a couple of hours ago." His eyes never left the display mounted a few feet above his head.

"Ok," I said, "play it."

"I want to be honest with you first, Commander. I almost deleted it. I wanted to, and still believe that I should have." Roger's body language was foreign to me, uncomfortably so. "But it's not my call."

"Play it," I repeated.

He hesitated as if he wanted to buy himself a little more time to think. "The video feed was heavily encrypted with an algorithm I've never encountered before. The broadcast stream was broken apart into multiple containers, each encrypted with its own key, then compressed back into a single file. I was able to hack it and piece it back together, some of it, to make it at least partially viewable. The quality is poor at best, and without months to work on it, this will be the cleanest it will get." Roger leaned forward to the communications panel and tapped the screen. The flickering blue washed away leaving the outline of a person, partially concealed by heavy pixilation and waves of interference. The picture was horrible, but the figure was unmistakable - Liriana.

The video froze sporadically throughout the message. The audio was choppy, missing words and phrases, and changed pitch without warning. Through all the visual noise, I could see her eyes, heavy and sad. Her weary face. She would talk for short bursts, turn to look behind her then continue with her broadcast. Her delivery was rushed, and her voice elevated.

"This message......Maxx......crew of the Beast. It's only......before our......contact with...... You need to know......allowing us to...... Tracking has been easy......ship is repaired...... Rothet is...lead away from... You......flush......well too late. ......this was......deal...... Cooper......but it...... Understand that......signed up...... You need to......do whatever you......for the safety......trust of others......Maxx, I'm......right all......JaC are too.....sorry...... I'm dying."

As if to intentionally provide additional torment, the video feed finished and froze on a clear image. An image that showed Liriana's face and her warm, brown eyes welling up with tears. The words 'I'm dying' played in my head, over and over. The audio ceased, and the picture faded, flooding the bridge in a shower of blue. I sat, rubbing my arm as I stared at the monitor.

"It's too unintelligible to be of much use," Roger said. I didn't respond. My teeth were clenched and I dug my fingers into the MXX letters inked into my right forearm. Roger continued. "I was afraid that you would read more into this than you should."

"Is that so?" I asked.

"Commander, I know how emotionally tied you are to Liriana," Roger said. "May I speak freely?"

"Why not?"

Roger knew I didn't mean it, but he continued anyway. "Against my better judgment, I'm going to say what I feel needs to be said. I'm afraid that you will make a rash decision based on what you just saw; a decision that could have a drastic effect on this mission, and the lives of the crew."

"Play it again," I said, my eyes hadn't left their vigil on the forward monitor.

"I didn't delete it out of respect of your command, but I don't see a reason to play it again. There isn't any useful information to be had in the transmission."

"I won't ask you again."

Roger released a sigh, placed the video into a loop, and leaned back in his chair. I don't know how many times I watched it - five, maybe ten. For the first few viewings I was sucked into the emotion of it, but over time I separated my feelings from the message itself. It was broadcasted with intent, with a meaning.

Roger pretended he wasn't paying attention as he scanned the ship's readouts and status updates. But I saw his eyes work to the corner of their sockets and his left ear tilted toward the speakers. He was just as invested in this message as I was. Liriana was a reliable and respected team member for years, and most of the crew, like Roger, resented the fact that I banished her.

I finally had enough, terminated the recording and slumped into the chair. "What do you think it means?" I asked.

"It's tough to say," Roger said as he continued to make himself look disinterested by reviewing the ships status reports.

"Damn it, Roger! Tell me what you think!"

"Who knows what the message means. There are too many pieces missing to even start to decipher it. All we know is that it was meant for us by the reference to your name and the *Beast*." Roger didn't try to hide his anger. He wanted to help her. He wanted to understand why she would reach out to us. But he couldn't hack the encryption, and inside, a small piece of him must have felt like he was letting her down.

"She mentions Cooper. Why Cooper? She also addresses contact, tracking, and safety. I know her message could have infinite meanings, but did she send this broadcast to warn us that Tompkins is tracking us down?"

"How the hell would I know?" Roger lashed out.

"Compose yourself!" I snapped back. "She wouldn't go through the trouble to send this if it didn't mean something important. Look at her face, damn it! Something bad is happening to her, and it may be because she's trying to help us!"

Roger sat quietly, his fingers curled together in his lap as if to hold them back from nervously working the panels. His chin was buried in his sunken chest and his eyes watched his right thumb rub across the top of his left hand.

"Liriana meant everything to me and Sarah. When you dropped her from the team, when you abandoned her, it was like you took my daughter from me and sentenced her to death." Roger looked up at me, his face drawn and white.

"I don't expect that you would understand why I did it," I said. "It was my call, and it was the right one. Everything I do is in the best interest of our current and future missions."

"Really, Commander? It was business then? Sometimes I wonder if that decision was based on what was best for *you*."

The room, now only filled with the noise of an electronic hum, became a tomb of uncomfortable silence. Roger wanted to delete the message, but couldn't. He cared about our crew and knew our only chance of survival was completing our mission. He knew Liriana's message would be a distraction, but he couldn't turn his back on her. She was family.

Roger broke the silence. "Is she really dying? Is that true?"

I nodded. "She over-JaCed and those implants are ravaging her body. They're slowly draining the life from her."

"How much time does she have?"

"I don't know," I replied. "I could help her if she'd let me."

Roger's eyes brightened. "How?"

I rubbed my arm. "I just can, Roger. Let's leave it at that."

Roger ran his fingers through his bushy hair and scratched at the back of his head. "My guess," Roger said, "and it's only a guess, is that Tompkins is closing in on us." He worked his hands from the back of his head and down to his shoulders where he started to rub. "She mentioned tracking, which I assume means that they are tracking the *Beast*. However, Ava confirmed that she was unable to locate any tracking devices and Tompkins' destroyer is not showing up on any of our sensors. Assuming there's moderate distance between our ships, it would take a tracking device of considerable size to broadcast our location. Something large enough that it would be difficult, if not impossible, to hide and to power. So I doubt they're using a device."

"A person then?"

Roger nodded. "Terra before she left? Maybe she's still here or it's somebody else. I've been watching the cameras the best I can, and I asked Tank and Ava to keep their eyes open for anyone or anything that appeared suspicious. We all came up empty. I followed your orders and was careful not to share any more information with the crew than what we had to."

"If someone on this ship is in contact with Tompkins now, it's too late anyway." I sighed and leaned forward in my chair. "Everyone on this ship knows our destination, but only you and I know the path. At least we have that."

"I agree that's a huge advantage, but let's assume for a moment that Tompkins knows our destination as well. It would make us much easier to locate. Maybe they set the explosives on our ship with a deliberate plan. They may know the extent of damage to our engines allowing them to make certain assumptions about our path, calculating our need to refuel while still avoiding as much risk as possible."

"I think that you're giving Tompkins way too much credit," I replied. "Besides, it's not Tompkins I'm worried about. It's Rothet – at least if he's still alive."

Roger raised an eyebrow. "Who is this Rothet? I noticed that Liriana mentioned him in her broadcast."

"It's a long story. He's a hired hand for Tompkins but he's more than just an assassin." I shook my head as if to clear out the cluttered thoughts. "There's something about him. Something I can't put my finger on."

Roger offered an accepting nod then changed the subject. "And what about Liriana's apology and her mention of Cooper?"

"I don't know. Maybe she's sorry that she joined Tompkins' team? Maybe she was reaching out to Cooper for some reason? I just don't know."

Roger furrowed his brow and sighed. "All speculation I suppose. There's no way I can break the encryption further. What we just saw is the most information we're going to get."

I rose from the commander's chair and gently patted Roger on his shoulder. "You did the right thing. Hang in there. This will all be over soon." As I started to walk toward the bridge door, Roger called out.

"And if Tompkins or this Rothet does attack us, what then?"

I paused, confused by his question. "What do you mean? We've already discussed a plan."

"If they attack, what about Liriana?" Roger said as his voice cracked. "We can't leave her. Not again."

I stood motionless as I searched for the right answer, but never found it. My hand scanned the biometric access panel on the door and I stepped from the dimly lit bridge into the flood of lights in the outside passage. The door closed behind me with a whir, leaving me standing alone in the hall, troubled by a new set of demons I may soon have to confront.

I was called back to the bridge only a few of hours after I'd left. Our biggest fear had become a reality. Tompkins was readying his attack.

Roger, Tucker, and I were drowned in the spray of the bridge's red emergency lights. The attack from Tompkins was about to occur, less than fourteen hours before we reached our drop point on Lotress. His destroyer was showing on our tracking sensors, and he was no longer making an attempt to conceal his ship, or his intentions. They were closing in on us fast, and they would be within targeting distance in less than fifteen minutes. The *Beast's* three remaining engines were fully engaged, yet Tompkins' destroyer was closing the gap between us as if we were standing still.

We had to wait two more hours before we could activate the remaining hyperdrive. We couldn't jump again. We couldn't outrun them. Our only chance was to shoot our way out of this. There was no doubt that the *Beast*, in her current state, wouldn't be able to match the firepower of their destroyer, so our luck rested on being able to land a few shots that could slow, or incapacitate his ship.

The *Beast* was equipped with twelve laser cannons, all of which were damaged by the saboteur. Tank was able to part them out and get four of the twelve cannons back online. I made the decision to disable the auto-fire and auto-targeting options and deployed four of our best remaining marksmen to manually operate them. One of the four was Tank, and I assigned the leadership of those men to him. Though the targeting speed of the cannons would be greatly reduced with human intervention, it erased any and all predictability on what they chose to fire upon and when. Tompkins wouldn't be able to set his defenses based on an algorithm that predicted the *Beast's* firing patterns.

Our laser cannons are focus beams, not pulse beams. When engaged, they emit a solid stream of laser fire that stretches from the tip of the barrel into infinity. They consume a massive amount of power which limits the duration of the stream, but once locked onto an enemy ship they're deadly.

Tompkins' was executing a well-planned strategy. We were in a desolate section of the Dark Quarter that's rarely traveled. There would be no interference here from the UG or scavengers, no pirates to swoop in at the end of the battle to pick through our remains. I was confident that Tompkins had been tracking us since the first day I set foot back on my ship, waiting for this exact moment to pounce.

I didn't know what to expect from Tompkins, so I prepared for as many scenarios as possible. We spread what men we had left across the ship to guard against a forced breach and the boarding of enemy troops; pinning our hopes of survival on deck hands and cargo personnel hastily converted into soldiers.

Our cargo hold was secured as best we could. The crates were restrained with extra canvas straps, nets, and steel bar locks to avoid any shifting or falling. We armed half a dozen men and placed them inside the bay to guard the cargo and protect the injured soldiers that remained aboard the ship. All of the pass codes for the doors were disabled, and we configured the readers to accept biometric scans only. All general access and transport passageways that led to the cargo bay were sealed with temporary tack welds on the doors.

Roger continued to pilot the ship, but to my surprise he allowed Tucker to take an active role in the defensive maneuvers. That scared me. Since the loss of Sarah, Roger hadn't willingly accepted another pilot's help, which told me that we were in for a very rough fight. One that Roger couldn't handle alone. It would be Roger's skill that would get us through this, but Tucker would play a key part with ship positioning and flight adjustments.

I hated space battles because I was out of my element. I was forced to rely on the skills of others, their fortitude and courage. My knives and blasters served no use, and the outcome was largely out of my control.

"We have less than ten minutes before engagement," Roger said.

I picked up my com and broadcasted a message to Tank and the other three marksmen. "Is everyone ready?"

"Yeah, we're ready," Tank said, then cleared his throat. "Between us,

Maxx, four cannons, running on limited power, are useless against a destroyer.

"We aren't going to win a shootout. Do what you can to disable their ship. Focus your fire on their engines, thrusters, and any visible cannons. I know it won't be easy, but we're all counting on you."

There were a few seconds of silence on the other end of the com. "Tell Roger to give us some decent firing angles. We'll do what we can."

I ended our conversation then held the com against my chest. I could feel the pounding of my heart. I had one more message, and this one was for the remaining crew of the *Beast*. "Everyone, I've asked you to prepare for what may be one of our toughest battles to date. In a few minutes we'll be standing toe-to-toe with a ship that is far superior to ours in every capacity, save one - the crew. We all understand the risks of our professions and the potential outcome of our failures. The rewards of our successes have kept most of you in my employment, but today we fight for our lives. We fight for each other. I ask you to stand strong and help your fellow soldier. Today is our day to write yet another storied chapter in our history. And like all our other battles, and all of our other missions, we will win. We know no other way." I disengaged the com.

Now was the time for all of us to act, to prove our worth and show our resolve when our backs were pinned against the wall. Tompkins was chasing a wounded animal that could no longer run, and now must battle to survive. We were about to find out if he was ready for the fight of his life.

The panels covering the meter-thick circular bridge windows were retracted, allowing us a full, unfettered view of the dark expanse of space. For a moment I was lost in its beauty. It drew me in like a child gazing up at the flickering stars on a clear night. When I was young I dreamed of this opportunity, to roam freely, untethered, uncontrolled, and living by my own volition. If I were to die today, I wouldn't have had it any other way.

"Less than two minutes until engagement." Roger broadcasted his message over the ship-wide communication system.

Silence devoured the bridge. Even the engines seemed quieter as if not to alert Tompkins of our location. The light of the stars dotted the darkness of space around us with their burning life, illuminating our path and helping us locate our enemy. And there they were, just off the portside of our ship. The heat from their white-blue afterburners was spotted in the distance as errant beams of starlight reflected off of the ship's titanium shell. The brightness of their afterburners calmed and dulled, and the starlight reflection off of the destroyer's hull changed to a stomach wrenching orange. They were firing on us.

The lasers punched their way through our plating and ripped sections of steel from our hull. A trail of metal broke free and spread out behind us, swirling in our wake.

"Close the bridge panels!" I shouted. Tucker was quick to follow my order. The panels ground together as they closed, rubbing steel on steel and interlocking at the midpoint of the glass. Roger initiated the battle ready sequence that plunged our ship into a darkened state, save some sparse pockets of backup lights and the flashing white and red emergency alarms. Initializing a battle ready state conserves all power for bridge functions, engines, life support, and cannons. Power is rerouted from everything deemed less critical unless it's manually rerouted, or until the battle-ready state is aborted.

"They're firing again!" Roger shouted. "Defensive maneuvers!"

Beads of sweat formed just above Tucker's arched brow. His look was a jumble of nerves, but his eyes were focused on the monitors, his hands were steady, and he performed like a professional. He adjusted power to the thrusters and exposed our underbelly just in time to take the incoming fire into our ship's lowest level.

I gritted my teeth. "Those weren't warning shots or tests to check our defenses. Those were fired with the clear intent of doing us in." I turned to Tucker. "Do your best to take all incoming fire into the lower levels."

Another volley of orange death lanced silently through the void of space and acknowledged its audible presence as it tore through a new section of our hull. The *Beast* rocked under the impact. Our lower levels were deteriorating into loose pieces of scrap metal. It wouldn't be long before our makeshift shield was sheered from our ship.

"We need your help!" Tank announced to the bridge using the ship's com system. "You have to draw them in closer before we fire back. These cannons don't have much juice available, and we need to make every shot count."

"We can absorb one, maybe two more direct hits," Roger said, "then we'll start to expose the meat of our ship."

"Deactivate the cannons topside and route all their power to the lower cannons," I ordered.

"Why power them down? " Tank asked with a hint of confusion. "That leaves us vulnerable topside."

"Exactly," I said. "I don't want anyone firing on the destroyer until I give the word. Roger, draw him in with defensive maneuvers. You know the areas of the ship we need to protect. Sacrifice the rest as needed."

The next few minutes were a display of keen reflexes and years of piloting intuition. The *Beast* wasn't a nimble vessel, especially in her damaged state, so evading oncoming laser fire was a true masterpiece in piloting. At the end of the last barrage, our hull absorbed the punishment of four more bursts of laser fire; one partial blow and three direct hits into our lower levels. The last blast rippled through the *Beast* with such crippling force that I was worried about the integrity of our hull. She couldn't take much more.

"Fire once from the lower cannons," I said.

"We don't have any line of sight on their ship," one of the marksmen said.

"I don't care. Fire!"

We fired two shots at the destroyer, neither of which came close to finding their target. We looked desperate, vulnerable, wounded, and without options. Tompkins must have bought into our apparent panic and ordered his pilots to shorten the distance between us to deliver their finishing blow. They adjusted their flight path just as our systems acknowledged their remote scans of the *Beast's* weaponry. Once they identified the two functioning cannons on the lower levels, they redirected the path of their destroyer directly over the top of the *Beast*. What their scans didn't detect were the two deactivated cannons mounted on the top, until it was much too late.

"Reroute all power to the cannons topside!" I ordered. "Tank, it's your turn now!"

Tank and crew opened fire and didn't disappoint. Both cannons found their target, cutting, melting and shredding the main thrusters and engine compartments of the destroyer. Our beams were locked onto Tompkins' ship and burned through the titanium with ease like paper on fire. The emergency lights dimmed, and the controls in the bridge flickered as the cannons sucked the power from the *Beast*.

They lowered the position of their ship and out of view of our topside cannons. Tompkins' returned a volley of fire. Seams split in the hull then metal plates slowly peeled away from the body of the *Beast*. Our ship looked like a lizard shedding its scaly hide as a stream of debris followed in our wake. Another round of laser fire hit us hard, rocked our ship, fluttered our lights, and converted the smooth hum of the engines to a gasping wheeze.

"We lost two more engines," Roger said as he scanned the status reports. "Fires have started in each compartment. The remaining engine will overload soon."

"Can we seal the rooms to contain the fires?" I asked. "The fuel stores…"

From the status monitor, I watched smoke pour from the engine rooms and spill into our lower compartments as the engines caught fire. The fires roared, fueled by the synthesized oxygen that pumped through the ventilation system, and ignited the hyperdrives' fuel tanks. Each engine room exploded in succession, punching gaping holes through the sides of our hull.

"Clear out all personnel and seal the engine rooms!" I ordered.

"We have to save the last one!" Roger yelled back.

"Forget the engine! There isn't anything we can do. Clear out those men!"

"I know the ship better than anyone else. If I can get to the engine room in time I can recalibrate the last engine's synchronization patterns. We can save it!"

"Stand down, Roger. There won't be anything left to repair."

Roger's eyes grew wider as he spoke. "If I just sit here, we're all dead!"

"If I lose you down there, we're dead anyway," I said as I picked up the com. "Tank, we're out of options on the bridge. If there's anything you can do, do it now."

"Maxx," Tank replied with a heavy voice, "unless he puts his ship back into our line of fire, there isn't a thing we can do. We have enough power for a single shot, but with the recent damage we can't reroute power to the lower cannons. If we can't turn the ship, I have no line of sight."

Tompkins' ship fired once more into the remaining engine room, disintegrating the compartment under a series of loud and violent explosions. The *Beast* floated aimlessly like a ship at sea, drifting forward, fueled only by our momentum.

"Do you want me to raise communications with their ship?" Tucker asked as he chewed on the inside of his cheek.

"No," I replied. "Keep us silent. There isn't anything I could say that would change his mind or his actions."

Our enemy hovered near us as if to savor his victory. The destroyer looked like a predator eyeing its kill, toying with us, waiting for us to squirm just one more time before it delivered the finishing blow. Our only option was to wait for that final strike to come.

"Activate all of the remaining cameras and route their feeds to the forward monitors," I said as I sat on the commander's chair. "There's nothing left to do but wait."

Seconds turned into minutes, minutes into an hour. Then, after the long wait, one of the destroyer's shuttles ejected from the underside of his ship and hurled toward us. The direction of the shuttle was deliberate, and though its purpose was unknown, it was obvious that it wasn't looking to dock. Its trajectory was off course and it wasn't slowing as it neared my ship. It was spinning at a high rate of speed when it struck the *Beast*, wrenching itself through the hull and twisting its way into the side of our ship like a screw into wood. It finally stopped with nearly half of the pod buried inside of the *Beast*.

"Explosives?" Roger questioned.

"Maybe," I said, "but why? He could've finished us off with laser fire."

A second shuttle was launched, then a third. Both collided with our ship and penetrated the hull. The thrusters on Tompkins' destroyer lit space with a dirty blue as it slowly turned away from us. Tompkins' ship drifted until the thrusters burned a greenish hue; the hyperdrives were activated and they were ready to make a jump. That slight bit of movement was all that Tank needed. The greenish hue was suddenly lost under a wash of red light; our lasers cut through the back of their destroyer and into their engines and hyperdrives.

Tompkins' destroyer initiated the jump sequence, but it was too late. Under a belch of smoke and a spray of glowing metal shards, the destroyer lurched forward then listed sideways as it attempted to carry out the jump. The green hue faded as the hyperdrives disengaged and went offline. Their exit was careless, and Tank's marksmanship set off an eruption of celebration throughout the ship.

I eased back into the commander's chair as the *Beast* groaned around me. Oxygen sputtered through the vents with a choking wheeze and the lights in the bridge flickered and dimmed. Roger retracted the panels from the windows but they came to a grinding stop after opening less than a couple of meters. The darkness of space peered into the bridge, ready to finish the job that Tompkins couldn't.

Our battle was over. Tompkins' destroyer coasted from our position at a speed that indicated severe damage to his engines. His remaining thruster spit a flickering, dull-blue light. As it limped away from combat, the fear that engulfed my crew was washed away by a collective feeling of relief. I knew better. Our situation was desperate.

I called Tank and Ava to the bridge to meet with Roger, Tucker, and me. Tank entered the bridge with a smile extending from ear to ear. He crushed me in an animalistic hug and tossed me onto the commander's chair.

Roger stood and approached Tank. "Now that, my friend, was some very precise shooting."

"Woohoo!" Tank screamed as he grabbed Roger by his thin shoulders. He shook him so hard I was worried his head would snap off. "Couldn't have done it without you, bud! Best damn pilot in the galaxy!" Roger cracked a rare smile and cupped Tank's hand to accept his congratulations.

"Give some credit to Tucker," Roger said. "It was his quick maneuvers that saved us all."

"Are we just going to sit around here all night stroking each other?" Ava asked. "If so, I've got things to do."

"Wow, what's the deal?" Tank said, drunk on a JaC induced surge of adrenaline. He let out a few more primal screams then rubbed Roger's hair until it was a snarled mess atop his head. When Ava didn't soften her stance, he started to approach her with his arms wide open. "Do you need a hug?"

"Take one more step toward me and see what happens," Ava said with a scowl. Her hand was wound around the grip of her pistol, the safety strap unbuckled and hanging to the side. "We've got people dead and dying from the attack and you celebrate like we've won something."

"I saved your sorry ass!" Tank shot back.

"Enough!" I shouted. "As much as I would like to say this is over, it isn't." I scanned the room, staring each of them down. "Tompkins had us dead to rights, but he let us go."

"He probably had weapon failures," Tank said.

"Not likely," Roger said, attempting to smooth his hair. "Our active scans reported full functionality on seven of his cannons including rotation, targeting, and auto tracking as well as sufficient power stores."

"He disabled our ship," Ava said. "Isn't that what he was looking to do all along?"

"If he just wanted to disable our ship for the cargo, he would've boarded us. Instead, he engaged his hyperdrives and was activating a jump." Roger shook his head from side to side. "He wasn't planning on docking us."

"His attack was deliberate and intentional," I said as I paced between the crew. "Whatever he was looking to do, he accomplished. Our biggest concern is what's in the pods that are lodged in our ship." I turned to Roger. "First, give us the damage report."

Roger gave up on his hair and cleared his throat. "There's no way that I can soften the blow, so I am just going to give you the facts…and they aren't pretty." The front facing monitor lowered under a cascade of sparks. The data was fed through the overhead com by the *Beast's* health monitoring system, accompanied by the detailed visuals of each major finding on the screen. The report was grim:

- *Engine One: Offline. Repair not possible.*
- *Engine Two: Offline. Repair not possible.*
- *Engine Three: Offline. Repair not possible.*
- *Engine Four: Disabled.*
- *Engine Five: Offline. Repair not possible.*
- *Engine Six: Offline. Repair not possible.*
- *Engine Seven: Offline. Repair not possible.*
- *Engine Eight: Offline. Repair not possible.*
- *Hyperdrive One: Offline. Repair not possible.*
- *Hyperdrive Two: Offline. Repair not possible.*
- *Fuel Stores: Fuel tanks lost. Fuel storage depleted.*

- *Docking Gear: Damaged. Repair not possible.*
- *Life Support Systems: Damaged. Sustaining current functionality on battery reserves.*
- *Hull Integrity Check: Level one breach. Repair not possible. Level two breach. Repair not possible. Severe damage to levels three, four, and five. Hull breaches in sectors two, seven, thirteen, and seventeen. Severe damage to levels fourteen and thirteen. Hull breaches in sectors seven and eight.*
- *Laser Cannons: Eight disabled. Four functional. Insufficient power stores for activation.*
- *Emergency Shuttles: One launched. Four damaged. Eleven functional units. One hundred and ten seats available.*

The ship's status reading was delivered like a surprise punch to the solar plexus, leaving everyone unable to breathe and gasping to regain composure. Damaged hyper chambers, lack of firepower, no maneuverability, no defensive measures - the list went on, and on, and on. Unfortunately, things were about to get worse.

"Roger," I said, "shut it down." Roger turned off the audio and video feeds without the slightest protest from anyone standing in the bridge. "Now give us the bad news."

"Fuck me," Tank said. He buried his face in his hands.

"The three modified shuttles that were launched from Tompkins' destroyer have fused themselves into the hull of the *Beast*," Roger said. He activated a live video feed of one of the pods and displayed it on the monitor. A solid two-thirds of the bulky shuttle had wrenched its way through the hull of the *Beast* and was still glowing molten hot around its edges. It looked like a bullet, freshly fired from the barrel of a gun, its metal body buried deep into the side of its target.

Zooming in on the image, Roger highlighted reinforced armor and surface welds that covered the shuttle. "Based on the initial review, it appears that Tompkins took extra steps to make sure we couldn't get access to the insides of these pods."

"Wonderful," Ava said. She chuckled nervously as she continued. "Are they filled with explosives?"

"Logically one would think, but that's not the case." Roger spun his chair to face us. "Each is equipped with a military-grade distress beacon - and all three are active."

"So, he disables our ship then leaves us beacons calling for help?" Tank asked. "Now that's fucked up."

I shook my head. "These distress signals are worse than explosives," I said. "Maybe worse than Tompkins' army of goons boarding our ship." I fielded a number of confused looks as I continued. "We're trapped, drifting in space with a cargo hold full of illegal Solonian goods. We can't activate our engines or jump into another sector. We're forced to sit here and wait for the Unified Governments to send us a welcoming committee."

"He never wanted our cargo," Ava said. Her voice trailed off as she spoke.

I nodded. "Maybe he got a better deal from the UG. By disabling our ship, he delivers the Solonian goods, and us."

Tucker's eyes widened. "We need to dump the cargo."

"And where would it go?" I asked. "We dump it into space and most of the crates will drift right along with us." I took in a deep breath. The muscles in my neck and back tensed as I continued. "If Tompkins is working with the UG, we have to assume he's already reported our location. The beacons are his insurance in the event we're able to move our ship."

"What about Terrell?" Ava asked.

"We've already been in communication with his ship. No matter how many credits I offer him, he won't touch our cargo."

"How long do we have before the UG is knocking on our cargo bay door?" Tank asked.

"To give you an exact number would be presumptuous as there are too many unknowns," Roger said.

"Just guess!" Tank roared.

"Our current position in the Dark Quarter is well outside of the UG patrolled sectors, but there's a station not too far from our location. Even if we assume the fastest ship in the Unified Governments' fleet is docked at that station, they won't be able to jump to our position."

"Why?" Ava asked. Her head was cocked to the side and her eyes pinched into a squint.

"They're too close," Roger said. "If they engage a jump they'll overshoot our location." Roger spun in his chair to face the console. He entered some data as he talked. "That's the good news anyway. The bad news is that even if they use standard thrusters they'll be here in under nine hours." Roger spun his chair around once more to face us. "If for any reason they have a ship closer than that, your guess is just as good as mine."

Tank grimaced. "So what's the plan, Maxx?"

"Roger and Tucker, I need you to continue to run ship diagnostics. I need to know what we can salvage and what's beyond our repair, down to the very last wire on the *Beast*. Start with the life support systems and work from there. Tank and Ava, I need you to round up some fusion cutters and open the cargo hold."

"For what?" Tank asked.

"It's time to find out what we're hauling."

The three of us stood under the towers of crates. All five hundred secured behind the extra strapping and steel bar reinforcements. Luckily, the barrage of laser fire from Tompkins' ship hadn't dislodged any from their secure housing.

"This isn't a good idea," Tank said, tugging on his goatee.

"Would you rather that we wait until the UG shows up so they can open them?" I asked.

"What if further ship diagnostics indicate that we're able to repair one of the engines?" Ava asked. "Engine four was reported as disabled. Maybe we should give Roger and Tucker a little time."

"There's no way we'll be able to fix that engine," I said. "We'll be lucky if we can keep the life support systems functioning." I pointed at the stack of crates in front of us. "We need answers, and possibly a bargaining chip. Both are right here."

"You open just one of those up and we're all as good as dead," Tank said. His face appeared pale and worn.

Ava looked at the crates then at me, shrugged her shoulders and turned her palms to the air. "It's your call, Maxx," Ava said. "I'm behind you if you want to open them."

Tank stepped between the crates and me. "Listen, you can't open those damn crates!"

"Look, Tank," I said as I placed my hand on his shoulder. "The Solonians already have death warrants waiting for all of us if we don't complete the mission, and this isn't going to make it any worse. The *Beast* is done. We'll never make it to Lotress in time to meet the deadline. Whatever's inside is going to give us some answers, and as slim as the chance may seem, a possible way out of this mess."

Tank sighed. "There's still a chance for us, and for you, if we leave these things closed. Whatever the hell is in them should stay that way."

"The only hope we have, to save us all, is sitting only meters away from us," I said, pointing at the crates.

"But, Ava has a point," Tank replied. "They could get engine four –"

I waved Tank off mid statement as my anger took over. "It doesn't matter! We're just deadweight, floating defenseless in the Dark Quarter. Let's assume, just for a second, that Roger gets that engine working. We still have three distress beacons fused into our hull and an engine that wouldn't be able to outrun the slowest freighter."

"But…"

I turned to face the cargo hold attendant, who I asked to man the picker, and raised my head upward in acknowledgement. He nodded at my request, lowered three crates from the top of the nearest stack and placed them in front of us. They were plain in appearance; sturdy boxes constructed of smooth wood and secured with metal spikes. The rubber seal around the lid was monitored by a tamper device that was mounted on the side of the crate. A small red light pulsed on and off as if to flash us a warning.

I located a maintenance bar resting on one of the lifts and removed it from its housing. The end of the bar was thin enough that I could push it through the rubber seal and jimmy it between the crate and lid. With a sharp jerk, one of the spikes popped free. The red light on the tamper sensor continued its steady pulse. I worked my way around the lid, lifting each spike free with as much care as possible. Tank and Ava didn't say anything, possibly worried that speaking would force me into making some catastrophic sensor-activating error.

I freed one side of the lid then rested the bar against the crate. I wiped the sweat from my forehead as I spoke. "I wish that the feed from Liriana was clearer. She may have been able to shed some light on this cargo and what we're in for."

Tank stuttered to get out his response. "Feed? What feed are you talking about?"

"She transmitted an encrypted video to our ship less than a day ago. That's why Roger sent you down here with the message to join him on the bridge. It's how we were able to ready ourselves for Tompkins' attack."

Tank's eyes shifted in their sockets as if he was searching for his next question. "What did she say? What was in that feed?"

"A lot, but only a small bit of it was decipherable. Roger was able to decrypt only a part of it, so the video and audio were choppy and incomplete."

"Why the hell didn't you tell us about it?" There was thundering rage building in Tank's voice.

I placed my hands on the lid and stared down Tank.

Ava, not wanting to get involved in the confrontation, picked up the maintenance bar and continued where I'd stopped. "I'll just finish this up," she said.

"Tell me!" Tank demanded and pounded his fist against his chest. "I asked you a question, and I want an answer!"

I stepped up to Tank. The bottom of his goatee stretched to meet my eyes. He looked down at me. The corner of his eyes quivered and his fists were clenched tightly at his sides.

"There wasn't anything in the message of any value," I said. "There was nothing to share."

"The last time I checked, I was an officer of this crew, yet at times you treat me like I'm a grunt." He turned to look at Ava. "Did he tell you?"

"Nope," Ava said, never letting her eyes leave the lid of the crate.

"And doesn't that piss you off?" Tank asked.

Ava didn't reply and kept working to free the lid.

"Whatever," Tank said. "This isn't the first time that you've cut me out of important information. You can't be trusted."

"And what the hell does that mean?" My temper grew to match his.

"Nothing," Tank grumbled, his voice trailing off. "It means nothing…"

"Say it, Tank."

Tank turned and spat. "You're too personally invested in Liriana, Maxx. You can't make any clear decisions about her on your own. You can't be trusted to make the right call when it comes to her." Tank cocked his head to the side, his neck cracking in response. "But it doesn't matter, Maxx. She'll be dead soon and there's nothing any one of us can do." His voice started out as a thunderous boom but by the time he was done speaking, it had trailed off to a barely audible whisper.

My vision tunneled on Tank. "If you ever address me like that again, or question my ability to lead, it will be the last time we work together. Is that understood?"

"By the looks of things, this will be our last time together anyway,"

Tank grumbled. He shifted his feet and took a single step back. His fists were still locked tight and the throbbing veins in his neck moved the collar of his shirt with each beat of his adrenaline-fueled heart.

"Holy shit..." It was Ava. I had been too engaged with Tank to notice she had freed the lid. She stood next to the crate, her arms dangled at her sides and the maintenance bar slowly slipping from her grasp. "Holy shit..." She whispered it under her breath, the two words full of fear and uncertainty. The metal bar struck the cargo room floor with a rattling clang.

"What the hell is it?" Tank asked. Ava stood still, frozen in place.

I had no idea what we had uncovered. Weapons, drugs, counterfeit items, implants, forged credits, precious metals? No matter what it was, I was sure we'd moved it before. When you'd transported as much illegal cargo as we had, the contents no longer shocked you. At least that was what I thought until I examined the inside of the crate.

The sides, bottom, and lid of the crate were lined with an inflatable synthetic plastic. A type of packing material used to seal and cushion its contents. Contained and secured by the bubbled plastic was the emaciated body of an adult male. He was naked, eyelids open and stitched to his brows, his arms pinned to his sides. Flaking stains trailed from the back of his head, leaving dried pools of dark red splattered throughout the crate. The rancid smell of death crept out from inside.

"What that hell?" Tank said, stepping between Ava and me. "What the hell is that? That ain't right."

As I knelt next to the crate my heart pounded like a drum in my chest. The corpse was somewhat preserved but shrunken as if dehydrated. There was no apparent mutilation, blunt force trauma, stab wounds or blaster burns, just a spray of blood around the lining - mostly around his upper torso and head. I picked up his right arm and laid his hand in mine. His joints were stiff, like the mechanical arm of a robot. The ends of his fingers were worn to bloody nubs and small bits of the packing material were wedged under what fingernails remained, scratched free from the lining around the inside of the crate. The rest of his fingernails were broken and lodged in the packing material or scattered in splintered pieces. I turned his arm over to expose a series of branded letters on his forearm.

"Help me roll him over," I said.

The crate was large, but the packing material was inflated to mold to the size of the body. It sealed around the man so tight that there was little room to move or shift. We pealed the skeletal frame from the puddle of dried blood, lifted him, and set him on his side. His arms and legs flopped down like lead weights as we turned the corpse over. There was a long, jagged incision that started at the base of his neck, ran down his spine, and ended at his lower back. It was sporadically stitched with a thick thread, not enough to stop the bleeding, but enough to keep his skin from peeling away from his back.

"Ava, go get John," I said. "He should be treating the wounded on the other end of the cargo bay." I tore the tamper sensor off the side of the crate. There were no wires connected and no active sensors to monitor the lid. The light continued its slow, steady beat. It was a fake. "Tank, help me open another crate."

I jammed the maintenance bar under the lid of the second box, lifted and pried two of the long metal spikes free. Tank growled under his breath, shoved his fingers between the gap in the lid and crate, and tore half of the lid free. With a few more pulls he fully opened the crate, tossing the sections of the splintered lid to the deck. Inside was a second corpse, a female with an enumerated forearm. We rolled her to the side to get a clear view of a wickedly long slice from the base of her neck to the small of her back. Her skin was puckered and haphazardly sewn together to hold it in place.

"The other one," I said. Tank exchanged a quiet look with me then dragged the crate in front of us. He bumped the other two aside and dropped it at my feet with a thump. We tore through the lid with less care than the last. Inside was another copy of the same, a dead body displaying a gruesome visage.

Ava returned with John trailing behind. His aged body was forced to carry his excess weight, and the run made his already rough voice winded and short.

"What do you need?" John wheezed. John was far from a doctor, but he understood the human body better than anyone else on my ship. Now just a cargo hand in my crew, his previous job was a torturer in the UG military. He'd seen things that would give people nightmares, and done things he'd regret until the day he dies.

"The Solonian cargo is nothing but dead bodies," I said. "I need you to analyze them, tell me how and why they were killed."

John was so winded that he took a knee in front of the crates to catch his breath. He arched his eyebrow as he peered inside one of the crates. "Not sure I'll be able to help, but I'll try." His nose puckered as he drew in the wafting stench of the rotting corpses. He pushed his way to his feet, covered his mouth and stepped back.

"What the hell is going on here, Maxx?" Ava asked.

"They're all slaves," I said. "Look at their forearms. Each of them is clearly marked. The incisions are the same on each, but I don't know what they're for." I raised the arm of one of the corpses then fanned out his fingers. The tips were crusted with blood and wore down to bloody stumps. "They were alive when they were packed in these crates. This one tried to claw his way out."

Ava covered her mouth and talked through her fingers. "And each one of these crates holds a human body." She rubbed her forehead and scanned the towers of crates that lined our cargo hold. "Five hundred corpses..."

"What if they're diseased?" Tank asked.

"If they are, then we're infected," I said. "The crates were sealed well enough with the rubber lining around the lid and this synthetic material to keep the rotting smell inside, but if they're carrying any disease it's been propagating through our ventilation system for months. If they're carriers, we've got whatever they have."

"I don't know how long they've been dead," John said in a rough, raspy tone, "but I can confirm that what the Commander said is true. They were sealed inside of these crates while still alive." John talked into a crate as he continued to examine one of the bodies. "More than likely they were alive when we took these crates from the Solonians."

My stomach rolled. Very few things rattled me, but the idea that we were hauling living people for days, eventually dying from lack of food, water, air or medical attention, was sickening.

I balled my hands into fists as I stared at the rows of crates; my cargo hold had transitioned into a morgue for five hundred people. The first three were UG slaves harvested from various systems across the galaxy, cut for some gruesome reason, and stuffed into crates. I had no reason to believe that the others would be any different. The evil of the Solonian Government knew no bounds.

"Why didn't they shout out for help, kick the damn lids, or rattle the sides of the crates?" I asked. "If only one of them would have done that, maybe we could've saved hundreds."

"I can't tell you for sure," John replied. "Maybe they were drugged? I don't know. I need more time to take a closer look at these corpses and incisions."

"John, that's your number one priority," I said. "Ava, I need you to work with Roger to find out how many of our crew he can spare. Get as many as you can and open every last one of these crates."

She squinted her eyes shut and drew in a deep breath. "Will do," she said.

"Anyone repairing the ship's life support systems or tending to the wounded are off limits. Everyone else should be down here working as hard and as fast as they can to open those crates. Understood?"

Ava acknowledged me with a tip of her head before lighting up her com.

I motioned to Tank. He stepped out of the sea of corpses and walked toward me. His face wore a look of concern. I figured it was as if I was staring into a mirror, not looking much different myself.

"Are you OK?" I asked.

He paused, almost as if he was searching for the right response. "Yeah, I'm fine." He peered over his shoulder then back at me. "This is the most fucked up thing I've ever seen."

I took another glance at the towers of death, stacked and secured in our cargo bay. "You and me both." I placed a hand on his massive shoulder and raised the fake tamper sensor in my other. "And to make things worse, we've been set up."

I summoned Tank, Ava, and John to meet with me, Roger, and Tucker on the bridge. Our moods were as dark as the dimly lit room.

"I'll need information, and everyone's input." I stroked the stubble on my face and massaged the knot out of my neck. "John, you're first. Tell us what you've found."

"I had a chance to analyze a few dozen bodies, and the story is the same with each." John's voice wavered as he talked; a disturbing sound from a man that used to induce terror for a living. "There's a deep incision along their spinal cords, and a number of smaller incisions at the base of their necks and lower backs."

"I doubt someone just carved them up for fun," Tank said.

John shook his head. "No, it was with a purpose. A distinct purpose." John turned over his hand and opened his palm to display the broken remains of a JaC. "At one time, they were all JaCed. Every one of them. I found this broken piece embedded in one of their spines."

"So they killed them and removed their JaCs?" Ava furrowed a brow. "That doesn't seem like a profitable enough venture for the Solonians."

"These were all poor and worthless slaves...," John said. He stopped mid-sentence and glanced up at me then lowered his eyes. "Expendables. These slaves weren't JaCed up on their own. I believe the Solonians were conducting experiments."

"What do you mean?" I asked.

"All of them were loaded with JaCs. At the base of their back, neck, and along the spine. At least a dozen per person. Maybe more. The tracks of the implants are scored into their bones and the nerve ending attachments are still clearly visible. Other than this fragment, all of the JaCs are gone. They were removed before they sealed them in the crates."

"Why?" I asked through gritted teeth.

"I don't know. If they were conducting experiments, why not burn them or bury them on a moon when they were finished? Why load them into crates and pay someone to transport them across the galaxy?"

"Their slave markings are UG brands," I said. "These people were UG owned slaves."

Ava closed her eyes and mumbled. "If we're caught by the UG with five hundred carved up UG slaves, we can expect much worse than a quick death."

Tank spit. "The UG ain't going to show us any mercy for this."

The room grew quiet as I turned to face Roger. "I expect that the conditions of the engines are as bad as originally reported?"

The look in Roger's eyes told us everything before he said a word. He paused and cleared his throat. "Seven of our engines and the hyperdrives were completely destroyed in the barrage of laser fire from Tompkins' destroyer. We ran further diagnostics on engine four and matched the readouts against any repair options. There's nothing we can do to fix it. You could give me a month, a full crew, and all the parts I need and I still couldn't fix it in time."

"So, we're fucked," Tank said.

Roger paused then nodded. "Yeah. We're fucked."

I let it soak in. Slowly. I sat down in the commander's chair and looked out into the darkness of space. Pieces of my ship floated around us like a metallic asteroid field. I knew what we needed to do, but couldn't say it.

My crew shouted out options in a panic. They were all a jumbled blur. *Ready our remaining troops to fight. Concede and surrender when the UG shows up. Send out our own distress signal. Try and work out a deal with pirates in the Dark Quarter.* They were all horrible options that led to the death of every man and woman on the *Beast*. The only positive was that some would be quicker than others. I waved my crew off, drawing silence in the room.

"How many operable shuttles do we have?" I asked. Everyone stood behind me as I gazed into space through the gap between the bridge window security panels.

Roger blew out a breath as he spun in his chair. He tapped a few buttons on his control panels and directed the results to the flickering forward monitor. Eleven working shuttles, one hundred and ten seats.

"That's not enough shuttles," Roger mumbled, "Not everyone will fit."

"Make them fit," I said. "I want every person off of this ship in less than two hours."

"Where are we going to go?" John asked. "We're in the Dark Quarter, Commander. Drifting shuttles in the Dark Quarter will lead to a worse fate than waiting here for the UG."

"I'll contact Terrell," I said.

Tank laughed. "He already turned us down. He's not going to dirty his hands with UG and Solonian business. Refueling our ship was one thing but harboring wanted UG fugitives is another."

"He'll help." I swiveled the chair and turned to face my crew. "Take all of my credits. Every last one of them and split them equally between the pods. I'll raise Terrell on the coms and let him know that my entire fortune in credits are his. All he needs to do is dock each pod to his ship to claim them." I shifted my gaze to Roger. "Let him know that after he recovers all of the pods, he needs to disperse the crew across the galaxy, with no more than three on the same planet, station, or moon. Spread everyone out. When the UG starts looking for us, it will be best for him and our crew."

Ava tilted her head to her shoulder. "Why don't you tell him yourself?"

"I'm not going with you."

"What do you mean?" Ava said with a pinched expression.

"I'm taking the fighter, and I'm going after Tompkins."

"You're what?" Ava widened her eyes. Tank shook his head and buried his face in his hands. Tucker sat quietly with his hands folded together in front of him.

Roger looked at me and flashed the slightest of smiles. "You're going after her, aren't you?"

"Who?" Tank talked at the ground. "Liriana?"

"I am," I said, and I'm going to kill Tompkins."

"There's no way you can do that on your own," Tank said. He shook his head from side to side, placing emphasis on each word as he spoke. "No. Way. In. Hell."

Ava pointed at Tank. "He's right, Maxx. You're going to take on Rothet, Tompkins, and his goon squad on your own?" She aimed her finger at me. "And you don't even know if Liriana will slit your throat the second she gets the chance."

I bent forward, placed my forearms on my thighs then folded my hands together. "You're right. It isn't going to be easy. I've made so many mistakes over the last dozen years, and this may be my last chance to rectify the biggest one of all. I have to try."

Tank tugged at his goatee, his eyes fixed on his feet. "This is suicide, Maxx, but I can't let you go alone. I've gone this far with you, been through too much to call it quits now. I'm in."

"Me too," Ava said before I had a chance to answer Tank. "To have even the slightest chance to pull this off, you'll need my help. I owe you, Maxx, and I'm not going to run. We'll take Tompkins down, or die trying."

"We're all in," Roger said as he placed his hand on my shoulder. John nodded his agreement.

I turned to Roger. "I have something more important for you to do, Roger. I need you to take the credits and make sure that Terrell holds up his end of the bargain."

A look of shock washed over Roger's face. "You need my help."

"Indeed I do," I said. "You need to take care of the crew. You're the only one that Terrell will listen to. Roger, you're the only one that can make sure he follows our agreement and saves the crew." Roger's eyes shifted away from mine, his jaw quivered. "I need you to do this."

He looked into my eyes. I could feel his pain. The loss of his wife, the loss of his friends, and the end of our run together.

"I'll do it," he said, "but you get her back. Just get her back."

"I promise," I said. "Tucker and John, I need you to go with Roger and the crew. Tucker will serve as Roger's backup and second in command. John, you know the UG better than anyone here. Help get the crew on planets where they will be the safest from the reach of the UG."

John grunted his acceptance.

"It's been good to have served under you," Tucker said.

I nodded then turned to face Ava and Tank. "The two of you realize this could be a one way trip?" Tank and Ava remained still as they waited for me to continue. "I'll accept your help on one condition. If we pull this off, both of you need to get as far away from me as you can. The UG and Solonians will scour every planet, moon, and space station in this galaxy until they find me. When this job is done, you'll never see me again. Understood?"

"Understood," Ava said softly.

"Yeah, whatever," Tank said.

I swallowed hard as I stood. I slid my hand across the back of my chair as I peered out the bridge window one final time.

"Roger," I said. My voice cracked as I talked. "I need to ask you one more favor before you lead the crew off my ship."

"Anything," Roger said.

"Set the *Beast* to self-destruct."

The three of us sat in the hauntingly quiet deck of the fighter, armed with as many weapons as we could carry. As much as I wanted to, I didn't linger in the *Beast's* halls or spend an extra moment on the bridge. I was about to lose the only true home I'd ever had, and the only family I'd ever known. Ignoring those thoughts, and the current circumstances, was the best way to move past the hurt.

We waited for Roger to give us clearance to depart from the *Beast*. The pistols at my sides, and the knives that rested across my back, provided me a sense of calm. Ava was seated across from me, her weapons already drawn from their holsters and gripped in each of her hands. Her elbows rested on her knees as she tapped the floor with the barrels of her pistols. A thin bandoleer of grenades crossed her chest. Her eyes were focused on the tops of her leather boots while she bit at her top lip. Ava hadn't said a word since she crossed the threshold from the *Beast* into the fighter. Her only responses had been physical - nods and shrugs.

I was fairly certain that the remainder of the *Beast's* available armaments were loaded onto Tank's hulking frame. I stopped counting at seven. His crown jewel was a repeating auto cannon that was as long as the height of an average man and powered by a fusion core generator. Under a full charge, the cannon would melt a hole as large as half a meter in diameter through a titanium plate. Once activated, the backlash of the radiation released from the barrel was enough to char exposed flesh and burn leather. Tank's healing JaC was the only thing that kept his skin from melting off his body. Tank also had a cross-band of explosives strapped across his chest, two long knives sheathed on his belt, and two pistols holstered to his sides.

235

The back of the fighter was loaded with some basic supplies wrapped in a tight bundle and secured to the deck. Next to that pack was a plasma torch and a self-expanding cordone plastic cap used to seal breaches in a ship's hull.

Roger's voice crackled through the overhead speakers, fighting against the buzz of static. "Is everyone set for launch?"

"We are," I said.

"Listen carefully. We modified your fighter's thrusters to supply a little extra boost. It will burn fuel quickly, but will more than triple your acceleration and closing speed. All unnecessary hardware and equipment have been removed to lighten the overall weight of the ship. That includes the second set of piloting controls, seats, backup navigation systems, and safety gear."

"That's great the fighter is fast," Tank said, "but how the hell are we going to find him?"

"Tompkins' ship is still showing up on the cusp of our tracking modules. His speed has been consistent since his departure, as well as his flight pattern - slightly erratic but maintaining a steady trajectory. Based on your fighter modifications, his rate of speed and distance from the *Beast*, I would expect you'll close the distance between us in less than a couple of hours. Of course that's assuming that he's unable to repair his engines before you get there."

Tank grunted. "Then we're wasting time with all this talk. Let's get rolling!"

"One last thing. I've uploaded his destroyer's schematics to your personal data transcoders. There's no way to know how many modifications they've made to that destroyer since Tompkins purchased it, but I highly doubt that they relocated any rooms associated with the ship's primary functionalities." There was a slight pause, then a change in Roger's voice, shifting from a matter-of-fact tone to slow-paced concern. "Your ship's vitals look good, and you're all clear for launch. Good luck to each and every one of you. I will miss you all."

"Take care of yourself and the crew, Roger," I replied, my voice trailing off. "Be safe."

I engaged the engines and activated the thrusters. The rolling static from the speaker ceased, and the cockpit was immediately consumed by the rumble of the fighter as it shook underneath us. We were enclosed in a steel shell, illuminated only by the pilot's controls that cast our thin shadows against the hull. Tank and Ava strapped themselves into the seats behind me, their solemn looks fixed out the forward bridge window.

The fighter lifted from the dock with an angry roar, spitting red fire from the thrusters. When we launched, the propulsion gave us a taste of what would be a long and unsteady ride. It was hard to control, and a struggle to maintain a straight trajectory as we emerged from the shadow of the *Beast*. I took one last glance at her before she was lost from my view.

"Let's discuss our plan of action once we reach Tompkins' destroyer," I said.

"We already know the plan, Maxx," Tank said with a sigh. "Break into the ship. Kill the bad guys. Save the girl. Did I miss anything?" He leaned back in his chair and arched an eyebrow.

"If it's OK, I would like a few more specifics," Ava said, shooting a glare at Tank. "Lay it on us, Maxx."

"Our objective is to commandeer two strategic points on the ship - the engine room and control station. By disabling the engine room we can make sure they can't move their destroyer out of the Dark Quarter or closer to a Solonian or UG ship."

"And the control station?" Ava asked.

"I want to prevent anyone from leaving their destroyer or docking to it. I'm not going to let Tompkins elude me this time. We'll break into two teams. I need both of you to take the control station, and I'll take the engine room."

"How the hell are you going to take the entire engine room on your own?" Tank asked with a grunt. "And even if you do, what are you going to do with it?"

"When I get to the engine room, I'll light it up with this." I nudged a pack of incendiary explosives strapped to my chair near my feet. "I'll seal the doors, then let the explosives do all of the work. You two need to disable the docking and launch controls permanently, but leave two shuttles active - one shuttle for each of you. Once you've disable the controls, launch the shuttles and leave."

"That isn't going to happen," Tank said. "We're not going to leave you there to fight off Tompkins' goons on your own."

"You will have to cut your way through a lot of his crew to secure the control station. It's a much longer path, and I expect you will draw most of the action. You'll have your work cut out for you, but when you succeed, there won't be much left for me to deal with."

"We can double back," Ava said with her fingers resting on her chin. "We can help you out."

"There won't be time. These destroyers have their oxygen scrubbers built into the engine room. Once I burn it down, she'll be lucky to hold an hour's worth of oxygen. Either way the destroyer becomes a coffin for everyone on board."

Tank smiled. "Now that sounds like a plan."

A look of concern crossed Ava's face. "But if we don't leave a shuttle active for you, you'll die…"

"I don't plan on going down with Tompkins and his team of goons," I said. "I'll take care of my business with Tompkins, find Liriana, and get off the ship. I'll manually override the lockdown on one of the shuttles – something I've done dozens of times." Ava narrowed her eyes at me as if she didn't trust what I was saying. "Set your coms to the secure channel, and under no circumstances will we contact each other unless there's an emergency. We don't want to give anyone on Tompkins' crew the ability to track our locations. This mission is going to be tough enough, so we need to keep every advantage that we have."

Tank nodded his response then shifted his focus to his weapons. He inspected the fusion core on his cannon, and followed the wiring and circuitry to ensure it was ready to fire the moment we boarded Tompkins' ship. He eyed Ava, his look meant to urge her to do the same. "This is going to get ugly, princess, but don't worry as I'll take care of you. Just stay behind me and let me do the work." Ava closed her eyes and sighed.

All that was left was the wait. We were actively tracking Tompkins' destroyer, and the location of his ship was getting closer with each passing minute. Tension hung in the air as everyone prepared themselves for the upcoming battle. Tank continued the meticulous review of his weapons; double and triple checking all of the major components, and grumbling as he made adjustments. Ava sat quietly as inaudible words rolled off her lips.

"We're closing in on their destroyer," I said, breaking the silence. "We need to start talking about our docking options."

"Maybe we can just ask them nicely for docking clearance?" Tank said with a smirk.

"There are two potential options, and various risks associated with each. We carved a breach in their rear hull with one of our laser cannons during their attack on the *Beast*. The breach is wide enough to maneuver this fighter inside, which should keep us safe from their cannons –"

"Sounds good!" Tank interrupted.

"But, it will require some extremely skilled piloting because I'll have to slow the fighter enough to penetrate the breach and come to an immediate stop once inside. It's a tough enough task to do with a standard fighter that has maneuverability, but we added additional boost to our thrusters and disrupted its weight and balance by removing key navigational and mechanical components. Those modifications will make it that much more difficult."

Ava shook her head. "I don't think I could do it. Even with my experience as a pilot."

"Forget it," Tank huffed. "I don't want to end up as a stain on the outside of Tompkins' ship. What's the second option?"

"We land the shuttle anywhere we can on the outside of the destroyer while avoiding the highest concentration of cannons. I'll activate the magnetic docking gear to attach us to their hull. I would expect that no matter where we land they will eventually be able to target us with their cannons and swat us off. It would require a quick docking and entrance strategy."

"How quick?" Ava asked.

"Maybe two or three minutes. It will take some time for the auto targeting system to recalibrate itself to differentiate us from the hull. They won't take the risk of an errant shot that damages their own ship."

"I'll take option number three," Tank said, waving his hands in front of him. "I don't like either one."

"There isn't a third option," I said, "unless you have some ideas."

The shuttle was silent. "Option two it is," Ava said.

Tank stood, striking his head against the curved hull with a loud, ringing thump. He closed his eyes as he talked. "So, after we land, we're going to float our way to a door somewhere? Do we have the gear for that?"

I shook my head. "Using the fusion cutter, we'll cut through the middle of one of the four magnetic landing gear, which are already marked on the floor below our feet." I traced a portion of one of the outlines with the toe of my boot. "We'll monitor which of the four landing gear has the most secure attachment on the flattest surface of their fighter's hull. If we cut the outline correctly, it should leave enough of the landing gear attached, and the melting metal should help seal around the edges of our cut. The fighter's internal life support systems should be able to compensate for the pressure changes and oxygen loss associated with any gaps between the two ships. At least long enough to get us inside their destroyer."

"And if we cut it wrong?" Tank asked.

"Our ship could release from their hull and suck all of our available oxygen through the hole we cut in the deck."

"Is that all?"

"Not quite. The first person through will be dumped into an unknown compartment of the destroyer and possibly into the hands of a number of waiting goons. The last person through needs to figure out a way to seal the hole behind them with that." I pointed to the self-expanding cap lying next to the fusion cutter.

"Why seal the hole?" Ava asked. "We may need it for a quick escape."

"We can't take the chance that our fighter will hold its magnetic dock or won't be destroyed by Tompkins. If the ship releases, and we're trapped in a locked room on the destroyer, we risk being exposed to space. Not sealing the hole is too risky."

Ava sighed and rubbed the back of her neck. "I'll prep for the cut while you find a suitable attachment point. You get us there, and I'll get us in."

"Once we breach their hull, I'll go in first. Tank you come in after me and help Ava seal that hole. Once we're inside we clear out the room and split apart. The schematics Roger uploaded to our data transcoders should be able to lead us to the control station and engine room. Understood?"

"Got it," Tank said. He sat in his chair and strapped himself in while his eyes shifted between the marked circles on the floor.

It was only minutes before we caught the glint of light from the hull of Tompkins' destroyer. Smoke poured from the thrusters of the giant ship leaving a dirty trail in its wake.

"Get ready!" I shouted. The lights from the fighter's controls dimmed, replaced by the flashing warning of red strobes. "It doesn't look like they're going to welcome us in."

Our only view into space was a small window at the front of the shuttle, reinforced with a cross of welded steel which divided it into four sections. I focused on the pair of monitors attached to the pilot controls, using both as my navigation panels. The forward window would only serve a teasing view to the passengers that had no control over what happened next.

It wasn't long before the window became an inward portal for the deadly light of their laser fire. It illuminated our ship and nearly blinded me with passing streaks of orange. The pilot's controls flickered off then back on as the bolts grazed the sides of our ship. Another volley of laser fire burned into the starboard side of the fighter and shredded her hull. It screeched out as if in pain

I shouted over the fighter's warning alarms. "Brace yourselves! We're coming in hot!" An array of laser fire tore into the rear of our craft, wrenching us sideways and filling the insides of our cabin with smoke.

"Our engines are done," I said. I banked the fighter toward the left and released the magnetic landing gear. "Get ready, we're about to engage!" Our fighter collided with Tompkins' ship and skidded across its hull under the stench of burning metal and friction. I magnetized the landing gear. The belly of our fighter hummed, lurched once, then stopped as if we'd struck an unyielding wall. Loose equipment hurled toward the front of the fighter and our bodies strained against the tightened safety belts that strapped us to the seats.

I scanned the landing gear data. "Circle three!" I shouted. "Go!"

Ava released her restraining straps, donned the protective goggles and oxygen mask, and activated the fusion cutter. It was all up to Ava now. Any deviation from a precise cut could leave us with a hole too small to fit through, or a hole too large that would suck all the oxygen from the fighter. We didn't have time for two cuts, so the first had to count.

I grabbed Tank's shoulder. He bent his head down and tilted his ear toward me. "I'm going in right after she gets that hole cut!" I yelled over the noise of the cutter and sparking circuitry. "Make sure you help Ava seal it closed as soon as we're all inside!"

A shot from one of the destroyer's cannons clipped the top of our fighter. The lights fluttered before we were plunged into darkness. Only the reddish hue of the fusion cutter lit the room where we stood.

"That was too damn close!" Tank screamed. He nudged Ava's back. She glanced up at Tank and watched as he circled his index finger. "Hurry it up or we're all dead!" Ava's eyes tightened behind the goggles.

"They hit the control compartment on the top of the fighter!" I yelled. "They're close to tearing the top off!"

Ava continued to cut, but her progress was masked behind the rising smoke that stung my eyes and burned my lungs. I was starting to worry less about dying from an imperfect cut than from the deadly fumes that filled our fighter. Oxygen pumped through the vents and into the compartment, swirling the smoke into twisting black clouds. The scrubbers were running at maximum output, and were struggling to keep up.

A second targeted shot skimmed across the top of our shuttle, shaving away metal plates. Successive laser fire followed every thirty seconds; which must have been the time needed to recalculate the blaster's target area. Each blast grew increasingly louder and closer to opening the top of our fighter to the darkness of space.

"Come on, Ava!" Tank yelled. "We're running out of time!" As if on cue, the light from the cutter vanished and our fighter filled with a rush of oxygen. A thunderous clang soon followed.

The outline of a circle glowed white-hot on the floor of our ship. Molten steel dripped like water into the compartment below. I slung the pack of explosives over my shoulder, took a deep breath, and jumped through the hole, plunging myself into darkness.

My fall was less than five meters; just long enough to give me time to adjust for a safe landing, but not so far that I would shatter bones when I landed. My feet absorbed the impact, and I tucked my chin to my chest and rolled forward with both pistols drawn. The room was engulfed in darkness.

I holstered one of my pistols and activated my data transcoder. I turned the device outward to illuminate the room. It was empty. Not a thing or person to be found. The walls were battered and dented and the deck was grooved and scratched, likely used for storage or transport.

I set the transcoder on the floor and stood underneath the hole, readying myself to assist. Tank's trunk like legs pushed through the opening as he lowered his gigantic frame into the room. His heavily wrapped left hand was clamped on the edge of the still hot circular cut while he dangled in the air. The sizzling sounds of burning cloth and flesh were heard from where I stood.

Tank reached up with his right arm, guided Ava out from our ship, and lowered her into my arms. I took my position under Tank, allowing his feet to engulf my shoulders. Tank pulled the plastic cap from our fighter and activated it's expansion, sealing the hole in the hull. Although it took him less than a minute, my shoulders and legs felt as though I was supporting him for days. He finally gave them the relief they were screaming for when he jumped to the floor. The weapons that were strapped across his back swayed and clattered together as he landed with a loud thump.

"Let's get moving," I said. "They'll be knocking down the doors to this room any second now."

"Does anyone know where we are?" Ava whispered.

"No clue," I replied. "All we know is that the control station is on the top deck, and the engine room is mid-level in the rear of the destroyer. We'll have to travel the corridors for a bit before we can get our bearings."

Tank made his way to the closest manual service door and pushed it open with the barrel of his cannon. The steel hinges coughed a rusty groan as he created enough room to allow us to pass through into the hall. The ship wasn't in alarm mode, and the corridors were clear.

"We're headed this way, Maxx," Tank said, pointing his cannon down the long hall to our left.

I nodded in reply. "It's best we split up here so we don't get pinned down in a single group. Remember our plan. Don't use the coms unless it's an emergency. After you've secured the control station, look for the quickest exit off the ship."

"Be safe, Maxx," Ava said as she touched my arm. She raised herself onto her tiptoes and placed a soft kiss on my cheek. "Thank you for everything you've done for me."

I brushed the hair away from her eyes, exposing the long scar stretching down the side of her cheek. "Just get off this ship. Don't let this be your last mission."

Tank reached forward and cupped my forearm in his hand.

"Good luck," I said, releasing my arm from his. "I couldn't have asked for a better friend." It was the first time I had spoken that word to a crew member. Tank squinted at me as if in disbelief then nodded his head.

I pressed my back against the corridor and slid to the first bend in the hall. The clatter of Tank's and Ava's weapons faded, until the only sound that remained was the buzz of the lights over my head.

The passage unfolded in front of me like a winding snake. I followed the pathway until I came to a ninety degree turn to the left. I shot a quick glance around the corner to confirm that it was free of Tomkins' goons then continued forward.

There was nothing unusual about the destroyer's layout, and it didn't take me long to identify where I was in relation to the engine room - one level above and roughly half the ship's width away. The schematics that Roger uploaded were spot on, and confirmed that Tompkins hadn't made any modifications to this section of the destroyer.

The absence of an alarm and the lack of armed personnel in the corridors concerned me. They knew that our fighter docked the outside of their ship and by now they would have discovered our entry point. It was possible they were doubling up on reinforcements in areas they deemed critical, but Tompkins wasn't the type to sit back and wait for the action to come to him. My only hope was that they weren't all swarming the top deck to ambush Tank and Ava.

Rounding another turn in the corridor, I paused when I heard two voices mumbling in the distance. I peered around the corner. Two goons, dressed in Tompkins' OWME uniforms, yacked at each other in the passageway. They didn't appear to be in a hurry. I gazed at my transcoder in an attempt to locate the nearest detour. The next quickest path to the engine room was to backtrack over half of my path, drop down two levels, and take the access stairs back to the other side of the ship – doubling my time to get there. I watched the two goons a few more minutes, hoping they would leave. My patience grew thinner with each second, and I needed to act. If Tank and Ava were to overrun the control station soon, it would be a fatal mistake not having the engine room secured as well, and the mission wasn't going to fail because of me.

The distance between us was well over twenty meters, and as much as I wanted to use my blades to keep my attack silent, I wasn't going to take the chance that one of them would draw a blaster on me before I reached them. With both pistols firmly in my grip, I raised them in front of me and approached the two goons. Both men turned toward me, fumbling for the guns strapped at their hips. Two shots from my pistols and the corridor was washed in green light. The laser fire struck their chests and both collapsed to the floor; their legs and hands still twitching from the blasts.

The noise of their bodies striking the floor, along with the hum of my blasters, would have every goon on the ship running to my position in a matter of minutes. Maybe I'd done Tank and Ava a favor.

I searched the corpses for something of use, an access card or a com, but all I found were some standard-issue blasters and a handful of credits. I left their bodies and moved on.

I traveled through two more corridors before I heard the rushed footsteps of a few goons chasing me down from behind. They fired a number of errant shots that sparked against the paneled ceilings and glanced off the passageway walls. I turned another corner, drew my knives and waited.

The goons were in a full, dead-on sprint, and weren't ready for me as they rounded the passageway. I plunged one of the blades deep into a goon's chest, and slashed a red smile across the neck of another. The third goon tried to stop, but his momentum carried his feet forward, sliding out from underneath him and bouncing his back off the deck with a forced exhalation of air. His head was shrouded by a cowl leaving only his dark eyes free to peer at my blades then back to the pair of silvered blasters clutched in his hands. He lit up the passageway around me; the heat from the laser fire scorched the air and blinded me under the barrage of light.

I twisted to the side, trying to make myself a smaller target and forcing him to track my movements. I lunged at him, lancing my blades down where he laid, but he was gone. My knives sparked when they struck the metal floor, and the force of impact jarred one free from my left hand. The pack of explosives fell off my shoulder and rolled to a stop against the wall. I heard the brush of cloth behind me. I spun from my knees and kicked his legs out from under him as he was attempting to stand, sending his body back to the deck with a loud thud.

I kicked one of his guns free. It spiraled across the grated metal and down the hall. I reached forward, grabbed and held the other. My hands shook as I struggled against his strength. I released my grip and rolled over the top of his body and locked his neck between my thighs. I cupped one hand under his chin and pressed the other against the side of his cloaked head, and with a quick pull and a powerful push, his neck swiveled and popped.

I brushed the sweat from my eyes and made my way back to the bodies of the two goons. They were equipped like the others, carrying only standard-issue weapons and some credits. The last of the three men, the one whose head I twisted like the cap on a jar, looked different. He was dressed in his own clothing and equipped with different gear - all of which looked distinct and expensive. There was no identification to be found, but the pale color of his skin and large bone features in his bubbled face gave away his race. He was Solonian.

The two pistols he was toting were hand crafted and feather light. The charge meters below the rear sights displayed a remaining one hundred and sixteen shots each. Any regular grunt would have more than two to one usage of the weapon in their dominant hand. The identical numbers on each blaster indicated he used each equally, and was proficient in firing from both hands. It was a sign of a highly skilled and aptly trained marksman.

I shook my head in disbelief. This wasn't some cheap hire. He was a purebred Solonian marksman, and the only way you get one in your employment is with the blessing of the Solonian Empire. Was it Aphe's intention to join forces with Tompkins from the start? If that was true, why not just terminate me and my contract before I left the space station? I picked up the pack of explosives, slung them over my shoulder and made my way down the hall.

I was only a few minutes from the engine room and started to pour over the details of how I would seal it. The panel itself wouldn't be hard to compromise. If I couldn't pry it free, I'd set explosives around the panel cover to dislodge it from its housing, then locate the two wire clusters connected to the door sensors. Next, I would trace the wires from each bundle that activated the open and close commands so I could force the door open, set the explosives inside the engine room, then fuse the close sensor wires together to force the door into a locked state. Easy, clean, and effective.

Realizing that I was drifting too far into my thoughts, I forced myself to break the trance, just in time to be greeted by a familiar voice.

"It took you much longer than I had...expected," Rothet said. He stood next to the engine room door, his body leaning against the access panel. His arms were folded loosely below his chest, both hands clenched and buried under his biceps. The pistol holsters on his hips were empty, and his two unsheathed, ebon blades rested against the wall next to his feet. He was free of his jacket, wearing only a tight knit shirt, loose pants, and a new pair of black, polished boots. He looked healthy; too healthy for someone that took point blank blaster fire in the center of his chest.

He raised his left hand and opened his palm as if to buy a few seconds before I killed him. That didn't stop me. I fired four shots. Rothet's movement was a blur of speed and my blaster fire only scorched the walls behind him leaving black marks where they hit.

As Rothet dodged my fire, he grabbed a device from his belt, activated it, and tossed it at my feet. The circular device rolled, magnetized and locked onto the floor. The lights in the corridor dimmed around me before going dark. I squeezed the triggers on my pistols but nothing happened. I raised them to my eyes and saw that both charge counter displays were blank. Rothet retrieved another item from his belt and dropped it as his feet. When it struck the floor it bathed the corridor in a yellow, flickering light.

"I must say, I'm more than a little disappointed in your lack of banter," Rothet said as he broke his stance, dropped his right arm from his chest and extended his fist in my direction. He spun his wrist upward and peeled his fingers back to display a blinking remote activation pad resting in his palm. His thumb hovered above it; the red pulsating screen gave the appearance of his thumb throbbing in pain.

I flipped the toggle switches on my guns and steadied my aim as Rothet spoke. "Listen carefully before you do something you'll regret. With a single press of my finger on this screen, I'll unleash a ring of strategically placed explosives that will separate the top deck of this ship."

"How about I just kill you and take the activation pad?" My grips on the pistols tightened as I pulled the triggers. I fired both guns, sending a spray of uranium bullets to each side of Rothet. The bullets struck the walls behind him, some detonating upon impact and others ricocheting down the corridor. Rothet didn't flinch, his hand stayed steady in front of him. They were only warning shots, not meant to find his body. I couldn't risk shooting a man holding a remote activation pad – especially one that could cause an explosion and possibly kill both Tank and Ava.

"Admittedly, that's one of your options," Rothet replied. "But are you willing to take that...risk?" His thumb circled over the top of the device as he continued. "If you do kill me, are you certain that I won't activate the detonation of the explosives when those bullets strike my body?"

"And why should I care?"

"Don't play me for a fool, Maxx. I know exactly why you're here." Rothet raised his hands at his sides to indicate the area around him. "I know what your purpose is, and I know that your team of two is attempting to gain access to the control station."

"You're making a number of assumptions. Are you ready to bet your life on it?" My pistols were aimed at Rothet's head.

"Is that how you're going to play this? You have a spy in your midst, and I know just as much about your intentions as you do. One of mine was watching your each and every move." Rothet's thumb rolled over the top of the screen. "We could continue to play this game, but time is...wasting."

"So you and Tompkins have it all figured out?"

"What about Tompkins?" Rothet's smile dripped with malice. "Do you really think I would let someone of his stature control me?" He shook his head as his smile widened into a tooth-bearing grin. "There aren't enough credits in this galaxy for me to bow to the likes of someone like...him. I used Tompkins to get what I wanted. Just like you, Maxx, he was a pawn in my game. And now he's...dead."

"Dead?"

Rothet angled a glance at the swords that rested against the wall. A coating of red colored the razor sharp edges of the blades. "I played him as long as I could, that was until he started to jeopardize my mission."

Rothet's eyes looked like back holes set in the darkness of space. I had no reason to believe he wasn't speaking the truth. "I would be lying if I said that I wasn't disappointed." I ran my tongue across my teeth. "What's your interest in the cargo I'm hauling?"

"Your cargo is worthless. I couldn't care less about that Solonian garbage that's stacked in your ship." He shook his head from side to side. "No, I'm after something much more valuable than that, and you're going to help me get it."

"I wouldn't be so sure," I said through gritted teeth. My hands gripped the pistols like tightening vices as I fought against the urge to pull the triggers.

"Oh, you'll…help. All in due time. I've already acquired one half of my prize long ago, but you're instrumental in obtaining the other half." Rothet pursed his lips and narrowed his eyes.

"What is it that you want?"

"For now? It's quite simple. You."

I tossed my pistols to the floor behind me and set the pack of explosives at my feet. Reaching behind my back, I drew the knives from their sheaths. The edged blades rubbed across the leather, ringing out like a song.

"If you want me, come claim your prize."

Rothet smirked, then deactivated the remote device and slid it into his pocket. He recovered his swords and spun them once around the outside of his body. He cocked his head to the side as if reading my body language.

"When you lose, I will make it so painful that you will wish that I had killed you. You'll be forced to help me finish my mission, and watch when I disintegrate the top deck on this destroyer then kill every last person on the *Beast*."

So this was what it had come down to, a final battle between Rothet and me to save Liriana and the lives of my crew. A true smile broke across my face for the first time in years.

Rothet was faster than the last time we fought. He was quicker in anticipating my every move, my positioning, and my offensive and defensive stances. It was as if our first encounter was no more than an exercise to learn my fighting style so he could program it into his brain and use it against me. I felt like his puppet, moved at his will, played with like a child's toy. Though when his playtime was done, I knew how it would end for me.

His ebon blades found my body countless times as they sliced cloth and flesh behind each arcing slash of darkness. A front kick caught me off guard; planted in the center of my chest, it vaulted me back into the corridor wall. It hurt like hell, but I kept the pain hidden the best I could. I pulled in short breaths and widened my eyes to clear the bright spots that dotted my vision.

"Why didn't you run?" Rothet said as he wiped a sheen of sweat that formed above his brow. When I didn't answer, he continued. "I know why you're here, Maxx. It's not your hatred for Tompkins that brought you. I know that you're here for…her."

I spit a stream of red from my mouth before I spoke. "I made a mistake, and I'm here to rectify it."

Rothet rolled his eyes to the ceiling. "I see. You're a hero then? An agent soldier finally seeing his true calling." He pointed one of his blades at my head. "Why, you're a new man seeking out his lost love."

A blaze of pain swiped across my side as Rothet's blades caught me again. A warm, wet sensation formed around my wound and trickled down the inside of my shirt. I pinned the flat of the blades against my forearms and shifted my right leg behind my left.

Rothet wiped away blood from the sleeve of his shirt and flicked it to the floor. My blood. "Maxx," his tone was condescending, "heroes only win in children's fairytales. There are no heroes in the Silor Galaxy." He lunged at me. I deflected his attack but his blade caught the top of my shoulder. "You're a foolish man, changing your ideals on a whim. You're forgetting who you are...what you are." Another slash caught the top of my thigh, but I was able to parry away the damaging force of the blow. "A man can change the blade in his hand, the gun holstered at his side, but he can't change who he is." I blocked his next two swings. The forceful slashes felt as though I was blocking sledge hammers instead of swords. He backed me against the wall under a rain of blows.

I swung wildly, desperate to put him on the defensive. My swing cut nothing but the sweat-filled air around us. He was toying with me. My next swing missed, leaving my back exposed to Rothet. A blunt blow struck me in the spine and drove me to the deck. He kicked one of my knives free then planted the heel of his boot on my other hand, twisting and grinding until my last blade was loosened from my grip. He used his sword to flick the knife away. I watched as my last hope for survival stuttered and sparked across the metal deck as it twirled away down the hall.

Rothet knelt beside me. The touch of his blade laid flat against my neck and the sharpness bit into my skin His hot breath bathed my ear as he whispered, "You have no idea what this is about, do you?" The sound of him licking his lips smacked in my ear. "You think this is about the death of hundreds of worthless slaves rotting in your cargo hold?" I clawed at the floor as Rothet sawed the blade lightly across my neck. "Or the personal grudge of a fat man who conspired with the most powerful Empire Nation in the Unified Governments to take you down?"

I started to reply, but Rothet chose not to listen. He pressed the blade against my skin and released a thin river of red that dripped down both sides of my neck and padded gently on the floor.

I spun to my side, his blade cutting deeper into my neck as I turned. I wrapped my arms around his and rolled Rothet into the wall with a loud thump. He was stronger and faster than me, but lighter. Leverage was all I had. I pinned him to the deck and thrust my knee into his neck as I held his arms tight and his blades away from my head. I pushed with all the strength I had. He struggled to fight back as his gasps for air turned to a gargled wheeze before he finally sputtered to silence.

Rothet's eyes closed as I pushed on his neck with all of my strength.

His arms weakened, his body started to go slack. When I thought I had won, his dark, soulless eyes opened and a thin smile stretched across his face.

He released his swords, reversed the grip on my arms and flung me into the wall across the hall. My head struck hard against the steel before I tumbled to the floor. Rothet's boot found my cheek then my ribs. He picked me up as easily as a child, lifted me over his head and drove me into the deck.

Rothet wrenched my arms behind my back until they nearly tore free from their sockets. I felt the touch of cold metal on both of my wrists before the crack of another blow was delivered to my head, shooting bright light into the backs of my eyes. Rothet shackled my ankles together as I lay stunned, my face resting in a pool of my own blood.

Rothet spit, stood, then picked up his swords and slid them into their scabbards. "Let me be honest with you, Maxx. I didn't see that...coming." I rolled onto my side, leaned my back against the passageway wall and watched him rub his neck. The bruised flesh was already healing.

"What now?" I asked. My head swirled and my vision flashed between light and dark. The restraints around my arms and legs were drawn tight and wouldn't give. I was at his mercy.

Rothet's eyes narrowed. His hand paused around his neck as he spoke. "You have something I want, and you're going to help me get it."

"Maybe you could release these restraints for me?" I rolled my head to the side and spit a stream of blood. My tongue flicked around my teeth, checking to see if they were all still there. "There's something I would love to give you right now."

Rothet laughed. "I was led to believe that what I'm looking for is on your ship, the *Beast*. After I disable this destroyer, we'll be headed there to pick it up."

"Good luck picking through what's left of her." Rothet kneeled next to me and tilted his head to the side, listening as I continued. "We set it to self-destruct."

"Ah, that," he replied. "I can guarantee you that she's still in one...piece."

"That's not possible..."

"We drained all the remaining power in the *Beast* by activating the power dampening units that were equipped in the pods we attached to your ship." I shifted my gaze to the floor as Rothet continued. "Let me guess. Your scans told you they were military-grade transmitters, correct? If so, my team did their job well."

"Without any power, my crew is helpless. The ship won't be able to generate oxygen or launch the shuttles. You'll kill them."

"And?" Rothet stood then folded his arms behind his back. "You really do care about your...crew." Rothet shook his head. "We engaged the dampeners as soon as you left your ship. It was a necessary step to make sure we kept it intact. I contacted your friend, Terrell. He'll keep any potential scavengers at bay and in turn, I'll permit his claim on all of the credits you promised him for saving your crew. As far as the oxygen scrubbers..." Rothet shrugged his shoulders. "The rest of your crew is of no use to me."

"Mark my words, Rothet. I will kill you."

"Maxx, as crazy as those words sound, I do believe that you think they're true." Rothet pounded this boot into my stomach. "But I don't think you're in the position to make threats, or promises."

I spit another stream of blood. "I never make promises I can't keep."

Rothet removed the remote activation pad from his pocket and eyed the device. His face was illuminated in a shade of pulsating red. "This couldn't have gone any smoother for me, Maxx. But to be honest, what I don't understand is why you would come back for...her." Rothet lowered the device and looked me in the eyes. "I was assured that you would, but why? Why risk your life for someone that hates you?"

I struggled against the restraints on my wrists and ankles. My answer to Rothet was delivered as a burning stare.

"So be it." Rothet crouched next to me then patted me on the cheek as he activated the remote detonation. Explosions erupted overhead; the hull of the ship buckled and shuddered underneath us. The passageways filled with the angry moans of bending steel and the furious bursts of oxygen propelled fire. "Maxx, things are about to get...fun."

I caught a flash of black and a hint of silvered steel from behind Rothet. Liriana stood only a few meters away, my blades clenched in her white-knuckled hands. I did my best to smile through the pain. "Rothet, I couldn't agree more."

I was helpless, bound in shackles and forced to watch as Liriana and Rothet battled in the corridor. Sparks showered the hall like red and white rain as their blades met at impossibly fast speeds. Neither of them was giving any ground.

"Take it easy, girl!" Rothet shouted between blows. "We're on the same damn side!" Liriana's only response came as a determined look in her eyes; a look that called for Rothet's death.

Liriana was quicker, faster, and stronger, yet Rothet was able to parry every one of her attacks.

"This is futile and you know it!" Rothet shouted out on a spray of spit. "Time is running out! The ship is collapsing around us! You were instructed to wait in the fighter! You aren't worth anything to anyone...dead!" His next two attacks found their home, once across her right arm and a second across her side. "Stop this foolishness, or I'll be forced to kill you!"

Liriana persisted, slashing and lunging with speed that was too quick to perceive. Her eyes never wavered from Rothet. She watched his every move as if studying and learning. The fight was a violent tangled mess of black, silver, and red - Liriana's blood.

Rothet's blades found Liriana on her shoulder and across her thigh. The floor was growing slick with her blood and her speed slowed as the fight progressed. I pulled at the restraints with all of my will, all of my strength, but only ripped my flesh and coated my wrists in blood. They wouldn't release. They wouldn't give.

Liriana lost one blade then another. Rothet's sword pierced her shoulder and struck the corridor wall. She didn't scream out, just placed her hands over Rothet's on the sword handle to stop the blade.

"This is no good," Rothet said. "Don't make me do this."

Liriana raked her nails across Rothet's face, from his forehead down to his chin. Rothet shrieked, then drove his other sword into her stomach, piercing her light armor plating. Liriana grunted and bowed her head as Rothet slowly pushed the blade through her.

"I didn't want to do this," Rothet whispered as his sword inched its way through her stomach and out her back. "This ruins…everything."

"How long have you been studying my fighting style?" Liriana said with a gasp. "You've been JaCed for me, waiting for this moment." Liriana closed her eyes and winced as a trickle of blood dribbled from the corner of her mouth.

"Yes, I have," Rothet said, "but I never planned to kill you. I didn't want this, but you left me no…choice."

Liriana lifted her head and locked eyes with Rothet. "Me either." She grasped Rothet's hand and drove the sword through her and into the wall, stopping only when the pommel rested against her stomach. Rothet was caught off guard and stumbled into her, pressing their bodies together. She grabbed his hand and shattered Rothet's wrist with a quick twist. Liriana wound her arm around Rothet's neck, spun him around and lifted him off the floor with a sharp snap. His body crumpled into a pile at her feet.

Liriana closed her eyes, sucked in a breath, and pulled the sword free from her shoulder. The blade clanked and rattled when it fell to the floor, flicking drops of red on the silver walls. She screamed when she pulled the second blade from her stomach. A stream of red followed its exit. She collapsed then curled into a ball. She clutched at her wounds, rocked in place and mumbled curses under her breath. Liriana took a deep, stuttering breath then dragged herself toward Rothet's body, the deck behind her streaked with a wet trail of red. She located the keys to my restraints and crawled her way toward me. She was able to get one of my hands free before she started to shake.

"You've lost so much blood," I said as I removed the shackles from my other hand and ankles.

Liriana rolled to her back, her hands covered the wound in her stomach staunching the free flow of blood like water leaking from a hole in a dam. "It feels worse than it looks," she replied through clenched teeth and a forced smile.

I gently lifted her back from the floor and brushed the hair away from her face. "Your healing JaC. Can it compensate?" Liriana replied with a slow shake of her head. The cuts were too deep, and the healing process wouldn't be able to close the wounds before she bled out. "I need to get you some help."

As I started to stand, Liriana touched my cheek. "You came for me," she whispered. "You came for me." Her voice was growing weak.

"I failed you."

She smiled as her eyelids fluttered. Her voice was a whispered gasp. "It doesn't matter. This is all that I needed."

There was a clatter of weapons, someone was advancing on us from down the hall. I scrambled to collect my blades and blasters, raised my pistols and spun to see Tank rounding the corner. His body was marked with black soot, burns, and covered in a layer of sweat. I holstered my guns and knelt next to Liriana. I brushed her face lightly with my fingers. "You're not going to die," I said as I scooped her into my arms.

"What the fuck...," Tank said, pausing mid-sentence as he looked around the hall. "What happened here?"

"We need to get her some help, quick!" I replied. I looked down at Liriana's still body; her breathing grew shallower by the second. The heat drained from her, carried out by the free flowing streams of blood.

"Did you kill him?" Tank's eyes shifted between me and Rothet's body.

"There's no time, Tank! She won't make it if we don't go now."

Tank knelt down and picked up the pack of explosives. "There's a UG fighter located in the shuttle bay not far from here. It's the only ship docked on this destroyer that would be large enough to carry a hyper chamber."

"A UG fighter on Tompkins' destroyer? What the hell is going on?"

"I have no idea. It was registered in their docking bay when we locked the shuttles down." Tank hooked his thumb toward the hall behind him. "Follow me." Tank turned and worked his way down the halls, scanning each door as we passed.

"What happened to Ava?"

Tank turned back to look at me. "Hopefully she's off the ship." He continued down the corridor, talking as we ran. "Everyone was dead, Maxx. Everyone."

"What do you mean?

"There were bodies everywhere. Ava and I followed the trail of death to the control station. A few dozen men littered the halls. Maybe more.

When we got there, the access door to the control station was locked shut. It took us about ten minutes to hack the panel." The ship lurched and rocked under a chain of small explosions. Tank stopped, braced himself against the passageway wall, then continued forward once the shaking stopped. "There wasn't anything to secure because the room was empty. We locked down all the shuttles except for two, closed the door and coded it to stay locked."

"Did you see Tompkins?"

"Maybe. We decided to take a detour to the bridge on our way out. It was gruesome, Maxx. Most of the bodies were hacked up beyond recognition. If he was one of them, you don't need to worry about running in to him ever again." Tank paused at a 'T' in the hall, checked his data transcoder and turned left.

"Why aren't you and Ava together?"

"It was my idea. I thought that if we both had shuttles on the opposite ends of this destroyer, we had a better chance of one of us stumbling into you." Tank paused for a moment. "I couldn't leave you here, Maxx."

My gaze shifted from Tank to Liriana. Her arms were draped across her stomach, the steady flow of blood slowing to a trickle. I couldn't tell if she was still breathing.

"There," Tank said, pointing at the UG fighter. "That's it."

My legs wobbled and my head spun from my own loss of blood. My joints ached and my body screamed with each step, but I didn't listen. I opened the access hatch to the fighter and stepped inside while Tank covered my back. The fighter was filled with equipment and supplies, stocked and ready for a long voyage. The hyper chamber was one room off of the cockpit.

I laid Liriana inside the hyper chamber and closed the lid. I activated the controls, held my breath, and waited. The chamber sealed under an exhaling hiss then initiated the scanning process. *"Stasis hibernation and human tissue repair activated. Lacerations located on the right thigh, lower torso, left bicep, and left forearm. Positive repair outcome confirmed. Damage to the left clavicle and scapula detected. Fractured bone and skin lacerations detected. Injury stabilized. Major trauma to the right kidney and pancreas detected. Broken lower right ribs number ten, eleven, and twelve. Repair possibilities unknown at this time. Blood loss critical. System shock likely due to severe trauma. Processing hibernation for stabilization."*

For a moment I was in a trance. The induced hibernation process clouded the inside of the chamber and fluttered her hair as it filled with gas.

A small pool of red expanded beneath her until the vacuum system engaged and filtered out the blood.

"We need to get off this destroyer," Tank said over the top of my head. I turned and looked up at him, offering a nod as my response.

"We've done everything we can," I said in an attempt to reassure myself more than Tank. "Let's get out of here."

From the cockpit we closed the access door and engaged the engines under a fierce rumble of smoke and flame. When I attempted to lift the fighter, it jolted underneath us and stopped, never disengaging from the dock. I reset our flight pattern and re-engaged. The fighter lurched, but wouldn't lift. Tank's eyes grew wide as he stroked the mass of hair under his chin.

"Well," I said as I worked the ship's control panels, "you and Ava did a fantastic job. This fighter is locked down tight." I scanned the readout display and tapped it with my finger. "And we've got a company of goons closing in on us."

"Son of a…"

"I don't know if we have the time for me to override the lockdown." I looked at Tank, then at his cannon propped against the hull behind him. "Cut off the landing gear."

"Hell yeah!" Tank shouted. He bolted from his seat and grabbed his auto-cannon as I activated the access hatch then followed him to the door. A stream of radiated laser fire burst from the cannon the moment the fighter's door slid into the wall. Bodies outside burst into flaming scrap, splattered on the walls and floor. Tank's shirt singed and pockets of skin on his arms started to dissolve and drip from his body.

"Tank!" I shouted. "Take out the landing gear! I'll cover you!"

There was a moment of fire that lit behind his eyes. A JaC triggered rage that left me wondering if he would even listen, or if he even cared. After a few seconds the docking bay finally grew quiet as Tank released the trigger on his cannon. The barrel on the gun glowed bright red, illuminating the entrance to the fighter. The only noise around us was the crackling and popping sounds emitting from piles of the goons' burning flesh.

Tank descended down the platform and I followed, both pistols drawn and ready. Tank cut off each of the three landing gear, slicing through the steel with ease. The fighter moaned then crashed down onto the docking bay. The right wing bounced off the deck and sent the fighter tilting back toward us, slamming the left wing only a meter from where we stood. It teetered back and forth like a boat in choppy water before slowly coming to a stop.

We ran back inside, closed the access hatch and re-engaged the flight pattern. The ship vibrated underneath us, shifting and shaking without the landing gear platforms. The fighter lifted, but not without difficulty, ripping a sizable section of plating from the belly of the ship.

"Minor damage," I said with a sarcastic smile. My eyes drifted to the oxygen and pressure sensors more than once.

"Look," Tank said as he pointed at the ship's diagnostics panel. "Someone's accessing this ship's navigational feed. They're downloading its signature so they can gun us down when we fly out of here."

I nodded my reply as I directed the ship toward the exit bay. Matching the reverse thrusters to the power of the forward thrusters, the ship bucked in place like a wild horse restrained against its will.

"We've got one shot at this. I'll hit that exit bay as hard and as fast as this ship will take us. We can only hope that the destroyer is damaged enough that their tracking system won't be able to lock on to us in time."

Tank's hands gripped the armrests, cracking and pealing the leather away from the frame. "Give her hell."

I removed the reverse thrusters and applied full forward trajectory. The fighter rocketed, pin-balling off the docking bay walls before I straightened its flight pattern. We shot out of the bay like a bullet from a gun.

A red glow showered over us as our ears were filled with the warning sirens of an imminent attack. Tompkins' destroyer had us locked in, with not one, but three cannons.

"Fuck me..." Tank said. It was the last thing I heard before a wash of orange flooded the cockpit.

The chaotic, self-serving lifestyle of an agent soldier was defined by risk and reward, taking on contracts no one else would touch. An agent soldier's loyalties lie with their jobs, and those who succeeded understood that crew members were tools used to complete them; no different than the blaster holstered at their side or their battle-torn ship waiting for its cargo hold to be packed with illegal goods. All of your tools were critical components in completing contracts yet dispensable when they'd become a burden or failed to serve their intended purpose. Your only friends were credits, and once you strayed from that philosophy it guaranteed only failure and death. We served together, yet we stood alone.

Those are the words I lived by, words I'd repeated over and over again. I believed in them. It was the only reason I was able to survive as long as I had. *So why did I stray from that path?*

This single, hollow thought consumed me as I caressed the cocoon of fogged glass and tarnished steel that encased Liriana. The sobering glow of the hyper chamber's two remaining status bars created a subtle, greenish hue in the otherwise darkened and smoke-filled room. "I promise you," I whispered, "it isn't going to end this way."

I winced as I placed my hand over the gash across the back of my neck. A stream of crimson trickled between my fingers and spilled into a widening pool atop the hyper chamber. Pulling in a painful, stuttering breath I glanced at Tank; his large, battered frame leaned heavily against the ship's hull as if he was attempting to prevent its collapse.

"Tank?" I questioned.

"I'll make it," Tank said, spitting out a mouthful of blood that left streaks of bright red on his thick, black goatee. "I've had much worse."

"Good. I didn't want you quitting on me now."

Tank's laugh gave way to aspirated coughing. "This doesn't look good for us."

I bowed my head. "We're alive. That's worth something."

Tank waded through the explosion of debris covering the floor and stopped next to me. I could see him from the corner of my eye but didn't let my gaze stray from Liriana's hyper chamber. Tank drummed his fingers on the glass. "Where the hell are we?"

"Nalid." My response sounded distant, even to me.

"Never heard of it, but I hate it already."

"It's one of the abandoned mining worlds located within the Ring of Six on the edge of the Dark Quarter.

"You sound like a tour guide." Tank smirked. "If you're right, there won't be any UG patrols looking for us here. That's a plus." Tank squinted as he tried to peer out one of the port windows. "I hate it slightly less now."

I didn't listen to a word of what Tank said. My attention was drawn to the lighted control panels of the hyper chamber. One by one the array of indicator lights hissed and popped, rushing in the sobering reminder that I needed a plan, and quick. I donned the UG officer's coat that I'd salvaged from the storage bay and brushed beads of sweat and blood from my face.

"Here's how I see it. Liriana's stasis equalizer is damaged beyond repair giving her hyper chamber less than eighteen hours of life support. Estuld, the closest colonized planet to our current location, is well over four jumps away - two full days of travel assuming we could get this fighter off the ground. We have dozens of fist-sized holes in our hull that will leak cabin pressure like a sieve, and to wrap it all up, the way that you're spitting blood I expect that you're bleeding internally from wounds caused by our crash landing."

Tank spat another stream of red and tugged at his goatee as he talked. "So, what's the bad news?"

I didn't answer Tank's question. I knew he wouldn't like my plan. On the way to the bridge I stepped through the displaced tentacles of wiring and fractured metallic plates that littered the passageway. Beams of blue sunlight intruded through the countless breaches in the ship's hull, illuminating my path.

"Maxx?" Tank questioned as he followed behind. "What are you going to do?"

"We need one of their stasis equalizers for the hyper chamber, and one of their ships," I said. As foolish as it sounded, I didn't have any other plan - any other choice.

"One of *their* ships?" Tank choked on his own words. "One of the UG's ships? You can't be serious?"

"I am."

Tank stepped in front of me; his enormous frame blocked the entrance to the bridge. "Forget it, Maxx. Calling in the UG is suicide. There has to be another way! We need to take some time and think this through."

"Time is a luxury we don't have. I'm not going to let her die. It's as simple as that."

"You're willing to continually risk our lives for hers?" Tank's corded muscles tensed and rippled through the torn fabric of his tight-fitting shirt. His neck cracked as he tilted his head from shoulder to shoulder. "You're a fool."

I stepped up to Tank, dwarfed by his brutish size. I fixed my eyes on his, and stood silent. Drops of blood welled up in the corner of Tank's mouth and dripped down the front of his shirt when he broke his silence. "You lost your crew, your ship, and nearly both of our lives with a series of horrible, compromised decisions. You're getting sloppy, Maxx. Real sloppy."

"The last time I checked, you weren't leading this operation."

"If I was, our crew would still be alive, the *Beast* would still be operational, and we wouldn't be in this mess."

"Is this how it's going to be?" I narrowed my eyes.

Tank's Adam's apple bounced with a deep swallow as he chewed on my words. I was his commander, yet Tank cared about what was best for him and his survival. Tank was a warrior; an unflinching killer afraid of no man. He'd beaten the best this galaxy had to offer, yet he knew me well. He knew my abilities and my determination when driven by a cause I believed in. I would fight until only one of us was left standing. I wouldn't back down.

Tank rolled his tongue over his teeth, spit on the floor by my feet then stepped to the side, opening the passageway to the bridge.

"We're running out of time." I bumped my shoulder into his chest as I entered the bridge.

Once in the cockpit, I diverted the ship's remaining backup power to the distribution panels. The battery unit arced in response and filled the bridge with the pungent odor of fused wire and melting circuitry. With a reverberating hum, the panels relented to the forceful rush of energy and sprang to life, triggering the computer's lengthy startup sequence.

"Listen," Tank said, "what just happened –"

I raised my hand to cut Tank off before he had a chance to finish. "It's done. I don't blame you for what you said. Forget it."

Tank nodded and spat another stream of red that contained dark, coagulated chunks. "Looks like it's drying up," Tank said. "I think my body is starting to heal."

"If only we could repair this ship just as quickly." I pointed to the forward monitors as I continued. "The concentrated patterns of their auto-cannon fire were focused on our ship's engine room and thrusters. I don't think they were looking to kill us, only disable our fighter."

Tank reviewed the damage reports that streamed across the monitors dangling from wire clusters and broken conduits. "I agree with you about the laser fire patterns, but why wouldn't they just kill us?"

"Rothet needed me for something," I said as I fumbled with the ship's emergency beacon. "His plan was to draw me in and capture me."

Tank blew out a sigh as his eyes searched the room. "So it was all part of his plan to lure you onto Tompkins' ship?" He scratched his head. "Why?"

"I don't know."

Tank looked at the hyper chamber then back at the emergency beacon in my hands. "You sure you want to go through with this?" Tank questioned.

I swiveled the chair to face the lonesome corridor that stretched into the compartment holding Liriana. The promising glow of the fully charged life support system was weakening, allowing darkness to consume the once illuminated entryway.

"I'll make you a deal, Tank. I promise not to ask you why you're willing to let her die if you don't ask me why I won't." I paused for a moment and locked my eyes with Tank's. After a few seconds Tank broke the stalemate and lowered his head. I activated the ship's emergency beacon and tossed the pulsating component on the seat of the pilot's chair. "If there are any UG ships patrolling the fringes of the Dark Quarter, they will lock onto this signal."

On my way back through the ship, I stopped by Liriana and placed my hand on the dome of frosted glass. Wiping away the building ice crystals, I watched her shallow breathing flutter the ends of her hair. She looked cold. Fragile. I couldn't let her die. I wouldn't. I'd lost everything. My ship, my crew, and my life as an agent soldier. I checked the charge packs on my pistols and adjusted the knives under my jacket. I was ready for the UG, and it was time I took something from them.

We stepped onto the loading dock platform of our fighter, shielding our eyes from the blistering, ash-filled currents of undulating air that bit at our exposed skin. The jagged, windswept landscape of Nalid was sheeted with layers of viscous, orange dust which created an uneven and perilous terrain. Two vibrant suns burst over the northern horizon and flooded the arid landscape with a smoldering bluish glow, highlighting a decrepit mining colony roughly three kilometers to the east.

"There," I said, pointing toward the structures while using my other hand to guard my face against the blowing elements. "That's where they'll land."

"You sure?" Tank questioned. "Why there and not closer to this ship and the distress signal?"

"The UG fighters are too bulky to land on this soft ground." I stepped off the platform and pressed my foot into the loose sand. "It's too unstable. The sand will swallow up their landing gear in seconds and would compromise their takeoff." I pointed to the mining town. "They'll seek flat, stable ground, and the best option is a landing pad in that town."

"What if they cut off their landing gear like us?" Tank chuckled as he brushed crusted blood from his face. "So, what's the plan? How do we welcome them in?"

"The emergency beacon will draw their attention to us. Once they land on Nalid, I'll greet them at the landing pad and secure a stasis equalizer and their ship. Once we have Liriana's hyper chamber fixed, we'll take their ship and get the hell out of here."

"Do you think you'll be able to get inside their fighter?"

"That's where you come in. They'll be focused on this UG ship and its distress signal. Their only option is to send soldiers by foot to recover us, leaving only a few of them behind. I will take them out, retrieve the equalizer, and meet you back here."

"That simple, huh?" Tank flexed the muscles in his arms and rolled his shoulders. "Easy to say, hard to pull off."

"I'm more concerned about how you can defend yourself when they arrive. I have the advantage of surprise while you're dangled as their bait."

"I think you underestimate me, Maxx." Tank's smirk was barely visible under the tangle of wiry hair. "If you're confident about the landing location, I'll move our ship into that valley to the south. There's only one way in and one way out. This may be her last run, but I think she has it in her."

"I can't stop them from coming. You will have to hold them off long enough until I can get back to help."

"I'll lace the valley entrance with so many incendiary explosives it will burn a hole directly to the core of this worthless planet. Don't enter their ship until you know they've triggered the trap. Even at your distance the explosion will be visible and audible. That way you can be sure that they didn't give up early and circle their way back to their fighter."

"I knew there was a reason I kept you around," I said, clasping Tank's forearm in mine. "Good luck."

"I've got the explosives, and you're the one heading into the belly of the beast. I'm not the one that needs the luck."

The ground was uneven, thick with blowing dust and ash that swallowed my feet with each step. The palms of my hands burned when I crawled up the rolling dunes, and the soles of my blistering feet ached. Shearing wind limited visibility, wildly flapping my jacket like a frenzied beast.

After an hour of travel, a towering mass of warped metal structures greeted me as I cleared the protective crest of dunes that sheltered the abandoned mining colony. Some of the buildings were intact, but charred from the intense rays of Nalid's twin suns. Others were vacant shells and broken skeletal husks, worn and weathered from years of neglect. Centered in the deserted city was a wind-blown landing pad partially devoured by Nalid's elements, and surrounded by a refueling station and two maintenance garages. Sliding down the hill, I plodded toward the garage closest to the landing pad, carefully brushing over my tracks.

The door of the shelter was askew, nearly broken free from its hinges and encased in a mound of powdered embers. Stripped of anything of worth, only scattered tools and metal scrap littered the floor of the garage. I pushed my way through the door and hunkered down inside, resting my back against the shed's ridged walls. It wasn't a great location, but it would provide a secure enough position and allow a clear line of sight to the pad.

I took a deep, calming breath and released one of my pistols from its holster. The gun felt awkward in my swollen hands. I fumbled to remove the power intake panel below the grip and worked four wires free from the charge pack, rewiring the intake by reversing the yellows and creating a jumper between the red and blue. The pistol hummed its disapproval as the green digits on the charge display retracted from sixty-eight to seven. I didn't have any plans to get into a fire fight, and wouldn't let the UG's battle armor stop me. One shot from this reworked pistol would erase any enemy, leaving behind just a stain and some memories.

I draped my jacket around my body like a protective cover, allowing the shadows of the garage to consume me. I tucked the pistol between my folded arms and sat quietly. There was nothing left to do but wait.

Tortured by the extreme heat and incessant moaning of the wind, I counted the passing hours. I started to wonder what went wrong, running every feasible scenario through my head. Did the distress signal stop working? Was the emergency beacon's pulse not strong enough to break through the heavy atmosphere? Were there no UG patrols in this area? Or, worse yet, did they find another landing area near our fighter?

I swiped my arm across my forehead to prevent the building sweat from trickling into my eyes. Retrieving the com from my jacket pocket, I attempted to raise Tank. The com's activity lights were strong, yet the only response was unwelcome silence. Maybe the return signals were absorbed by the shed's walls and Nalid's elements. An unexpected chill overcame me in the extreme heat, creeping down my back and settling in to gnaw at the base of my spine. Any hopes of saving Liriana diminished with each passing second, yet there was no other plan and no other option. I had to wait it out.

Late into the fourth hour of my watch, a rumble materialized above the shed, vibrating the walls and bouncing the tools and metal scrap near my feet. Outside, the winds shifted and swirled counter-clockwise while sand exploded from the planet's surface, clearing the landing pad of windblown debris. I wondered how long the garage would hold under the force of the ship's thrusters. I knew my ears couldn't take much more. Finally, battered landing gear peeked through the clouds of cinder revealing the nose of the ship, clearly marked with the insignia of the UG. They were here.

Belching red flame, the fighter's landing gear bounced off the surface of the pad before the pilot cut the power to the engines and quieted the thunderous tremors. Flashing lights dotted the ship's underbelly, highlighting its battle scars and lighting the hiss of steam that poured from its vents. I could feel the pounding of my heart inside my chest as the seal of the access hatch broke. Synthesized oxygen spilled into the atmosphere while the platform groaned as it engaged with the landing pad. The pain of my wounds disappeared, washed away by a flood of hope.

The first of the UG soldiers stepped outside the ship, clad in battle-tested armor with a UG logo emblazoned across his chest. He clutched a bulky laser rifle in his hands, and an array of electronic devices and grenades hung from his belt. Across his shoulders were the markings of an enlisted specialist; the UG's elite of the elite. They didn't deploy specialists for general recovery or reconnaissance missions, so it was obvious they were extremely interested in recovering whoever owned the ship we took from Tompkins' dock.

Three more soldiers emerged from the fighter to join their companion, each protected by the same armor and equipped with similar weapons. The roaring winds drowned out their conversations, their heads nodding and arms pointing to the south. When the discussion ended, three of the soldiers departed from their fighter and trudged toward the distress signal. A fourth remained behind to guard the entrance of their ship. All was going as planned.

My hand tightened around my pistol's grip as the UG specialists passed within a few meters of my position. The devices on their belts swayed and clattered against the walls of the shed. I held my breath and fought to keep my aggression in check. Once they cleared the area, their ship was left with only a single soldier to protect it. I resisted rushing to attack, knowing I had to be patient if my plan was to succeed.

The remaining specialist stood his ground, guarding the entrance to the fighter like an obedient dog. I thought he had spotted me in the garage when the visor of his helmet stayed fixed on the shed's door as if he was peering at me through the darkness. His cold eyes became visible, revealed when the winds stilled and the sun penetrated the hardened plastic shield. My finger brushed against the trigger of the pistol, but I waited until his gaze relented. He didn't know that I was here - yet.

I waited for more than an hour until the bluish air of Nalid reddened and charred black, carrying a deafening roar and a rolling wave of heat. Tank's trap worked, though the blast seemed strong. Too strong. Molten shrapnel fragments rained against the walls of the shed as I sprang from the enclosure and fired at the soldier. The weapon's chamber crackled with energy then released a blinding bolt of amber that sliced through the dense air and popped the soldier like a dirty soap bubble, painting his remains against the side of the ship.

I charged through the vacated access hatch in search of the remaining crew. The ship was a UG Class B fighter that could transport up to six crew members, which meant there were potentially two more soldiers inside. Without hesitation I worked my way through the sparsely lit corridors; my boots clanked against the mesh deck as an eerie orange glow radiated from under the hallway and cast swaying shadows in the tight corridors. The passageway buzzed with overhead com static and the smell of death slowly crept into my nostrils.

My last gasp of air came in heavy with the putrid tang of decaying flesh. My stomach tumbled as the odor grew thicker and hung in the air. Sweat streamed down the back of my neck like small winding rivers. I paused and placed my forehead against the hull while covering my mouth and nose with my free hand. The metal of the ship provided some relief, cooling my body and steadying the trembling of my hands.

I heard the slightest rub of metal on metal and turned in time for my face to catch one of the soldier's fists. All of my teeth felt as though they were loosened in my mouth. He swung again, this time catching air before his hand struck the wall of the corridor with a crunching thud. He sent a second punch to my midsection then pinned my gun hand against the wall.

I drove my knee into his armor-covered stomach and drew my second blaster. Before I could raise it and take aim, he swatted it free from my hand with an annoyed grunt. The blaster struck the ground with such force that it cracked the grip and shorted the charge pack. The back of his hand caught my face again, leaving a streak of searing pain in its wake. His grip tightened on my gun arm as though he would crush my bones into dust. I spun sharply to the left, and twisted my arm out of his grasp; ligaments and tendons cracked and popped in my shoulder. I was free.

I released one of my blades and slashed a whisper of steel across the seams in his armor, drawing blood under his arm and at the base of his neck. Retreating from the whirling blade, the soldier eyed my moves with careful measurement. He unsheathed a knife from his belt and lunged at me. I dodged his attack and lopped off three fingers from his right hand. His knife and severed digits rained onto the floor. As he clutched at the wound I drove my knife through a gap in his armor and lodged the blade deep into the inside of his forearm and through his elbow. He didn't make a noise, only staggered away, allowing me enough time to recover my pistol. I raised my blaster and fired a single shot at his exposed head. It burst into a meat-filled haze of red mist and the remaining trunk of his body collapsed to the floor.

My wounded arm swelled, and I moved it a few times to make sure my shoulder was still attached. I gripped the blaster in my left hand and dangled my right arm at my side as I forced my way down the corridors.

The odor of death grew more pungent with each step. I searched a few storage compartments and locked bays until I stumbled into the area that contained the reason for the smell. There were more than a dozen bodies, dismembered and skinned. Most of them were unrecognizable; they were cut beyond recognition and had been decaying for weeks. My stomach roiled. I covered my mouth and nose, backed out of the room, then sealed the door. The UG's brutality knew no bounds.

I spotted a hyper chamber's lights illuminating a room at the far end of a hall. I entered the compartment and found the final soldier suspended in stasis. Peering through the fogged glass I spotted numerous injuries, burns, and cuts on his muscular frame. These men weren't just sent from a battle cruiser or space station. They had been roaming the Dark Quarter for some time and were sent here for a specific purpose.

I pressed the stasis equalizer's release button and initiated the timed discharge sequence. As the last of the power trickled from the unit, the hyper chamber slowly ejected the long, sleek cylinder from its housing. Treating it as if it was a fragile piece of glass, I removed what was left of my torn jacket and wrapped it with care.

The murderous warrior remained still, showered by the life-giving green hue of the chamber's status lights, all of which would soon grow faint and turn the protective cocoon into an unyielding deathtrap.

I recovered a pistol from a storage locker on the other side of the room. With the heel of my boot I broke the grip and stripped the power intake, charge components and component wiring. I wound the wiring around the door release latches and looped them back to the power intake device. Applying a surge of energy from the charge component, the latches ignited under the intense heat then fused with small wisps of smoke. Preserving the hyper chamber guaranteed access to a fully functioning unit for Liriana when we traveled off of Nalid. As for the UG soldier, a slow, painful death brought about by insufficient life support was more than he deserved.

While preparing for my journey back to the ship, I couldn't help but think of the countless innocents violated by this pack of wild animals. As I stepped out of their fighter, I cradled the stasis equalizer under my arm as though I was protecting a newborn child from the unforgiving winds. "Rest in peace," I whispered under my breath in hopes that the tortured souls of these soldiers' victims were now set free. "This is just the start. More of the UG will be joining you soon."

A sea of fiery debris and a path of scorched soil clearly marked the entryway of the mountainous valley. The soft footing of Nalid grew more rigid as I walked toward the ship. Fire licked at my flesh while I attempted to clear the oily smoke from my eyes.

Dozens of bodies were scattered amongst the wreckage, lying in twisted piles of arms and legs. I knelt near one of the corpses and used my blade to examine his burned and disfigured features, slowly rolling his arms and head from side to side. A rush of panic consumed me. Their charred remains were marked with the partially visible insignia of the OWME. Somehow Tompkins' goons locked onto our encrypted distress signal. If Tompkins' remaining crew was able to escape the destroyer, and were here at the same time as the UG, what was the chance that Tank was able to take them all out? How the hell would Tank be able to fight off a contingent of highly trained UG specialists and Tompkins' goons?

I raised my head in time to catch the silhouettes of two figures sifting through the ruins, their identities distorted by endless waves of heat. The din of the roaring blaze was soon joined by the shifting footsteps of unknown visitors attempting to conceal their presence while advancing upon me from behind and to my left. A click of a blaster safety release was all I needed to hear to confirm their intentions.

I spun to greet them; a streak of silver leapt from my hand and lodged deep into the throat of one of my attackers. With a choking gurgle and a spray of red, the soldier dropped to his knees before he crumpled onto Nalid's surface. The second figure was on me before I had a chance to draw my other knife. A swoosh of air followed the butt of a rifle to the back of my head, splintering my skull with shards of pain and knocking me to the ground. I rolled to my feet and turned to face my attacker.

"Captain," I said as I spit. His name burned in my mouth. "For some reason I'm not surprised."

"MXX," he responded. His face was stoic as if set in stone; his white film-covered eyes searched me over as they shifted in their sunken sockets. "You've caused more problems than any of us would've expected." The Captain spun the rifle back into his hands and pointed the barrel at my head. "How about you hand me that little trinket?" He pointed the rifle at the stasis equalizer, then back at me.

I glanced at the device, still cradled like a child in my arm. "Don't tell me, Captain, that you've been tracking me all his time in hopes that I would procure a stasis equalizer for you?"

"I don't have much patience for your sense of humor." The Captain's face pinched into a snarl. "I need that equalizer."

"Those UG specialists, they weren't under your command, were they?" The corner of his eye twitched when I asked the question. "What was it that made you turn your back on the UG?"

"You may not be familiar with this situation, but the person with the gun gets to ask the questions. Hand it over." The Captain raised his hand, stretched out his thin fingers and curled them in a beckoning motion.

"The fighter we took from Tompkins' destroyer was yours, wasn't it?" The Captain's white eyes fixed on me. "The UG doesn't look too kindly on traitors, Captain. You'll find yourself running from planet to planet for the rest of your sorry years."

The Captain shrugged his shoulders and smirked. Wrinkles spidered under his eyes and split his skin in a web of cracks and crevices. "Does it look like I have a lot of years left?" His hand was still outstretched, waiting for me to hand him the equalizer. Behind him, another figure was making their way toward us. The outline of their body was distorted behind the wall of heat and flame.

I looked at the stasis equalizer and shook my head. "You'll have to kill me for it."

"Ahh, so there's the...rub." A man stepped through the wall of flame and took his position by the Captain's side. It was Rothet. "You know that we don't want you dead, Maxx. I think I've been quite clear about that. We need you, but of equal importance is our need for that stasis equalizer."

"You're dead." The words spilled from my mouth as a muted whisper. "I watched Liriana shatter your neck and spine."

Rothet raised his arms to the side, spun toward the Captain and back to me. "Obviously, I'm quite alive."

"Liriana?" I questioned. "Tank?" What have you done with them?"

"I'm right here, Maxx." Even though the voice came from behind, the deep, booming words of Tank were quite familiar.

I closed my eyes and sighed. "I don't suppose you came to help me?" My back faced Tank while my gaze moved between the stasis equalizer, Rothet, and the Captain.

"Of course I did," Tank said. "But first you have to help us."

"Us?" My mouth grew dry as I tried to speak. "So it wasn't Terra?"

"It was Terra," Rothet said, "until she went…AWOL. She was one of mine when you so graciously took her under your protective wing. She was a good girl, did what she was told, until she suddenly went dark on me the day she left your ship."

"Tank," I said, "why did you kill Cooper? You're nothing but a coward to take the life of one of your friends."

"Friend is a word I'm not familiar with." Tank grunted and blew out a breath. "He was going to cause problems, so I killed him on Tesid when I had the chance. I crushed his head then burned his body like a heaping pile of trash." There was a long pause before Tank continued. "And I would be lying if I told you that I didn't enjoy it." I could feel Tank's smile even though I couldn't see it.

I turned; one hand locked around the equalizer, the other on the grip of my holstered pistol. Tank was bearing mixed armaments of the OWME and UG. There was a rifle slung over his shoulder, a pistol strapped to his thigh, and a long bandolier fitted snugly across his chest. Most of his injuries had been healed by his JaC, leaving drying scabs and light scars. The other more grievous wounds had been cleaned and bandaged.

"How long have you been working against me, Tank?" I asked. "How many people have died because of you?"

"It's been a while." Tank said. "A long while. What's worse is that the galaxy's greatest agent soldier never suspected me." Tank raised his arm and opened his hand. "Just give us the stasis equalizer."

It was then that everything fell into place. The three had been working together ever since I accepted the Solonian mission. It was all a setup to draw me out into the open. They used Tompkins to fuel my hate, and Liriana to fill me with regret and doubt. Rothet, Tank, and the Solonians were all in on this deal. They didn't want the UG involved, so they needed someone on the inside to keep me alive and out of their hands. The Captain.

"You're searching for the compensation JaC," I said. I turned to face the Captain. "That's why you needed me alive and helped get us back to the *Beast*. You aided our escape off of Paxcel and from Tesid. You worked the UG over from behind the scenes keeping them off my back until the JaC was located." My eyes shifted to Rothet. "You used Tompkins, knowing he would do anything to take me down. His credits and resources helped fund your part of the mission. Incorporating Tompkins and Liriana was a play on my emotions." I turned to look at Tank. The expression on his face was one of amusement. "You helped me all along playing your part as a loyal soldier, knowing that I was the only one that could get us back to the *Beast*. Without me you would've never found my ship or the compensation JaC. Once we were back onboard, you and Terra searched for the JaC, but the two of you couldn't locate it - not with the crew roaming the ship and so much area to cover. So you worked with Rothet to disable my ship and lure me into his waiting arms, leaving the *Beast* vulnerable and without my command."

"Those are all good theories," Rothet said, "but placed together a few days too...late."

My eyes shifted back to Rothet. "You're all under the Solonian's employment. The cargo I'm hauling was an intentional setup. The Solonians leaked the information to the UG that I was in possession of mutilated bodies of their slaves. Those bodies were meant to keep me on the run, and once you recovered the JaC, I would take the fall. The UG's focus would be on those slaves, giving all of you, including the Solonians, a free pass."

"The plan was solid and clean," the Captain said. "It still is."

"Let me guess. You haven't been able to locate the JaC?"

"It's only a matter of time before we find it," the Captain said. "We've deployed a small army aboard the *Beast*, all equipped with JaC scanners, and they're searching for it now."

"If you so much as touch one of my crew –"

"What I told you back on Tompkins' destroyer was true." Rothet cut me off before I could finish. "Your crew is dead, Maxx. We drained the power on your ship, trapped them inside and waited for them to...suffocate." My hand tightened around the grip of my pistol. I pulled the gun from the holster and flipped the switch to the uranium rounds. "Tsk, tsk, Maxx.

Let's not be too…hasty."

"You raise that gun, and Liriana dies!" Tank's voice boomed. "Don't tell me you've come all this way just to see her die."

"So this is it, Tank?" I replied. "All the years you've served under me and this is how it ends?"

"You're a fool. A damn, stupid fool." Tank's response carried the weight of building anger. "We're agent soldiers, Maxx. We're not friends. It's the credits. Don't you remember why you got into this game?"

"And Liriana?"

"She's the one missing piece to this puzzle, isn't she?" Rothet said. "The bodies resting inside the *Beast's* cargo bay are evidence of five hundred failed Solonian experiments. Liriana's ability to accept ten JaCs, and live, is nothing short of…monumental. The unmatched technology of your compensation JaC, coupled with her uniqueness, has the Solonians very interested in the possibilities."

"So you hand her and the compensation JaC over to the Solonians and let them conduct their tests?" My finger brushed against the pistol's trigger. "All for a few credits."

"What they do with her is of no consequence to me," Rothet said as he raised his hands at Tank and the Captain. "To any of us. And they're willing to pay us more than an empire's ransom when we deliver them."

My eyes fixed on my exposed right forearm, brandished with MXX in bold, black ink. "I promise this isn't going to end well for any of you," I said. I placed the equalizer gently on the ashen surface of Nalid then backed away from the unit. "You can have the equalizer, but I won't tell you where I've hidden the JaC on the *Beast*."

Tank smiled, but his tense muscles gave away his true feelings. "You believe that keeping the location of the JaC secret will save her?" Tank picked up the equalizer. "We'll find the JaC. You know we will. You may buy Liriana some time, but you won't save her from the Solonians nor their intentions for her."

"You know me well enough, Tank. You can hold me against my will and torture me every minute of every day, and you won't break me. The information on the location of that JaC will die with me." My eyes tracked Tank as he moved next to Rothet and the Captain. The image of the three would be forever burned into my mind. Tank freed the stasis equalizer from the jacket. Its sleek surface gleamed in the flames and the rays of Nalid's twin suns.

"This wasn't how it was supposed to play out," Tank said as he lowered his rifle. "If we take you back with us, I know you'll die in captivity and never speak a word." Tank turned to look at Rothet and the Captain. "If he was able to escape, or share the JaC's location with someone else who could recover it first, our entire mission would be for nothing."

"You're confident the compensation JaC is on his...ship?" Rothet questioned.

"Absolutely," Tank said. "He offered Liriana the chance to join us back on the *Beast* to get it implanted. It will just take some time to locate it."

"Then kill him."

I couldn't fire on them and risk the chance of damaging the stasis equalizer. Instead, I held onto the grip of my pistol knowing I would never use it. All things eventually come to an end. My life was worth nothing, and giving Liriana a chance to live was all I had to offer. If they gunned me down my body would rot away, slowly devoured by the elements of Nalid until it flaked apart and scattered in the winds of ash. No one would mourn my passing, and I didn't care. This was the life I chose, the life of an agent soldier.

Tank raised his rifle and squeezed the trigger. A flash of light, followed by darkness.

I woke, welcomed by a planet now enveloped in a shroud of black. I was buried by the powder-filled currents; dust and ash were matted against my wounds. Cold breezes chilled my body raising gooseflesh on my exposed arms and stiffening my joints. Struggling against the waves of nausea coursing through my body, I rolled to my knees and forced myself to my feet. The laser fire didn't kill me, but left behind a mark of burned flesh and painful internal wounds that pulsed inside of me.

I spun away from Tank's blast, and that timing saved my life. Tank didn't finish the job. He had to know that I was still alive, yet he chose not to kill me.

The once raging fires in the valley were mere flickers of flame, casting random points of light on the planet's surface. I was left alone in a field of debris littered with fractured metal and sprinkled with lifeless corpses.

For a moment the tattooed letters on my forearm seemed darker than the lightless skies. I could feel the compensation JaC resting behind the ink; the key to Liriana's salvation was with me all of this time. I recovered the remains of the UG officer's jacket and slid it over my throbbing shoulders. Hunched over, I scratched through the sand until I located my pistol and blades. Pain surged through my body with relentless fury. I clutched my side and collapsed to the planet's surface.

At that moment, I made two promises to myself. I would find Liriana and take her from the Solonians. Then I would hunt down Rothet, Tank, and the Captain, and kill each one of them.

I sat, thrust the knives back into the sheaths, then peered out at the ocean of sand in front of me. In the darkness it would take hours to find the mining colony and the UG specialists' fighter. It would take months to heal my wounds, and perhaps years to find them. But it didn't matter. I had made two promises. Both of which I planned to keep.

ABOUT THE AUTHOR

DONALD SCHLISING is an author of science fiction and horror with a number of published short stories and creative works to his credit. *MXX: Agent Soldier*, the first book in the series, is his first published novel. Donald lives in Wisconsin where he's an active and award-winning photographer and IT professional.

ACKNOWLEDGMENTS

My thanks to Jesse, Mitch, Kristina, Jamie, Nina, and Eric. It's an honor to call them my friends. To all the men and women who serve, or have served, in the United States Armed Forces. Your service, dedication, and patriotism provides me the freedom and opportunity to do what I do. The rest of you I will thank in person.